Praise for
Shades of Mor...

"Will Marnie and Taylor, torn apart sixte... ...ago, find a way to overcome, seemingly impossible barriers and find happiness? *Shades of Morning*, superbly crafted by veteran author Marlo Schalesky, presents a sense of family and love that will touch the reader's soul. The book is a memorable journey into a woman's heart and the lessons she learns about real family loyalty. Reader, prepare yourself for a surprise ending!"

— IRENE BRAND, best-selling author of *Love Finds You in*
   Valentine, Nebraska, and *Made for Each Other*

"*Shades of Morning* is magical! Full of the wonder of love, *true* love. It surprised me on every page. I loved it!"

— DEBORAH RANEY, author of *Almost Forever* and the
   Clayburn Novels

"Each of Marlo Schalesky's inspirationally unique stories are 'like a box of chocolates—you never know what you're gonna get' and *Shades of Morning* is no exception. From the first page, I fell for the beautifully drawn and flawed characters, and by the end, I wanted to hug them, especially Emmit. What an angel."

— TAMARA LEIGH, author of *Nowhere, Carolina,* and *Leaving*
   Carolina

"*Shades of Morning* is a gripping story of grace and forgiveness in the face of years of secrets, half-truths, and running. Yet it is so much more. Marnie and Taylor became people I cared about from the opening pages, yet I wondered how the tangled web of their past could ever unravel to show the promise of a future. And the image of God revealed in the prose speaks to me even now after I've reached the end."

—CARA C. PUTMAN, author of *Cornhusker Dreams*

"Poignant. Heartfelt. Compelling. This latest novel by Marlo Schalesky is a touching testament to the power of love, forgiveness, and second chances. *Shades of Morning* is an unusual love story with a twist—and what a twist! You'll love it. But be sure to have a box of tissues close at hand. This would make a great movie! (Are you listening, Hollywood?)"

—LAURA JENSEN WALKER, author of *Becca by the Book* and
    Turning the Paige

"Marlo wrote an engrossing story told with her signature richness and beauty. Her characters lived and breathed—I connected with them immediately—even as they displayed the messiness of real life. *Shades of Morning* will touch your heart and remind you of God's enduring hope, love and redemption. It's a treasure!"

—CINDY MARTINUSEN-COLOMA, author of best-selling novel
    Orchid House and *Beautiful*

SHADES *of* MORNING

Other Books by Marlo Schalesky

Fiction
If Tomorrow Never Comes
Beyond the Night (Christy Award–Winner
for Best Contemporary Romance)
Cry Freedom
Freedom's Shadow
Only the Wind Remembers
Veil of Fire

Nonfiction
Empty Womb, Aching Heart

MARLO SCHALESKY

SHADES of MORNING

A NOVEL

MULTNOMAH
BOOKS

SHADES OF MORNING
PUBLISHED BY MULTNOMAH BOOKS
12265 Oracle Boulevard, Suite 200
Colorado Springs, Colorado 80921

This is a work of fiction. Apart from well-known actual people, events, and locales that figure into the narrative, all names, characters, places, and incidents are the products of the author's imagination or are used fictitiously. Any resemblance to current events or locales, or to living persons, is entirely coincidental.

ISBN 978-1-60142-025-1

ISBN 978-1-60142-287-3 (electronic)

Published in association with The Steve Laube Literary Agency, LLC, 5501 North Seventh Avenue #502, Phoenix, AZ 85013.

Published in the United States by WaterBrook Multnomah, an imprint of the Crown Publishing Group, a division of Random House Inc., New York.

Multnomah and its mountain colophon are registered trademarks of Random House Inc.

Library of Congress Cataloging-in-Publication Data
Schalesky, Marlo M., 1967–
    Shades of morning : a novel / Marlo Schalesky. — 1st ed.
       p. cm.
    ISBN 978-1-60142-025-1 — ISBN 978-1-60142-287-3 (electronic)
  I. Title.
    PS3569.C4728S53 2010
    813'.54—dc22

                                                    2010001948

Printed in the United States of America
2010—First Edition

10 9 8 7 6 5 4 3 2 1

To Jayden
My own unexpected gift

The Sun of Righteousness shall arise
With healing in His wings.

Malachi 4:2, nkjv

Prologue

utumn snow fell like fat angels fluttering to earth.

Emmit sat on the snowbank, his eyes closed, his head tipped back. He was a snowflake too, drifting on the breeze. Cold nibbled at his wings. Ice kissed his lashes. He stuck out his tongue and caught a flake. Why did the snow always melt away just when he finally got some? He reached up and scratched his too-small ears with a too-small hand. Then he adjusted his heavy, Coke-bottle glasses.

Something whispered in the wind. He held his breath and listened with all his might. He could almost hear the voices telling him that today he was fifteen years old. It was a big number. They all said so. He was a big boy now. All grown up.

And that meant it was time for the prayer to be answered. Not some little prayer about sniffly noses and friends at school. Not one about nice weather or where to park a car. This prayer was important. It was about love. It was about family. And God always answered those.

Especially today.

Emmit wiggled deeper into the snow. The flakes fell in heavier clumps. He opened his eyes and waited.

The pretty light would be coming soon. The big whirring one on top of the truck that picked up the garbage from the cans on the street. He liked the light. Round and round. Round and round. It would come.

A screen door slammed. He looked back over his shoulder. A puffy white coat stood on the doorstep with a matching hat perched atop wisps of brown hair. The coat waved.

Emmit waved back. That's how a mom should look. White coat, pink smile peeking from between collar and hat.

"Mighty cold out here, sweetie." She motioned toward the snow as she spoke.

Emmit grinned. "I wait for pretty light."

She nodded and trudged to the mailbox by the street. The box creaked when she opened it.

Then the pretty light came with a chug, a squeal, and the grinding of gears. The light turned and turned, made its way around the corner and up the street.

Emmit watched it. "Pretty light! Pretty light!" He called out to her, but she didn't turn.

She stood there, hunched over a stack of white envelopes in her gloved hand.

The wind gusted.

The whirring light rumbled closer. Closer.

Then it happened. A little thing. A simple thing. It shouldn't have mattered at all. But it did.

An envelope skittered from her hand and blew into the street. She went after it.

He stood. "Stop!" But he couldn't stop it. Couldn't stop her. And worse, he couldn't stop the lights.

Her boot hit ice. It slipped from under her. Envelopes mixed with the angels in the air. Fluttering, flying, drifting on the breeze.

But they weren't angels. Not at all.

Emmit yelled and yelled. But it didn't help. So he closed his eyes, plugged his ears. He held his breath. But that didn't matter either. He still heard the terrible squeal. The dull thud.

And then, the awful silence.

He peeked out and saw her, a still, white blob on a dirty, white street. The whirring light stopped.

Emmit sat down and cried into the drifting snow. But that didn't make any difference either. She didn't get up. She didn't move. No matter how much he cried.

Later other lights came. Red and blue and more yellow. Lights on a black-and-white car. Lights on a big red fire engine. Lights on a white van with the letters A-M-B-U-L-A-N-C-E printed real big on the side.

They weren't pretty lights. He didn't like them at all.

He shivered. But no one noticed him. They just buzzed around the new lights like bugs. They weren't bugs. But they still buzzed and shouted and flew away.

And he just sat there, tears freezing on his cheeks, a cold fist rubbing his wet nose. How could this be the answer to prayer? This didn't seem like any answer at all.

This seemed like everything gone all wrong.

He wiped the ice from his face, lay back in the snow, and moved his arms and legs up and down, up and down. Three times to make the image of an angel in the bank.

A perfect angel. A snow angel. Just for her. Because she was what a mom should be. Because he loved her too. Because she was gone.

The new lights took her.

And then the snow stopped falling.

1

Marnie Helen Wittier hated baby showers. She also hated her middle name, but that was another story. What mattered now was that despite her intense dislike of powder pink balloons, little crocheted socks, and cheap plastic baby bottles, she now wove in and out of handmade tables at her own coffee shop, offering floral-dressed women fresh pumpkin-shaped cookies and specialty lattes.

The only thing worse would be if she had to wear one of those foo-foo dresses. But a gal had to draw the line somewhere. If not at pink balloons and pastel teacups, then at least at swaying dresses and—gasp!—high heels. She wouldn't be caught dead in heels.

But she could put up with pretty tulips on the tables, the pink and white streamers, and that ridiculous It's a Girl! papier-mâché sign, because this shower was for Kinna Henley. And if anyone deserved the perfect baby shower, that woman did. After all last year's troubles piled onto years of infertility, Kinna had earned the best shower Marnie could think of. That's the only reason she'd said "of course" when those ladies from the church asked to hold the event here.

Still, that didn't stop her from snatching a pink napkin, scrawling the words *Hosting a baby shower...what was I thinking???* on it, and stuffing it in her pocket. The napkin would go into her box of regrets later. A reminder to never, ever do anything this stupid again.

Marnie delivered her last latte to a woman dressed in a particularly agonizing shade of fuchsia, then hurried back to her spot behind the coffee bar. Her reflection shot back at her from the mirror behind the bar— short, spiked hair, dyed jet black, and dark plum eye shadow to match. The look would have worked perfectly with a nose ring, except she couldn't stand to get one. How on earth did people blow their noses with that thing sticking in there? So she'd settled for an extra sterling silver stud in her ear and called it good.

She supposed she ought to try out a more conservative look, now that she was turning thirty-five, but so far she hadn't gotten up the nerve. Besides, it was too fun shocking the old ladies at church. She grinned, then stuck her tongue out at the image in the mirror. That was more like it. Marnie Wittier would not let one baby shower get her down.

She put her hands on her hips and turned back toward the room. Half was a coffee shop, the other half a small bookstore, separated by a wall and wide french doors. Marnie smiled. Her favorite things: books and coffee. And people enjoying both. Right now the crowd of pink-cheeked church women gathered on one side of Marnie's Books and Brew while a few other customers lingered on the other. Kinna was opening gifts. At least the baby was a girl. Marnie could handle a shower full of pinks and yellows.

But not blue. Lord knew she'd never be able to face blue.

On her right, Marcus wandered the aisles of the book section, straightening and shelving the latest box of Christian fiction she'd ordered. He had a piercing—in his eyebrow, not his nose—and his hair stood out in all directions. Good kid. Honest. Even if his head looked like the wrong end of a mop. He grinned at her and she smiled back.

Old Joe cleaned the table they'd use for a book signing that evening. And just coming through the door was the new girl from Oklahoma she'd hired. Poor thing, mother named her Daisy. Daisy from Oklahoma, with corncob-colored hair and cornflower blue eyes. She'd be lucky if she survived two weeks in California. But everyone deserved a chance. Even a girl named Daisy.

Marnie sighed and gathered some cookies from the tray on the counter. She glanced at her employees and customers. They were her friends, her family. What a family should have been. Not that she knew anything about that. Foster homes didn't teach her a whole fat lot about family. But she was great at packing a suitcase in forty-five seconds flat. So the whole foster-home thing wasn't a total waste.

She threw the cookies on a plate, then scooted out into the room. Pretty soon she'd have to add another table in the coffee part of the shop. She had plans for two more. One made from, of all things, coffee cups and another covered with crayon drawings from her customers' kids. She'd protect the drawings under a glass tabletop. The cup table would sit next to the driftwood table, and the crayon concoction would nestle between the auto-parts table and the one made out of toothpicks. She loved those tables. All of them. They were hers. They were special. They were…they were home.

Laughter drifted from the group of women. Marnie smiled. She couldn't help it. Yeah, this was a baby shower. But it was worth it to see the change in Kinna. And not just in the size of the woman's belly, but in her eyes. In her soul. Something that happened last year. A miracle, she'd said.

Well, Marnie didn't know much about miracles. Mistakes maybe. And accidents. And stupid, monstrous mess ups. She knew a lot about those. But miracles? Those were for other people. Good people. Like Kinna and Jimmy. Not for single coffee-shop owners who a long time ago had run away from the place she'd hoped to call home.

Don't worry, God, I'm not looking for any miracles. Her gaze shot up to the ceiling, and she winked.

Half a second later, the floor jolted. The walls shook. Glasses jiggled, the row of autumn pumpkins shuddered, and two stacks of paper cups tipped and fell. Marnie widened her stance and allowed the ground to rumble beneath her.

Conversation stopped, and in the jingling quiet came a sharp squeal. Daisy. The floor stilled. Voices took up where they'd left off. And life rolled on, just as before. Except for the cornflower girl huddled beneath the tinfoil table.

Marnie suppressed her grin as she sauntered toward Daisy and helped the girl up from beneath the shiny table. You could always tell who the out-of-staters were. Poor kid.

The girl's eyes were as big as the pumpkin cookies. "Th-that was a big one, wasn't it?"

Marnie patted her arm, then cocked her head toward the church women. "Listen."

A moment later, the numbers came.

"Four-point-three." That guess came from Kinna.

A sharp voice spoke next. "Naw, that was at least a five-point-six."

"Five-point-zero even, mark my words."

A Vietnamese woman named Mai stood, though you could barely tell she was standing. "What earthquake?" She shook her head and put on her thickest accent. "I no feel a thing. You white girls such pansies."

They all laughed.

Then a single, old, trembling hand rose from amid the group. Josephina.

Marnie leaned closer to Daisy. "Are you listening? Here it comes."

Josephina's quavering voice silenced the others. "Four-point-eight."

She stuck her gray head out from the group of women. "Turn on the radio, *mija*."

Marnie clicked on the news. After a few minutes, it came. A deep-timbered voice said, "Reports of a four-point-eight earthquake centered outside Castroville." Not too far from Marnie's in Pacific Grove.

Everyone clapped, including the customers on the far side of the room.

Marnie put a finger under Daisy's chin and closed the girl's mouth.

Daisy's tone dropped to a whisper. "How does she do that?"

Marnie chuckled. "She's lived in Monterey County since her *familia* came over the border in the early 1930s. Rumor has it Josephina was three years old, and she hasn't set foot out of the county since. Been here for every last earthquake that's shaken the coast. The woman's a phenome-non." Marnie slapped her hands together and raised her voice over the dwindling applause. "Okay, Josephina's special tea for everyone, on the house."

They all cheered.

It had taken Marnie eight tries to get the tea just right. "You have to make it just like *mi madre* used to make it," Josephina kept saying, and ever since it had been a customer favorite. Marnie's special mix.

The bell jingled from the front door. Marnie looked up. A purple-shirted man pushed through the opening. He turned. No, not a man, just a kid. A pimply-faced boy with a silly purple hat to match his plum purple shirt, with an electronic clipboard balanced on his arm.

He waved at her. "Hey, Marnie."

She lifted her eyebrows. "Scott? You got a new job?"

He grinned and pointed at some tiny lettering on his shirt. "We do it faster."

Marnie stepped toward him. "Who are you looking for?"

"You."

Marnie blew her bangs off her forehead with a quick puff of air. Thank goodness. She'd been waiting and waiting for that new bean grinder from Italy. She rubbed her hands together. "Well, where is it?"

Scott pulled a slim envelope from beneath the clipboard and held it out to her. "Here ya go."

"That's not a bean grinder."

"Huh?"

Figured. "That it? Just an envelope?"

"Yep. Sign here."

Marnie took the plastic pen, signed, and watched as Scott tucked the clipboard back under his arm and strode toward the door. He threw another jaunty wave over his shoulder.

"Got a new toffee nut," she called after him. "Come back later and try it out."

"New books too?"

"A whole shipment came in just this morning."

"It's a date." The door thudded shut.

A date. She shook her head. Her friends were always teasing her about dates, because everyone knew Marnie Wittier never, ever went on a date. And she didn't go to the beach either. Those were her rules.

A series of *ooo*'s and *ahhh*'s rose from the women. Marnie glanced at them. Kinna held up a complete set of pink Onesies. Striped pink, flowered pink, pink polka dots, and even one with little pink monkeys. Good grief. Call out the pink police.

Marnie turned away and reached for the letter. It was in a beige linen envelope, heavy, official. Expensive. Who would be sending her something like that? She flipped it over to the front.

The air escaped the room. Time sucked in an empty breath. And

Marnie sensed her world tipping around her. *No…* Slowly, so slowly, she extended her finger and touched the fancy attorney's logo on the envelope's upper-left corner. A crescent wave, a block *C,* and a flat line like the shore on a calm day. Her arm moved as she traced the name beneath. His name. But it couldn't be. Shouldn't be. Must not be. And yet…

Marnie blew out a long breath. The earthquake had come. The real one, more real than any earth tremor, than any tipping cups, than walls that shuddered and stopped. A single logo, a single name. They rocked her world. And if she were to measure, she'd call it an eight-point-oh for sure.

She closed her eyes. *It's not real. It can't be.* Her life was good now. Finally. She was surrounded by people who cared. People who just knew her as Marnie, the friendly Books and Brew owner. That's all they knew, all they needed to know. But the man whose name would be inside that envelope knew something else. He knew who she used to be. He knew everything. Well, almost everything anyway, including the fact that she'd once loved him.

Or maybe he didn't, because she never did tell him so. She'd run away from him first. Run away and left love, left hope, behind. But she brought the pain with her. The pain, the guilt, the regret. She'd kept those locked in a seashell-covered box on a top shelf in her little cottage too close to the bay.

Marnie snatched up the letter and stuffed it into her pocket. It burned there like hot espresso. But she couldn't open it. Not here. Not now. Seeing that logo was enough. Because after all these years, it had happened.

He found me.

2

*J*f Taylor Cole had a gun, he would have shot it dead. But he didn't have a gun, and it wasn't the phone's fault he had to make this call. To *her*.

Good thing she wasn't home. Now the phone could live another day. Taylor grimaced and adjusted the crazy jester's hat on his head.

Of course, a successful attorney ought not get all stupid over a single phone call, even if he was just a lousy estate planner. But this would have been the first time he'd heard her voice in over fifteen years. Fifteen long years of him silently repeating Rhett Butler's famous line: "Frankly my dear…"

What a crock.

He tugged on the edges of his hat and glanced outside his office window. Dozens of jack-o'-lanterns glittered down the main street of Clam's Junction, Maine. Windows glowed in the dimming light. Music from Tim Burton's *The Nightmare Before Christmas* played from the pharmacy across the way, and farther down, deep booms echoed from the candy shop. The streetlights, covered in fake spider webs, glimmered in the descending dusk and sent strange shadows wavering over the cobbled road.

Taylor smoothed the orange and purple satin over his chest. Then he stood. The bells on his shoes jingled. He breathed out a long sigh. The kids would be coming soon. Thank goodness. He looked forward to this night all year.

Some people called it the devil's night, but not Taylor. What better opportunity to connect with the town's kids and let them know how special they were? He didn't have any children of his own, but on this night all the kids were his. And tonight, especially, he needed that.

He reached out and squeezed the squeaky red nose he'd wear in a few moments when he, like dozens of other business owners down First and Main, handed out treats to rosy-cheeked kids with wide grins and wider pillowcase bags. They did it every year.

Tonight it was snowing. Huge, fluffy flakes covered the street in a blanket that made it seem more like Christmas than Halloween. Of course, he loved Christmas too, when he dressed up like Santa Claus and brought brand-new youth Bibles and coloring books to the kids down at the shelter. Holidays were great.

Phone calls, though, not so much.

He glared at the phone. *Thank You, God, that she wasn't there.* Of course, he'd have to try again. But not now. Later. Unless he pulled out that old BB gun and silenced the phone forever. He grunted. With his luck, the pellets would ricochet off and bean him in the nose.

He sat back and formulated an excuse to give his assistant, Nancy. "The phone just exploded," he'd say. "That's why I've run into a little trouble getting in touch with the aunt from California." A little trouble. Ha. But Nancy had finished the final paperwork for the guardianship transfer, so all that was left was to talk to *her* and to send Emmit. And that was more than just a little trouble, whether his phone stayed intact or not.

Taylor rubbed his hands on his new Dockers, then picked up the big red nose and pressed it on his face. A knock sounded on the big front door of his main office. He jumped. The time had come. Finally. He hurried to answer it.

A geisha girl, a goblin, and a bumblebee stood on the step outside. "Trick or treat!"

Taylor adjusted his hat and leaned toward them. "Amy, what a breathtaking Japanese princess you make. You've stolen this emperor's heart." He put his hands over his chest and pretended to be love struck.

Amy smiled with a mouth full of braces and twirled to show off her dress. "Mom made it. Isn't it beautiful?"

He tapped her freckled nose. "You're beautiful."

She pushed up her glasses. "You always say that."

"Because it's true." He paused and grabbed a handful of Jesus Loves You pencils and mini chocolate bars from the bowl by the door. "A pencil for you and, let's see, an Almond Joy, because you're such a joy to all of us."

He joked with the other kids and plopped pencils and candy into their bags too. The last one he peeked inside.

It looked like the pharmacy was giving out Dora the Explorer bandages this year. And it appeared that Patti from Sweet Shots candy store had decided on her famous chocolate-covered pretzels. In the bag underneath the pretzels was a tiny sucker from Ted's Hardware. Ted always was a cheapskate. But there weren't any candy apples yet from Sandy down at the antique store or popcorn balls from Jim's Grocery. It seemed that the kids were starting at the north end of downtown this year and working their way south. His office was about halfway.

"Thanks, Mr. Cole." The kids jogged down the steps.

Taylor turned for another fistful of candy. Usually Emmit joined him for their yearly ritual of handing out treats. But Emmit didn't want to spend time with him so much anymore, not since he'd found out that Taylor was the one who would send him away.

Tightness squeezed through Taylor's chest. "He belongs with his aunt." He said the words out loud and prayed to believe them. He almost did. Problem was, his life was unraveling again. Bits fraying off until the whole thing became loose and shapeless in his hands. And after he'd tried so hard to weave together something that made sense, something that would hold tight, at least tight enough for one phone call to the woman who had snatched his dreams and vanished. And now, even after fifteen years, she could pull a single string and everything he'd put together fell apart again.

That just stunk.

God, You can't possibly be asking me to face this loss again, to give up the one person I've come to love.

But God could, and God did, and God was. And worse yet, Taylor's job was to make it happen. And stay behind again, alone. Some things never changed.

Taylor glanced at the ghost ascending the stairs and gave a fake shiver. "Mighty scary costume this year, David."

The boy peered out from the sheet. "How'd you know it was me?"

"The shoes." He pointed down to white high tops with bright orange stripes.

David glanced down too and chuckled. "I guess they do give me away."

Taylor reached for a pencil and candy. "Dark chocolate for the man fresh from the grave." He dropped it in.

"Thanks, man."

Taylor turned his attention to little Cassie with her cowgirl hat askew and a cast over her left arm. Her lower lip trembled.

He lifted her chin with one finger. "What's wrong, little cowgirl?"

"I broke my arm. Now my costume's all ruined. David says you can't ride horses with a broken arm."

"What does a ghost know? He's dead."

She peeked up at him.

"Besides, aren't you a famous bronco rider? I bet you broke your arm riding the wildest horse in the west."

Her eyebrows furrowed. "But we're in the east."

"That horse done threw you clear from west to east." He tried a Texas drawl. "But you got the best of him. Rode him tame in the end."

Cassie giggled.

David grunted. "It was a bike."

Cassie scowled at her older brother under the sheet. "Mr. Taylor says it was a horse, and I rode him good. It was too my horse. Her name's Pixie."

David shook his head. "That's the name of your bike."

Cassie held out her bag. "I'm a big, bad bronco rider. So there." She stuck out her tongue at her brother.

Taylor put a pencil and two pieces of candy in her bag. "Okay, cowgirl, let's see that cast."

She lifted it toward him.

He gave a mock gasp. "Why, what's this? Hasn't anyone signed it yet? Can I be the first?"

Her eyes grew wide. "Would you?"

Taylor laughed, grabbed a pen, and signed his name with a flourish. Then he sketched a bucking horse and wrote, "To the best bronco rider in the west or east."

Cassie held up the cast to her brother. "See, David, it really was a horse. Mr. Taylor drew it right here. Look."

David shook his head and walked back down the stairs toward the street. "Well, we can't argue with Mr. Taylor, can we? Come on, Cas. Let's show all the other people your bronco-rider costume, complete with the cast."

She followed, then paused and waved back with her good arm. "I'm gonna come out and see your horses real soon, Mr. Taylor. Just as soon as my arm's better."

"I'll have the black saddled and ready." Taylor watched her skip down the sidewalk beside her brother. The black loved it when kids came to ride him.

Of course, that was Emmit's fault too. The boy had fallen in love with that horse when he was five, on their first visit to old man Sanders's ranch. Taylor had taken Emmit out there on their way to the circus. He'd just needed to get a couple papers signed. He didn't know at the time that one stop would change their lives.

He remembered how he jumped out of the car and rushed over to the passenger's side before Emmit could get out and run off. The boy had just gotten out of the hospital after another surgery. Kids like Emmit often had heart problems. But the surgery was supposed to fix that, and it seemed like it did. But it couldn't repair his speech or all the other disabilities associated with his condition. Emmit hadn't said a single word since getting out of the hospital. Everyone tried to get him to talk, but nothing worked.

Until he saw the horses. They changed everything. Emmit stepped out of the car and stopped, his mouth agape, his arms hanging limply at his sides. Then he raised one hand and pointed at a tall, black horse in the pasture beyond. His eyes grew wide.

Taylor put his arm around the boy's shoulder. "Do you like the horse?"

"Beautiful." Emmit breathed the word, the first word he'd spoken in over a month. Then he bolted toward the fence as fast as his five-year-old legs could carry him.

Taylor raced after him. The horse sauntered to the fence and nuzzled Emmit's hand.

"I love horse. I want horse." He turned to Taylor. "Uncle Tay, I have horse?"

Emotion clogged Taylor's throat as he swept the boy into his arms and held him so he could pet the horse's mane. Every Saturday following that, Emmit insisted Taylor bring him to see the horses. After a couple months, Sanders let him ride the black, with Taylor leading the horse by a rope, of course. But you would have thought Emmit was in heaven by the huge smile on his face and the stream of words tumbling out of his mouth.

"He's big horse, Uncle Tay. I ride him. I like to ride. I ride every day. Do they ride horses in heaven? I bet angels ride horses. This is a nice horse. His mane is black. I pet him. Good horsie. I love you, horsie. I give you carrots. Did you bring carrots, Uncle Tay?"

Then one Saturday Taylor caught him telling a new foal all about the chocolate-covered pretzels he'd eaten after lunch. That's when Taylor knew for sure the horses had cured Emmit. And in some ways, they'd healed Taylor too, at least a little.

So when Sanders moved north to live with his daughter, Taylor bought the ranch and had lived there ever since, tending the horses, riding Misty, and dreaming of seeing the horses heal more children besides Emmit. So far, though, that dream hadn't come true. And it looked like it never would. Because now Emmit was leaving. And he would take the dream with him.

Why can't I ever hold on to the things I love?

"Trick or treat!"

The shout jarred Taylor out of the memory. He blinked and turned to the next group of kids trotting up the steps. A big-eared Dumbo, an astronaut, and— His breath stopped.

And a little girl in black leather pants, a biker jacket, and a helmet perched atop her head.

Marnie.

He should have known she'd haunt him, especially on a night like tonight. Even though she was older now, different. She had to be. She wasn't that young, sassy girl he'd once known. The one he once promised to stick by, no matter what. Promised to do right by, and failed. Miserably.

He should have known her memory would show up here to accuse him. If only he'd shot that phone when he had the chance.

She'd done okay on her own, though, without him. At least that's how it looked from his research on the Internet. It had been simple really. He'd just Googled *Marnie* and skipped past the references to the old Alfred Hitchcock movie. And there she was, smiling at the camera in front of a quaint little coffee shop in California. Marnie, sixteen years older but still stunning. Still with that feisty smile, with one eyebrow raised, her arms crossed over her chest, as if daring the viewer to judge her.

So like the girl he remembered. And not like her. The Marnie he'd known would have looked a lot like the little girl begging candy at his doorstep. She would have had a helmet under her arm and wouldn't have paused long enough for a picture to be snapped. Her hair would have been long and deep brown. But she still would have had that same challenge in her eyes. Just like she did that summer so long ago.

That single summer that changed everything.

"Trick or treat!" The kids shook their bags.

Taylor put on a smile, tossed candy and pencils into their pillow-cases, but he didn't see them. Not really.

All he saw was Marnie, her hair spread out on the pillow the last time he'd seen her. Marnie, who he didn't do right by after all.

And now it was happening again. Pain and loss. Doing wrong. Doing right. Either way, nothing would ever be the same.

Because she was here. The woman he'd once loved. That's the ghost who came knocking at his door tonight. And no pencils or chocolate, geishas or goblins, would chase her away.

3

Sixteen years was a long time. But not long enough. Not hardly. Taylor knew it as his hand reached into the candy dish. He knew it as the streetlights flickered in the ever-darkening night. He knew it as the little kids came and went, as the night wore on and the monsters at his door grew older, as the chocolate waned and the moon hid and the sky spat snow into the blackness. Sixteen years and he still couldn't forget. Not a single look, a single word, a single tremulous hope.

Taylor was twenty-three that summer. Young, stupid, and on a quest to "find himself" after his second year in law school. A tough year when he'd volunteered at the local legal aid because he was going to help the children.

He didn't help anyone. Not even close. Instead he did more harm than good, and in the process he feared he'd lost his soul. Turned out, all he really lost was the good sense his mama had given him.

He rented a tiny cottage on the beach outside a town he'd found on a map. A little place called Clam's Junction, hundreds of miles from the bustle of his home in New York. He told his mom he had to reevaluate his life, told himself God would show him what to do.

But it wasn't God who showed him. It was Marnie. She taught him to hope again. Taught him to see. Gave him back his vision. And then snatched it away.

Still, he didn't know any of that as he sat there at the edge of the beach, barefoot with his fluorescent green hat low over his eyes to block the midmorning sun. He just stayed there, digging his toes into the sand and watching the waves swoop in and out across the vast, rocky shore. He turned a small stone over in his hand and rubbed his thumb over its smooth surface.

What am I going to do? God? Give me a sign.

He didn't get a sign. All he got was the roar of a Harley behind him. He turned around, and there it was. A magnificent machine rumbling in the cottage driveway. And astride it sat a slim figure dressed all in black. Dark sunglasses, leather chaps, black boots.

The rider revved the Harley's engine one last time before turning it off. A hand reached up to remove the helmet and out swept a wave of long, dark hair. She dismounted the bike and set her helmet on the seat. She faced him, fists on her hips, wind in her hair.

And he just sat there with his mouth agape, like some kind of dumb-struck schoolboy in *The Breakfast Club.*

"Nice hat. You're the lawyer?"

"Uh, um, duh…"

She laughed, a full, throaty sound that coaxed a smile from his lips and ended with a funny little hitch at the end. "You'll stun the court with that brilliant banter, after your hat blinds them, of course." She strode toward him. Still with that smile. That same lively, challenging grin.

He stood and brushed the sand off his hands. The stone dropped to the ground.

She stopped in front of him. "I thought lawyers had an answer for everything."

"Who are you? The judge and jury?"

"You wish."

"I do."

She laughed again. Same full sound, same little hitch. She pulled off her sunglasses and stuck out her right hand. "Marnie Wittier. I'm with the family who lives across the road."

Ah, from the landlord's family. He didn't remember them mentioning a daughter. "Taylor Cole. You own the cottage, huh?"

"Not exactly."

"You know, it doesn't have a shower."

One eyebrow lifted. "Too bad, tough guy. You'll have to take baths like the old-timers. You'll live." She paused. "Unless you're planning to sue over it."

"Naw, I think I can manage."

She crossed her arms. "See, that's how I can tell you're not a real lawyer. A real lawyer never says he's not going to sue."

"How do you know?"

"I watch TV. Besides, you look a little wet behind the ears. Or maybe you just got back from a short swim in the surf." She motioned toward the waves.

"I wish I had."

"Lawyering's tough business, huh?"

She had no idea. No clue how the law could be bent, massaged, turned in ways that would have seemed crazy to him a year ago, and crazier to his practical mother. He'd been so passionate, so...so naive.

He'd wanted to be a lawyer ever since he was a kid, watching reruns of *Matlock* on the tiny television in his room. All his friends were into the brand-new MTV, but he loved how one old gray-haired guy could bring justice into a world gone wrong. And somehow, that justice brought peace, rightness.

He wanted to be that guy, not necessarily as a defense attorney, but as some kind of lawyer who brought that same rightness to the underdog, especially to kids who didn't have things as good as he did. Kids like his friend Jeremy, whose dad hit him if he didn't get all As. That's why Taylor was going to grow up, be a lawyer, and stand up for the little guy.

Too bad it didn't work out that way. Not only was the law nothing like it was portrayed on television, but he was no Matlock.

He grimaced and glanced at the woman in front of him. "I suppose. At least that's what I'd guess after my second year of law school."

"That bad?"

"Worse."

"Well, what'd you expect? They say the only thing lower than a lawyer is a politician." She bent over and picked up the smooth stone he'd dropped.

"I'm not the scummiest form of life yet, that what you're saying?"

Her eyes sparkled as she suppressed another laugh. "Not yet." She cocked her head at him. "What kind of law do you want to practice?"

He sighed. What did he want? He used to know. Used to think he'd learn the law, defend the kids, save the Jeremys. But instead he'd learned the loopholes, defended his grades, and saved nothing at all. Not even his dignity. He rubbed his hand over his chin, then stuck his hands into the pockets of his shorts. He couldn't meet her eyes. "You know, defend the poor, help the needy."

"Well, Robin Hood, you gonna rob from the rich to give to the— Oh wait, to give to the lawyers, right?" She tossed the stone from her right to left hand, then pointed it at him.

He glanced up. "You really know how to flatter a guy."

"I call 'em like I see 'em."

"And it looks like I'm on my third strike." And he deserved it.

She grinned. "I may have to change my mind about you lawyer types. You've got spunk."

"You do too."

"I have to."

"Why?"

She paused for a moment, then shook her head. "Because I'm a girl."

He watched her, almost positive that what she said wasn't what she had first thought. She had been about to say something else. Something true. He pulled his hands from his pockets and slapped his palms together. See, he wasn't totally incompetent as a would-be lawyer. At least he could tell when someone was switching her story midstream.

She poked the rock at him. "What's your excuse?" She tossed the stone up again.

"Being a lawyer, of course." He let her drop the rock into his hand, then he slipped it into his left pocket.

She nodded. "Okay, Mr. Lawyer, how 'bout helping a girl find her missing mom? You do that?"

"That's PI work."

"Lawyer-in-training can't help, huh? Some Robin Hood you are."

He rubbed his foot in the sand. Damp grains oozed through his toes. "Who's the girl? You?"

She stared out over the waves. "Maybe." Marnie wasn't smiling. She turned back and pinned him with her gaze. "Tell me about your family."

His family. Well, that was safe. What was there to tell? "Dad's an engineer. Mom does interior design. Got two brothers. One's a pastor. The other thinks he's going to be a writer, at least until he discovers there's no money in it."

Marnie frowned. "See. It matters."

"What does?"

"Where you come from. Who you come from. A person's gotta belong."

He shrugged. "I dunno." Didn't seem to help him. Not this last year anyway.

"I do. Kids gotta know if they've really been thrown away like a piece of trash."

She said it so calmly, too calmly. It sent a shiver through him. "How long's she been missing?"

"Since I was ten, ten years ago." She crossed her arms. "Ever since then, it's been foster homes until I got out on my own." Her eyebrows rose. "So, can you help or not?"

"Well…" He never could resist a kid in trouble. "I guess—"

The squeal of tires interrupted him. A horn beeped. Both Marnie and he turned toward the sound. A small silver Toyota hummed down the gravel driveway in front of the cottage. It stopped next to the Harley. A moment later, a woman burst from the driver's side. Her long, honey-colored hair flew around her flushed face as she approached them, shouting as she came.

"Marnie, don't you dare!"

Marnie grimaced. "Come off it, Rose."

Rose's blue eyes narrowed. "You will let that boy alone. Do you hear me?"

Boy? Taylor's shoulders stiffened. "Who's that?" He spoke in an undertone.

Marnie blew out a breath. "My beautiful, perfect, older sister. Who else? And yes, I know, we don't look anything alike, even though there's only a year between us." Her voice hardened. "And yes, she has a boyfriend."

Like he cared. But the way she'd said it, his almost-lawyer instincts tuned in again, warning him. There was something in the way she turned her head away, lifted her chin just a hair. Something in the way her jaw line tensed.

Rose stormed closer. "Marnie, you listen to me." She halted and threw her hands up. "Don't tell me you already—"

Marnie cut her off. "What if I did?"

She stabbed a finger in Marnie's direction. "You better not have."

Both women's voices raised, one to a shriek, the other lower, taunting. "What's it to you?"

Rose's voice hit another octave. "Oh, I don't know, maybe that she's my mother too. Ever think of that?"

"So?"

"So, I am not going to be known as *that* woman's daughter."

For one long, awkward minute, the sisters glared at each other. Taylor shifted his weight from one foot to the other. Was that the phone ringing? Only his cottage didn't have a phone. Maybe he'd left the stove on or his laptop unplugged or the water running. Something.

Before he could think of a good excuse for escape, Rose shook her head and whirled toward him. Her voice lowered to a normal pitch. "She's impossible." She put on a sweet smile and lifted her hand. "I'm so sorry you got caught in the middle of this. My sister can be very impetuous. I'm Rose, as I'm sure you heard."

He took her hand, briefly. "Taylor."

"Yes, I know. Mom told me."

What? "Mom? But I thought..." He motioned between the two women.

"I mean our foster mother, of course. The one who owns this cottage and lives up there across the road." Rose pointed. "The one who fed us, clothed us, took care of us." She glanced at her sister. "Our *real* mom."

Taylor took a step back. "Oh." Maybe he'd left the iron on, except he never used an iron in his life. Try again. His favorite television show was on? Except the cottage didn't have a television either. Out of luck. He glanced toward the cottage's back stairs.

Marnie flung her hands out and huffed. "Give it a rest, Rose. We were only with Doris for three years."

"I was with her for three. You were there for four before you turned eighteen and were on your own, remember?"

"How could I forget?"

"You seemed to have forgotten plenty, not the least of which was how Doris never kicked us out, never just vanished, has been there for us. And that's saying something."

"Yeah, like what?"

"Like we aren't some kind of garbage tossed to the curb, no matter what you think or say."

"I've never said that."

"Really?" Rose's voice became all cool and reasonable.

Marnie swallowed.

"And why don't you give it a rest? Permanently. I simply don't see why—"

"Yes, you do."

"No, I don't, Marnie."

"You want me to explain it again…*now*?"

Rose tossed a horrified look at Taylor. Her tone lowered to a hiss. "Not in front of him."

Taylor cleared his throat. "I'll just go in now"—he motioned in the direction of the cottage—"and have a shower, uh, I mean, a bath."

A slight smile flickered over Marnie's face, then was gone. Still, he almost thought he saw her wink at him. But now she was again facing her sister.

"Don't worry, Sis. If I find our mom's some raging lunatic, or worse, a liberal, I won't let anyone know."

"It's not that."

Marnie lifted both eyebrows. "Oh?"

Rose tilted closer. "Okay, so maybe it is. If she comes back in our lives, what do you think my chances will be with William, then? You will not ruin this for me, Marnie. Not like last time."

"Doug was a total loser. Had a great car, and that was a pretty nice yacht, but the zits, ew."

"Knock it off."

"Come on, Rose, he was a total letch. I didn't think you could do worse. But then I didn't know Fancy-Pants William."

"You be quiet about him."

"Then you leave Taylor and me alone."

"Oh, *Taylor* is it? What, you've known him for three minutes and you're all buddy-buddy already?"

Taylor started to inch toward the cottage door. Too late.

Marnie looped her arm around his. "Yeah, that's it. We're a new item. Didn't you know? I'm going to marry a rich lawyer. And William is only, what? Oh yes, the son of a banker."

Rose pursed her lips. "Fine, just fine. Bat your eyes at the new lawyer-boy, get what you want, find our useless mother. Just don't come crying to me when everything goes wrong and you find out that you were better off not knowing."

"Stop it."

Rose shook her head. "Finding our mother is not going to help you one bit. We don't need her. She'll just make things worse. For you, for me, for everyone."

Marnie looked away. "And don't forget William."

"He's not the only reason."

"Don't worry, I won't cry, and I certainly won't come to you."

"Don't be a fool, Marnie." Rose spun on one dainty heel and stomped off.

Marnie watched her go, then turned toward Taylor and let go of his arm. For a moment, he wished she hadn't. "Sorry about that. Didn't know you were in for a cat fight on your first day, did you?"

"I've seen worse."

"Really? Must have been some nasty cats." She grinned at him. "So, you still want to help me find my mom?"

"Nope."

She scowled. "Not you too? Come on, help me."

He shook his head. "I don't need to."

"Why not?"

Taylor watched Rose's car back up the driveway and swing out into the road. It crossed in a sudden jerk, then sped up the long, narrow path to the other house—the main house where their foster mother lived. The house where people knew secrets they kept from the girl standing next to him. That's what his lawyer instincts told him. And he knew he was right. He turned toward Marnie. "Why not? Because your sister already knows where your mom is."

He never forgot the look she gave him then. Fury, betrayal, and a single glance of a sorrow so deep that it changed him, drew him, determined every move he'd made after that. Because for that one breathless instant, he had seen into her soul.

4

Nothing was more annoying than the incessant ringing of a phone. Especially when you were dreading who might be on the other end. Marnie shuffled, as slowly as possible, down the small path that led to her little rented bungalow. She shifted the bag of takeout chow mein and pot stickers on her hip and slowed her pace even further. *I'm not home.*

The phone kept ringing. On and on and on.

She stopped and watched the cutesy sea décor that decorated either side of the path. A fake heron, a log-and-rope border, a sandy flower bed scattered with shells. Her landlord thought it was homey. Marnie thought it was corny, but that was okay. As long as she didn't have to have a half-sunken replica of a boat in her living room, she could stand one in her front yard.

Inside, though, was all hers.

She sighed and started again for the front door. Early evening shadows played over the wood as she reached the door, unlocked it, and stepped inside. Here, there were no wood carvings of birds, no ropes, no logs, no ships. But there weren't photos either, or trinkets on the shelves, or fun little reminders of a life lived happily ever after. The walls were bare. The shelves mostly empty. The windows shuttered, without curtains. There wasn't even a single pumpkin in honor of the season.

Marnie shut the door behind her, locked it, then moved to the kitchen. She dropped the food on the table and tossed her backpack next to it. Chow mein could wait.

The phone stopped ringing. *Thank You, Lord.*

She slid down into a hard-backed chair and stared into the other room. A spartan couch lined one wall, with an old CD player on a table next to it. Only the bookcase showed life. There, Max the iguana lay in a shaft of sunlight. He was grayer now than green and only turned his head a quarter inch and flicked his tongue at her as she entered.

Today she didn't call out her normal greeting. She just stared at him. He stared back from between books piled every which way on either side of him. Tall books, short ones, paperbacks, hardcovers. They were her friends. The ones she could pour out her heart to. The ones who asked for nothing in return. Them and Max. They were safe.

But in the middle of the bookcase sat a box. The box. One-foot long, nine-inches high, covered with shells, and carved out of bits of old driftwood. It was anything but safe. But it was still precious.

She stood and walked to the box. Beyond she could see the small second bedroom she'd converted to a workroom to make her coffee-shop tables. Light still trickled from the tall glass doors that led from the far end of that room onto the back patio. And farther down the hall stood her own bedroom, just as stark.

She paused before the box. Then she pulled the baby shower napkin from her pocket and slipped it through the opening in the top of the box. She gave the lock on the front a quick tug. Solid. Firm. The box was getting full, though. Over fifteen years of regrets was a lot to hold. A lot to keep sealed, shut away. Forever.

That's why the box was precious—it held the portion of her life she kept locked up so no one would know, no one would guess. Locked so tight that sometimes she thought even she might forget. Except she didn't.

Well, maybe someday.

Maybe never.

What will I do when the box is full?

She touched the box again, let her fingers linger on the rough surface, then she turned and strode back to the kitchen. She dropped into her chair and grabbed for the container of pot stickers. It had been a long day. Too long. It was good to be back home, away from pink napkins and shiny balloons. Good to be wrapped in peaceful silence. Or it would be silent, except for Max scraping his way slowly down the ramp from her bookcase and the envelope shouting for attention in her pocket.

Marnie pushed away the pot stickers and pulled out the envelope. She touched the return address again. Maine. So he'd gone back there, and stayed. Even after all this time. He always said he would.

And he did.

But she didn't.

She escaped. Back then, Pacific Grove was as far as she could run. She'd boarded a bus and kept on going until she couldn't go any farther. And still, it wasn't far enough.

She turned the envelope over in her hand. She'd have to face it. Open it. Read the words he wrote. But how bad could it be? It had been so many years. Too long for him to now reach into her life and shake it. Too long for anything he would say to matter.

Yeah, right.

Marnie took a deep breath and slid her finger under the flap. The sound of rending paper echoed off the kitchen walls. The envelope opened.

She pulled out three pieces of fine linen paper. Thick, rich paper. His paper.

They trembled in her fingers. Her gaze lingered on the logo again, now taunting her from the top of the first page.

Taylor Cole, how did you find me?

But of course he found her. He was good at that. Still, it had taken him fifteen years. She ought to be over him. She ought not to care anymore. Hadn't she put nearly everything he'd given her into her box of regrets? Hadn't she locked them all away? But didn't forget them. Didn't forget him.

She pictured him again in her mind. Did he still look like the same young guy with the dark brown eyes and windswept hair? Did he still love hats? And did that one silly lock still fall over his forehead? Did he push it back when he was nervous? His hair might be graying now. And maybe he cut it differently. Maybe he'd even lost it. And maybe he'd moved on from hats. Fifteen years was a long time.

Still, she couldn't help imagining him as he'd once been. On fire to do what was right, to defend her, to get the truth out of her sister and discover where her mother had gone. What a useless errand that had been. But there was no way they could have known it then. Not as they sat there in the tiny cottage living room with those few old photos spread before them.

He straightened the only picture she had of her mother, an old black-and-white blurry one with her mom pregnant and a cigarette in her mouth. "So, you think your mom's in on it? Your foster mom, I mean?"

Marnie flopped down on the couch opposite him and tossed her motorcycle helmet onto the recliner. "Maybe. She'd do whatever Rose says. Just like everybody else."

"And the agency has no information?"

She smacked her forehead. "Gee, why didn't I think of that? Maybe the *system* has everything I need…*not.*"

"Okay, so they don't know anything."

"Our mom skipped town years ago. We came home from school to our ratty little apartment and she was just gone. Neighbor called Child Protective Services and so began the string of foster homes."

"Did they try to find your mom?"

She shrugged. "I guess. But she left no forwarding address, no nothing. And I don't suppose anyone tried very hard. Why would they?"

"Because they cared."

Marnie grimaced. "Yeah, right."

"So, why'd she leave?"

"Who knows? That's what I want to find out. I need to find out."

Taylor looked at her a long time. "Why? Why not just let it go like Rose says?"

This time, it took a long time for her to answer. She wasn't sure she could trust him. Not yet anyway. But then he looked at her, touched the brim of his Minnesota Twins baseball cap, and smiled just enough for the dimple in his right cheek to show. "Why are you helping me anyway?"

"I got a soft spot for kids in trouble. Now answer the question."

"Am I on the stand, Lawyer-Man?"

"Would it help if you were?"

She smiled. "Okay."

"The truth."

"Of course the truth." He'd have seen through anything else. She took a deep breath. "Mom said something to me that day before she vanished. Rose was already out the door, heading to the bus stop. Mom stopped me, grabbed my chin, and forced me to look her right in the eyes. Then she said something."

"What?"

Marnie shook her head. "I don't know. I can't remember." She clenched her hands together and leaned toward the table between them. "But sometimes I think if I just knew that one thing, I'd understand everything that happened. I'd get why she just threw us away and never looked back. It had to be important, had to explain, didn't it?"

"I don't know."

"I've got to find out. Otherwise…" Otherwise she'd go on wondering, questioning, believing that love was something for others but not for her. Never for her. Because she wasn't worth it. Her own mother didn't love her enough to stay. "I just have to find her, that's all. I have to know."

Taylor nodded. "Well, someone knows where she is now."

"My sister."

"Yep."

"And she's not telling."

"Nope."

"Anyone else?"

"God."

She blew a raspberry with her tongue. "Fat lot of good that does. He's not telling either."

Taylor raised his eyebrows. "Have you asked?"

Something in the way he said it—all matter-of-factly without the slightest bit of hesitation—stopped her snappy comeback. Her mouth hung open for a moment, and then she sputtered out, "Wh-what?"

He cleared his throat. "Have you asked?"

Yuck, that's what she thought he said. "Oh, come on, you're not going to get all Billy Graham on me, are you?"

"And if I am?"

She crossed her arms over her chest. "Well, I won't like it."

He laughed. "Yeah? So sue me."

Her scowl broke to a grin. He could always make her laugh at the craziest moments. As if he saw more than she did, believed more than she did, and feared a lot less. But fear was her secret. No one else was supposed to see that.

Except she suspected that sometimes, or maybe a lot of the time, he did.

She poked a finger in his direction. "Okay, I deserved that, Mr. Lawyer-Man. Still, praying hasn't done me a whole lot of good yet."

"How do you know?"

She gave him a stern look and settled back into the couch. "You met my sister, right?"

"She's okay."

"Okay? She's perfect, didn't you know? That's what I get for my prayers. This"—she glanced down at herself: the worn leather pants, the tough black boots, the T-shirt with the name of the local bar plastered across the front—"and a perfect sister."

"Aw, you aren't so bad."

"Fooled you."

"You really think so?"

Her mouth clamped shut over anything else she would have said. Because she didn't have anything to say to that. He was right. There was no fooling Taylor Cole.

Silence wafted through the room and blew out the back door. Taylor spoke again, softer this time, gentler. "So, are we going to pray or not?"

"If you insist." Were those her words, coming out all meek and quiet-like? Maybe. Or maybe she was just tired. Yeah, that was it.

"Don't you believe in God, Marnie?"

She shrugged. "I dunno. I guess I do." She believed in a great, big God out there somewhere. Keeping the planets aligned. Helping folks like Mother Teresa and that guy trying to feed the starving kids in Africa. But so what? What did that have to do with her? What did *He* have to do with her?

"Then let's do it." Taylor closed his eyes. He didn't fold his hands.

Weren't you supposed to fold your hands? And worse, he tilted up his chin to pray instead of facing his feet. Marnie was sure you were supposed to peek at your toes when you prayed. That's how they always did it at the Easter and Christmas services she went to with her foster families.

"Lord, please help us to find Marnie's mom. And give us the courage to deal with whatever else we encounter when we do. Mostly, Lord, give us the courage to face the truth."

She needed that prayer then, more than she knew. Back there as she sat opposite him in the little seaside cottage. And she needed it now too. In her little bungalow with his letter hot in her hand.

Well, God, here we go again. Please, give me the courage to face the truth.

Marnie opened her eyes and allowed her gaze to travel to the letter's first line.

"Dear Miss Wittier…"

She swallowed and forced herself to continue.

"We regret to inform you that your sister has passed away…"

Marnie's breath stopped. The letter dropped from her hand.

5

mmit was invisible. At least that's what he wanted to think. Because he liked the big office with the soft carpet and the lady with gray hair and round glasses who rat-tat-tatted on her computer keyboard behind the desk. He liked the pretty green plant that grew next to the glass walls of the big office. He liked the stacks and stacks of books and binders and the rich smell of ink and old paper. But most of all he liked Mr. Cole.

Too bad he didn't look so happy today.

Emmit squatted next to the big glass office wall and peeked through the slats of the shade on the other side. Mr. Cole's office. And Mr. Cole sitting behind his big, shiny desk. Wearing a real fancy tie, and a real nice hat, and a real sad frown.

Poor Mr. Cole.

Dear God, make Mr. Cole happy again soon. Please.

Emmit frowned. He used to be able to pray better. He remembered that. It was hard to pray now. Real hard since that bad day when the nice light came and brought the bad sound and the ugly lights. Things hadn't been right since then.

But maybe God would help.

Because Emmit had lost something. Something important. And that's when he stopped being able to pray good.

God, help Mr. Cole.
God, help Emmit.
God?

~~~

Could a hat tell a kid that he'd miss him? Could it say that Taylor would keep the boy here if he could, that if he had another choice, he'd never send him away? Taylor hoped so. He prayed so. But now as he let his fingers linger over the brand-new Aussie cowboy hat on his desk, he sighed. It was a silly gift, really. A hat that matched the one Taylor used for riding. Emmit would probably think he'd lost his mind. But it wasn't his mind he was losing, it was his heart. Again.

Lord, how can I send him away? How can I stay here without him, without anyone?

But he had to. Rose wanted it that way. He heard her say it herself when she came in about her will. "If anything ever happens to me, I want you to make sure Emmit goes to Marnie. Promise me, Taylor."

"I've put it in the documents. Don't worry."

"Promise me. You'll find her, and you'll make sure you send Emmit."

Taylor nodded. "Of course."

But he'd never expected anything to happen to Rose. He never expected it would be his job, his duty, to send Emmit away. If he had…well, it wouldn't have changed anything. But, oh how he'd miss that boy.

And all the hats in the world couldn't fix that.

Taylor glanced at the single picture on his desk—Emmit grinning into the camera with Misty by his side. Taylor's Misty, the only woman besides his assistant Nancy in his life. Chestnut hair, deep brown eyes, and a love for sugar and carrots. Other women had come and gone. The pianist from church, the real estate agent from the next town over, Dr. Shultz's daughter fresh from grad school. But none of them filled the hole inside him. Only Misty understood. Only she didn't demand, didn't judge, didn't ask for more than he wanted to give. And that's because she was a horse. And Emmit loved that horse every bit as much as he did.

That's why he hoped the boy would see his gift of a hat and understand. But how could he? Emmit wouldn't remember the first time Taylor had given him a hat that matched his own. Emmit wouldn't remember how his seven-year-old eyes had grown big and wide, how he clapped his hands with delight and put the hat on crooked. He wouldn't recall how little-boy Emmit had run around the room singing about being a real cowboy, then worn the hat for three months straight while mucking stalls and feeding carrots to the horses, at school, in church, and even to bed at night. Emmit wouldn't remember. But Taylor did. Because for three solid months, he could almost pretend he had a son.

But he didn't. No matter how often he wished it.

And now the time had come. Loss and pain were knocking on his door again, and all he had to fend them off was one silly hat and a heart full of dead wishes.

Taylor put the lid back on the box holding Emmit's hat, then pulled out the top drawer of his desk. Inside was a menagerie of plastic kaleidoscopes, toy trucks, cheap dinosaurs, tiny dolls, and mini jars of blowing bubbles all mixed in with every color of lollipop available. Taylor kept them there for any kids who visited his office with their parents.

He grabbed a root beer lollipop, unwrapped it, and stuck it in his mouth. Then he listened to the loud ticking of the clock from his bookcase, the tapping of Nancy's fingers on the keyboard in the outside office, and the squeak of the outer door as someone opened it. The tapping stopped.

The inner door to his personal office opened a moment later. Nancy's head poked through the opening. "He's here."

"Give me a moment."

Taylor touched the box again, straightened a stack of papers on his desk, and allowed his fingers to rest on the airline ticket on top. He'd gotten that for Emmit too. Because he had to. Not because he wanted to. If only the boy would believe that.

Next to the ticket was another box that held a number of Emmit's favorite things—chocolate-covered pretzels from the shop down the street, a photo album of his mother, the fuzzy *ABC* book he'd loved as a kid.

"Love covers over a multitude of sins," the Bible said. He hoped that was true too, because he'd loved Emmit ever since Rose placed the baby in his arms, looked at them both, and said, "Stay, Taylor, for Emmit's sake." And then she cried.

He never could resist a plea like that, especially when the baby, fresh home from the neonatal intensive care unit, reached out and waved a floppy fist toward his face and burped milk all down the front of Taylor's shirt. He looked into those baby-gray eyes and knew he couldn't walk away.

Funny how he'd come back to Clam's Junction for Marnie but found Emmit, full of physical problems, struggling as a baby just to survive. Rose needed him; Emmit needed him—they needed someone anyway. And he was there, hurt and broken too and still wanting to make things right. Still with a love for kids in trouble. And Emmit was in a lot of trouble even back then.

So he stayed. It was only going to be for a year or so at first, just until Marnie returned, like he was sure she would. He'd wait, help

Emmit and Rose, and lend a hand to old man Bailey with his estate-planning practice.

But a couple years turned into three, then four, then five. Then Mr. Bailey had his heart attack, and the business went to Taylor. And Marnie never came back. And Emmit grew into a little boy who called him Uncle Tay, wore a matching hat for three months straight, and made him think that this one thing, at least, had gone right.

But now Rose was gone, he was losing Emmit, and it was his job to send him to the woman who had stolen Taylor's heart once and now would take it again, leaving him with nothing. Nothing at all.

Taylor stood, pulled the lollipop from his mouth, and rewrapped it. Yes, it was time. "Nancy, can you send in Emmit now?"

Emmit shuffled through the doorway, sat in the chair closest to the window, and looked outside. He just sat, with his arms crossed over his chest and his legs crossed on the seat in front of him.

Taylor shook his head and walked to the other side of his desk. Emmit wasn't that innocent little baby anymore, and he wasn't the eager little kid who wanted nothing more than to ride horses and feed them sugar cubes with a hat just like his Uncle Tay's.

He was a teen who had just lost his mother.

"Hello, son."

Emmit didn't even glance at him. "Not your son."

I know. I wish you were. Taylor's throat tightened. "I've got your airline ticket ready." He picked it up off the desk.

This time, Emmit did look up. His eyes narrowed and his jaw hardened. Then it trembled. "Won't go."

Taylor grimaced. He'd been afraid of this. His voice softened. "Why not?"

Emmit's face turned pink. "'Cause I prayed."

"What does praying have to do with anything?"

"Prayed for, prayed for family." His voice lowered and cracked. "Real family."

"Oh, Emmit." Taylor knew when Emmit had started praying for that—five years ago when Craig moved out of Rose's life and Emmit didn't even have a pretend daddy anymore. "Your Aunt Marnie will be your real family now."

Emmit's chin rose until he was looking Taylor right in the eye. And for once he spoke clearly, his words sharp and despairing. "I prayed you would marry my mom. I prayed you would be my dad."

Taylor's heart leaped into his throat and stuck there. He dropped the airline ticket and strode toward Emmit.

Emmit rose. "I don't get it. I prayed and, and…"

And instead of gaining a family, you lost what little family you had. Taylor put his arms around the boy and drew him close. "I'm sorry. I know. I wish…" He couldn't finish. He didn't dare.

Emmit sniffed and cried, just a little, into Taylor's shirt, like he did when he was a small boy and his favorite Tonka truck got run over by the neighbor kid.

Taylor put his hand on Emmit's head and let him cry for Rose, for lost prayers, for the dream that would never be.

God, why couldn't You just answer his prayer?

After a minute, he patted Emmit's back and attempted to smile down at him. "Hey, I got you a hat." His words came out shaky. "One just like mine." He cleared his throat, then walked back to his desk, opened the lid to the hatbox, and tilted it toward the boy.

Emmit rubbed his nose on the back of his hand and swallowed. "I'm not seven."

Taylor nodded. "I know."

"So?"

He looked away. "I just thought, well, I don't know. Something of home to bring with you." *To remember me. To remember us. Oh, Emmit, there's nothing I'd like better than to be your dad.*

Emmit glanced at the windowsill and refused to look in Taylor's direction. He sniffed again and rubbed his nose until it turned red. "Don't need a hat."

"I just thought—"

"I still won't go."

Taylor sat against his desk and blew out a long breath. "She's a good person, Emmit. You'll like her. She makes cookies at her coffee shop." Cookies, good grief, like that was going to convince a fifteen-year-old kid to travel across the country to an aunt he'd never met. *That the best you can do, Cole? Some dad you'd make.*

Emmit shot him a look of pure hopelessness, then stared at the windowsill again.

Yeah, I know. You won't go. But you have to. "Look, you can just try a visit at first. Maybe you'll like it."

Emmit tugged on his ear, then stuck out his bottom lip.

Taylor plopped back into his chair. "We've already purchased the ticket. You've never been on an airplane, have you?"

Emmit sighed. "No."

"It's fun."

He grunted.

Teenagers…it would be hard enough if Emmit were a normal teen, full of rebellion and anger and grief. But as it was…well, this was even harder. He looked at the kid, scraggly hair trailing over black-framed glasses, a modest sprinkling of pimples, and a jaw line hard with desperate determination.

"Won't go."

On better days, Emmit had a great smile and a laugh that could move even the hardest heart. But not today. And not for a long time. He missed the boy's smile.

Taylor leaned forward. "I know, and I'm sorry. But she's your guardian now. I think you'll like her. Here, try on the hat." He took it out of the box and held it out in Emmit's direction.

Emmit glanced at it but didn't take it from Taylor's grip. "It's black."

"I know."

"My other one was brown."

"This one's from the Australian outback."

"Mom took my other hat. Said I couldn't wear it to church no more."

So that's what had happened. Taylor always wondered.

"No one will take this one."

The bottom lip slipped in, just a bit.

Taylor walked back around his desk and sat down. He rested his elbows on the desk's surface. "Did I tell you I knew your aunt Marnie when she was young?"

Emmit didn't look at him, but Taylor thought he saw his jaw soften, at least a little. The kid was listening. And that was a start.

"She like hats?"

"She used to."

"Humpf."

Taylor tilted back in his chair. "Let me tell you a story about hats." He drew a long breath. "I remember one morning when she came racing around the corner on that big Harley of hers. She loved that Harley. This time, she had two big, white buckets hanging from the handlebars. Clamming buckets. She was bound and determined to have a clambake that night because I'd told her I'd never had a clam in my life."

"You said it was about hats."

"Listen, you'll see."

Emmit rubbed his foot over the carpet and settled back into his seat. He stared out the window, pretending not to listen.

"So we were going clamming. Only problem was that it was a nasty day to be out on the beach. Wind was howling, surf slamming into the rocks along the shore, clouds dark and gloomy. But your aunt, she didn't care. We said we were going clamming and that's what we were going to do. She'd already bought the butter and vinegar. So there we were with our big ol' buckets and this huge shovel she'd pulled from behind my cottage. The thing was two sizes too big for her, but she hauled it out over the sand anyway."

Emmit turned his head ever so slightly toward Taylor.

"We plodded up and down the beach looking for those little air holes clams make. And I was a little bit behind her, not really looking for clam holes at all." He paused and waited to see if Emmit would ask what he was doing instead.

He didn't.

"I was watching the way she walked, her arms swinging free and her hair shimmering like a dark wave down her back. Man, I loved to watch her walk. Weird thing to notice, I know. But there was just something about it, about her." He sighed and imagined it again in his mind.

"We walked and walked and didn't find any clams. She told me my big, bad lawyer ways were scaring all the clams away. I told her it's those big, bad riding boots she insisted on wearing. She said clamming's no fashion show. I said good thing because boots didn't go with raggedy shorts and a sweatshirt. Even a guy knows that. She said clamming didn't go with Yankees hats either, and by the way, she hates the Yankees. I told her hats made more sense than boots. She was about to make some snappy comeback when she spotted it. Our first clam air hole."

Taylor glanced at Emmit. The boy's arms were still crossed, but his shoulders were more relaxed and his breathing had slowed. He was still listening. Waiting for Taylor to continue.

Taylor suppressed a grin. The Marnie he knew could win over even her worst critic…like she was doing now, even over the distance of sixteen years. *Ah, Emmit, you have no idea what a knockout she was, even in those ridiculous black boots.*

He could see them again, clearly in his mind, as the memory came to life.

She grabbed the huge shovel and started digging. And digging. And digging. She turned over the sand. But nothing was there. Just gooey wet sand.

Taylor motioned toward the goo. "He's burrowed away, Marnie."

She scowled. "Not fast enough."

He laughed. "It heard you coming with those boots."

Marnie pointed the shovel at him. "You just watch and learn, Lawyer-Man. I'll get that clam yet." She kept digging. "Maybe we won't eat this one. I'll keep him for a pet."

He snorted. "Some pet."

She didn't stop digging. "Better than nothing."

He stared at her. "A dog's a pet. A cat's a pet. A clam is not a pet. Everyone knows that."

She leaned on top of the shovel and gave him a look he'd never forget. Sad and angry and hopeless and maybe a bit resigned. She grabbed the shovel handle again. "Foster kid, remember? I was never able to have a pet." She didn't look at him at all when she said it.

He swallowed. "Never? Not even a fish?"

"Never."

He stood there.

She dug some more. Dug and dug and dug.

And finally she got it. Tiny little thing it was. She held it up in her palm, all full of seawater and sand. Then she swiped his hat, turned it over, and plopped that wet, gooey, slimy clam right in the center of it. "Knew that hat would come in handy."

They laughed as water dripped out Taylor's hat and the clam just sat there in the middle.

Marnie put the hat back on his head, clam and all, and grinned at him. "Told you I'd get it."

He grinned back. "We're feasting big time tonight."

She stuck her tongue out at him, pulled off the hat again, plucked the clam from the top of his head, and put the hat back. She dropped that clam in the hole she'd dug and walked away.

They never did get any more clams that day. Instead they went to the store and bought some, then came back and cooked 'em up and dipped 'em in her butter mixture. Tasteless things, they were, but the best clams he'd ever had.

Taylor walked over and rested his hand on Emmit's shoulder. "We didn't take home a single clam, but you know what I learned that day?"

"Huh?"

"Never wear hats clamming." He watched to see if Emmit would smile.

He didn't, but Taylor expected he was close.

"I also learned that even if things don't turn out like you want, sometimes it's still not so bad." Taylor put on his own smile and hoped it covered up his pain. "You'll see."

Emmit didn't move this time, and he didn't grunt. That was a good sign.

Taylor patted his shoulder. "Okay, I'll just try to give Marnie one more call and let her know when you're coming. You wait out with Nancy."

Emmit stood and walked toward the door. As he drew close, he paused and took the hat from the box. He glanced at Taylor. And almost smiled.

Taylor escorted him out the door to the chair near Nancy's desk. "It'll just be a minute."

Emmit nodded and sat down.

Taylor returned to his office, shut the door, and dialed her number. He held his breath. Again. The phone rang and rang and rang. Again. But it was no use. No one answered, not even a machine. *Doggone it, Marnie, why do you have to make everything so difficult?* Well, at least some things never changed. He grimaced.

He stood and returned to the door, then opened it and called for Emmit.

He waited.

Nothing.

"Emmit, come on."

Just silence, except for Nancy tapping on the keyboard and a huge delivery truck rumbling by outside.

"Emmit?"

The tapping stopped.

Nancy peeked around her computer screen. She pushed her glasses up on her nose. "He's gone, Mr. Cole."

"Gone?"

"Left as soon as you shut the door. Said he was meeting someone."

"I told him to wait."

She shrugged. "There was someone just outside, so I thought—"

"Did he say when he was coming back?"

Nancy paused for a moment before answering. "He said he wasn't."

"Why didn't you stop him?" Taylor raced to the outer door and looked down the long sidewalk. Emmit was gone. Completely, totally gone. And if Nancy was right, he wasn't coming back.

Not again.

6

*N*o way. No how. No, no, no. There was no chance Marnie was going to be the guardian of some fifteen-year-old kid. And a boy. Ugh. Rose wouldn't ask that of her. And God wouldn't either.

Would You?

Marnie took the letter out of her pocket, where she'd kept it for two long, endless days. She glanced at the rows of recipe books on her office shelves, the kind notes from customers that hung from her corkboard, and the pile of new boxes filled with the latest releases from one of her favorite publishers. Sounds drifted from the main room outside. The clank of coffee cups—the ceramic ones she kept for her regular customers—the ding of the oven in the back. The screech of a chair being pulled out, and the ring of the cash register. *Thank goodness.* Normal sounds. Sounds that meant her world really wasn't going to be turned upside down.

She laid the letter on her desk and smoothed it flat. She read it again. But the words hadn't changed. Not since the first time they'd punched her in the gut in her bungalow, not since she'd gone over them again in bed that night, not since yesterday as she sat looking out toward the ocean, or that morning when she crumpled it up while drinking a cup of hot tea.

Her sister was dead. And now she was the legal guardian of someone named Emmit. She hadn't talked to her sister in over fifteen years. And now she was supposed to be the parent of a kid she'd never known existed? Just like her sister to go and die and, and—

Marnie's throat clogged. *Oh, Rose...* She sniffed. No, Marnie had shed enough tears over her sister already. Years worth of them. Still...

She flattened out the wrinkles in the letter again. She would just have to write a polite letter declining. Surely they'd understand. He'd understand. She'd shut the door on that part of her past once and for all. Again. A simple letter. Or better yet, a fax.

She opened her desk drawer, pulled out a piece of coffee-shop stationery, complete with a tiny icon of a cartoon coffee cup reading a book, found a pen, and began.

"Dear Mr. Cole—"

The pen stopped. Quivered.

This was ridiculous. She gripped the pen tighter, forced it back to the paper. "I received"—she tapped her fingers on the edge of the page—"your letter." The pen dropped.

Dear Taylor, I received your letter. How can my sister be dead? How can I be the legal guardian of a boy I've never met? How can you reach into my life after all these years and make my heart break again?

Were you there when my sister died? Your letter only said she'd been in a coma. Why didn't anyone contact me then? Maybe I would have come back to see her. One last time. Or maybe I wouldn't have.

Why didn't you find me earlier? Why did I let you find me now? Leave me alone, Taylor Cole! I don't want to raise a son. I can't. I don't want to remember. And I don't want to write this stinkin' letter where every word makes my heart want to bleed.

Marnie grabbed the stationery with its seven words written on the front and slapped it facedown on her desk. She snatched up the pen and wrote in big, scrawling script on the back, "Not seeing Rose before she died." She folded the paper into an awkward square, then jammed it into her pocket. She'd feed the box on her shelf at home later.

An old man shuffled into the office. He stopped short. "Sorry, Marnie. Just emptying trash cans." He stuffed his cleaning rag further into his back pocket.

"Come on in, Joe." Marnie smiled. That man loved to clean. Never seen anyone like him. Most wouldn't have hired a guy fresh out of prison that way, with that awful scar down his face and that funny gait of his. But he'd worked hard for her. And people deserved a second chance.

Everyone?

No. Not everyone.

Not me. The words hung in her mind, unspoken, barely thought. She crushed them, wadded them up, and threw them away. Then she stood. "Joe, could you please—"

A crash sounded from the main room. Breaking glass, a loud thud, a high-pitched squeal.

Daisy.

Marnie raced down the short hall and into the coffee shop. Broken ceramic coffee cups littered the floor, coffee pooled in a large puddle, and her wooden table covered with bumper stickers lay on its side, cracked down the middle. Only the ragged ends of a few stickers held it together. And there, kneeling in the middle of the mess, was Daisy.

Fat tears rolled down the girl's face as she glanced up and caught Marnie's gaze. "I'm so sorry, Miss Marnie. I just, I don't know what happened. It just…"

Marnie eased around a tipped chair. "Collapsed?"

"Well, yeah. No. I sort of bumped it first. And then, and then…" The girl took a big, stuttering breath.

"And then it tipped?"

"Yeah. Well, no. Then the coffee spilled on the floor. I was setting it on the table. Wasn't empty, and then, and then…"

"Then the table fell?"

"Yeah."

Marnie's eyebrows lifted. "Well, no?"

"No." Daisy chewed her lower lip. "I tried to stop it, but I slipped in the coffee."

"And grabbed the table, and the table fell and broke."

She nodded. "Yes. I'm sorry. But you know, the Bible says everything always turns out good if you, if you, if you just love God."

"Does it?" Of course it didn't, but Marnie wasn't going to correct the girl now. Not with her sitting there dripping with brown liquid and surrounded by bits of broken ceramic.

"And every cloud has a silver lining."

"Bible says that too, huh?"

"I-I think so."

"And He's got the whole world in His hands?"

Daisy smiled. "Yeah. That's right."

Good grief. Marnie tiptoed through the mess, then took Daisy under the elbow and helped her to her feet. "All right, let's get this mess cleaned up, and you too. Try not to cut yourself."

Daisy sniffled and rubbed her hand over her nose. It was such a childlike gesture Marnie had to smile.

Marnie turned, but Joe was already mopping up the coffee, picking up the cracked table, and sweeping up bits of broken glass. He'd also brought a stack of clean rags. She tossed one to Daisy, then took another, knelt, and started to sop up the liquid that had trickled under the bubblegum table.

Behind her, the door creaked open. The bell sang out. Marnie glanced up. She almost expected it to be Taylor. That would be about right—just the way she'd want to meet him after all these years, coffee staining her apron, soaking into her knees, a sopping rag in her hand, and a young girl sniffling and muttering something about God opening doors and closing windows beside her. Yep, that'd be just about perfect.

Except it wasn't him.

Of course it wasn't. He wouldn't come all the way across the country to find her. There was no reason for him to. Except…

Just for an instant, a memory passed in front of her vision and she saw him there, just as he had looked sixteen years ago. His hat swept off his head by the ocean breeze, a bucketful of clams in his hand, jeans rolled to midcalf. He stopped dead when he saw her. Stood there so long the next wave came in and practically knocked him face first into the sand.

Then the cold Atlantic rushed out again and left him tottering with his bucket and Levi's dripping. But he didn't care. And neither did she. He'd been a sight to behold. But that was a long time ago. She straightened and touched the letter in her apron pocket.

If he were to come through that door now, after all these years, would she run to him, or would she run away? Again.

Marnie set her wet rag on the glass top of the bubble-gum table. She'd do neither. She'd just kneel here with her mouth hanging open and coffee stains down her bright blue apron. Then she'd get up and ask him whether he wanted decaf or regular…and she'd give him decaf anyway. Decaf, with just a dash of chocolate. Exactly the way he used to like it.

But it wasn't Taylor at the door. It wasn't even the pimply-faced delivery boy, Scott. It was Mr. Karloff, the landlord. And there was never a silver lining in that cloud, no matter what Daisy might believe. "Mr. Karloff, how good of you to stop by." Ugh, forced friendliness always sounded so cheesy. She staggered to her feet.

Mr. Karloff stared at the spill, then he narrowed his eyes and turned his froglike face toward her. "Rent six days late."

Marnie wiped her hands on her apron. "I'll have it to you this afternoon." Somehow.

Mr. Karloff mumbled something in broken English about too many employees and lack of business experience, then stomped up to the counter.

Marnie sighed. The man might be right. But each of her employees was more than just hands and feet and the work they could do. They were family. Yes, even Daisy. And you didn't just send family packing. She shuddered and touched the letter in her pocket. Beside it was that folded-up piece of stationery with her own words scrawled on the back.

Family…like she had any idea of what that word really meant.

Marnie turned toward the counter. "Daisy, take Mr. Karloff's drink order, please. On the house." It was always on the house. One day that man would pay for his own coffee, but if she didn't offer, he'd just stand there glowering at whoever was taking his order and finally say, "You not know who I am?"

Today, however, she could use every cent that came in. Even his. She shook her head and bent down to set another chair aright. Maybe she could take today's receipts and pay the rent. Then she could scrape together enough to pay Marcus, Daisy, and Joe on Friday. She'd have to delay paying herself again. But that was okay. Rent on her bungalow wasn't due for another week. And anything could happen in a week. Right?

Mr. Karloff turned back around and dug his hand into his suit jacket. He removed an envelope and tossed it on a table between them. "Almost forget. Letter come for you."

Marnie tried to force another smile but failed. "Thank you for picking up my mail." The last word came out as a low, grating sound.

"You are welcome."

Marnie twisted another rag around in her hand. *God help me, or I'm going to—* She spotted the logo on the envelope. *Not again.* She dropped the rag. Her fingers reached toward the letter, Mr. Karloff forgotten, the sounds of the milk steamer dimming, the wet cling of her pants over her knees now only barely noticeable.

He had come. Taylor had indeed come through that door, only in paper form.

She turned over the envelope and slit it open. Inside was only a plain piece of paper, no posh letterhead, no linen finish. Just normal white copy paper. She unfolded it. And there was his handwriting, slanting across the page.

Dear Marnie, it read. Not *Miss Wittier,* just *Marnie.* Her heart thudded.

I know my first letter came as a shock. I've tried to call. It's
been too long.

The writing changed a bit, as if he'd paused, then started up again.

Look, I'm sending Emmit to you on Friday. I've already
got his plane ticket. Rose wanted it this way. I know you'll
take him. If you don't, he'll go into foster care, and I can't
believe that even sixteen years would change your mind
about foster care. We'll take care of the paperwork later. I
don't expect the transfer of guardianship to be contested.
After all, there is no one else but you to take care of
Emmit. And now I've got to get him on that plane. His
flight info is included below. Tell me you'll be there.

I'll be there. He knew her too well. Even after all these years. She glanced down at the letter one more time. Right above his name, a few words were scribbled out. She could read them anyway. *"I've never forgotten..."*

She closed her eyes. *And neither have I.* And that was the problem.

～∿

He didn't want to be here. But he was here anyway. With the afternoon sun glinting off the snow on a little yard onto a little house with the shades pulled and no one home.

Taylor adjusted his hat and trudged up the steps to Rose's old house. It hadn't been sold yet. The red and blue Realtor's sign was still in the front yard, the lockbox still hanging from the door handle. He reached in his pocket and pulled out a key. He unlocked the door and stepped inside. It smelled musty in here. Like unwashed socks and old pizza cartons. He wrinkled his nose.

He shouldn't have sent that letter. It had practically killed him to write it. *"There's no one else,"* he'd said and left off the words screaming though his mind: *except me.* He'd have taken Emmit in a second. But that's not how the law worked. He wasn't the boy's father. He wasn't even his uncle. He was nobody.

Besides, Rose had been so insistent when he'd written up her will. Emmit was to go to Marnie, and that was that. And now he was committed. Emmit had to be on that plane. But what would Taylor do if he couldn't find the boy? He'd left messages at school, with friends, with the family who had watched Emmit while Rose had been in a coma. Taylor told them all he needed to see Emmit. Told them about the plane ticket to California sitting on Nancy's desk at the office, waiting to be used tomorrow. Told them that Emmit couldn't stay here anymore. Still, one of those people was hiding him. Had to be.

Taylor wandered down the hall into Emmit's room. The bed was made, the closet half-cleared, drawers tucked shut. He stepped to the dresser and opened a top drawer. Empty. He opened another. Only an old pair of mismatched socks met his gaze. Nothing would help him here.

He stalked back down the hall to the kitchen. Here things weren't as tidy. A greasy cardboard pizza box lay open on the counter. A nearly empty cup of soda wept onto the Formica counter, and wads of pepperoni-stained napkins lay scattered on the floor near the trash can.

One more day. That's all he had to find Emmit and get him on that plane. Sometimes, Taylor wished he could just walk away, forget it, leave Emmit here with a family who would care for him. It would be so much easier. But he couldn't. And it wasn't only because of the will. He still had to do what was right. Because once, long ago, he hadn't.

This time he wouldn't fail her. This time it would be different. Hard. Impossible. But right. For Marnie. And for Emmit.

Taylor turned away from the pizza carton and noticed a bit of paper sticking out from beneath an empty mug on the counter. *That* hadn't been there yesterday. He walked over and picked up the note. Seven words were written in barely legible block-style writing:

I AM FINE. LEAVE ME ALONE. — EMMIT

Taylor threw the paper back on the counter. He knew it. That boy was with someone, and that someone wasn't returning his calls. Keeping the kid away from big, bad Lawyer-Man who was going to send Emmit all the way across the country. Of course, whoever it was thought he was just doing what Emmit wanted. Thought he was being compassionate. But that person didn't know. Didn't understand.

Well, someone better get a clue before Child Protective Services found out. And then that foster care threat wouldn't be so empty after all. But that wasn't going to happen because Emmit would be on that plane. No matter what.

Taylor took the note and slid it into his inside jacket pocket. He may need it later. A lawyer never threw anything away.

The front door creaked open behind him. He whirled toward it. A man with long, brown hair entered.

Taylor sighed. "Hi, Craig." Speak of the devil.

Craig smoothed his hand over his ponytail. The man was always doing that. Taylor hated it. "Nancy said I'd find you here."

"So, what do you want?" Taylor tried to keep his voice even, steady. What Rose ever saw in this guy...

"Gotta get those papers signed to place Emmit into the system."

"He's leaving for his aunt's in the morning."

Craig pulled his ponytail over his shoulder and tugged on the end. "Really? You found her?"

"Yes."

"Well?"

"Legally—"

"Don't give me that legalese mumbo jumbo, Cole. Rumor has it the boy's gone missing. And we at Child and Family Services have a real problem with that." He leaned over and tapped Taylor on the chest. "And Rose would too. You know that."

Ice tumbled through Taylor's veins. "Missing? Who said anything about Emmit being missing?" That man always had an inordinate interest in Emmit, more than the few years he'd lived with Rose warranted. Someday, Taylor would get to the bottom of that.

"Your assistant mentioned—"

"Nancy?"

"She—"

Taylor's mobile phone rang. He glanced at the screen, then put up a finger to silence Craig. "This is Nancy now." He flipped open the phone. "Hello?"

"Mr. Cole, I just wanted to let you know that Craig came in a while back. I'm sorry."

"I know." He grimaced.

"But while I was out picking up the mail, someone else came in and picked up that ticket you were telling me about."

"Are you sure?"

"Quite."

Taylor grinned. "Thanks, Nancy." He shut the phone and turned toward Craig. "Well, it's all set. Emmit will be going to his aunt's in California, as per the will. We won't need to put him into the system."

Craig's eyes narrowed. "Something funny's going on here, Cole. I'm watching you."

Taylor leaned back against the kitchen counter and envisioned Robert De Niro pointing at his eyes in *Meet the Parents*. "Don't you have something better to do than watch a lawyer do his job?"

Craig chuckled. "I'm a government worker, remember? We never have anything better to do." He turned and sauntered out the door. "Call me tomorrow."

Taylor took a deep breath. Everything would be just fine. Tomorrow Emmit would be on that plane, and Taylor could get back to his normal, lonely life—just a horse named Misty and him. Then he could forget about the woman who lived three thousand miles away and the boy he was sending to her. He could forget the mistakes he made sixteen years ago and the sins he committed. He could forget…but Marnie wouldn't.

Forgive me, Marnie. This was the only way.

7

*H*e was late. And there was nothing Taylor hated worse than being late. Especially today. But he couldn't help the rubber-neckers on the freeway, or the little old lady who pulled right in front of him on the two-laned highway, or the fact that every single light had turned red just as he approached it.

And then, of course, there was the line to reach the ticket counter at the airport in which every person in front of him seemed to have some insurmountable problem that couldn't be solved by a few quick clicks on the computer consoles at the front.

But finally it was his turn. He rushed toward the bright-faced woman beckoning him to the empty spot in the row of consoles. The very last spot in the long line of them. Figured. He reached her and blurted out the flight number.

She tapped the keyboard behind the counter. "I'm sorry. That plane has boarded already."

Taylor huffed out a breath and pushed the hair off his forehead. *Of course it has.* "I need to know if a certain passenger boarded. He would be under your unaccompanied minor policy."

"I can see if he checked in. His name?"

"Emmit. Emmit Wittier."

A couple more taps. Her brow furrowed. "Hmm, now that's odd."

"Odd?" His stomach clenched.

"He didn't check in. But I see his ticket was used." She tapped some more. "I'm sure it's just a computer glitch. Someone must have entered the information incorrectly." She picked up the phone next to her station. "Let me just call the gate."

"Can't I go to see for myself?"

The plastic smile again. "I'm sorry, sir. Nonpassengers aren't allowed past security unless they're accompanying a minor."

"I just told you—"

"Then he must have been accompanied by an adult, correct?"

Taylor clenched his fists. The woman was right. If Emmit had boarded, someone must have taken him through security and to the gate.

"I'm sure everything's fine."

She was sure. Taylor wasn't. He glanced toward security. A short dash and maybe he could make it past. Yeah, and get tackled by men with batons and hauled off as a terrorist. All because of curious drivers, a little old lady, and bad traffic-light luck.

"Thank you." The woman hung up the phone. "Yes, a boy named Emmit boarded the plane. Apparently everything's fine, sir. And according to our records, his aunt will be picking him up at the gate in San Francisco. Can I help you with anything else?"

He rubbed his face. Emmit was fine. He could put this whole thing behind him. Finish up a few legal loose ends. Get Craig off his back. Make sure Emmit's things were shipped out to him. And forget.

Everything would be okay. He repeated the words to himself, and still he had a hard time believing them. Probably because this had happened before. Only that time was at a bus station. That time he was following Marnie, even though he was two months late. Still, he tried to track her. But she didn't know it. Never knew he had tried to get her back.

He should have known things wouldn't go right that day. Nothing ever went right at bus stations. He'd learned that the summer before, when Marnie and he set out on their fool's mission to find her mother, because somehow finding the woman would solve all the mysteries and make Marnie whole.

That hadn't happened. But he'd hoped finding her would at least help, at least show he cared. That's what he was thinking that day he first visited the bus station nearest to Clam's Junction.

Marnie stood a bit apart from him, her fists on her hips, her hair pulled back from her face by a black scrunchie. She wore no makeup. She rarely did in those days. She didn't need it. She flashed him a dazzling smile. "Thanks, Taylor, I owe you one."

He pulled his Ray-Bans from his collar and put them on, then he tugged his baseball cap lower over his eyes. His pager buzzed. He didn't even glance at it. "You'd better wait to see what your mother's like before you thank me."

She laughed. "But you found her, right?"

He shrugged. "I dunno. I think so. I sent the ticket anyway. So we'll see. God's going to help us."

"Really? Why should He?"

Good question. Maybe because Taylor didn't want to mess up again like he'd done last year at Legal Aid. Then his stupidity had cost a couple their home. Now it could cost Marnie her mother. "He just will, that's all." *He has to.*

Taylor moved closer, trying not to sniff too deeply the scent of diesel or to look too closely at the scuffed tile floors beneath dim fluorescent lights. Trying not to study the people too carefully—the woman with the twin toddlers who were having a fit, the man with bird's nest gray hair who looked old but wasn't, the lonely teen girl who swung her booted feet under her seat and never glanced up.

Above, the PA system droned, the lights flickered. The door opened. An old couple tottered in. A drunk man staggered out.

And still Marnie and he waited. *God, don't let me blow this one. Let it be her mom. Please, please, please.*

It had taken him the better part of two weeks to dig through the records to find a list of possibilities. And then all he knew was that her first name was Helen and her last name had been changed back to a maiden name he didn't know. It had taken another week and a half to track down a decent address of the one he thought might be her.

Unfortunately, there were several "Helens" with older daughters in the system, and none who seemed willing to be helpful. This one he'd found had been mostly incoherent, but he'd sent her a ticket anyway, begged her to come. Yes, he'd promised, he'd pay for everything. And she'd get a fancy dinner out of it. Just come.

She said she would.

She'd better.

A bus rumbled around the corner outside and chugged down the street toward the station. Marnie inched closer to him. Her hand touched his arm. Gentle, trembling. She sighed. "Well, here we go."

"Here's looking at you, kid." He pretended to tip his hat.

She chuckled, with her signature little hitch at the end. He loved that. "You're a good guy, Taylor Cole. I'm glad we're friends."

Friends. He wanted to be more. "Good guys finish last."

"Not always." She let go of his arm. "Okay, I'll bet you a quarter she'll be wearing a yellow shirt."

He grinned and tried on a Western drawl. "You think I'm a betting man? You gotta know when to hold 'em and know when to fold 'em."

"You gonna take the bet or not, Kenny Rogers?"

He dropped the accent. "Okay. I've got a dime on black."

"A nickel on green."

"A penny on blue, with sandals."

Her eyebrows darted up. "Birkenstocks?"

"Flip-flops."

"All right, smarty-pants. I say a skirt, not pants."

He shook his head. "No way. How about a New Kids on the Block T-shirt? From the eighties."

"That's Old Kids on the Block now. But I'm in. I'll give you a dollar if she comes out wearing anything close to Jordan or Jonathan Knight."

"A dollar? Cheapskate. How 'bout a kiss? You know what Mae West says, 'A man's kiss is his signature.'"

"What is this? Old West week? You just keep your lips in their holster, buddy. There ain't nobody going to be signing here"—she wiggled her fingers in the direction of her mouth—"for a long time."

Taylor threw back his head and laughed. It was a running joke. Him teasing for a kiss, her refusing.

"I only kiss frogs," she'd say.

And he'd respond, "And I'm already a prince, right?"

"Sure. You're the lawyer formerly known as Prince."

And so it would end. But he'd get his kiss someday. And when that happened, it would mean something. It would be real.

The bus pulled up in front of the station.

Her hand gripped his arm again.

The brakes squealed. The doors thudded open. Taylor touched her hand. "You ready?"

She nodded.

"Let's go." He opened the door and let her step outside before following her. They took three strides toward the bus, then stopped. Waited. He held his breath.

An old man and woman came out of the bus. Then a young woman with kids. A teen boy. A middle-aged man. A woman in her fifties.

Taylor moved forward. "Helen?"

The woman looked up. Sharp eyes. Colored hair. "Excuse me?"

"Are you Helen?"

She shook her head. "No. Sorry."

Taylor stepped back.

Marnie inched closer to him. "She said she was coming, didn't she?"

Sort of. But people didn't always do what they said. Still, now wasn't the time to remind Marnie of that. Instead, he waited.

More people disembarked from the bus. Twice more he approached women to ask if they were Marnie's mom. None were.

And then the bus was empty.

Marnie turned away. "She didn't come."

"Maybe she wasn't your mom anyway."

"Maybe." She sighed. "God didn't help us."

"He will."

"When?"

"Maybe next time."

She glanced at him. "If you say so."

God, where are You?

She hardly said a word all the way back to his little seaside cottage. He said he was sorry; she said it wasn't his fault. Nothing came easy. She knew that. And then they rode in silence. And he couldn't think of a single old television quote to make her feel better.

He'd blown it. Even though she said he didn't.

He still felt he was to blame, and not just for that time at the bus station or the next time either, but now, as he stood here in the airport terminal and watched the airplanes take off into the sky. Now, as he tipped his head up and prayed that Emmit really was on one of them and everything really would be all right. Maybe this time things would be different.

This time, they had to be.

~~~

"Going on an airplane, an airplane, an airplane. Going on an airplane. Fly up in the sky." Emmit sang the song to himself, under his breath.

Then he sang it louder.

The woman in the seat next to him wiggled and turned her face away. He tapped her on the shoulder. "I fly in sky."

She glanced at him and her lips turned up. But it wasn't really a smile. He knew the difference.

"I go on airplane!" He announced to the seat in front of him, then to the man across the aisle, then to his shoes. Nice shoes. They were almost white, except for where he spilled ketchup earlier. He tucked his feet up and crossed his legs on the seat. He stuck his thumb over the ketchup spot. He made airplane sounds with his mouth. He reached up and pushed one of the buttons above him. It lit up. He loved the lights.

A moment later, a nice lady with a bright red smile stopped in the aisle and leaned toward him. "Can I get you something?" She turned off the pretty light.

"I angel. I fly in sky."

"Would you like some juice?"

"Doughnuts!"

"I can bring you some pretzels."

"Do I like pretzels?"

"Let's find out." She winked at him, then went back down the aisle.

Emmit waited. "I like pretzels. I like airplanes." He paused and frowned. "But I want to go home. I go home now?" He spoke to no one.

And no one answered.

He unfolded his legs and tipped forward in his seat. "My home has pretty lights. I like lights."

The woman near the aisle glanced his way and nodded. She got up and moved to another seat.

Emmit watched her go. She wore gold shoes. That was funny. If he had gold shoes he would laugh. The woman wasn't laughing. Maybe she was a sad woman. Maybe she didn't like to fly in the nice, soft clouds. Maybe she wasn't going home.

He rubbed his nose and adjusted his glasses. Maybe Emmit wasn't going home either. His brow furrowed again.

The plane slowed, tilted slightly. A voice came from the sky, saying something about starting a descent. He didn't know what a descent was. But it felt like the plane was going the wrong way. It was going down.

"I want to go up."

No one listened.

His breath came faster. He wasn't going home. He wasn't going up. He wasn't…he wasn't…his face turned hot. He flailed with his hands. He hit the back of the seat in front of him, then the seat next to him. He hit and hit and hit.

Then the nice lady came with the pretzels. She tried to hand them to him.

He stopped hitting. Pretzels. He liked pretzels. And he liked lights. He reached up and turned on the light again.

This time, the lady didn't turn it off.

"Going on an airplane, an airplane, an airplane…" Emmit's song filled the cabin again. And still the plane headed down.

─∿~

Waiting. That's what Marnie was doing. And pacing. And watching out the window at the tarmac. Waiting. A day, an hour, an eternity. Well, ten minutes actually. Moving back and forth in front of the gate, hoping his plane would land soon. Hoping it wouldn't. Just waiting, with the gal behind the counter eying her suspiciously like she was a suicide bomber or something. Like she didn't belong.

But she'd gotten special permission to come to the gate to meet the boy. She showed up early as directed. She went through security not once but twice. And she hadn't muttered one word of complaint, even though her stomach was doing the hula and she felt like she'd eaten a pound of espresso beans straight.

And still that woman stared at her from the other side of that prim counter and shot out a million questions with her eyes. *Who do you think you are? What are you doing here? You've got to be kidding me. With that hair and that getup? What kind of mother do you think you're going to make?*

Marnie crossed her arms over her chest. Okay, so the woman wasn't actually staring. It was more like she'd glanced up in Marnie's direction and now was tapping again on her keyboard. She probably hadn't thought a single one of those things.

But she should have.

Marnie fidgeted with the big cardboard sign in her hand. Crazy that Taylor hadn't even sent her a picture of the kid. Just a brief description: Messy hair, glasses, five foot two, short for his age. "You won't miss him," he'd said. That sounded ominous.

So here she stood like some kind of fool holding a white sign with *Emmit* written in black Sharpie on one side. Ridiculous. The paperwork would come later, the letter said. His boxes would come later. Everything would come later. Well, almost everything. But not late enough to give her time to get used to the whole idea of having a kid to raise, someone else in her home, and a boy in her life. A boy like, like—

No, she wouldn't think of that. Just what the kid needed, to get off the plane to an aunt who was having some kind of meltdown. No one deserved that.

He's just lost his mom, Marnie…your sister.

He deserved a break today, just like the old McDonald's jingle used to say. Maybe she'd take him there. Did teens today still like Mickey D's? She was too busy running her shop to keep up with that sort of thing. Clothing and hairstyles, maybe. Books and coffee mixtures, definitely. But fast-food restaurants? Not a chance. That would come later.

For now, she just had to meet the boy at the gate and make him feel at home, like the letter said. At home. Good grief. Like she even knew what that meant. Had Taylor forgotten everything? His last crossed-out sentence flashed through her mind. Maybe he hadn't forgotten. Maybe he remembered too much.

Taylor Cole, haven't you forgiven me yet? Haven't I forgiven you?

Maybe that was coming later too. Later. Fifteen years seemed late enough. Yet here she stood in front of two big doors leading down a long hall. Waiting. For what? A boy? A son? She trembled. Maybe she was waiting for redemption.

Poor kid. Living with her was asking a lot of him. Would that bit of purple coloring she'd added to the tips of her hair freak him out? He was Rose's son after all, so there was no way he'd be used to "unnatural hair colors," as determined by acceptable people. Rose wouldn't have changed *that* much in all these years.

Marnie grimaced. She probably shouldn't have added that purple last night or wore the purple eye shadow to match this morning. And the jeans and tight black T-shirt? A nice flowered dress would have been better. Except, of course, she didn't own one. Never had. And, God willing, never would. She shuddered.

Well, the kid was in for a bit of shock. Maybe he'd get on the next plane and run back home. Then she could forget about this whole mess and not feel guilty either.

Run back to foster care?

She sighed. No, that would never do. She'd have to find another way. Surely Rose had friends. Not family, of course, but someone who wouldn't mind raising her son. And what about the kid's father? The letter had said no father was mentioned in the will. But still, wasn't there some guy in Rose's life who wanted to keep her kid? Finding a good home for a fifteen-year-old boy couldn't be that hard. She'd find someone. Soon. Then she could go back to her life and leave the past locked away where it belonged.

But for now, she'd just have to try to be warm, welcoming. It wasn't the kid's fault he had some useless wild woman for an aunt. She practiced a smile. Blech. That would make him sick for sure.

Who knew, maybe he was one of those cool kids who wore jeans and black T-shirts himself. Maybe he'd think she was cool. Maybe having him here wouldn't be the biggest, most horrendous nightmare she could possibly imagine. Maybe God wasn't using this to rub her nose in all her past sins and mistakes.

Yeah, and maybe rent money would fall out of the sky and her bungalow would magically grow another room. Then she wouldn't have had to spend last night clearing out her table workroom, installing extra locks on the tall glass doors, and making it into a bedroom for her nephew. Maybe he'd be happy here and she'd find in him everything she was missing.

Yep, that's what she was waiting for. Not a plane, not a boy. But some kind of miracle.

Fat chance.

Outside the window, an airplane taxied up to the long tubed hallway. A man on the ground waved lights in his hands to guide it to the gate.

Marnie wrapped her arms around herself and rocked back and forth on her heels. She glanced at the woman behind the counter. The woman smiled and nodded.

It's here. He's here.

The waiting was over.

Oh, God…help.

A blue-jacketed man pushed opened both doors and propped them wide. Sounds echoed up the long hallway. Creaking, groaning, a clang. Then the sound of footsteps.

Marnie took a step back. She held up her sign. It shook.

A little girl skipped up the ramp. A woman in a wheelchair came next, pushed by an old man. Then a boy with Down syndrome, holding a flight attendant's hand.

Marnie looked past them all, watching for Emmit, waiting for the fifteen-year-old kid who would barge into her life soon. He'd be coming up that hall any second. She gripped the sign tighter.

The little girl leaped into a woman's arms just outside the gate. The old man wheeled the woman past her. The flight attendant let go of the Down syndrome boy's hand.

And then it happened.

The boy flew straight toward her. The sign tumbled from her fingers. His body impacted her, drown her—glasses sticking into her chin, blond hair sticking up her nose, warm arms gripping her in a fierce embrace.

"Here I am." The words, thick and muffled, tickled her ear.

"Emmit?" The word squeezed from her in a single breath of disbelief.

"Auntie Mar-ee."

She swallowed and looked into eyes as blue as the sky. Eyes smiling from behind thick glasses.

Great, just great. This was her miracle.

8

E mmit sat in the driveway with his legs folded up and his arms crossed in front of him. He'd been sitting here a real long time, rocking forward and back, forward and back. He didn't like the driveway. It was hard. It hurt to sit here. And it was just getting bright too, with the sun shining off all the ugly gray right into his eyes. When he first sat it was dark. But the sun woke up. Still, he wasn't going to get into the car. He wasn't. He wasn't. He wasn't. Not yet.

So he was going to sit here. No car. Didn't matter what Auntie Mar-ee said. He wouldn't do it.

She squatted in front of him. "Come on, Emmit. I've got to go to work. You'll like it there. I promise."

People made lots of promises. They didn't keep them, though. Just like Auntie Mar-ee wouldn't keep this promise. She couldn't. You shouldn't make promises you can't keep. Somebody used to say that. Maybe God said that.

Emmit liked God. God was nice. Except... He frowned. Except God made him come here, to Auntie Mar-ee. And sit on hard ground where there wasn't any snow to make angels. He missed the angels.

"Get up, Emmit. Let's go." She'd said that lots of times now. Maybe five. Maybe a hundred. A hundred was a big number. She'd yelled it too. He didn't like it when she yelled.

She yelled anyway.

Emmit kept rocking. Then he started to sing, real lowlike. *"Everywhere Mary went, lamb was sure to go."*

Auntie Mar-ee made a funny sound, like air blowing through her teeth. "That's right. You be the lamb, and I'll be Mary. Okay? I'm going to work. You come too."

Emmit stared at a crack in the driveway. "No."

"Emmit!" That was a yell.

Forward and back. Forward and back.

"Come on. I can't be late."

People said things that weren't true. Emmit knew that too. Auntie Mar-ee could be late. She would be late. God would make sure of that. *"His fleece was white as snow."* Snow was nice. He wished there was snow here. He used to fly and flutter like snow. But not anymore.

"Emmit?"

His backside was getting all tingly. He wanted to get up.

Not yet.

He rocked faster.

Auntie Mar-ee was prettier when her face wasn't all bunched up like that. He liked it better when she smiled. She wasn't smiling now. There was something sad in her smile, though. Like her smile had to lift weights no one could see. Emmit could see them. Almost anyway.

God, make Auntie Mar-ee all better, please. Make the heavies go away.

God would do it. God loved Auntie Mar-ee. God loved Emmit too.

Auntie Mar-ee shook her head, then sat beside Emmit. She pulled up her legs and wrapped her arms around them. She rocked forward and back, forward and back.

Emmit watched her. Then he got up, got into the car, buckled up, and grinned at her. "Let's go, Auntie Mar-ee."

Her cheeks turned a funny red color.

He patted his seat. "Mary had a little lamb."

She sighed, rose, and got into the driver's seat. She started the car and glanced over at him. "This is never going to work, you know."

The car rumbled beneath them.

He reached over and patted her hand. "I love you, Auntie Mar-ee."

She smiled, and Emmit's insides went all warm and happy.

~~~

Down syndrome was a whole lot more sweet and syrupy in the movies than it was in real life. In the movies, Down's kids were cute and funny and lovable. In real life, they made you want to scream and pull out your hair. They crossed their arms, stared at the ground, and refused to budge. They didn't make you say, "Awww." "Arrgh" was more like it. *Arrgh, ugh,* and other words she wouldn't say aloud. They never showed *that* in the movies.

She should have known Emmit wouldn't be anything like that cute kid who used to be on the TV show she never watched back in the early nineties. What was it called? *Life Goes On.* But real life didn't go on. It stalled in the driveway when she was late for work. Because Emmit was nothing like Corky. She could tell that already.

Lord, why in the world are You doing this to me? What did I ever do to You to deserve this? She paused and made a face. *Okay, don't answer that. But still…*

Of course it would have been better if she hadn't started this morning with a promise to herself, and to God. She wouldn't be like those rude, cranky people who treated special-needs kids like they were some kind of pariahs. Oh no, she would be patient, thoughtful, and kind until she could find him a new, better home.

Patient. She should have known right then and there she'd never live up to that promise. Patient lasted about five minutes after Emmit refused to get into the car to go to Books and Brew. Thoughtful lasted another ten, and kind went out the window at twenty. And still Emmit sat on the pavement with his arms crossed, his eyes down, his body rocking back and forth, back and forth, back and forth, for a full hour.

She hollered, she screamed, she stomped up and down and made a complete fool of herself. It was ugly. But he didn't care. He just sat.

And now, finally, he was in the car. Sitting there humming in the passenger's seat of her restored VW Bug. Humming like nothing had happened. She slammed the door shut and stared at him. There he was, happy and ready to go, just as if the past hour had never happened. Crazy, yeah, that was it. And crazy was contagious.

Emmit grinned at her.

She turned away and started the car, then wrapped her hands around the steering wheel so tightly her fingers hurt. *Come on, God, this is nuts. You can't expect me to take care of a Down-syndrome kid. Or any kid, for that matter. You remember…*

She swallowed the thought and slammed the Bug into reverse.

Emmit hummed louder.

She glanced over at him. "This is never going to work, you know."

For one long moment he looked into her eyes. And she saw something in his. Something deep, and old, and profound. For a breath, she thought she saw eternity.

He touched her hand. "I love you, Auntie Mar-ee."

Her throat closed. He couldn't. Not now. Not when she was so sure she couldn't do this. Not when she'd just spent a half hour wheedling and another half hour hollering. How could he not hate her? And how could he melt her with a few simple words? No, she wouldn't let him. He would only hurt her, disappoint her. Just as she would do to him.

Some people were meant to love. Others only watched from the outside and wondered. She was supposed to be in the latter group. Because once, a long time ago, she had a single chance at love. One glimmering, impossible opportunity. And she'd blown it. Big time.

And still, her traitor lips smiled at him.

He smiled back.

She shoved her foot against the gas pedal and zipped out of the driveway.

Emmit didn't care. He just hummed.

Marnie grimaced. She would really have to teach him another song. She flicked on the CD player. The voice of Nichole Nordeman filled the Bug's tiny interior. Words asking "What if you're wrong?" Asking, "What if it's love?" Ugh. She skipped to the next song.

Emmit sang louder, out of key, and still with the words to "Mary Had a Little Lamb."

She turned off the CD player.

The Bug rumbled around a corner. Off to Marnie's left, sunlight danced along the surface of the bay and cast shards of light into her eyes. The gulls were out this morning and even a few sailboats.

Emmit stopped singing. He leaned toward the passenger-side window and pressed his nose against the glass. "Pretty boats."

"The wharf will be coming up soon. Plenty of boats to see there."

"Those boats not pretty. Only boats way out floating pretty."

She shook her head. "Why's that?"

"God makes boats to float on ocean. Not to be all tied up next to shore."

"There's a nice breeze today for sailing."

"God makes wind. He makes boats. They float. That's why they're boats."

A tiny smile brushed Marnie's lips. "I suppose so."

"I'm made to sing."

No kidding. She fought the urge to say it aloud.

Emmit didn't notice. "God makes me sing. I sing nice."

Her eyebrows rose. She wasn't going to touch that one. No way. The Bible said to make a joyful noise. Noise, well, that was right on, at least.

Emmit turned toward her and pushed up his glasses. "What God make you to do?"

Mess up. She frowned. Now where did that come from? "Make coffee."

Emmit crossed his arms. "And doughnuts."

"No, not doughnuts. I don't make doughnuts at the store."

"Doughnuts."

Great, he was getting stubborn again. "No. No doughnuts."

"I like doughnuts."

Marnie groaned and pulled into the parking lot. She glanced toward the front door of Books and Brew. The line was out the door. She turned down the first row of cars. And, of course, there was nowhere to park. Just her luck. *Some help here, Lord?*

No one pulled out. No space opened.

Of course not.

She circled the lot twice more, then pulled into a fire lane. She'd move the car later. In the meantime, she had to get in there and get that line back down to reasonable. From the looks of it, it hadn't moved in minutes.

"Look. Funny people." Emmit pointed at the line.

Not funny. Cranky. Impatient. And probably planning their trip to Starbucks tomorrow. Service, that's what Marnie's was known for. Well, not really. It was mostly known for atmosphere, cookies, great coffee, and the best books. But service ranked up there too. Until today, that is. Until Emmit.

"Let's go, Emmit." She shut off the car, hopped out, and hurried toward the front door of Books and Brew.

Emmit didn't follow. He stood just outside the car, staring at the curb. His brows furrowed. "Red."

She huffed. "Yes, it's red. Come on."

"Red. Bad."

She pressed the heels of her hands into her forehead and drew a long, deep breath. *I will not yell again. I will not throw a fit right here where all my customers can see it.* "Emmit." She shuddered. Her voice sounded ugly. She cleared her throat and tried again, nicer this time. "Emmit?"

He looked at her.

She pointed toward the building. "Let's have a doughnut."

His shoulders straightened. "Doughnut!" He hurried toward her.

Her face warmed. What was one little lie? It wouldn't matter.

She pushed past the line of people, some familiar, others not, most with arms crossed and scowling faces. A tiny woman perched on tiptoe to see the front of the line.

"Hi, Renee."

The small nurse plopped down and turned toward her. "Oh, there you are. What happened, you get a flat tire?"

Marnie grimaced. "Yeah, something like that."

Someone grabbed her sleeve. She looked around. Emmit.

He tugged on the material. "Where doughnut?"

For a Down's kid, he had a memory like an oversized elephant. Or maybe they all had good memories. She didn't know a single thing about Down's kids except they must like sitting in driveways and eating food with holes in the middle. Oh yes, and singing mind-numbing nursery songs.

He pushed his glasses up on his nose. Then he smiled.

They probably didn't all have that room-lighting smile, though. Or such clear, blue eyes. "You need to sit right over there." She pointed to a table made from driftwood. It sat in the far corner of the shop.

Emmit pointed to a different table. "I like that one." The crayon table. Of course he'd want that one; it was right in the middle of the room.

Two more customers pushed through the door. One craned his neck around the chubby man in front of him. "Hey, what's the holdup?"

Renee turned. "Marnie got a flat tire."

"I didn't..." Oh, what was the use?

"She's here now, ain't she?"

"Give her a break."

Another voice rumbled from farther back. "Who's the kid?"

"I dunno."

"Marnie?"

Feet shifted. The line moved. A little, just a little.

She glanced to the front. Daisy stood at the cash register with a fake smile and panic in her eyes. Marcus panted behind the espresso machine, his hands a blur as he tried to make a dozen drinks at once. No one was manning the bookstore. No, Joe was there, emptying boxes and straightening books. She would really have to train him behind the counter. But not today.

Marnie took Emmit's arm and guided him toward the crayon table. "Sit right here and I'll bring you a treat, okay?"

"Okay. People grumpy." He looked away when he said it.

"Yes, they are."

"I see books."

"Yes. You can look at the books later. For now, you stay right here. I'll be just behind that counter." She patted his hand, then rushed toward the back of the counter. She threw on her apron and tied it in the back. Then she hurried to the cash register.

Daisy pushed back a strand of golden hair. "Thank goodness you're here."

"Sorry."

"Who's that?" She nodded toward Emmit.

"My nephew. Did you put in the cookies?"

"Are you kidding?"

"I'll do it."

"But…" She motioned toward the line.

A woman stepped up. "Josephina's tea, please. Decaf."

Marnie marked the cup. "Got it."

Daisy made change. "The cookies have to wait."

Marnie shook her head. "See the seventh guy in line?"

"Yeah."

"That's Sam. He'll want one dozen chocolate chip, two dozen oatmeal, and a half-dozen plain sugar cookies for the office."

"Oh. You'd better go put in the cookies, then."

Marnie picked up a cookie sheet from under the counter and turned toward the door to the kitchen.

A shout stopped her. "I don't want cookies. I want doughnut!"

Marnie dropped the sheet. *Oh no.*

"Doughnut! Doughnut, doughnut, doughnut!" He pounded his fists on the tabletop.

Customers turned and stared.

Not again. Not another mutiny.

"Doughnut." His hand came down again. A crayon flew off the edge of the table and whacked Sam on the side of the head. A yellow crayon. Maybe Sam liked yellow. Marnie hoped so.

Emmit scrambled up on his chair. "Doughnut, doughnut, doughnut!"

She raced around the counter toward him. "No, Emmit. Shh…"

He glared at her. "You promise."

"I know." That would teach her to lie to him. Talk about backfiring.

He jumped up and down. The chair tottered.

Marnie grabbed his arm. "You're going to fall."

"Doughnut!"

"How about a snickerdoodle? I'll make a snickerdoodle." Those were always Rose's favorites.

"Hmm." He stopped jumping.

"Just sit, okay? Please…" *I can't do this. This is insane.* She settled him back in his chair, all the while sensing the stares of her customers, the shock of Daisy and Marcus, the indifference of the God who should have kept all this from happening.

Who was she kidding? This would never work. Emmit would be the death of her, her coffee shop, her well-managed, safe life. She couldn't take care of him, even for a few weeks. No way was she prepared. Rose couldn't expect that from her. Not after what had happened before. This all had to be some crazy joke. Or a nightmare. Yeah, that was it. She was dreaming. She had to be. She reached over and pinched herself in the arm. "Ouch." Well, that ruled out dreaming. But not insanity. *God…*

Emmit stopped shouting. And started singing.

She was definitely losing her mind. And soon, everyone would know it.

A hand touched her shoulder. She turned to see Daisy standing behind her. Marnie's eyes flew to the line. "The customers…who's…?"

"Let me take care of him, Marnie. You take the orders. The Bible says 'a friend in need needs a friend indeed!'"

It didn't, but it sounded good anyway. "But…"

"I have a cousin with Down's."

"But…" For a moment, an image of Daisy huddled beneath a table, shaking from a small quake flashed through Marnie's mind. Daisy was silly, flighty, and, and…and looking calmly into Marnie's eyes.

"Let me. It's okay."

Everyone deserved another chance. And besides, what choice did she have? Marnie nodded and backed away. Funny, now she was the girl shaking beside the table after an Emmit-quake, and Daisy was the calm one with her hand extended. Oh, the irony…

Daisy placed her hand on Emmit's arm and helped him down from the chair. She leaned close and whispered something to him.

He sat and grinned.

Marnie rushed back to the counter. Normally, she loved working the register. Loved the people, the personalities, remembering orders, reading faces, coaxing smiles. But today, faces were a blur, smiles were scarce, and old Barkley had to repeat his order three times before she got it right. He ordered the same thing every day. This was crazy.

From the corner of her vision she could see Daisy leading Emmit over to the books. The bell on the front door jingled. Well, at least that meant the line wasn't out the door anymore. She looked around a customer to see the blue uniform of a police officer. "Hey, Mike." He'd be ordering for half the station.

Mike waved in her direction. "Lots of business today, huh?" He got in line and motioned toward the parking lot. "Hey, Marnie, some idiot parked in the fire lane right outside your shop. Don't worry, I gave him a ticket. Shoulda given him two for blocking access to your place like that."

Marnie rubbed her forehead. She should have known. "That's my car, Mike."

"That beat-up old Bug?"

"Yep."

He stared at her for a minute, then shook his head. "What are you doing parking there?"

"Long story." She grabbed a cup from the stack and marked it. Double white mocha, no whip, organic milk, three pumps.

The woman in front of her tapped Marnie's hand. "Decaf."

"What?" She refocused on the front of the line.

"I need that to be decaf. I'm nursing, remember?"

Marnie blinked. "Decaf. Of course. Sorry, Kinna." She marked the box.

"You all right?"

"If I said yes would you believe me?"

"Not a chance."

Marnie smiled. "It's just that he"—she motioned toward Emmit, now sitting cross-legged in front of a bookshelf—"was so not in my plans."

Kinna chuckled. "If there's one thing I've learned, it's that God doesn't care a whole lot about our plans. He's got His own."

"This craziness is His plan, huh?"

"'I know the plans I have for you, declares the LORD'—with the emphasis on the *I*'s."

Marnie swiped Kinna's card and sighed. God's plans. Well, she deserved this. God was getting back at her for mistakes made, sins committed, regrets hidden away in a locked box.

A hand reached over and took Kinna's cup from Marnie's grip. The hand trembled. She turned. "Joe?"

Old Joe stood there, his cleaning rag in one hand, the cup in the other. "I'll take care of my daughter-in-law here." He winked at Kinna.

She smiled back. Joe gave the cup to Marcus, and stuffed the rag in his back pocket. Then he turned back to Marnie. "That your boy over there?" He nodded toward Emmit.

She grimaced. "He is now."

"You go make them cookies. I'll take the orders."

"But…"

"Go on now."

"You don't know how."

"Been watching. Ain't that hard. Mark the little boxes, hand the cup to the kid. Take the money and make change."

"But…"

"Just 'cause I'm an ex-con don't mean I'm gonna rip off cash from the register."

"I know that, Joe."

He rubbed his hand over his scarred cheek. "No ya don't, but you'd give me a chance anyway, wouldn't ya? You'd let me try. Wouldn't assume I'd steal."

She smiled. "Of course. You know that."

"You help folks all the time. Now's time for us to help you."

A strange tightening came to Marnie's chest, a strange stuffiness in her nose, an odd dampness in her eyes. She sniffed and looked away.

And there was old Mrs. Gates, with her same powder blue dress as always, same white orthopedic shoes, same worn blouse with little yellow sunflowers. She was in the book section, just like every Wednesday and Friday. She'd go over to the bookshelves, pick a book, order tap water, and read for forty-two minutes. Then she'd put the book back until the next time. It took her a month to finish a book, and by that time it was so dog-eared and spine bent it couldn't be sold. But Marnie never said anything.

Mrs. Gates patted the scarf over the curlers on her head, adjusted her tiny, round glasses, and leaned over Emmit. She handed him something. A book, an expensive one from the children's section. "Just put it back when you're done, sweetie. That's what I always do."

Emmit grinned, happy again. Daisy glanced over at Marnie and winked.

Marnie turned toward the kitchen.

"Marnie?"

She turned back to see Josephina standing behind her.

"You okay, mija?"

"What do you suppose this hits on the Richter scale?" She pointed to Emmit, then motioned toward the line.

"This? Why it's just a little tremor, that's all. Two-point-three."

A tremor? Did that mean the big one was coming? Great, just what she needed, a little old lady prophesying doom. Problem was, Josephina was always right.

Emmit stood, carried his book carefully back to the crayon table, and opened it. Then he ripped out the first page and threw it in the air like a kite.

Marnie closed her eyes.

He tore another page.

Yep, the big one was coming. She really had to get him a new home, and quickly.

9

Three hours. For three long, excruciating hours from nine to noon Taylor had been sitting behind his desk listening as Myrtle May Collins divvyed up her meager possessions between her relatives. It took forty minutes to decide who would get the toaster. Another twenty-five to decide on the china she'd bought piece by piece on special at the grocery store. Little Ellen May was getting the china because she'd been named after Myrtle. Little Ellen was fifty and had her own china, but that didn't seem to matter. For the last hour, Myrtle agonized over her salt-and-pepper shaker collection, and now it was Mixie, the cat.

Taylor fiddled with his pencil. He put it down, picked it up, drew a face on the yellow pad in front of him. He twirled it and put it behind his ear. He took it down again and drew a mustache on the face.

"Mixie needs a good home."

"Perhaps you'd like to have someone else make these types of decisions for you. We could name—"

Myrtle gasped. "Certainly not!" Her fingers fluttered to her breastbone. "Can you imagine Marge getting her hands on my shakers? Why, the rest of the family wouldn't get even a pinch of salt."

"I see." He hoped she couldn't hear the tightness in his tone or the not-so-silent sigh at the end of his words. Probably not. He suspected her hearing aid was turned down.

He leaned forward and pretended to be listening. *Estate planner. What was I thinking? I could have been a defense attorney. Or a prosecutor. Surely dealing with murderers would be easier than this.* But he'd never really wanted to be a defense attorney or a prosecutor. He'd just wanted to help kids, kids like his best friend Jeremy.

He remembered the day Jeremy was saved. And it wasn't through prayer, or a pastor, or a kind friend. A lawyer saved him. The lawyer who had fought for Jeremy's grandma to gain custody. That man had made a difference. And Taylor knew he could make a difference too. So, what was he doing here, dealing with old women and their pets?

Taylor stared past Myrtle's head at the photo hanging on the wall behind her. An ocean at dawn, a beach, a castle washing away in the sand, and a man walking alone away from it. The picture made his chest heavy, but he hung the print anyway. It was a reminder, a still shot in time of what could have been and wasn't, what should have been if only he had stayed true, done right, all the way to the end.

Myrtle's voice broke through his thoughts. "Or maybe I should give Mixie to my sister. She's always had a thing for cats. But she's got that horrible little mutt."

"Hmm…" He nodded and kept looking at the picture. If he stared hard enough, the man would blur, then disappear. The ocean would calm, the sand castle would grow whole. Then he would remember.

"Are you listening, Mr. Cole?"

Taylor refocused. "Of course."

"I said Annette keeps her house so well dusted. Mixie should go to her."

Great, she was giving a cat to a clean freak. "The cat to Annette. Got it."

"And tell her he should be dusted at least three times a week."

"You want her to dust the cat?"

Myrtle's eyes widened. "Of course, silly. He's a ceramic cat."

It took all his resolve not to groan aloud.

"Moxie, however, is made from porcelain. Do you think I should make sure they stay together?"

"Um."

"But Moxie fits better with those new curtains of Edith's."

The sky in the picture was clearing.

"And then there's Mitzy."

The water brightened.

"And Harold."

The man faded.

"He's a dog."

In a moment, she would come. A woman with long, dark hair and a quiet laugh with a hitch at the end. She'd walk beside him, and they'd hold hands. She'd rescue him from this purgatory of Mixies and Moxies and Harolds. And maybe, just maybe, this time the man wouldn't let go.

It hadn't started there, though. Not on the beach with the waves lapping, the sun peeking through the fog, and tiny mussel shells scattered at their feet. It started in a dirty alley behind an apartment complex, with the sun beating straight down on them and a scribbled address clutched in his fist.

Marnie stood beside him, her hair caught up in a long ponytail and sunglasses hooked in the neck of her oversized shirt. She stood on tiptoe to peer through the knothole in the fence and into the back of the apartment in front of them.

"Are you sure this is it?"

He turned his hat backward. "It's the address the guy gave me."

"But the mailbox says someone named Lily Costas lives here. And I don't know, the place looks, well, weird."

Taylor shrugged. "Maybe she didn't change the name on the box. Or maybe she's going by Lily now. And what do you mean by weird?" He rested his arm against the wooden fence and looked around him. Trash littered the alleyway. Stylized letters in blue and red spray paint sprawled over the fence and told him where he could go. The adjacent fence sported gang symbols and other words that would've made his straight-laced mother threaten soap soup if he'd ever spoken them. He shifted his weight.

"A torn sheet is being used as a curtain and about fifteen overflowing ashtrays are in the backyard."

"Randy said this was the woman."

"I don't know about this Randy guy."

"My dad said he's a good PI." A rat scuttled out from behind the stuffed garbage cans a few feet away and scrambled through a hole in the fence. Taylor shuddered.

"I thought *you* were going to find her for me." She glanced back at him and poked him in the chest.

He grinned. "If it goes well, I still want the credit. If not, it's all Randy's fault." He stepped closer. "Can you see anyone?"

She peeked back through the hole. "Not yet."

"We can always talk to the manager first, just to see—"

"There she is!"

Taylor cringed at the excitement in Marnie's voice. It was true he wanted to find her mother, but he couldn't imagine anything good coming from finding her here. He squatted and peered through another knothole. A dead rosebush blocked his view. It still had thorns, but the leaves were brown and dry. A warning, perhaps.

He stood back up and pressed closer to Marnie. "Let me see."

She backed away.

A cat jumped on the fence. Skinny thing. It glared at them, then hissed. Another warning. But he didn't take it. Instead he peeked through the hole and spied a woman in a ratty T-shirt with pajama bottoms. *Oh, man, don't let* that *be her.*

"What do you think?"

He glanced back at Marnie. "Does she look familiar?"

"What's she doing?"

He watched the figure pass in front of the sliding glass door, then out of sight, then back again. "She's lighting a cigarette."

"And don't tell me she just poured herself a drink."

He grimaced. "Well, yeah."

"Figures."

He cleared his throat. "Let's go talk to the manager. It's probably not her."

"I think it is."

"Why? Does she look like who you remember? That picture you gave me was no good at all."

"Sorry." She sighed. "I don't remember very well. Move over. Let me see."

He did.

She looked through the hole. "This woman's hair is grayer and short. She's skinnier too."

Hairstyles changed. People lost weight. "See, maybe it's not her."

Marnie straightened and put her hands on her hips. "Well, I'm going to find out." She pushed away from the fence, strode past three bent garbage cans, and turned down the walkway alongside the apartment.

Taylor jogged to catch up. "This is a bad idea." A very bad idea. And it didn't take a law degree to figure that out.

She tossed her ponytail over her shoulder and glanced back at him. "Maybe. But here goes nothing."

Or everything.

He slowed.

She sped up. A moment later, she turned the corner to the front of the apartment building and was standing at the broken screen door. She opened the screen and knocked on the wooden door. She knocked again.

The door opened.

Muted conversation tumbled back toward him.

The door slammed.

Marnie moved away. Her shoulders slumped as she rejoined him on the walkway. "That went well."

"Not her, huh?"

"I didn't know a face could turn that color."

"Fuchsia or beet?"

"Watermelon, except for the nasty scar on her upper lip." Marnie shook her head. "You'd think I asked her if she was a hooker or something."

"Maybe you did."

"No, I just wanted to know if… Oh, I get it. I guess a 'Hey, am I the kid you abandoned?' question could be taken like that."

He threw his arm over her shoulders and squeezed. "What'd she say?"

"She said she"—Marnie's voice took on a whiny tone, with a bit of a drawl—"ain't never had no crummy little brats, so I should just get out of here and leave her alone."

"Maybe that's a blessing."

"Strike two for us."

"So, it really was Lily Costas, huh?"

Marnie shook her head. "Nah, that was just the name on the box, like you said. This woman's named Helen, just not Helen-who-left-two-daughters-and-said-something-important-to-the-younger-one-before-she-left."

"We'll find your mom." He tried to keep the relief out of his voice. He wouldn't wish that woman on anybody. He guided Marnie toward the car, his arm staying around her shoulders, casual, friendly, as if he meant nothing by it. Except he did.

Rather than going straight to the car, they turned and walked toward the beach. Toward the craggy rocks, toward the soft lapping waves, toward the wooden boardwalk and pier that stretched out over the water. The sun was just starting to dip behind the line of buildings behind them, casting the dim glow of twilight over the wood and waves. They crossed an empty parking lot and sauntered out onto the pier. There, they paused, rested their elbows side by side on the railing, and gazed out over the ocean.

Finally Marnie spoke. "It's not too much to ask, is it?"

"What?"

"To find my mother. It's not like I'm asking that she be all wonderful, or we have this weepy Oprah-moment reunion or anything."

"No?"

She threw him a glance from the corner of her eye and smiled. "A Jerry Springer moment would do."

He chuckled. "I was almost expecting that back there." He motioned toward the apartments behind them.

"You didn't answer my question."

He turned and contemplated her for a moment. "Well, that depends who you're asking, I guess."

She cocked her head. "Aren't I asking you, Lawyer-Man?"

His throat tightened. "I, um, well…"

She grinned. "I'm just kidding. You know what I mean."

He did. She meant she was asking God. And He wasn't responding. And Taylor didn't have any answer to that.

She folded her hands and stared out over the water. "People get healed from cancer, have miracle babies, get money in the mail when they're on their last dime. God answers their prayers. Big prayers. So, why not me? Am I really asking too much?"

Taylor sighed. "My mom always said you can't compare apples meant for pie with apples meant for candying."

Marnie turned her head toward him and scowled. "So, I'm being serious for a change and you're talking about apple pie?"

He moved closer. "She meant that each of us has our own life path, our own journey God lays out for us. God's vision and purpose for one person isn't the same as for someone else. So we shouldn't be surprised when He answers our prayers differently or leads our lives in different ways." Taylor smiled. "At least that's what she said when my brother got to see *Raiders of the Lost Ark* and I was stuck home with the flu."

"Poor baby."

"Well, it was pretty unfair, don't you think?"

She chuckled. "Kinda insensitive, don't *you* think, talking about your mom when I don't have one?"

His stomach dropped. "Oh no, I'm…"

She punched him in the arm. "Don't say it. You know I'm joking. If you turn into one of those pansy guys walking on eggshells, I don't think I'll be able to stand you." She went back to leaning on the railing.

He let out a long breath. "Yeah, well." He moved closer until their arms touched. "Still, this whole mother-finding thing isn't easy."

A breeze rustled over the water and blew strands of her hair over his face. She smelled sweet, like honeysuckle.

She straightened. "It's cold here. Let's walk." She blew into her hands, then rubbed them together.

"Here." He took her hand and put it into his jacket pocket. "That'll warm it up." He put his hand in too and twined his fingers around hers. They made their way down to the beach, ambling along, quiet, thoughtful, her hand tucked securely in his. It was the first time he held her hand. Other men would be looking to find a way to get her to the bedroom, but for him, just then, holding her hand in his was enough. It spoke of more to come. Of silent promises, of whispered hope. And for that instant, he could almost sense God smiling.

Too bad it didn't last. Too bad the man let go.

Taylor's mind jolted back to the present as Myrtle rapped her fingers on his desk. "Harold should definitely go to Wilma."

Taylor blinked.

"After all, that woman needs a man in her life."

The picture shifted, solidified, and went back to showing just a man, a lonely beach, and a sand castle washing away in the surf.

Myrtle grabbed a tube of lipstick out of the huge sack she called a purse and applied the red paste to her mouth. She pressed her lips together with a loud smack. "Don't you agree, Mr. Cole?"

"Umm..."

She squinted her eyes. "Not very talkative today, are you, son? You feeling all right?"

Taylor rubbed his hand over his forehead and let his gaze slip out the window to avoid staring at the lopsided lipstick. Outside, cars puttered past. Someone's horn beeped. Bits of snow fluttered from a somber sky. A truck pulled away from the curb. And there, across the street, a boy stood. Scraggly hair, glasses, hands stuffed into a jacket two sizes too big. Taylor leaned forward and pressed his hand against the pane.

The boy looked just like Emmit.

~~~

My name is Emmit. Emmmm. It. He rolled the name over in his head, then said it aloud. "Emmmmm…it. Emmit!" He liked that name. Someone told him it meant truth. Who told him that? He couldn't remember. That was a long time ago. Back when he could sing right. Now the songs sounded funny. And he couldn't remember the words. But he sang anyway. The song he remembered. Singing was fun. He sang about Mary and the lamb. It was a good song. It made him happy. He loved the lamb. He missed the lamb. He remembered that.

He left the lamb the day the bright whirling lights came.

Sounds came from the other room. *Tap. Tap. Tap.* The squeak of a chair. *Tap. Tap. Tap-tap.* Auntie Mar-ee would be in there for a while. She was tapping letters into the skinny box.

Emmit liked boxes. Big boxes. Small boxes. Brown boxes. White boxes. Boxes for shoes. Boxes for toys. Boxes that held his favorite Captain Crunch cereal. He liked those boxes almost best. Just almost, because there was another box he liked best of all. Right now it was sitting high-high-high up on a shelf between lots of books. But maybe he could climb up that shelf and get that box. Pretty box. Big box. Made out of funny wood and covered with seashells all glued on. He liked it. Pretty brown and white colors and pieces that didn't fit so good together. Mar-ee looked at that box every time she passed it. She didn't touch it. At least he never saw her do it. And she never, ever opened it.

He pushed his glasses up his nose and scratched his ear. It was a nice box. Maybe something nice was in it. He sat on the carpet and folded his legs up in front of him. Beside him, a big window grabbed the light and spilled it all over the floor. He scooted over until the light spilled all over him too.

Then he studied the bookshelves. *One. Two. Seven. Five.* He could climb those.

The tapping in the other room stopped.

He looked up at the great big lizard sitting on a shelf in front of him. He liked the dragon. The dragon was named Max.

"I better hurry, Max."

Max blinked.

Emmit pushed himself up, then scurried over to the shelves. He patted Max on the back, felt the knobby smoothness, then put his finger to his lips. "Shh. Don't tell Auntie Mar-ee."

Max was a good lizard. Max wouldn't say a word.

Emmit stuck out his tongue. *One.* He put his foot on the first shelf. Max watched, real quiet. Good Max. *Two.* He pulled himself up. A book fell. *Seven.* He climbed higher. Another book thudded to the carpet below. Then a stack toppled down. *Five.* He grinned and grabbed for the box.

He had it. It was big for his hands. He tucked it under his arm best he could and shimmied back down. *Four. Eight. Six. Jump!*

The box dropped. It made a big sound. He snatched it up. Then he sat back down in the sunlight and opened it, ever so careful-like. Ever so quiet.

"Emmit? What are you doing?" Mar-ee's voice came from the other room.

He frowned and didn't answer. He stared into the box. Bits of paper. Ugly, scrawled words. A piece of a postcard. A picture. A plastic sword. A dirty silver chain with a heart on it. Funny things. But they didn't make him laugh. They made him sad.

"Emmit?"

He dumped them out on the floor and pushed his hand through them. A napkin. A strange, round shell. And lots of little shreds of paper. Sad things. Very sad things.

He shoved the box away and grabbed one of the fallen books. Then he started to sing.

10

*Y*ou always did like secrets, Taylor Cole, but this is ridiculous."
Marnie muttered the words under her breath, then pounded
them into the e-mail, her fingers slamming into the keys with fierce
strokes. She stared at the computer screen, stared at his name there in
black and white. Stared, and still could barely believe it.

Her sister, her perfect sister, had a Down-syndrome son. It seemed
impossible, but the last week proved it to be true. Because Emmit was
here, and everything in her life had changed because of it, because of him.

"I love you, Auntie Mar-ee."

The words came back to her, and with them a strange softening inside her. She shook off the feeling. This was crazy. Insane. She couldn't
raise a son. No way. And especially not one with problems.

God knew that. He'd known it for fifteen years. So, what kind of
game was He playing? He and Rose. What was she thinking? Had she
married then? Went ahead and married that stupid, annoying piece of
dog— Marnie cleared her throat and refocused on the screen.

No, Rose was gone. God wasn't answering. All she had left was
Taylor.

"You should have told me." She frowned and deleted the words. Despite everything, Taylor didn't owe her anything. After all, phone lines

went two ways, and so did roads and airplane flights. But she hadn't ever dared to try any of them, not to reach Taylor or even Rose. She'd never had the guts to find out what happened after she left all that behind.

And now Rose was dead. And this strange boy was here. And Taylor Cole was no longer just a memory. Things weren't safe anymore. Marnie shivered.

From the other room, a sound came. Emmit treading with heavy feet and humming some off-key tune. "Mary Had a Little Lamb." It was always "Mary Had a Little Lamb." He loved that song. After six solid days of it, she was starting to hate it.

And that wasn't the only thing. Yesterday, Emmit took every last piece of silverware out of her kitchen drawer and spread it out over the floor. The day before, he squirted out half the hand soap from the bathroom dispenser and finger painted the walls. The day before that, he tore up all the fancy swirled rye she'd just bought from the bakery and tossed it to the birds. Apparently the gulls told him they were hungry for her special blend. And all the time, he smiled and hummed that agonizingly out-of-tune song about Mary and her lamb.

And while he rearranged her drawers, décor, and everything else about her days, she spent every spare moment on the Internet trying to find information on taking care of a Down-syndrome kid. She'd discovered kids with Down's were stubborn. Well, she figured that out on her own. They had smaller ears and hands. They often had bad eyesight, and they didn't like change. Too bad for that because there was nothing she could do about it. And some, like Emmit, loved music.

She sighed and refocused on the screen. Her fingers moved.

You could have warned me. Or is this some kind of retribution for running off, for keeping secrets of my own?

I deserve this.

I don't deserve this, you know. I can't do this.

I have to. I know I have to.

You've got to find this boy another home. I can't keep him.
That should have been obvious. But not foster care. Find him
someone who understands him, who can love him. Find him
someone better than me.

She erased the last sentence. *There's no one but me. I know that.*

You've done some crazy things, Taylor Cole, but this tops
them all. And after fifteen years. Fifteen years. I hoped you
would have forgotten. I hoped you'd forgiven. I guess not—

A loud thud sounded from the other room. Then another. And another. Marnie shoved back from her tiny desk and glanced through the
doorway behind her.

Thud.

She couldn't see him. She should have known not to leave him alone.
Even for a moment. "Emmit? What are you doing?" She stood and turned
toward the door.

No answer.

"Emmit?" She hurried through the doorway. *Oh no.*

He sat in the middle of the living room floor with his legs folded up
and his body rocking forward and back. Books lay scattered all around
him. He picked one up, held it high over his head, and dropped it. Then

he looked up and smiled his dazzling smile. He was beautiful when he did that. Beautiful and maddening.

"His fleece was white as snow!" Emmit clapped his hands and laughed.

Marnie shook her head. "Not again, Emmit."

"Books. Love books." He picked one up and opened it upside down. "I read."

A smile brushed her lips as she walked over, turned the book upright, and placed it back in Emmit's hands.

He sighed. "No pictures."

"Tomorrow we'll get you some good books with pictures. I just got in a new shipment for the shop."

"And doughnuts."

"Cookies. No doughnuts."

"I like doughnuts."

She suppressed a groan. "Snickerdoodles."

"Okay."

"So, you're going to get right in the car tomorrow when it's time to go to—?" A horrible sight stopped her words. Her mouth went dry. He couldn't have. He didn't. Her gaze riveted to the spot where her special box was supposed to be sitting on the bookshelf.

Max was there.

The box was gone.

"Emmit?" Her voice shook. "Where's Auntie Mar-ee's box?"

Emmit grinned. "Pretty box."

"Yes. Where is it?" She fought to keep her tone steady, calm. It rose anyway.

He pointed to a spot beside the couch. "Pretty box. Ugly paper inside."

Marnie's heart thudded like a ten-pound tome hitting the floor. Despite the lock, the box was opened. Her things—papers, tiny objects, reminders of times best forgotten—lay scattered on the carpet. Mementos of her regrets, private, personal…secret. But no longer.

"How did you get it unlocked?"

He didn't answer. Again.

Her hands trembled. She turned back to Emmit. And there he sat, still smiling bright enough to light the room, still holding the book upside down, still just as happy, just as innocent, as if he hadn't spread all the dark corners of her life all over her living room floor.

Her vision tunneled. She wanted to yell, scream, fly over there and—

But it wouldn't do any good. She'd tried that already and it hadn't helped one bit. Emmit never understood that he'd done anything wrong.

She blew out a long breath, a calming breath. Out. In. Out. It didn't help either. And there was no way she was going to sit cross-legged with her fingertips together and say "oohhmmm." *Aarrggh* maybe, but not *ohm*.

She walked over, bent down, and picked up the box. She turned and held it out to Emmit. *Stay calm. Don't shout.* "Don't touch this." Her voice wavered. "Never touch this. Okay?"

"Mary had a little lamb."

Aarrggh. *Calming breath. In. Out.* Her grip on the box tightened. *He doesn't know any better. He doesn't understand.*

Neither do I.

Marnie set the box on the coffee table, then squatted and scooped up the bits of paper from the floor. She dumped them all back in her box. She tried not to look at them. It was best not to see. That's why she never opened the box. Never. She picked up the napkin from earlier in the week and stuffed it back in. Then a pen, a photo, a necklace, a dried rose petal, and a dozen other small items. Items that whispered and wooed, called her to remember.

No. Not now. Not ever.

She closed the box. A bit of silver caught her eye. The lock, half-hidden beneath the couch. She picked it up and squeezed it in her fist. Then she relocked the box, stood on tiptoe, and placed it at the very top of the bookshelf, out of Emmit's reach. She glanced at the iguana. "Max, you keep him out of this, okay?"

Max blinked.

"Auntie Mar-ee."

She looked over her shoulder.

Emmit was standing now, his arm outstretched. He wiggled his closed fist. "For you."

She turned and held out her hand, and then he dropped something into it. A sand dollar. Small, worn, almost pink. She froze, then slowly turned it over. There, written in black block letters was a single word: shame.

The one word that started it all.

Don't remember…

But it was too late now. The memory would come. And with it, the humiliation, the regret, and the awful emptiness of knowing it was only the beginning.

God, why couldn't You just answer his prayer? Why couldn't we have just kept the past buried? Buried in a box on a shelf forever. But it wasn't buried. Not really. It never had been. Never would be. She knew that. God knew it too, but honestly, why couldn't they just keep the box locked and pretend. *Well, God?*

Marnie sniffed. God never had been One to leave things alone. Not like Rose. If it were up to Rose, the past would have stayed hidden forever, if only to protect her image among her friends.

But back then, Marnie was the shoveler, the one who insisted on digging things up when it would do no good to have them revealed. Back then, she was a fool. Especially that night.

The stars were just starting to sparkle in a darkening sky when Marnie and Taylor strode into the country club lobby. Her boot heels clicked on the fancy marble floor. Her reflection shone from a dozen gilded mirrors. Long dark hair, a touch of makeup, a flowing dress, and a smile phonier than Washington politics.

Some song by Boyz II Men drifted out of the doorway of the main room. Even from here she could see the champagne fountain, the table laid out with silver trays of food and decorated with rare orchids, and beyond, shimmering ice sculptures in the form of sea creatures.

Ridiculous. Opulent. Stupid. The only thing redeeming about it was Taylor agreed to come with her to this pretentious event. If it weren't for Rose and her Richie-Rich boyfriend, Marnie wouldn't be here at all.

"It's a party to show off his new custom racing boat," Rose had said. "He's going to introduce me to all his friends." There had been a little breathless whine at the end of Rose's sentence.

"So?"

"So don't mess this up for me."

"I can't mess it up if I'm not there."

Rose let out a delicate sigh. "He's already invited you. You can't just not show up."

"Watch me."

"Come on, Marnie. He was really nice to invite you. It's going to be soooo fancy."

"Oh, wow." Marnie's voice turned dry. "I'm so excited…*not.*"

"Just come for a little while, then you can go back to your leather and motorcycles."

"Oh, can I wear my riding clothes?"

Rose scowled. "Wear something classy. Borrow something from my closet if you have to. Just don't embarrass me, okay?"

"What am I, three years old?"

Rose flipped her hair behind her shoulder. "Sometimes I think you are. So behave, will you?"

"I'm not coming."

"Yes you are."

"And I won't behave."

"Yes you will."

"You can't make me." Good grief, now she really did sound like she was three.

"Yes I can."

"How?"

"You want to know something about Mom, right?"

Marnie's eyes narrowed.

"If you come and you behave, I'll tell you what I know."

"Promise?" Marnie stuck out her pinkie finger.

"Promise." Rose wrapped her pinkie around Marnie's and shook it, just like they'd done when they were young.

And that's how it happened. That's why Marnie stood here now before a doorway that led to lavishly laden tables and tight groups of expensively dressed twentysomethings. That's why she stared through her reflection in a half-dozen windows to see a fancy racing boat bobbing on the waves outside. That's why she endured the dress that was too tight, the mascara that was too thick, and the earrings that were too long. But she drew the line at the shoes. No way was she going to wear some horrible knockoff designer heels.

Marnie looped her arm around Taylor's and lifted her chin.

He glanced at her. "You ready?"

"I hate this."

He grinned. "I know. But Rose is going to hate those motorcycle boots more."

She grimaced. "I did wear a dress."

"It looks great. Doesn't go with the boots, but…"

"I couldn't borrow Rose's shoes too. She wears a six."

"I'm sure she'll forgive you."

Marnie raised an eyebrow. "Yeah, right. When cows sprout wings and fly with the pigs." She reached up and brushed her hand over the lapel of his sports jacket. "You look good though."

"Thanks. It's my lawyer costume."

"You look mah-velous, dahling." She put on a fake accent and didn't say more, didn't tell him that he really was breathtaking in that perfectly tailored suit, with his wavy brown hair, for once not hidden beneath a hat, and warm, chocolate-colored eyes. She'd always been partial to that shade of dark chocolate. Well, maybe not always, maybe just since meeting Taylor. But of course, she wouldn't let on. That would ruin everything.

His arm was warm against hers as they slipped into the room and moved toward the tables laden with fifteen types of food she didn't recognize. Bits of odd-colored goo, crackers with gross-looking black stuff, and at the end of the table, fancy stemmed glasses. Orchids lay scattered between crystal dishes on top of tables covered not in cheap linen but fine, delicate silk. She strengthened her grip on Taylor. Beside him she was confident, comfortable, safe.

His arm tightened in response.

Marnie stared at the tables, then leaned closer to Taylor. "My kingdom for a bowl of Doritos or a plate of Double Stuf Oreos."

He grimaced. "No such luck."

"I'm starved."

"Me too."

She plucked up something that looked like a chocolate wafer covered in creamy mousse. "Well, at least there's chocolate." She popped it into her mouth, then choked and spat it back out again. "Not chocolate." The words sputtered from her lips.

Taylor chuckled. "Don't let Rose see you spitting out the hors d'oeuvres."

She glanced down at the brown yuck in her hand. "Hors d'oeuvres? Somebody call the caterer because I think they're serving dog food."

His eyes sparkled as brightly as the stars emerging outside. "It's pâté."

"Pah-tay? Do I have to stick out my little finger and sip tea when I say that?"

He grinned. "I'd like to see that."

"Fat chance." She wrinkled her nose. "This stuff isn't pâté, it's pot-tee."

Taylor's face turned that funny shade of pink like it always did when he was trying not to laugh too loudly. "Can't take you anywhere."

She giggled, then covered her mouth with her clean hand. "What am I going to do with this stuff." She raised her other hand and frowned at the gross brown mess. "Get me a napkin."

"Rose is looking this way." Taylor's voice dropped to a whisper.

"Oh no." Marnie glanced up. And sure enough, there was Rose, dressed in the perfect shade of off-white to complement her complexion. Of course, Rose wouldn't call it off-white. It was something like eggshell, or cream, or ecru. To Marnie, it just looked off-white. She turned her back to hide the pâté from Rose's view. "Napkin?"

"Too late." Taylor lifted the edge of the tablecloth. "Here."

"You're kidding."

"You'd better turn around quick and smile, or she'll be over here wondering what's wrong."

Marnie reached under the cloth, her fingers just brushing Taylor's. For a moment, their eyes met and held. Her skin tingled.

"Hurry."

She caught her breath and wiped off the pâté under the cloth, then quickly turned toward Rose and wiggled her fingers in a little wave.

Rose matched her false grin with a tight smile that never reached her eyes. Then she turned back to the tall blonde beside her.

Taylor reached over and took Marnie's arm again. Warm, confident, comforting. "Come on, I see the bar. Let's get some 7UP."

"Shirley Temple."

Taylor pulled Marnie away from the pâté and hurried her toward the bar. He moved nearer and whispered in her ear. "That was close."

"Rose was stupid to make me come."

"She didn't want to be here alone."

Marnie scowled up at him. "What are you talking about?" She motioned toward the groups of hoity-toities gathered around the room. "I'd hardly call this alone."

His gaze swept over the groups, then returned to pierce Marnie. "Isn't she? Think about it."

"I don't want to think about it. I want a Shirley Temple."

"You're all she has, Marnie. She doesn't belong here any more than you do."

"She thinks she does."

"Really?"

"I want two cherries in my drink."

"You'll have to see the truth sometime."

"But not today."

He shook his head. "Soon."

They wove between groups chatting about nothing until they reached the bar. A minute later, Taylor handed her a Shirley Temple poured into a fine crystal goblet. She lifted it until the light shone through the glass. A Shirley Temple in crystal, now that was pretentious. She stood close to the wall with Taylor at her side.

Out there were women who looked like something out of a fashion magazine. Women with thousand-dollar dresses and professional manicures. Women with perfect makeup, perfect hair, and perfect figures. Women with perfect families, perfect homes.

Women totally unlike Rose and her. Maybe Taylor was right. So, what was Rose trying to prove?

Marnie moved closer to Taylor. "How soon can we get out of here?"

"Not soon enough."

"Let's go cliff diving." Taylor looked great in swim trunks.

"There aren't any good cliffs around here."

She sighed. "Snorkeling?"

"In the dark? And you don't snorkel."

"No time like the present."

"This is snorkeling, didn't you know? Don't you feel like your head's not quite above water?"

She made a face. He was right again. He was always right. And he knew how she hated this. Hated the way the lights danced off the tile and crystal. Hated the sounds of fake laughter. Hated the smell of food she wouldn't feed to her cat, not that she had a cat. No pets, that was the rule. And most of all, hated the way it all made her feel on the inside—like she wasn't good enough, like she never would be. She should have never, ever let Rose talk her into this.

A group of three women sauntered by. As one, their gaze slid down to her boots, then back up again. Marnie shivered. Ugh. Maybe she should have tried some pumps after all.

In the background, the music shifted to some incoherent song by Coolio, a song completely out of place among the silk, orchids, and nasty pâté. They ought to be playing Hootie & the Blowfish. She loved Hootie.

Another gaggle of women walked by. They too glanced down.

Marnie scowled. "Good grief. Who knew footwear would be so fascinating around here?"

Taylor snorted. "What? Now you care?"

She crossed her arms. "No."

"Come on, we can stand over there." He motioned toward a spot behind the tables with the ice sculptures. "No one will see your feet then."

"No one would notice anything next to those gaudy things."

He swept his arm forward like a footman in a fairytale. "That's what we're counting on. You first, m'lady." He smiled and she looked deep into those chocolate eyes and couldn't help but smile back. Taylor understood; he always understood. She'd known him for less than a month, and yet it seemed that he could read her soul.

Her cheeks warmed. She turned away so he wouldn't see, wouldn't guess how much he affected her. "Gee, thanks." She squinted at the three huge figures with small sand dollars scattered around the base of each. A bottle-nosed dolphin, a giant seashell, and a big-beaked pelican. She scooted behind the pelican.

"This thing is ridiculous. Can you imagine someone paying for this?"

"It's quite a work of art." Taylor touched the pelican with one finger.

"Until it melts. What are they trying to say with things like this?"

"That they're worthy."

She huffed. He was always saying cryptic things like that. Trying to make her see, think, understand. But she didn't want to understand. She just wanted to hate these things in peace. "Yeah, well, what do I have to do to be worthy in this crowd?"

"Eat pâté and wear outrageously expensive heels."

"And kiss up, just like Rose?"

"Maybe. If you want her to tell you what she knows about your mom."

"Fine, then, I'll kiss up." Marnie leaned over and pressed her lips to the bird's backside. That'd show them.

Her mouth stuck.

She pulled back. Her lips didn't come free. Oh great, she was showing them all right. Showing them what a backwoods idiot she was. Rose was going to kill her.

"Marnie?" Taylor hissed beside her. "What are you doing?"

"Help," she whispered from the side of her mouth.

"What?"

"Help me."

"Stand up."

"I can't."

A strange choking noise sounded beside her. Taylor. If she could see him, she'd bet his face would be pink. Really pink. Traitor. She tried to glare up at him, but couldn't manage it. Her mouth was pressed too tightly to the bird's back end.

Footsteps moved away. A moment later, cool liquid poured down her cheek, over her mouth, freeing her.

But not before her sister and all her new friends saw.

The sickening sound of cultured laughter rang through the room, and suddenly Marnie was the sorry little foster kid again with mismatched shoes and a hole in her coat, the kid the moms whispered about, the one who wasn't good enough to play with the normal kids.

Marnie's gaze found Rose's and clashed.

Rose's face turned the color of a very red rose. Marnie could almost see the steam coming out of her sister's perfectly formed ears and condensing on those sparkling earrings she said were diamonds. But Marnie knew they were really just cubic zirconia.

Rose strode up to her. Her eyes narrowed. "You promised." Words spat from between clenched teeth.

"Sorry."

"You're going to pay for this."

"I know." Marnie picked up a sand dollar from the table and slipped it into her pocket.

The first memento. Later she would write on it. Later she would slip it into a box that would soon fill with memories too much like this one. Later she would lock that box, hiding away the sand dollar. But never the memory. Never the regret. That she would carry with her always. And the consequences of what Rose would say next. Simple words that somehow would change everything. Words spoken in a room full of perfect strangers.

"Have you no shame?"

A little comment. A little dig. It shouldn't have mattered. But it would. It would become the first in a long line of little things that would lead to an inevitable conclusion.

Yes, she deserved this. Deserved it, because she'd worn boots when she should have worn heels. Because she kissed the backside of an ice pelican. Because all she had was shame and her sister didn't know it.

Shame that led right here, right now, to a fifteen-year-old Down-syndrome boy and a box of regrets that should never, ever have been opened.

She should have known better. Then and now. She should have been better, smarter. She should have been the person Rose wanted her to be.

But that wasn't possible, not at the party all those years ago and not now with Rose's son sitting in her living room needing Auntie Mar-ee to make things all right. As always, she was letting Rose down. Some things never changed.

Marnie glanced back at Emmit, then retrieved the box and dropped the sand dollar into the hole at the top. She checked the lock and shoved the box back on the top of the bookcase. Then she touched Emmit's arm, walked into the other room, and deleted the e-mail to Taylor Cole.

11

Emmit? It couldn't be. And yet… Taylor dropped his pencil and leaped from his chair.

"Mr. Cole?"

He grabbed his Aussie hat and shoved it on his head. "Excuse me, Myrtle." He tossed a glance in her direction, then darted around the desk, through the doorway, and past the receptionist area. He rushed out the building and skittered down the short flight of stairs to the sidewalk. A blast of icy wind slammed the door behind him. He looked both ways, then jogged to the corner. His gaze flew across the street.

But the boy was gone. Vanished.

Taylor stood on the sidewalk as November snow slanted across his face and caught in his lashes. He shivered. He would have turned up the collar on his coat and bundled it around him, except he'd left it hanging in his office.

All right, God, what are You trying to tell me with a fake vision of Emmit?

He glanced up toward his window. He had seen someone, hadn't he? A kid had been standing right here across the road. A kid who looked right into his window, right at him. But the boy may have only been seeing his reflection in the glass. Yes, that was it. The kid had been glancing at himself. And of course it wasn't Emmit. It couldn't have been. The snow must have obscured Taylor's vision. He rubbed his eyes.

The only problem with his theory was he could see into his office right now. Myrtle stood by his bookcase, and by the looks of things, she was checking his law books for dust. She was sure to find some. He grimaced and let his gaze wander back over to where he thought he'd seen the kid. Right in front of the tiny bakery where they served his favorite doughnuts. No one was there now. But… He stepped forward and narrowed his eyes. Something was fluttering in the snow. A folded piece of paper.

Taylor waited for an SUV to pass, then strode across the street. Funny that a piece of paper would have fallen just where he'd seen the boy. He bent over, picked it up, and unfolded it.

He almost dropped it again. Because there she was. Black hair, quirky half smile, dark eyes that even in a photo captured and held his. Her arms were crossed, her head tilted. The Marnie's Books and Brew sign was just behind and above her. Her dream come true. He stared for a full thirty seconds, then folded the paper down the center and creased it. Something odd was going on. This was the picture he'd given to Emmit to show the boy what his aunt looked like. So, how did it get here, half buried in the snow?

The gray sky still tossed out flakes of ice, coming down now at an angle that slipped down his collar and chilled his skin. He tucked the picture into his pocket and stepped from the curb.

A horn blared. He jumped back. A truck rumbled by. Taylor caught his breath. *Pay attention, Cole.* He checked for traffic coming both ways, then stepped into the street again. He hurried across and back to his office.

Myrtle was still there.

"Honey, you need to take a look—"

"At my books. I know."

"You know? But—"

"Thank goodness you're not leaving Mixie, Moxie, or Poxie to me." Yikes, did he say that aloud? He winked to soften his words.

Myrtle blushed. "Silly young man. The dog's name is Harold, not Poxie."

Taylor stepped closer and took Myrtle's elbow. He guided her toward the door. "Don't worry about a thing. I'll have your trust done in no time, and all the ceramic animals will go to just the right homes."

She fluttered her nonexistent eyelashes at him. "Promise, Mr. Cole?"

"I promise. Come back next week, and I'll have everything drawn up and dust free."

She patted her hair. "You're such a kidder."

He helped her out the door. "Just let Nancy know when you'd like to come in to sign." He gave her a final smile, then retreated to his office and shut the door behind her.

His e-mail program chirped. New mail. He sat at his desk and turned the computer screen toward him. Her name flashed at him. Marnie Wittier. She was haunting him again. In pictures and now in words.

He tilted closer to the computer's screen and soaked in her words. He paused at the third paragraph. *"Find him someone better than me."*

Taylor reread the words on his screen and scowled. The good news was that Emmit was there. The bad news was that Marnie didn't sound like the girl he had known. And yet…

No, she was just overreacting. He knew it would be hard but not impossible. Still, the Marnie he'd known was not one to overreact. She called 'em like she saw 'em. That's what he'd loved about her. No guessing, no pretense, no putting on airs. Even when her sister was dating that fancy-pants what's-his-name, Marnie was still his Marnie—motorcycle boots and all.

He pulled out her picture again and stared into it. So much the same, yet so different too. She should have been happy, with the little coffee shop and bookstore she'd always wanted. With the spunk that made him fall in love. But there was a shadow in her eyes. A sorrow only he could see. Or maybe he was the only one who saw it because he wanted it to be there—wanted her to miss him like he'd missed her.

Maybe he should have gone out there with Emmit, should have found out for himself what Marnie was like now. Did she still prefer Doritos and Double Stuf Oreos instead of caviar and champagne? Did she still wear boots? Would she love a kid who wasn't perfect? Would she give him a chance?

The Marnie he'd known would have. She'd have given him a first chance, a second chance, and a third. So he'd give her time. Give Emmit time to settle in, and the two of them to get comfortable with each other. It was just good that the boy had gotten out there where he belonged. Taylor'd almost begun to panic, almost started seeing things. The paper crinkled in his hand. He dropped it onto the desk. Then he poised his fingers over the keyboard and began to type.

Dear Marnie,

His hands shook. Could he do this? Could he cross the cyber-bridge to her after all these years? What could he say? *I see you've found your dream. I never did find mine.* No, it wasn't her fault he became an estate planner instead of the high-powered advocate for the kids he'd once imagined. It wasn't her fault he took the easy way, made a living, and didn't dream anymore. It wasn't. Except that it was.

Hers, and his.

God, why did I let her get away? Why couldn't I have just been the friend she wanted, the one she needed. Why did I have to push to be more? I was supposed to be the one person she could trust. But in the end, I didn't love her enough to do what was right, or at least stop from doing what I knew was wrong. Why couldn't I have just hung on? And why didn't I get a second chance?

He sighed. It was an old question. He'd asked it a hundred times over the years. He'd never gotten an answer. No matter how often he repented, God still stayed silent and Marnie still stayed gone.

Until now.

He steadied his fingers. He wouldn't write any of that. Wouldn't tell her how his faith kept pole-vaulting between guilt and despair. Wouldn't tell her how he'd stayed in Maine thinking God would answer and Marnie would come home. Wouldn't mention how many times he'd made a plan, then unmade it because maybe, just maybe, she'd be coming home. But he just kept on believing and not believing. And he still hung on to this aggravating estate-planning practice because he didn't dare do anything else.

No, he wouldn't type about that. None of it. But he could right the recent wrong he'd done her by sending Emmit out there with no instructions, no insights, no clues as to how to make the transition easier for them both.

No wonder she was writing to him like she did. Maybe if he'd told her that Emmit liked to ride horses, and his favorite musician was Jeremy Camp, and he loved to paint on real canvas, that would have helped. So he could tell her now. And maybe he could send some of those chocolate-covered pretzels from the shop on the corner.

That's exactly what he'd do. He rolled up his sleeves and slapped his hand on the desk. The paper with Marnie's picture jumped. He turned it over, folded it again, and tucked it beneath his desk lamp. He frowned and pulled it out again. On the back in the corner, a phone number was scrawled in black ink.

He tapped the paper with his fingers. Then he picked up the phone and dialed the number.

A sleepy voice answered on the other side. "County records. Birth certificates. How can I help you?"

"Sorry. Wrong number." Taylor hung up. Something was going on. Something that a good lawyer would ferret out to discover the truth. A good lawyer like he used to be. Or at least like he once imagined he would become. A good lawyer who would ask questions like, "Why would Emmit be calling county records?" And, "What would he find there when he did?" And, "What does this have to do with the woman on the other side of the paper?"

Taylor shut his laptop and closed his eyes. Too bad he wasn't that lawyer. He didn't want another mystery. He was tired of them.

They'd dogged him ever since Marnie ran away. He'd asked Rose about Marnie, but she wouldn't give a straight answer. Eventually he stopped trying because deep down he was afraid she'd left because of him. Because she couldn't trust him anymore.

The world would have shrugged its shoulders at his sin. "Who was he hurting?" it would say. But he knew the truth. He didn't do right by her, and he paid the price. Sin was sin, no matter how acceptable in the world. It shamed him.

And now he was so tired of secrets. Tired of evasions. Tired of loss. Sometimes it seemed that's all he knew anymore, the secrets of clients, their deceptions, their perceptions. What was true, what was real? He was just tired. That was real enough. Weary of wading through it all.

Maybe he needed a vacation. He'd heard California was nice this time of year.

The pretty box was gone. Auntie Mar-ee had moved it. Emmit sat on the floor, crossed his legs, and rested his chin on his hands. Then he thought. He thought real hard. So hard his glasses slipped down his nose and made him see all funny. He pushed them back up. There, now he could see Max.

He waved at Max. Max didn't wave back. Lizards didn't wave. Everybody knew that. Even Max.

He could see all those nice books with all their shiny covers. Funny how Auntie Mar-ee didn't keep any pictures of people. Everyone he knew had pictures they put out. Auntie Mar-ee didn't even have one.

He frowned. Pictures didn't matter. The box mattered. He had to find that box.

He scooted over and sat in the rays of sunlight that fell through the window. It was warm here. It didn't snow. There were no snow angels. Only him. He missed them. Missed the soft sound of their wings fluttering to earth. Missed the soft whispering sound of their voices. Missed the soft coolness when they kissed his cheeks. But Auntie Mar-ee needed him. She needed him real bad. That's why he couldn't go home. Not yet. No matter how much he missed it.

He had to stay here and find that box.

Auntie Mar-ee's voice skipped out to him from the other room. "Emmit, go get your shoes, please. We need to go to the store."

He lifted his chin and called back to her. "Bookstore?" He liked the bookstore. Books were good. He didn't like the cookies so much, though. He even tried poking a hole in the center of one, but it still didn't taste like a doughnut.

"No bookstore today. We're off, remember? There's something I want to pick up somewhere else."

"Where?" He looked back over his shoulder.

Her voice softened as she stepped into the doorway behind him. "It's a surprise."

He smiled. He loved surprises.

Maybe Auntie Mar-ee loved them too. He turned back and opened his shirt pocket with two fingers. He peeked inside. There, all folded up, was a funny green paper with a word written on it. It had come from Auntie Mar-ee's special box. He pulled it halfway out and studied the word. He couldn't read it. It was important, though. It had to be because she wrote it on money. And people thought money was important.

He slipped the bill back into his pocket and patted it. He'd show her later. Now wasn't the right time. But soon, he would. Then she'd be real surprised too.

Good thing Auntie Mar-ee liked surprises.

~~~

Thank you, Taylor Cole.

Marnie scrunched the printout of his e-mail in her hand and reached for a Jeremy Camp CD on the store's shelf. It was a few years old, but that wouldn't matter. She'd already bought a used iPod and cheap speaker system to go with it. On credit, of course. How she was going to pay for it, she didn't know. Anything to get Emmit off that song about Mary and the lamb. If a guy named Jeremy Camp could do that, then it was worth the cost of five iPods and a dozen CDs.

She waved out the shop's window to Emmit who was still sitting in the car. He waved back. That meant he happened to be happy. His moods were one of the hardest things to get used to—sometimes he was the sweet, cooperative Emmit, and other times he was the sit-in-the-driveway-and-flail-and-hit Emmit. And she still couldn't predict which one she was going to get. He bounced against his seat, his mouth moving. Singing. Again. So now was the moment.

She pulled out her phone and a scrap of paper and quickly dialed the number of the local group home she'd looked up on the Internet. It had seemed wonderful, with photos of residents laughing at a car show or with their arms around one another, swaying to the music at a music festival. The Web site promised an "active social calendar" as well as twenty-four-hour care and supervision. It was perfect. They even had their own sweatshirts.

Still, she suspected Emmit wouldn't like the idea. Another change, another loss. It would be hard. But it was right. She could visit but not be responsible. Everyone would be better off that way. Just yesterday, she'd left pasta boiling on the stove, and of course Emmit bumped into it and burned himself. He'd woken up crying twice last night. And then he filled the toilet up with toilet paper and kept flushing until the whole thing overflowed. Clearly he wasn't happy living with her.

And she was losing her mind.

The phone rang. Rang and rang and rang. No one answered. She hung up. They'd just have to go there and hope the surprise of the CD would soften the surprise of suggesting a group home.

Marnie gripped the CD in her hand, pulled out her car keys, and strode out to the curb.

Five minutes later, they pulled up in front of an old Victorian house. She threw the Bug into Park and turned toward Emmit. "You stay right here, okay? I'll just be a minute."

"What is this place?"

"It looks nice, doesn't it?" She glanced outside. Unfortunately it looked nothing like the picture on the Internet. Where the flower garden was supposed to be, weeds grew up and tangled through the fence. The cute little swing that had held the smiling elderly couple was broken. The lattice had fallen, and most of the grass was dead.

"I don't like it here." Emmit crossed his arms.

"It's real nice." Her voice cracked. Well, maybe it was nice on the inside. Because this had to work out. It just had to. "I won't take long. I promise."

"You don't like it, Auntie Mar-ee. Ugly here. We go."

She got out of the car and slammed the door behind her. She hurried to the front porch, trying not to see the peeling paint, the cracks in the walkway, or the gum wrappers littering the once-lush grass. She paused and knocked on the door.

Like with the phone, no one answered.

She knocked again. Louder, harder. Again. Nothing. Something wasn't right.

Faint sounds came from inside.

She pounded on the door until her fist smarted.

Finally the door creaked open. A woman in an old T-shirt, with a cigarette hanging from her mouth, stood glaring at her from the other side of the door's opening.

Marnie swallowed. Words fled. Her stomach turned. *This isn't like that time.* She forced down the bile rising in her throat and pretended to smile. "Is this where the group home is?"

The woman puffed on her cigarette, then spoke through clenched teeth. "Closed down a couple months ago. Didn't ya see the big sign?" She pointed to the front window. "For lease. That shoulda given you a clue."

Yes, she supposed it should have. How could she have missed that? "Did they move somewhere else?"

The woman pulled the cigarette from her mouth and tapped the ashes onto the porch. "Who do I look like? Paul Harvey? You think I got the rest of the story?"

No, you look like... Marnie clamped her mouth shut over the comment.

The woman grunted. "Didn't move, just closed. Now I gotta get back to my cleaning. I think someone peed in the back room and never wiped it up." She glanced behind her. "Stinkin' job. Boss says he's doing me a favor." Her voice lowered to a mutter. "Some favor. Cleanin' up pee and only the Almighty Himself knows what else." She gave Marnie one last glare, then shut the door. The sound echoed all the way to Marnie's soul.

She backed down the steps. Slow. Careful. Unbelieving. Closed. Now what was she going to do? Keep him? That would never work. Send him to foster care? Never.

God, You should have thought twice before taking Rose. There's no way I'm up for this. You've got to find someone else.

Marnie turned away from the ramshackle house and stumbled back to the car. Emmit was still there, smiling, rocking, and listening to his brand-new CD.

She opened the door and sat in the driver's seat. Her hands gripped the steering wheel. Strains of "I Still Believe" swirled around her. Did she? Did she still believe, even now? Yes, she still believed that God cared, that He was faithful, that He gave second chances. To everyone, that is, except her.

"We go now."

"Yes, we go now."

"Good."

She started the car.

Emmit touched her arm. "Now, my surprise."

She turned toward him.

He reached into his pocket and pulled out a dark green dollar bill. He unfolded it and placed the bill between them. But it wasn't a dollar bill. It was a two-dollar bill, with the word *CHEAT* scrawled in black letters across the front.

"Surprise!" Emmit grinned.

Marnie slammed the car into reverse and promptly ran over the curb.

wo dollars. The price of a life. Of two lives, maybe. Sold cheap under swaying lights, because Marnie Helen Wittier had a plan. She should have known right then that it was a dumb one. When did any of her plans ever work out? But she hadn't figured that out yet on that balmy night all those years ago when she first touched that stupid two-dollar bill.

Taylor parked the car and came around to open her door. She stepped out into the glow of the streetlights and turned toward the pier. Out there, a shiny yacht rocked on the waves. Glimmers of light danced over the dark water and threw eerie shadows over the sides of the boat as it bobbed just inches from the dock.

The distant hum of an engine floated through the air, mixing with the chatter of voices, the smell of diesel, and the lapping of water against smooth wood.

The car door slammed. Then he was beside her. This time, though, he didn't hold her hand. She wished he would. But she didn't reach out for his either. She just strolled toward the yacht, breathed in the musky scent of his cologne, and wished. Music from the boat blared louder. The party was already long started.

Taylor's hand brushed her arm. "I see I made us late. Sorry about that. VBS ran over."

"Ran over what? And what's VBS?"

He grinned and pulled a toy bazooka from his pocket. "Ran over-time, I mean. VBS is vacation Bible school. I volunteered to lead the eight-year-olds." He blew the bazooka. "Today we talked about how God's kingdom is like a party. So we had a party, complete with decorations, games, and all the fixings."

"Is that why you still have cupcake on your cheek?" She reached up and wiped a crumb from his face.

"Hey, I was saving that for later." He winked at her and slipped the bazooka back in his pocket. "Just in case this party we're going to isn't as fun as the one I came from."

She crossed her arms. "It does sound like VBS is a lot better than this." She waved toward the yacht.

"We don't have to go to this you know."

She glanced over at him, noting again his casual polo shirt, unbuttoned at the neckline to show a bit of the bright red T-shirt underneath. She smiled. The T-shirt was Taylor's bit of defiance. Rose hated red. She said because it was a garish color. But Marnie knew the truth. It was less about the color and more about being teased incessantly as a kid by her younger sister about red roses and sticky thorns.

Marnie could still remember the song "Red Rose-r, red Rose-r, she sends thorns all over" sung to the chant of the Red Rover kid's game. It was an awkward little rhyme, but at six years old she'd thought herself very clever for making it up without any help. Rose didn't think it half so clever, especially when Marnie would sing it when Rose's "way cool" friends were over. And, of course, that made her sing it all the louder and often with the accompaniment of a drum made from a round Quaker Oats oatmeal box.

Marnie's smile tipped to one side. "I guess I owe her one. Besides, she begged." Her brows furrowed. "I guess she really likes this guy. Or at least his money."

"Did she tell you anything about your mom?"

"Not after the last fiasco."

"And this time?"

"Just that she changed her name. Fat lot of good that does us."

"I couldn't get anything out of her either. You sure you want to keep trying, especially after what we found at those last apartments?"

Marnie raised her eyebrows at him and didn't answer.

"Anyone ever tell you you're crazy?"

"All the time."

He laughed. "Well, it's not news, then. But any info we could get out of Rose would be. Maybe if tonight goes well…"

Marnie scoffed. "And the likelihood of that is?"

"Can't be much worse than last time." Taylor's voice lowered to a whisper.

A chill slithered through Marnie's gut. "Here's hoping."

"Listen, if you want to leave, just give me the sign, and we'll get out of there. Go grab some real food like hamburgers or pizza."

The light above them flickered. She slowed and put her hands on her hips. "What sign?"

He stuck out his tongue.

She chuckled. "Yeah, that's real subtle." She dropped her arms. "But don't worry, I've got a plan. Tonight, I'll get Rose to tell me what she knows."

"Really? How?"

"You'll see." Marnie smiled into the darkness and quickened her pace.

Taylor stopped.

Marnie turned around. There he stood under the quivering glow of the streetlight. His arms were crossed, his chin lifted, his lips pressed tight to suppress his grin. A curl flopped over his forehead beneath his hat. He reached up to push it back. She liked it better down. He recrossed his arms. "The real question is, when are you going to stop bringing me to these stupid things and let me take you on a real date?"

Her eyes narrowed. "I don't do real dates, remember? Too risky."

"Just pizza and a movie, then."

"Which movie?"

"Umm...*Batman Forever*?"

"Well, I do like superheroes. And that Val Kilmer is yummy."

"Great, now I have to compete with a guy who has a girl's first name." He held up a hand to stop her response. "Next Friday. No excuses. You owe me for having to come to this uptight gig. And I want to ride on the bike."

She nodded and continued toward the boat. "Okay, no excuses. And I want popcorn. The big box."

"Deal."

"And I'm driving."

"Party pooper."

She stopped before the yacht. On the deck, the same twentysomethings from the last party milled around in small groups. Women wore bracelets that sparkled as brightly as the champagne glasses in their hands. They laughed in high-pitched voices through lips painted ruby red. Fake fingernails fluttered to low necklines dotted with diamonds, pearls, and gold.

She shuddered, then glanced down at her same old boots and suppressed a grimace. Only one thing would make her face this crowd again—the hope of getting the truth out of Rose at last. At least there wasn't any tempting ice this time, and she'd be sure to remember not to eat anything she didn't recognize.

Taylor touched her elbow. "Now or never."

She straightened her shoulders. "Let the games begin."

They stepped up onto the boat. Three seconds later, Rose spotted them. "Marnie, Taylor, over here." Her voice sounded strange, blurred.

Marnie hesitated. Her gaze snaked around a group of giggling women to spy Rose sitting with others at a round table covered with green felt. Cards and coins were scattered over the table's surface. Next to Rose sat her fancy-pants boyfriend, studying his cards. Marnie looked closer. Good grief, the guy was even wearing one of those ridiculous scarves around his neck like Fred on *Scooby-Doo*.

Rose scowled in her direction. Sometimes Marnie thought her sister could read her mind. But at least they were playing cards. That's what mattered.

She wove her way toward her sister.

Rose motioned to a couple of empty seats. "Join us."

Taylor took a step back. "No thanks."

Marnie sat down. Her boots scraped against the smooth deck.

He leaned over and whispered in her ear. "What are you doing? You hate cards."

She looked up at him with a tight smile. "Remember what I said before? Tonight I'm going to play. And I'm going to win."

The guy one seat over from her slapped his palm on the table. "We'll see about that, sweetheart. Put your nickels where your mouth is." He snorted. "Not literally, of course."

Marnie wrinkled her nose. That guy—Jim, Chuck, Greg, she couldn't remember his name—was drinking more than simple champagne. She could smell that much. She pulled three dollars from her pocket and exchanged them for nickels. Funny how the rich guys always played for so little. Rose had said it was because they wanted it to be just for fun, or at least boasting rights. Pride, apparently, was more important than money.

Of course, they played for other things too—the use of a sports car for an evening, the phone number of a favorite girl, a fancy dinner date, a Saturday on the speedboat, and sometimes, the revealing of secrets. That's what Marnie was banking on tonight.

For that, even playing a hated card game was worth it. At least they were playing Texas hold 'em. She knew the rules for that one, so all she had to do was wait. And get lucky.

She waited for two hours. Hand after hand after hand. Betting and folding, gaining a nickel here and there, losing more, the boat swaying, Taylor milling around and tossing her glances, as if she'd turned into some kind of space alien. Rose was watching her too, slipping her puzzled looks now and then, wondering, questioning, daring not to ask.

And then it happened. With her nickels diminished to two short stacks, she finally got the hand she'd been waiting for. She bet on the turn. Ten of hearts. And on the river. A nine. Hearts again. A queen-high flush. And she knew, just knew that Rose had the straight.

Marnie pushed her nickels all in.

Rose leaned back. "Are you sure?"

She was. Rose would raise. Liquor-Guy would fold. And then she'd sweeten the pot.

Rose called.

Marnie put her hands over her cards and tipped forward. Her eyes caught Rose's. "I tell you what, if you win, I'll stop searching for mom."

Rose caught her breath. Her eyes widened. "Promise?"

"And if I win, you tell me where she is. Deal?"

Rose raised her chin and gripped her cards more tightly. "Deal."

Liquor-Guy tapped his cards on the table. "What about me?"

Marnie didn't spare him a glance. "You should just fold."

Instead he tossed in a two-dollar bill. "I'll bet that. And if I win, I get a date. And I get a ride on the Harley of yours."

Marnie didn't take her eyes from Rose as she laid down her cards. "Flush."

Rose turned pale. She laid down the straight. "Marnie, you're going to be sorry. You don't know…"

From the corner of Marnie's vision came a flutter of white, a movement of cards. She ignored it.

Liquor-Guy cleared his throat.

She looked over. Her breath stopped. No. It couldn't be. Not when she was so close. But there they were. The king of hearts. And the four. She'd lost. How could she possibly have lost?

The guy winked at her. "I win." He gathered up the nickels and tossed her the two-dollar bill. "You can keep that, as a reminder of our date." He tilted back in his chair and laughed. Then he ran his hand over his long hair.

Her stomach turned.

Ascot snickered. A strange sound. A guilty sound.

Marnie glared at him.

His face flushed.

Then hers did. "Did you slip him a card when I wasn't looking?"

Ascot shrugged. "Of course not. Why would I do that?"

She stood.

So did Rose. "Don't be silly, Marnie. You lost, that's it."

Marnie gripped the edge of the table. "Well, I'm out then." Stupid, stupid, stupid. She'd get out of that date somehow. No way she was going anywhere with longhaired Liquor-Guy. And no way she was letting him ride on her bike either.

But she had. Eventually she had. And that cost her a lot more than just a few nickels. It cost her Taylor Cole.

~~

He could almost see the chill in the air. Taylor's breath rose like a fog before him and mixed with the breath of his horse as they turned from the trail and headed back toward his ranch. Sunlight peeked over the trees and turned the meadow between them and the barn into a sea of glistening diamonds. The snow had stopped sometime in the night, leaving a perfect blanket over the pasture.

Misty snorted and shook her mane.

He reached down and patted her neck with his gloved hand. "You know we walk toward home."

She snorted again.

He always told the kids it only took one good run to make a horse barn sour and a month of walking to fix it. Still…

Taylor tightened his legs around Misty's bare sides. He leaned forward.

She quickened her pace.

He clucked. Once.

She broke into a smooth, perfect canter. The breeze blew his breath behind him and chilled his cheeks and nose. The weather was perfect, exhilarating. And Misty was perfect too. She was the only one of his four horses who could move directly into a glasslike lope, skipping the teeth-jarring trot. He loved her for that and loved to ride her bareback on mornings just like this, just the two of them, and the cool air, and the rising sun, and the hope of a new day.

God, why can't life be like a ride in the snow? In life, it seemed you couldn't avoid the rough trot. And too often it lasted for more than just a few strides. He wished it didn't have to be that way. He wished life could just be lived without mysteries and Myrtles, without doubts and disasters. He wished he could just be a simple horse rancher and forget about practicing law.

Now where did that come from? Hadn't he learned that it was no good to wish? No good to dream.

Marnie.

It only took one simple e-mail from her to get him dreaming again. What kind of idiot was he? If he wasn't careful, he'd start imagining groups of disabled kids coming to his ranch to learn to ride and take care of the horses. And worse, he'd imagine Marnie at his side, teaching them, and Emmit grinning up at him as he saddled the black for the kids. Just like a real family.

Those were dangerous dreams. Crazy dreams. He was a lawyer. He'd been a lawyer, he'd always be a lawyer, sorting out ceramic cats and collections of teapots. He'd never be John Wayne or Lorne Greene on *Bonanza.* He was just Taylor Cole, estate planner, without a wife, without kids, without the family he'd always wished for.

Misty leaped over a fallen tree trunk and quickened her pace. They broke over the rise. Tufts of grass poked from beneath the snow like promises of spring to come.

Taylor sat back, and Misty slowed to a quick walk. He squinted and put up a hand to block the glare of the sun off the ice. There, near the fence closest to the house, a figure stood.

Emmit?

Taylor blinked. No. He was seeing that boy everywhere. This guy was taller, his hands tucked into a thick coat, a hat pulled down over his ears, and—he sighed—a long ponytail sticking from beneath the hat. Great. What was he doing here? Emmit was gone, so why did Child Services need to keep poking around? Still, Craig and he were friends, sort of.

Craig waved as Taylor came closer. "Hey, you're out early."

Taylor grimaced. *So are you.* He reined Misty toward the fence, then dismounted. "Kinda chilly for a social visit."

Craig smoothed his hand over his ponytail in just the way that irritated Taylor the most, then rested his hands on the top rail. "Yeah, when have I come out here just for fun?"

"Well, two years ago for my Christmas party. And the year before that for Emmit's birthday."

Craig pushed back from the fence. "You were serving those fresh lobsters."

"You're blaming it on the free food?"

Craig laughed. "Sure. Any excuse will do."

Taylor unbuckled Misty's bridle and removed the bit from her mouth. He tossed the headstall over his shoulder and patted her neck.

The horse nuzzled him once before she trotted toward the barn.

Taylor turned back to Craig. "Okay, so what's up?" He hopped the fence and motioned toward the house. "You want some coffee? All I got is decaf, but I've got great mocha to go in it."

"Nah. Been waiting for twenty minutes. Gotta get going."

"You couldn't have just called?"

Craig tugged on his ponytail again. "Tried. Phone's off."

"So?" Taylor started toward the house.

"So, um." Craig sucked his teeth a moment before continuing. "Nancy tells me you've asked for Emmit's birth certificate." He hurried to catch up.

Taylor didn't glance his way. "Yeah?"

"So, you seen it?"

"No."

They reached the porch. Craig's hand gripped Taylor's arm. "Let it lie, Cole."

Taylor paused. "What do you mean?"

Craig fidgeted. "I mean, don't go poking around where you aren't wanted. Emmit's gone to his aunt's, and I guess that's where he should be. What's done is done."

Taylor shook off Craig's grip. "I thought you wanted to put him in the system."

He took a step back and adjusted his wire-rimmed glasses. His voice lowered. "I never wanted that."

"Could have fooled me."

"Did you take anything from Rose's?"

"What business is that of yours? You took all your stuff with you when you moved out five years ago."

Craig tensed. "Just answer me, Cole."

"I took some old pictures."

"What for?"

"I'd planned to send them on to California. Emmit ought to have some of the pictures from when he was little."

"Yeah, well, okay then. Just…"

Taylor grabbed the doorknob on his front door and twisted it. He turned back toward Craig. "So, I have your permission then?" His tone dripped.

Craig reddened. "I didn't mean it that way. It's just that Rose made me promise to make sure that Emmit was okay if anything ever happened to her. I owe her that."

"And that's why she left him to Marnie?"

Craig glared at him. "She had her reasons for that too, but that doesn't mean they were the right ones."

"Aren't you late for an appointment or something?"

"Yeah, I guess so." Craig backed down the stairs and moved toward his car.

Taylor waited. He never could figure out that guy. Maybe he had nothing to do. Seemed that way sometimes. He'd just show up, like at Emmit's baptism years ago, at his junior high graduation, at a Fourth of July picnic they'd had at the beach. It made sense when he was living with Rose. It made a lot less sense when he wasn't. It was like the guy was pressing his way in, wanting to belong but too awkward to do it right. He'd always been that way, even back when they shared parties on fancy yachts and he cheated at poker games.

Craig reached his stripped-down BMW and turned back around. "One last thing, Cole. I've just gotta know."

"What's that?"

"Were you really going to marry Marnie Wittier before she ran away?"

Taylor shivered. "What's it to you?"

Craig stuffed his hands into his pockets and looked away. "Just answer me."

"Yes."

Craig shook his head, got into his car, and drove away.

Taylor watched him go. Then he went into the house. The stack of photos he'd taken from Rose's sat on the kitchen table. That was funny. He was sure he'd left them on the counter, right next to Marnie's address. He picked them up and leafed through them. Emmit, with his crazy hair and glasses, turning three; riding his first horse at six; grinning at the camera with his two top teeth missing. And there were pictures from the picnic at the beach, and the Christmas party, and that play they'd put on at Emmit's school.

Taylor flipped through the pictures again, searching for one when Emmit was a baby. There weren't any. His three-year-old birthday was the earliest photo he had. Well, they would have to do. Taylor would get those photos sent out later.

He walked over to the counter where he'd put Marnie's address. It was gone. The small velvet box was still there, though. The same one he'd dug out from the back of his socks drawer last night. Dug it out, opened it, and stared at the contents for a good hour. Stared, remembered, wondered why she'd left it behind.

He'd closed the box last night. Now, it was open. He touched the small diamond, ran his finger over the white-gold band. He didn't need to read the words etched inside. *Clamming together…Marnie & Taylor.* Cheesy. But back then he thought it was clever.

Taylor shut the box and turned to the pile of mail he'd brought in last night. He was sure he'd seen…yes, there it was. The envelope from the county registrar. Sometimes it was handy to be a lawyer.

He opened the envelope and pulled out the certificate. No father listed. He'd expected that. After all, fancy-pants William would never admit he'd fathered Emmit. Taylor glanced further down the sheet. Strange. Instead of the physician's signature, a nurse had signed. Taylor knew the name, a friend of Marnie's foster mom, who used to work in the maternity ward. It was odd, but still, there had to be something else. Something that Craig knew and didn't want him to find. Something like…

Taylor's eyes widened. He read the filing date again. Then he folded up the copy of the certificate and tucked it in his pocket.

How could Emmit's birth certificate have been filed two months before he was even born?

Rose Wittier, what did you have to hide?

13

*M*arnie stood on tiptoes and slipped the two-dollar bill back into her special box. She peeked behind her. Good, Emmit wasn't watching. This was the third time she'd hidden the box somewhere in the house. The last two times it took less than an hour for him to find it. The boy may be challenged in some areas, but he was a genius at box hide-and-seek. He found it behind the towels in the bathroom cupboard. He discovered it in the pot on top of the fridge. And no doubt he'd find it again hidden here on the top shelf behind the retro record player in her room.

Mothers were supposed to have eyes in the backs of their heads, but not fifteen-year-old Down-syndrome boys. Still, she was beginning to think Emmit wasn't as limited by his disabilities as she'd thought. At least when it came to turning her life and her world upside down. He was an expert at that.

She twisted around on the chair and watched him through the open doorway. He didn't look up. He continued poking at a bit of peeling paint on the windowsill. He pulled off a long strip and held it up to the light. Then he smiled.

She sighed. She'd better hurry and take that away before he put it in his mouth and got lead poisoning or something. That would be just her luck. She balanced on the chair. "Emmit, put that down, please."

He did. But not the easy way. Emmit never did anything the easy way. This time, he crunched up the paint peeling and tossed it into the air. White specks caught the light and fluttered in a million directions. Tiny enough to have to require the vacuum, but not so small as to be ignored. Figured.

Marnie turned back around and pushed the box behind some books stacked to the side of the record player. There, it was perfectly hidden now. Surely this time… She stepped off the chair, grabbed it, and swung around.

Emmit stood just behind her.

She stopped. "You didn't."

He pointed to the top shelf. "Why you do that, Auntie Mar-ee?"

"Good grief, Emmit. Can't you just leave my box alone?"

He frowned. "Not good grief. Bad grief."

She set down the chair and rubbed her hands over her forehead. "I don't want you to touch that box. Ever. Okay? You leave those things alone." Of course, she'd told him that before, about a hundred times, and it hadn't stopped him. Wasn't doing the same thing and expecting different results the definition of crazy? Well, she was definitely crazy. Certifiable.

Emmit moved farther into the room, his gaze never leaving the spot on the high shelf. "I like to touch them."

"The things in the box? Why?"

Finally he looked at her. "Ugly things. I make them pretty." He smiled. "I like the sun."

Sometimes he made no sense at all. "You just let them be, okay?"

He sat on the floor and folded up his legs, just like always. "You don't like them. Why do you keep them?"

Why? It was a good question. She ought to just throw it all away. But she didn't. And she wouldn't. "I guess it's because, because…" Her voice lowered to a mere whisper. "Because they're who I am."

Emmit pushed his glasses up his nose and stared at her for nearly a minute. Then he pulled a rumpled piece of paper out of his shirt pocket. He set it on the floor and flattened it out with the side of his fist. It wasn't paper; it was a napkin. A napkin shaped like a flag and printed with colors of red, white, and blue.

Marnie caught her breath. Another stolen item from her box of regrets.

Emmit tapped the paper and spoke slowly, deliberately, with an emphasis on each word. "Auntie–Mar-ee–not–napkin." His brows bunched.

Marnie sat on the floor next to him, crossed her legs, and rested her back against the bed behind her. She reached over and picked up the napkin, then twirled it in her fingers. "Aren't I?" *I wish you were right.* But a napkin was just what she was, what she'd always been. A bit of cheap paper used to wipe up someone else's spills and then be thrown aside.

"Pretty colors."

She smoothed the napkin against her leg. "You like the red, white, and blue?"

"Auntie Mar-ee red, white, and blue?"

Yeah, maybe she was. Scarlet with sin, pale with shame, and blue from all the mistakes she'd made and could never undo.

"Auntie Mar-ee's shirt is purple." He stated the fact as if it settled the point. Then he slapped his hands together and held one out, palm up. "Mine."

"You want the napkin?"

"Give me."

She turned it over to the back side. In tiny letters around the outer border were the faded words *Not good enough.* Never good enough.

"Let's go to beach. Emmit love beach."

Marnie shut her eyes. "No. I told you, I don't go to the beach." *Ever.*

"Then tell me story."

She ran her fingers over the miniscule words. "Once upon a time there were three little pigs." *Named Marnie, Rose, and Taylor. And they all made their houses out of straw.*

"Not that story."

She glanced at him. "What story then?"

"Napkin story. I hear that." He smiled again, crossed his arms over his chest, and waited.

The napkin story. Well, why not? She folded the napkin in half and set it on the floor between them. She gazed into the colors until the memory came to life. "We were all invited to my foster mother's for a Fourth of July party. She loved to invite all the important people to her parties, and that day was no exception."

Emmit rocked forward. "You important."

A faint smile tipped her lips, then fled. "No. I was one of the *others*. I was there so I could better myself by mingling with the VIPs. Very important persons."

"Mar-ee important person." He nodded once.

Marnie knew that look. It meant she shouldn't bother to argue. Emmit had made up his mind. "I went to the party with my sister, Rose, and my good friend Taylor."

His face brightened. "Mr. Cole. I know him."

"Yes, you do."

"I like him. More than doughnuts."

Me too. She hurried on before Emmit could start asking about doughnuts. Or about Taylor. "You should have seen it. There were red, white, and blue colored balloons. And plates, cups, and napkins to match."

"Your napkin."

"Yes, my napkin was there. It was sitting on the end of the buffet table next to the yard where some people were playing a game called croquet."

"Mar-ee no play croquet." He shook his head in big exaggerated movements.

"No, I didn't."

"Why not?"

She would never get through the story this way. "I don't like games. Now, as I was saying, I was standing there drinking tea and watching my friend Taylor play croquet with the mayor's sister, who was a maternity ward nurse, and my foster mom. Her name was Doris—my foster mom, not her friend the nurse. I can't remember the nurse's name." And she didn't want to. "Anyway, Doris always loved to play with her guests." *If they were important enough.*

"But not with Mar-ee."

Never with me. "No." Marnie cleared her throat. "Our pastor was there, and the son of the mayor, and a couple councilmen."

Emmit blinked.

She could tell he had no idea what she was talking about. "Well, Taylor was staying at my foster mom's cottage by the sea that summer, and she was asking how he liked it."

"He liked it a lot."

"Yes, he did. How did you know that?"

Emmit shrugged.

"Then they talked about the church where Taylor's dad was a deacon, and the lawyer he was clerking for in town, and the places they'd both been, the countries they'd visited, the famous people they'd both met."

"You drank tea."

"Yes, while I stood there drinking mint iced tea. Doris always liked to serve tea."

Emmit scooted closer to her and laid his head on her shoulder. He sighed.

She did too. "And then she wanted to introduce him to the councilman's daughter, Analisa."

"She pretty?" he murmured.

"Yes, she was." Very pretty, in a Barbie makeover sort of way. But of course Doris thought Analisa was everything a young woman should be. After all, Analisa wore sweet dresses trimmed with lace and dainty ecru pumps with matching silk stockings. Analisa was a lot like Rose, except Analisa had red hair and carefully concealed freckles. But neither of them would have been caught dead in biker boots.

Marnie's gaze fixed on the napkin until she could almost see again how Doris had taken Taylor's arm to lead him to the far side of the lawn where Analisa was sipping her own tea from a fancy china cup and chatting with Rose and William. Then her foster mom glanced back and caught Marnie's eye. Marnie knew, just knew, what that look was supposed to mean. Analisa was the fancy china plate Doris would later use for dessert, and Marnie was the balled-up napkin she held scrunched in her hand. Taylor deserved more than a patriotic cookie on a crumpled napkin. He was a fine-china man.

That's when Marnie turned away and closed her eyes. Because it was true. She'd been wrinkled up and cast aside by her own mother. Rejected. Thrown away. Despised. That's what was real. Unless… If she could just find her mother and find out for certain. Maybe there was another answer. Something in the words her mother whispered to her on that last day. Maybe they would give another reason, a good reason, why her mother had to put Marnie and Rose into foster care. Maybe her mother loved her after all. And if that were so, perhaps she could be more than just a throwaway scrap. Not china maybe, but at least sturdy stoneware. Stoneware in black boots.

"Taylor like Mar-ee. Not pretty girl."

Marnie glanced at Emmit. Her lips pulled into a half smile. "Gee, thanks." But he was right. Taylor did like her, even if she wasn't on par with stoneware, let alone imported china. He proved it a few moments later. She'd turned and found him behind her, with her foster mom still at his elbow.

"There you are, dear," Doris crooned. "You have a spot on your shirt." She picked up a napkin and dabbed at Marnie's collar. "Couldn't you find something to wear that wasn't black? Honestly, you'd think it would kill you to get in the spirit of the holiday."

Marnie pushed away Doris's hand. "I didn't have time to sew a dress out of the flag like Analisa did."

Doris sniffed. "Don't be ridiculous. Hers is from Saks. Besides, it's against the law to make a dress from the flag."

Taylor stepped closer. "Well, not exactly."

Doris waved her hand at him. "Hush, Mr. Cole." She turned back to Marnie. "Now, Marnie dear, why don't you go inside and get more of the nice ginger-peach tea." She fluttered her fingers toward the sliding door.

Marnie turned and ran straight into Taylor. His arm jarred. His cup flew into the air, and raspberry tea glinted in the sun like falling rubies. Those rubies broke all over the table, Taylor's white shirt, and Doris's shiny red pumps.

"Marnie Helen!"

Taylor snatched a stack of napkins from the table. "Sorry. My fault."

Doris sputtered.

Taylor grabbed Marnie's hand and shoved a fistful of napkins into it. He pulled her down beside him. "Quick, start wiping. I think it'll blow over above us."

Marnie grimaced. "You don't know Doris. Good woman, but appearances are everything." She sopped up the droplets of tea from her foster mother's shoes. Then the shoes skittered away.

Taylor grinned at her. "Well, at least we got rid of her."

"At the cost of your shirt, I think."

He chuckled. "Good thing it's a three dollar special from the Hanes outlet. You think Doris would have been pushing me at that fancy chick if she'd known that?"

Marnie giggled. "Probably not."

"Next time I'll tell her, then. Of course, if you'd just played croquet with me, you could have saved me the trouble."

"I hate croquet."

"Scaredy-cat." He soaked up the last of the liquid with another napkin.

"Show-off."

He took a dry napkin and tucked it into her shirt pocket. "There, now you're in the spirit."

"It's not the same as a color-coordinated ensemble from Saks."

"It's better." He said it so firmly she almost believed it. Almost.

Emmit tilted forward and tapped her knee. "You miss Mr. Cole."

The colors on the napkin before her sharpened and came back into focus. *Yes, I do.*

He looked up at her. "Your face sad."

She put on a little grin. "I'm sorry. It's the napkin's fault." And it was. That's why she kept these things locked away, so she wouldn't remember, wouldn't be reminded of the things that hurt too deeply for words.

"Bad paper. I put in trash." He reached for the napkin.

She grabbed it first. Emmit was right. This napkin was an ugly thing. And yet, she couldn't throw it away. She hated it. Needed it. Feared it. She could never be free of it.

He held out his hand. "I have it now?"

For one breath, one single moment, she was tempted to give it to him. To cast it away. But she didn't. Of course she didn't. Instead she stood, pulled the chair over to the shelves, and carefully placed the napkin back in the box where it belonged.

Emmit stood too. He started to walk away, then paused and glanced back through glasses that made his eyes look small and sad. "You not napkin, Auntie Mar-ee. You pretty purple flower."

She shook her head. There were no purple flowers in her box. Not one. But for that moment, she wished there were. Because then maybe she could believe him. And then everything would change.

14

The cardboard box dropped with a loud thud onto Taylor's credenza. He stared into it. It wasn't a big box, barely larger than the kind that held files. Too small for the whole of someone's personal possessions, too small to hold the mementos of a lifetime. But this was all that was left of Rose's things. Emmit's few possessions had been sent to California. Then, as per Rose's will, her furniture, appliances, books, and electronics were donated to the local church. Her files had been cleared out and old papers thrown away. Her pantry items were given to the homeless shelter, and her clothes donated to The Salvation Army. Only this box remained. A collection of sad little trinkets that once meant something to someone, and now meant nothing at all.

He glanced into the box and saw a funny sign from Emmit's third birthday. He picked it up. The corner had been chewed off, and the teeth marks were still visible. Emmit had almost choked that day. But Taylor dug that piece of cardboard out of his throat before it got lodged in his windpipe. The boy was fine.

But Rose had still cried.

He dropped the sign back into the box and lifted out a painted rock with a tiny label. "Women's Retreat 2001 — He is my Rock. I trust in Him." The painted pink rose on it was faded now, and part of it had chipped away. He replaced the rock and pushed aside a few photo albums, some Christmas cards that were pictures of families from the church, and a postcard from a missionary in Madagascar. Then he dug past a few recent bills and a crocheted potholder until he got to a dilapidated lump of brown felt. He picked it up and smoothed the cloth. Emmit's old hat. So Rose hadn't thrown it away after all.

Taylor sighed and placed the hat on his counter. It looked sad there, lonely. Just like him. "I found it, Emmit." He whispered the words to no one. "I'll keep it for you until we see each other again."

Taylor sniffed, then returned to the box and kept digging until he reached the bottom. Stuck in the corner seam was a tiny hospital wristband. Taylor picked it up. It read "Wittier, Baby Boy" with the date of birth scratched out with black ink. Finally here was something intriguing. He twirled it in his hand. What did it mean? Why was it here?

What are you doing, Cole? He ought to just shut the box and walk away. Why would he need to unravel mysteries from a time he only wanted to forget? Of course, he never really forgot. And that was the problem. If there was anything Taylor loved, it was the truth. Discovering it, uncovering it, and living by what he found.

But he was finding that truth was scarce when it came to what had happened fifteen years ago. Why had Marnie run? Who had fathered Rose's baby? And what did it all have to do with the date of Emmit's birth? Maybe nothing. Maybe everything. Maybe the birth certificate and the wristband were just flukes. Mistakes made by someone at the hospital. Maybe they didn't mean anything at all.

Or maybe they did.

And now the truth was calling to him, bidding him to discover, uncover. Because if Emmit really was born two months earlier, he would have been born before Marnie left. And that mattered. He always assumed she'd run away because of him, what he'd done, and that stupid ring. But what if it was because of Rose? Or Emmit?

Taylor smoothed the wristband in his palm, stared into it, turned it over, and twisted it around his thumb. No, Marnie wouldn't have run from a baby like Emmit. Unless…unless she somehow believed that something was her fault. That would alter everything.

That time when she had run over Doris's newly planted roses with her motorcycle, she stuffed the branches back in the ground and rode off for three days. And once when she'd thrown in a load of laundry for him after their day at the beach, Taylor came back with the pizza they were going to share only to find a pile of wet towels in the laundry room, the floor sparkling clean, and a fat piece of duct tape holding the washer's drain tube firmly in the drain. Marnie was nowhere to be found.

But to run away for fifteen years? How could one little baby cause that? And now Taylor had sent that little baby-turned-teen after her. No wonder she objected to having him come. Except she'd claimed not to know about Emmit. So, what was true? What was real? And what made the woman he loved run away all those years ago?

Too many questions, not enough answers. Then and now. He dropped the wristband back into the box and rubbed his hands on his thighs.

Lord, make me Columbo so I can figure out this mystery. Columbo, with a cool hat but without the rumbled raincoat and unlit cigar.

The computer beeped. Taylor turned and glanced at the screen. New mail. He walked over and sat down. Marnie's name stared out at him from his In Box. He clicked on the message.

Have you found some other home for Emmit yet? What about his father? Did Rose ever marry William like she wanted to?

Well, I thought I'd let you know that Emmit started school today. I got him enrolled, and he seems to enjoy it. Apparently the few other kids in his class think he's smart, so he's all pleased with himself. I'm pleased too because he was getting pretty bored at Books and Brew all day. Rent's going up this month, so I need to figure out how to bring some more money in, which is hard to do with him hollering "Doughnuts!" all day long.

You should have warned me about the doughnuts. And by the way, the painting was a disaster. What were you thinking?

First of all, real canvas is expensive, especially if most of the paint isn't going to make it to the canvas anyway. All the newspapers in California wouldn't have been enough to keep that kid from making the biggest mess you've ever seen. Good thing I needed to repaint my walls anyway, though bright purple wouldn't have been the color I chose.

And second of all, he painted his glasses yellow because he said he wanted to see the sun. He's been going on and on about wanting to go to the beach to see the sun. I tell him no, he can see the sun right here. I don't go to the beach. I don't want to go. We don't have any clams here.

Taylor paused his reading. He didn't go to the beach much anymore either. It hurt too much. Did she avoid it for the same reason? Did she still wonder what it would have been like, what they would have been like, if only she'd not run away? He sighed. They'd never know. Either of them.

Lord, why couldn't it last? I thought there would always be clam holes in the sand, promising good food, good times to come. I thought I just had to have faith and everything would work out right. I went back to school, back to Legal Aid, tried to do the right thing. I did what I was supposed to. Why didn't it work?

Because I sinned.

But God forgives.

So, why didn't Marnie?

Taylor rubbed his eyes. God never answered that question. He knew because he'd asked it a thousand times. Why couldn't Marnie just have stayed? Why couldn't she have given him another chance? Why couldn't they have just been together, for always?

But always turned out differently. And there was no going back.

So for now, he kept reading.

Anyway, he painted his glasses. Then he painted mine. My new on-clearance-or-else-they'd-cost-a-fortune Maui Jim's. I cleaned the lenses, but I'm never going to get all that paint out of the cracks. No wonder the teachers at school gave me strange looks when I brought him in this morning. They hurried him off right away like they were afraid my weirdness was contagious and rubbing off on him.

Maybe they're right.

Taylor grinned. At least it sounded like Emmit was settling in nicely. Good. For a moment there…

Anyway, I think Emmit misses you. I miss you too. Only I'm not going to tell you that because I'm going to delete this e-mail just like I did the last one.

The e-mail ended there. No signature, no final words. She must have punched Send instead of Delete. Well, he was glad for that. He moved forward and rested his elbows on the desk. He grabbed the mouse and hit Reply.

> Marnie,
> I thought you loved purple. Wasn't that always your favorite color?

He grinned. Purple and black. Seemed like everything Marnie had owned was one of those two colors. Deep, dark purple, not that girly lavender color. She used to have a dress... Taylor rubbed his eyes again to get that image out of his mind. That's all he needed, to start imagining a young Marnie in that plum-shaded dress. He refocused on the screen.

> Painting glasses doesn't sound like Emmit. Try the canvas
> again. This time use those rolls of painter's plastic for the floor
> and walls. Get him to paint the ocean. He's good at that.

Really good. Taylor had a small painting Emmit had done in his office. Of course, it looked more like swirls of gray and green than an ocean, but Rose had told him it was an abstract so it didn't need to look like the real thing.

> And, no, Rose never did marry William. He ended up leaving
> her. Said he didn't want to be "trapped," whatever that was
> supposed to mean. After that, Craig took an interest. It was
> like he felt guilty or something. They ended up living to-
> gether for several years, but Rose kicked him out about five or

so years ago. So, no, I haven't found anyone else to take
Emmit. And I'm not looking either. He belongs with you.

And he did. Taylor didn't know how he knew it, but he knew it.
Every lawyer-truth-detecting sense he had told him so. Emmit was supposed to be with Marnie. They needed each other. And Taylor, well, he'd
just have to be alone.

The petition to transfer guardianship was uncontested, and
the judge didn't bother to ask for a continuance, but I've still
run into a couple paperwork glitches here. I'm hoping you
can clear them up for me.

Not exactly true, but close enough.

Was Rose pregnant fifteen years ago when you left? Had she
had Emmit yet? Sorry to bring up old times, but I was hoping
to file all the papers and close this case.

There, hopefully that was subtle. Raise no eyebrows. Prod no
wounds. That was his philosophy.

Did you get the pretzels I sent? They're Emmit's favorites. I
hope they didn't come melted. Wish I were there.

He erased the last sentence, checked it, and pushed Send. He rolled
back in his chair and tried not to think of her in that purple dress. He
tried for about thirty seconds, then the image came anyway. It filled his
mind and made his breath come just a little bit faster.

He had to beg her to come. After all, it was a black-tie event and she wouldn't be able to wear those boots. The firm he was clerking for that summer was a sponsor of a charity event for the local children's hospital, so he was expected to attend. Could she please come with him so he wouldn't be bored out of his mind? That's what he'd told her anyway. But the truth was, he had a plan. A crazy, wild, truly out-of-his-mind plan. And after just two months of knowing her, that night was supposed to be the night.

He should have known that only she could pull off wild and make it work. He was just stupid.

But he finagled a second ticket for her, rented a tux, bought a new black bowler hat, and waited for her to appear. They were supposed to meet at the event because he had to promise to help set up in order to get the ticket. And now the setup was complete. A hundred helium-filled balloons bobbed halfway between ceiling and floor. Streamers fluttered. Clowns made animals from skinny balloons of every color. Kid's songs dribbled from speakers. "Row, Row, Row Your Boat." "Old MacDonald Had a Farm." The "Hokey Pokey." And his favorite, "He's Got the Whole World in His Hands."

And back then, he even believed it. He was counting on it. And he shouldn't have.

Taylor sighed and let the memory of the room flow through him until he could hear the songs again and see the rubber ducks that floated in fountains in all four corners of the room. Meanwhile mountains made of teddy bears peered down at men in tuxedos and women in fluffy taffeta and expensive silk. Women wearing too much makeup and teased hair. He could smell the hairspray and expensive cologne. Flowers and fruit and musk and cultured laughter floated around him, mixing with tinny children's voices singing about the little bitty baby in His hands.

Taylor turned, walked toward the huge glass doors, stopped, and waited. She'd be here soon. Any moment now. He reached into his pocket and touched the tiny velvet box he'd put there. Crazy. Crazy, crazy, crazy. And definitely stupid. But tonight magic was in the air.

Or maybe just excess aerosol.

He cleared his throat. A taxi pulled up to the curb. The car door opened. And there she was. His Marnie. High heels, gently waving hair, and that perfect dress setting off every curve—high neck, sleeveless, hem to her ankles with a slit to the calf. She came closer. He held open the door.

Then she was beside him.

He held out his arm.

She smiled and tucked her hand beneath his elbow. "This better be worth it. These shoes are killing me."

He squeezed her hand against him. "It will be."

"I like the décor. Do we each get to take home a rubber duckie?"

"I'll sneak one for you if you like."

"Promise?"

"Of course."

She laughed, not a practiced, cultured laugh like the women around them, but her free, happy, real laugh with the ending hitch that made all his tension drop away.

"Come on, meet my boss."

"That's kind of risky, don't you think?"

"Oh, I think he'll behave. No promises on that, though."

"That's not what I meant."

"I know." He winked at her. "Too late, here he comes."

Mr. Runkey wove across the room toward them. Like always, his pants were too short and he tugged at his tie. Taylor tried to see him like

Marnie would—an older gentleman with his tux jacket buttoned wrong, his tie still crooked, and a terrible habit of patting down his comb-over whenever he got nervous. He was patting it now.

"Cole! Who's this lovely lady?" Mr. Runkey hurried the last few steps with chubby hand extended.

Taylor leaned toward Marnie. His voice dropped to a whisper. "Nicest guy in the world, but you'll have to wash your hand afterward." He put on a big smile. "Mr. Runkey, how nice to see you. This is Marnie Wittier."

Mr. Runkey engulfed Marnie's hand in his. As usual, he'd put on too much cologne, which clashed with the scent of his hair gel. "So pleased to meet you, young lady."

Marnie smiled. "Taylor says the nicest things about you, Mr. Runkey."

"Oh, call me Walt. And Taylor's a good man. Don't know if he's good enough to deserve such a pretty lady on his arm, though. Tell me, is he the kind of man who treats his girlfriends right?"

Marnie glanced up at him. "I expect so, but we're just friends."

"Friends?" He elbowed Taylor in the ribs. "What's wrong with you, boy? You aren't one of those funny guys are you?" He narrowed his eyes and looked Taylor up and down.

Taylor's face warmed. "No, I like women, if that's what you mean."

"Good, 'cause this one's a keeper." He nodded toward Marnie. Then he shook his head. His tone lowered to a murmur. "Just friends, she says. Young people these days."

Taylor straightened. "Well, I'm working on convincing her otherwise, Walt."

He scowled. "You call me Mr. Runkey. Only she can call me Walt."

Marnie laughed. "Taylor warned me that you might not behave."

"Did he now? Well, it's the wife's fault. Usually Judy keeps me in line." He patted his coat.

Marnie moved closer. "Here, let me fix that." She unbuttoned his jacket and rebuttoned it the right way. "There. Perfect."

He turned pink. "Thank you, young lady. After thirty years of marriage, seems I can't even dress myself with Judy gone."

"Gone?"

"Oh no, I didn't mean gone." His voice dropped. "Not gone as in dead. Heaven forbid." He patted his hair.

Taylor grabbed a glass of red punch from the tray held by a passing waiter. "Where did she go?"

"Visiting her sister in Ohio. Three weeks. I've lost six pounds." He grunted. "Eating nothing but peanut butter and jelly. Thank the good Lord this event comes with dinner. Unless..." He glared at Taylor. "Don't tell me."

Taylor wrinkled his forehead. "I'm afraid so."

Mr. Runkey's shoulders sagged. "I should have known."

Marnie frowned. "What?"

Taylor glanced at her, then pointed to the childlike decorations. "The theme doesn't just extend to the balloons and music."

Her eyes widened. She snickered. "Oh. PB&Js for dinner, huh?" She touched Mr. Runkey's shoulder. "Sorry."

He sighed. "The sacrifices I make for charity. Well, one more week and it's steak and potatoes for me again."

Marnie smiled. "You miss her."

"I miss my meat and potatoes." He winked at her. Then he patted down his hair. Again. "A man just isn't himself when the woman he loves is gone. Ain't that right, Cole?"

The box in his pocket suddenly felt heavy. "That's right, Mr. Runkey."

"So you better keep this little lady in your sights, eh, boy?"

He wanted to. But it wasn't always so easy. Maybe after tonight, all that would change. Taylor shifted. The doors opened behind him. A whoosh of air rustled the multicolored tablecloths and sent the balloons spinning.

Mr. Runkey wiped his fingers over his head and smiled. "Ah, our guests of honor have arrived." He clapped his hands. "Time to mingle."

Taylor turned to see kids coming into the hall. Bald kids, burned kids, kids in wheelchairs with tubes sticking out in all directions. He took Marnie's hand. "Come on."

They approached the children.

She stopped to talk to a little girl with both legs in casts. He moved on to a boy with a patch over his eye and scars on the left side of his face.

After fifteen minutes of talking to four different kids, he looked back to find her watching him. She didn't smile. She just stared at him with an expression he'd never seen before. Softness and pride and longing. Love. It had to be love. He was counting on it, though she'd never even breathed that word in his direction. Hopefully she thought it though, and felt it. He sure did.

He waved at her. She waved back, then picked up a little girl so the child could reach the string of a pink balloon floating near the ceiling. The girl giggled and grabbed the balloon. Marnie tied the string around the child's wrist and kissed her on the forehead. She turned away. On purpose. Taylor knew it was on purpose so he wouldn't see the emotions she usually hid so well.

And that boded well for his hopes and plans.

The music lowered. The microphone squealed through the sound system. Someone tapped it. A dull thud echoed through the room, followed by a voice. "Please, if everyone will take their seats…"

Taylor made his way toward Marnie. They came together by the bubbling fountain near the doors. He reached in, plucked out a duck, and handed it to her.

She squeezed it until it squeaked. "You always keep your promises?"

He draped his arm over her shoulder. It felt good there. "I try." He pointed to the scattered colors against the ceiling. "I can get you a balloon too, if you want."

"No thanks."

"Oh, I forgot, you met my boss. So you've probably had your fill of hot air for the night."

She laughed and leaned against him.

The box in his pocket pressed into his side.

Tonight. Everything would change tonight, he hoped. He had it all planned out. Dinner together here at the children's event, a short stop to window shop, then the main part would be ready. He'd show her how much he loved her and he'd kiss her for the first time. After that, if all went well, he'd pop the big question.

It was a huge risk. But it was worth it. She was the one. She was everything he wanted—kind, honest, funny, beautiful. And she made him a better man, because when he was with her, life was big and wild and wondrous. God was big and wild and wondrous too. And unpredictable, not the tame, dull God that fit nicely into the second pew at church.

Someone started talking from the podium in front. Taylor guided Marnie to the nearest table. Two hours later, everything was going as planned. Dinner had been eaten, boring speeches made, he hadn't dropped jelly on his tux, and she still had the rubber duckie. Finally the event was over.

Taylor took Marnie's hand and led her outside. It was eight thirty and the sky was just turning from gray to black. They walked to his car, her hand still tucked in his. He opened the door for her. Then they drove away.

It took her three minutes to discover they were going the wrong way. She sat up in her seat. "Hey, this isn't the way home."

"We have a couple stops to make first." He peeked at his watch and pulled into the parking lot of the Harley dealer.

Her eyes narrowed. "What are we doing here?"

"A little window-shopping. I'm thinking of getting a bike."

She crossed her arms. "You are not."

He raised his eyebrows. "You never know." He opened the car door and jumped out. "Come on, humor me. Which one do you suggest?"

She got out and sauntered over to the giant windows. She cupped her hands and peered inside. "You'd better hope a cop doesn't come by."

"We aren't doing anything wrong."

"It doesn't matter if you're doing something wrong, only if you look like you're doing something wrong. Haven't you learned that yet?"

"I guess not."

"Well, I have." Her voice lowered.

He stood close to her and looked through the window too. A dozen bikes stood at angles across the showroom floor, lit by the faint glow of the safety lights within. Taylor's breath fogged against the glass as he watched Marnie from the corner of his vision. "So, what do you think?"

"I think this is the bomb."

"The bomb?"

"Yeah, they've got the newest Fat Boy. Wicked."

"I knew you'd like it."

"Ooo, and look at that sweet little baby in the corner." She elbowed Taylor. "Did you know they replaced the FXR frame with the Dyna? I'm going to miss the FXR."

"So, what do you think, a little one or a Fat Boy?"

"Definitely the Fat Boy. Look at that silver."

"What about the black one?"

"You can't afford the black one, Taylor."

"I can't afford any of them."

"What are we doing here?"

Biding our time. He checked his watch. Perfect. "Let's go."

"Where?"

"You'll see." He turned her, then jogged toward the street.

She hurried after him. "Where's the fire? I'm wearing heels, remember?" She moved toward the car.

"Not that way."

"What?"

He went back, took her hand, and pulled her toward the sidewalk. "This way. Run!"

She laughed. "You're crazy tonight." She bent over and pulled off her shoes. "This better be worth it. And I'm never, ever borrowing heels from Rose again." She pushed the shoes into his chest. "Here, you carry these, Crazy Man."

Crazy? Yeah, he was. And he was only going to get crazier.

Together they ran down the street, her in her bare feet, him clutching her ridiculous shoes in one hand while the other held hers. Lolling buildings drooped on either side of them. Above, streetlights sputtered and winked. A breeze picked up bits of litter and tossed them into the gutters like ticker-tape from some bygone parade.

He held her hand tighter while his limbs shook and his mouth went dry. They jogged around a corner. They were almost there. Almost. Along this new street, the stores were dark, silent. Except for one. They turned toward it. A truck sped past and was gone. One car sat in the parking lot.

Other than that, everything was empty. Except the store with its lights blazing.

Taylor slowed to a walk.

Marnie stopped beside him. "What's this?"

He stopped too, then grinned. "Guess."

"Tom's Pet Palace? I'm thinking a pet store." Her eyes narrowed as she studied him. "You *are* crazy, aren't you?"

"Certifiable."

"They're open?"

He nodded. "I bribed them."

"Why?"

"Because. You'll see." Taylor led her inside.

Tom stood behind the register. "Evening." He nodded with a smile so big his face looked like a white fence with a boy's eyes peeking over the top. "Happy shopping." He snickered.

"Thanks." Marnie hesitated.

Taylor looked up and saw the banner that was rolled up at the top of the front windows. Later, at just the precise moment, Tom would unravel it. Confetti would fly. And there, in shiny red, white, and blue would be the question. The big honkin' question. *Oh, Lord, let her say yes.*

He took a deep breath, then pulled her farther into the store, past the bags of dog food, past the shimmering glass tanks, past the stacks of wired cages, to the back end of the room.

And there they were. Puppies, kittens, fish, hamsters, lizards, parrots, bunnies. He halted. "Merry Christmas."

She stood next to him, her gaze wide eyed now, roaming over the pets. "It's July."

"Happy Birthday, then."

"My birthday's not until September."

He turned her toward him and took both her hands in his. "Pick one, Marnie."

"What?"

"Pick one. A pet. Whatever you want."

"But…"

"I'm getting you your first pet. You can have one now. No more foster homes, no more allergies. No more moving around from place to place. Do you know what I'm saying?"

A smile crept over her face. She turned back to the animals. "Anything I want?"

She didn't understand. Not fully, not just yet. But she would. He brushed her hair back with his fingertips. "Anything. A cute little puppy, a kitten, a parakeet, whatever."

She pointed to the top shelf. "I want that."

Taylor looked up to where she pointed. A green monster stared down at him. "You're kidding."

Tom sauntered up and rested his fists against his sides. "She pick yet?"

Taylor pointed. "She wants that thing."

Tom frowned. "Dude, you're doomed." He peered at Marnie. "You sure you want Max there? Iguanas grow to be like five feet long and can live up to twenty years. Maybe a nice hamster instead?"

"He's perfect. And I don't like rats."

"Hamster."

"What's the difference?"

"Snake then? Or a cute little lizard?"

Marnie walked over to the shelves and stared up at the iguana. "My first pet. He's gorgeous." Her face glowed.

Taylor sighed. "We'll take the monster. And a tank, and some food, and whatever else we need."

"A heating lamp, a rock—"

"Just package it all up before I change my mind."

Marnie turned and regarded him for a long moment. "You're serious, aren't you? You really are going to get me an iguana."

"I am and—" His words cut off as Marnie threw herself into his arms. His hat knocked to the floor. A muffled "thank you" sounded in his ear. And all he could see were full lips and shiny hair. All he could smell was the sweetness of her perfume. All he could taste was the longing of her breath mingling with his.

His hand moved to his pocket. His fingers tightened around the box. His other hand reached up and curled around her neck. He drew her closer, closer, his eyes on hers, their lips nearly touching. And then—

Her phone rang.

She jumped back and dug in her purse. She pulled out the phone and pressed it to her ear. "Hello?"

Silence.

Her eyes caught his. Her body trembled. "It's Doris. Rose had a heart attack."

And that was the end of his perfect plan.

15

Emmit threw his hands in the air and twirled to the music. He closed his eyes and swayed and dipped. He tried to sing, but the words didn't come out right. So he hummed and danced and listened to the man in the black box sing about the Beautiful One.

He'd tried to paint a picture of the beauty he remembered. But it came out all wrong. The colors weren't right. The purple spilled, the yellow got all over the glasses, and Auntie Mar-ee took the paints away. All he really wanted was to see the Son. But painting was hard. The picture in his head was too fuzzy, and his hands wouldn't do what he wanted.

But his ears still worked just fine. And his body could still move to the music. He could dance to the One he loved. The One he adored.

Emmit loved this song. When he heard it, he could almost see, almost remember. He used to sing this song once. For real. Why couldn't he make the words come right anymore?

Clouds were in his head now, that was why. Funny dark clouds that made it hard to see. But he could still remember some things, especially when the music played. He remembered the snow. He remembered the ocean. He remembered God.

So it was okay that God sent him here to Auntie Mar-ee. It was okay that he couldn't fly in the snow anymore. It was all okay. Because he loved

God, he loved Auntie Mar-ee, and he loved the way the music made light dance through the room to cast away all the shadows.

So he listened, and he moved, and he let his heart sing.

~~~

Marnie was getting old. She knew it because the music was blaring in Emmit's room, and she was marching over there to tell him to turn it down. That's what old ladies did. They grumbled about the filth on television, kids' haircuts, kids' clothes, and the volume of their music. Next thing she'd be dying her hair blue and prodding disrespectful youths with her cane. She may as well go buy a bottle of Geritol and install safety rails in the bathroom.

Still, the music *was* loud, and if she knew Emmit, he was probably in there cutting up the brand-new drapes so he could see the sun better. He was always talking about seeing the sun. "Go to beach, Auntie Mar-ee, and see the sun." "Look through doughnut hole. See the sun?" "I like sun." "Sun good." "I see sun." "Where's sun?" Poor kid, he wasn't used to all this coastal fog. No wonder he missed the sun.

But that didn't mean she wanted the new drapes to be turned into ribbons. Of course, she'd hidden all the scissors, but that didn't mean he hadn't found a pair. That kid could find anything, but only if she'd hidden it from him. Ask him to put on the shoes sitting right in front of him, and suddenly he'd turn blind. But hide away a bottle of glue, or her craft scissors, or a box of mementos, and the next thing you knew, glue was spilled all over the kitchen counter, the drapes were cut up, and your secrets were spread out like toys all over the living room floor.

She quickened her pace. "Emmit, turn that thing—" She stopped in his doorway.

Inside, Emmit's eyes were closed, his arms raised, his face glowing. He danced in slow circles around the room in time with the music. Sunlight glinted through the glass door, drapes intact, and spilled over his feet.

Marnie watched, breathless.

Emmit swayed and twirled. He moved in front of the glass. The light shone around him, made him glow like some kind of angel straight from heaven. In that moment, he was the most beautiful thing she'd ever seen. And for one instant, she wished she could twirl with him, free, happy, unencumbered by doubts and regrets. Never dizzy.

What would it be like to live like that? Maybe someday...

Behind her, the computer chimed. She glanced back to her laptop on the kitchen table. Someone had sent her an e-mail. It could wait. She turned back to Emmit. The song changed, and so did his dance.

But maybe the e-mail was from Taylor.

Emmit stopped, opened his eyes, and smiled at her. "I love the sun, Auntie Mar-ee."

"I know you do."

"Sun warm, bright. I remember." He ambled over, sat in front the window, folded up his legs, and stared up into the sky. He sat there for forty-five seconds. Then he looked back at her and pointed out the door. "You go now. I sit."

She smiled. "Okay." *Just don't cut up the drapes.*

"I be good boy."

Promise?

He turned back around and again gazed into the sky.

That was as close as she was going to get to a promise. She walked back down the short hall and paused at the kitchen table. She glanced at her computer. It *was* Taylor. She pulled out a chair and sat down. She clicked on his e-mail. In an instant world, she still loved e-mail. It gave her time to think, digest, write what she wanted, and then erase it. She scrolled down.

Her fingers froze as she stared at the screen. There was the e-mail she'd deleted, pasted onto the bottom of his. *Oh no.* She glanced at the bottom. "I miss you too." Ugh, there it was in black and white. And he'd read it. She put her hand over that part of the screen and groaned. *Lord, I pray that he didn't see this section. Please, don't let him have read that.* If he did… She grimaced and glanced at his answering note.

More painting. She shook her head. Not a chance. Pretzels? Yes, she'd gotten them, and they were melted. Plus Emmit hated them. *Sorry, Taylor.* Rose pregnant? Hardly. Rose was always the careful one. And yet… Marnie paused. Rose must have been at least a few months along and kept it secret. Maybe she'd just hidden it behind bulkier clothes. Leggings and oversized T-shirts were popular back then. It was easy to hide a little bulge. Maybe Rose wasn't Little-Miss-Perfect after all. Maybe she was just Miss-Nearly-Perfect-With-A-Big-Secret. Besides, after Taylor left to return to school, everyone was keeping secrets. Too many secrets, too many lies.

At least he didn't say anything about her missing him. Unless it was in that last line. She shivered. The real problem wasn't her missing him, or questions about Rose, or suggestions about painting. The real issue was the question of paperwork. What did he mean? It sounded like her guardianship of Emmit wasn't official yet. Maybe there was still a chance someone else would take him. Then he'd go back where he belonged, and she would go back to her old life. Her box would be untouched, her drapes intact, her spare room turned to a workroom again. She would be alone.

Marnie looked down the hallway into Emmit's room. He still sat there, bathed in the sunlight. He glanced back over his shoulder and waved at her.

She waved back. Crazy kid. Give him a few more days and he'd have wormed his way into her heart. And that was dangerous.

I can't love you, Emmit. I can't. I'll only end up hurting you. Hurting us both. If I love you, I'll lose you for sure. And it will be my fault. Just like before…

All these years she tried to forget, to tell herself Taylor had moved on, that it didn't matter. She told herself that she'd moved on, she didn't care anymore. She didn't love him. Didn't love anyone. Never had. But still she wondered. Had he found someone else? Was he married now? Did he have kids? He should. He deserved a beautiful, wholesome wife. He deserved kids like those who came in picture frames at the store. He deserved so much more than she could have ever given him.

She should have known that long ago on that night. She should have told him so. But back then, the night was full of promise, the air full of hope. Then it had changed to fear. But still, it was magical. And he was her hero. For that one night, there was no paper in her box of regrets, no trinkets, no little reminder of what should have been. That was the night she knew she loved him. But she never, ever told him so.

Maybe it was because of the boots. For once, they stayed in her closet at home while she wore some useless, strappy things with heels like toothpicks. She thought she'd never survive the night in those ridiculous things, but for him, she would have done anything.

Still, he didn't know that and she didn't let on. Because if she did, things would go too far. The sorry little foster girl would be brought home to Mommy and Daddy. She couldn't have that. There would be questions and sidelong looks and talk about former girlfriends who were more worthy.

That's what happened to Rose every time. Rose kept thinking the next time would be different, but it never was. The guys would date her for a while for her looks, take what they wanted, then cast her aside. Rose would blame it on something Marnie had done, but they both knew better. Girls like them didn't marry the good guys. Girls like them didn't marry at all.

And yet, she had worn the shoes and worried that they told too much. He would guess. But she slipped on those strappy heels anyway and then pressed her finger to her lips and told them to hush, not to whisper her secrets to the world, and especially not to Taylor Cole.

But shoes can't be trusted.

She should have realized that when she stepped from the cab and those shoes rushed right to his side. But all she could think about was how great he looked in that tux, the warmth of his eyes meeting hers, and how his five o'clock shadow made him look even more a man.

The shoes were quiet as she mingled and said the appropriate things to the appropriate people. And then the kids came.

Kids scarred from burns, bald from cancer, with oxygen tubes and pale faces. And Taylor loved them all.

She paused to talk to a girl in casts. He moved on and knelt in front of a boy with an eye patch and facial scars. The girl handed her a pen.

"Aye, matey. Cool patch." A few feet away, Taylor put on a pirate accent.

Marnie watched him from the corner of her vision as she signed the girl's cast in fluorescent purple ink.

"You need a parrot." Taylor pulled off his hat and looked inside. He pulled out some brightly colored thing and squeezed it. It squawked.

She laughed. So did the boy.

Taylor ruffled the kid's hair and moved on to a girl without any.

The girl stared at the floor.

Taylor touched her chin and lifted it. "What's the matter, beautiful?"

"Nothing."

Marnie sketched a picture of her girl on the cast, then a horse beneath. She handed back the pen.

The girl squinted down at the drawing. "You're good at that."

"You like horses, don't you?"

"How did you know?"

Marnie touched the silver horse figure hanging from the girl's neck.

"My *abuela* gave me that when I had to go to the hospital. I was supposed to learn how to ride horses this summer."

Marnie pointed to the picture on the cast. "You'll get your chance to ride. See, that picture's a promise."

The girl's eyes turned wide. "Really?"

"Really. You just need to get better."

"I will!"

Marnie turned to the next child, her attention split between the boy in the wheelchair in front of her and the man a few feet away. He teased. He told jokes. He laughed with each kid. He pulled gifts from his magic hat. A carved train whistle for a boy who had gone blind. A make-your-own mosaic for a girl in a wheelchair. A sun catcher for a boy strapped to a mobile hospital bed. Taylor was everything she'd always suspected him to be. A man who cared, who overlooked surface imperfections, who saw into the soul. He was a man who could make her fall in love.

And that was dangerous.

Taylor's voice drifted over to her as he paused again before the girl with no hair. "Now are you going to tell me why your smile's asleep?"

"I'm ugly."

"What? You say you're bubbly?"

"Not bubbly."

"Whew. I thought I would have to put you in a popper."

A tiny smile curled the girl's lips. "You're weird."

"I know."

"I'm ugly because I forgot my wig."

"You don't need a wig. You're gorgeous as you are."

Marnie looked over to see him sit down and take the bald girl onto his lap. "Do you know what bird is most beautiful and majestic?"

"What's *majestic* mean?"

"It means like a princess."

"A peacock?"

"Nope. A bald eagle. It's even our national bird." He set her down, stood, and then bowed low before her. He kissed her hand. "Your Majesty."

She giggled. "I'm not really a princess."

"I say you are. In fact, you're so beautiful that only you are pretty enough for this." This time he reached into his pocket and took out a stunning silk scarf. He tied it around the girl's head. "You make that scarf look good."

He glanced up and caught her staring at him. Her face turned hot. He saw her. Really saw her.

And in that instant, she saw in him the God he'd been trying to show her. The One who looked at baldness and saw beauty. The One who gave and heard and cared and knew. Knew her and loved her anyway. Was it true? Could it be?

Could she be the bald princess and God the One with the beautiful scarf? *God, is it real? Are You like Taylor Cole? Do You really care about me?*

Taylor did.

What if God did too?

And for that moment, she could almost imagine it was true. She could almost believe she loved them back. God, who gave His Son like a scarf to cover her shame. Taylor, who gave himself when she'd done nothing to deserve a man like that.

So she watched him and could hardly breathe for the wonder, the possibility.

His eyes held hers.

And then she turned away and prayed he hadn't seen too much. Prayed that her eyes hadn't betrayed her even more than her shoes.

Later that night, she'd take off those shoes and run beside him. She'd pick out Max, the only pet she'd ever had, and she'd get a phone call that would change everything.

What would have happened if that call hadn't come just when it did? She stood there, phone pressed to her ear, listening to the hysterical tones of her foster mother's voice.

"The ambulance took her away. We don't know what happened. She just collapsed. The EMTs said heart attack. What are we going to do? I'm at the hospital now. Get down here. It's St. Jude's. She's still in Emergency. Hurry."

Marnie could almost see the sweat beading on Doris's upper lip, the way it always did when the woman was in a panic and couldn't offer a cup of tea.

"The doctors keep asking me questions, and I don't know what to say. She was fine, and then she wasn't. I don't know anything else. She just came over for dinner. My special chicken cordon bleu. I know you don't like that dish, so we didn't ask you over too. She collapsed just before we served the special rose tea; you know the one she particularly likes."

"Our Rose. Not the tea. What happened to our Rose?" If Doris kept talking about tea, Marnie would never get a straight answer.

"I told you. I don't know. I told them I didn't know. Three doctors, two nurses, and the EMTs. I. Don't. Know."

"But it was her heart."

"That's what they think."

"And?"

"And she's in surgery. That's all. Get down here. They want to know about history, and her parents, and, and, and I don't know what." Doris's voice rose to a shriek.

"I'll be right there." Marnie closed the phone.

Taylor touched her arm. "Is she going to be okay?"

Marnie shook her head. "Doris doesn't know. Rose is in surgery. Can you take me to St. Jude's?"

"Of course." He turned to Tom. "We'll pick up the iguana and stuff tomorrow, all right?"

Tom nodded. "Sure, man." He looked at Marnie. "Sorry about your sister. They say a pet is good for the heart."

Marnie tossed him a smile. "Thanks."

Twenty minutes later, Marnie sat with Taylor and Doris in the hospital's family waiting area. She undid the buckle of her shoes, then buckled them again, unbuckled, buckled, unbuckled.

A doctor opened the door and stepped inside the room. "We got it in time. We expect a full recovery." He looked at Marnie. "Are you the sister?"

She stood.

So did Taylor.

"She's going to be okay?"

The doctor rubbed his chin. "For now."

Marnie stepped forward. Her shoe stayed behind. She stumbled and caught Taylor's arm. Unbuckled. Dratted heels.

The doctor motioned toward the chair. "Have a seat. Let me explain what we know."

Marnie sat back down.

The doctor moved closer. "Your sister had an aortic aneurysm. When they rupture they're usually fatal, but your sister got lucky. Hers only tore."

"Is it fixed, then? Or will it happen again?"

"We repaired this rupture, but there's no way to know if she'll develop another aneurysm."

"Which would be like a ticking bomb, right?"

"Right. Sometimes this condition has a genetic component. We noticed that Rose has a bifid uvula."

"A what?"

The doctor opened his mouth and pointed down his throat. "You see that?" His voice turned funny as he formed the words. He closed his mouth again. "That flap that hangs down in the middle of your throat is called a uvula. Usually it's one piece, like mine. Sometimes, though, it can be cleft, or split, like Rose's."

Marnie frowned. "And mine. So what?"

"Do you have a history of heart conditions in your family?"

"I don't know."

"Any history of cleft palate, cleft lip?"

"I don't know."

"Joint pain?"

"I don't know."

"Similar aneurysms?"

She groaned. Now she knew what Doris had gone through. "We don't know much about our family."

Taylor sat forward. "But your mom does."

"We don't know—"

"Rose does."

Marnie stared at the doctor. "How important is it?"

"I suspect some kind of genetic disease. But I need some family history to get an idea of what we're looking at."

Marnie gripped her knees. "She'll tell us. She has to."

The door opened again. A nurse popped her head through the opening. "She's in her room now. She's pretty groggy still, but the family can see her." Her eyes caught Marnie's. "Follow me."

Marnie followed.

Taylor hung back.

Doris clutched the arms of her chair and shook her head. "I'll wait."

Marnie turned toward Taylor. "Come with me. Please." She glanced at the nurse. "It's okay, isn't it?"

"Your sister's been through a lot, so make sure you don't stress her."

"We won't."

The nurse led them to a room at the end of the hallway. Marnie went inside first.

Rose lay on the bed, her eyes closed, her hospital gown askew.

Marnie could just see the edge of the stitches from the cut over her heart. Her hands shook. She stepped closer and gripped the edge of the bed railing.

Rose opened her eyes. "Marnie?"

"Shh. It's going to be okay."

"I don't feel very good." Rose closed her eyes again.

Marnie touched her arm. "We need to know where Mom is, Rose. Our real mom. The doctor needs to ask her some questions to get you better."

Rose turned away. "No. I don't want anything to do with her."

"It's important."

Rose sighed.

Taylor cleared his throat. "There's a woman living in New York."

Rose's breathing quickened. "That's not her." Her voice cracked.

Marnie touched Rose's forehead. The skin seemed cold, clammy. "Where, Rose?"

"She's right—" Rose's back arched. Then she began to convulse.

Nurses rushed into the room and pushed Marnie and Taylor out. One slammed the door shut. From inside, she could hear the patter of feet, the beep of machines, the urgent tones of voices kept low. Her eyes sought Taylor's. "I'm scared."

He took her in his arms, held her close.

She wrapped her arms around him. The lumps in his pockets pressed against her. He still had toys left from their night at the banquet. They really were magic pockets after all. She glanced up at him. "You don't have something in those pockets for me, do you?"

He didn't answer. He just held her closer as they waited together for Rose to live or die.

Rose lived. But that was years ago. Years since a peanut-butter-and-jelly banquet beneath a balloon-covered ceiling, a trip to a pet store, being held in his arms while she trembled with fear. Years since she saw the truth about God in the eyes of a man. Years since he almost kissed her, and she would have kissed him back.

Years. So, how could she still be in love with Taylor Cole?

16

Secrets. Lies. And a vision of thick glasses on a boy's face. It was the vision that drove Taylor. Because it couldn't be Emmit. Of course it couldn't be. And yet…

Taylor had seen him again that morning getting on a bus. The kid looked so much like Emmit. Messy hair peeking from beneath a baseball cap, backpack slung over his shoulder. The kid glanced back, for just an instant, and Taylor just knew it was Emmit. Then the bus doors closed.

Taylor ran toward him, but the bus took off in a puff of smoke. And he was left standing there with the image of the boy's face seared into his mind. The image of Emmit, who was three thousand miles away painting walls and watching the sun set over the Pacific.

Reason returned. *I'm losing my mind.*

Either that, or God was trying to tell him something. Tell him that this thing wasn't done yet. Taylor wasn't done with Emmit, or Marnie. Maybe he never would be. At least until the mystery was solved. Two mysteries—what happened fifteen years ago to drive her away from him, and why he kept seeing a boy who looked like Emmit now.

Maybe Doris could help with at least one of those.

He hadn't seen her in years. When he first moved back to Clam's Junction, he'd drop by occasionally to see if Doris had heard from Marnie.

He was so sure back in those days that Marnie would return. But months turned to years, and he got so he couldn't stand the way Doris would give him that look, shake her head, say she was sorry, and offer him a cup of tea.

He'd asked a lot of questions back then and gotten a lot of answers. But none were the ones he was really looking for. How could Marnie have left him? Why didn't she wait? Who was she really running from? They'd told him she'd changed while he was gone. They told him not to look for her. They told him he wouldn't want to.

He didn't believe them. Until he discovered she left him no note, no address, no way to contact her. Max was gone, her memento box gone, but she left his ring behind.

That's when he knew she left him, and he suspected she wouldn't return. Still, it took years before he really accepted it. Years before he stopped watching for her bike to come up the street. Years before he stopped scrutinizing every woman with long, dark hair. And years before he ran out of questions for Doris.

Yet now he found himself here again, standing outside Doris's door, ready to knock and reopen old wounds.

He really had lost his mind.

He knocked anyway.

Doris answered. Her hair was a lighter shade of Clairol now, her makeup a bit thicker, but other than that, she looked just as she always had. Same haircut, same slimming skirt that didn't slim quite enough, same furrow right between her brows. "You came. I knew you would."

No hello, no smile, no mention of all the years between them.

"May I come in?"

She moved back and motioned him inside. It wasn't a welcoming gesture.

He stepped through anyway. "How did you know?"

"Craig. He came by earlier. Said you found Marnie. Said you sent her Emmit. Mumbled something about promises to Rose. Would you like some tea?"

He smiled. Some things never changed. "No, thanks." He moved into the sitting room and sat on the end of the couch. "What did Craig want?"

Doris perched on the edge of the Victorian settee and fiddled with the doily covering the arm. "To be a fool. I told him to leave it alone."

"What do you mean?"

"And I'm telling you the same thing, Taylor. Leave it alone. It's bad enough you sent that poor boy out there. But what's done is done. You remember that."

He wove his fingers together, rested his elbows on his knees, and leaned forward. "Isn't it time for the truth?"

She jerked back. The doily wrinkled. She straightened it, smoothed it, pressed it into the fabric of the chair until the padding dented. "Leave it alone, I said."

"Emmit deserves better."

Doris gripped the arms of the chair until her knuckles turned white. "Yes, he does. But it's too late now, isn't it? You've sent him to her. Sent him, when the last thing Rose would have wanted—"

"She put it in her will. And made me promise as well."

"She's a fool too."

"Why did she do it, then?"

Doris's tone went up an octave. "I don't know! How can I know? I'm just a foster mother. I don't have anything to do with anything. I never did."

A lie. Again. He could tell by the way her voice trembled. But Doris always mixed the truth with a lie so it would go down easier. Or so he couldn't tell the two apart. She was good at that, an expert. "Why don't you think Emmit should have gone to Marnie?"

"She won't want him." Doris turned her head away. Her voice lowered to a whisper. "She never did."

Taylor studied Doris's expression. Fear. No, anger. Or something far more bitter. "So, Marnie knew about Emmit?"

"What?" Doris's face paled. "Why do you say that? Of course she didn't know. We made sure—" She swallowed and pressed her lips together. "I'm having some tea. Are you sure you don't want any?" She stood.

"Doris, please."

"Tea?"

"No."

She rushed from the room. A moment later, the ding of a microwave sounded from the kitchen, followed by the clanging of a spoon against ceramic.

Taylor waited. And waited.

Doris returned, teacup in hand. "You're still here."

"I need some answers."

"You always did. And I still don't have any to give."

"You don't have them, or you won't give them?" That was always the question. All those years ago, and now as well. And now he wasn't sure he truly wanted the answers. They might be too hard to bear. But it wasn't for himself that he sought to know, to understand. Now it was for Emmit. "Enough time has passed. What can there still be to hide?"

Doris again balanced on the edge of the settee. "There's no use digging up the past. Nothing good will come of it. Nothing can."

Taylor stared into her face. Lies. Secrets and lies and more lies. He was so tired of them. "You lied to me."

Doris flushed. "What are you talking about? I never lied."

"You said Marnie ran away from me, that she didn't want to see me anymore. She'd changed her mind about us. You said that's what it was all about. You lied."

Doris held her cup in both hands and stared at the amber liquid inside. "Lies aren't always a bad thing."

"A lie is a lie."

"It can also be a mercy."

"Is that what you told yourself? Did you drive her away?"

She looked up, caught his eyes, and held them in a steady gaze. "Listen to me. Everything that happened was Marnie's own fault. She left you, she left all of us. She didn't want to come back. And good riddance I say. You deserve better. We all do." She licked her lips. "And Emmit does too."

"I don't believe you. Tell me the truth."

"The truth?" She laughed, a cold sound, sad and regretful.

He heard words echoing in his head. *I want the truth! You can't handle the truth!* Tom Cruise and Jack Nicholson in *A Few Good Men.* Maybe Jack was right.

Doris set down her cup and tipped forward. "Let. It. Go."

"I can't."

Her eyes narrowed. "Then I'll tell you this: You get him back, Taylor Cole. Do whatever you can to get him back. Don't you dare leave him in the hands of that, of that…" Her teeth clenched.

"Doris?"

"Of that murderer."

The word dropped between them and shattered like fine china.

～∾～

Sometimes, if Marnie sat very still in this very back pew, if the lights were dimmed very low, if the voices very soft, if the guitar thrummed a certain song…sometimes, if she closed her eyes at just the right moment, she could almost remember what it felt like that summer to fall in love. In love, not just with Taylor Cole but slowly, bit by bit, with his God. She could almost recall the hint of wonder, see a glimpse of the beauty, nearly taste the saltiness of the sea, and hear the gentle break of waves, and sense again the almost-presence of a God of love.

But that was before she'd written the words of 1 Corinthians 13 on a tiny piece of blue paper and stuffed it into her box.

Love protects.

Love trusts.

Love hopes.

Love endures.

But love failed. And yet, even after all these years, she couldn't let it go. So she came to this same church every Sunday. She sat in the back pew. She listened to the music. She slipped a twenty into the offering basket. She heard the sermon. She shook hands. But she never, ever sang.

Still, she came. She hoped. She wished one day God may notice her, one day He might show her how to be free. One day He might just show up and forgive her. For real, not just in words. Someday He may overlook her shame and love her again.

Someday, but not today.

Today she would sit silently in the back just like every other Sunday. She would mouth the words to the songs; she would slip out at the end. No one would stop her, no one would be disturbed, no one would care.

And that's the way it ought to be. She didn't deserve better.

Marnie settled deeper into the pew and listened as some perky little thing in her twenties stood up front chirping announcements. A potluck, a car wash, a mission trip to Mexico, a women's Bible study, workers needed in the nursery.

Beside her, Emmit fidgeted. Marnie fidgeted too. Emmit fiddled with the bulletin. He folded it up and threw it in the air. She caught it and scowled at him. He grinned back. He scooted down the pew. She scooted after him. He picked up a hymnal. She took it from him. He lifted up his shirt and stared at his navel. She didn't dare do the same. He hummed; she shushed him. He tucked his feet up and pulled apart the Velcro on his shoes. *Skritch-scratch, skritch-scratch, skritch.* She scooted back down to the far end of the pew and pretended not to notice.

However, the couple sitting three rows up weren't fooled. The man glanced over his shoulder. The woman turned around and glared.

Marnie's face flushed. "Sorry." Her voice whispered over the enthusiastic announcement of who would be the next retreat speaker.

The woman turned back around.

A hand touched Marnie's arm. Josephina slipped into the pew beside her. Marnie leaned toward her. "You don't want to sit here. Lots of action in this row."

"It's not even a two-point-one in my book," Josephina whispered back. "Barely a tremor."

"Not according to them." Marnie nodded toward the couple in front.

"Not your fault she had lemons for breakfast. That sour look doesn't have anything to with your sweet *hijo.*"

"Not son, just nephew. *Sobrino.*"

"Hijo now." Josephina wiggled her fingers at Emmit.

He beamed back and burped.

Josephina chuckled, then moved closer to Marnie. Her voice grew even softer. "I brought him a doughnut for afterward." She pointed to the gigantic bag she called a purse. "I know how he loves them." She put her finger alongside her nose. "And I brought wet wipes too."

Marnie smiled. Wet wipes. She had a whole stack in a plastic bag in her own purse, and in the car, and at Books and Brew, and in the bungalow. Because she'd read that having a Down-syndrome teen was a whole lot like having a toddler. Except Down's kids never grew out of it. Messy face, messy hands, messy shirt, messy everything. Yesterday she caught him picking his nose and wiping it on his sleeve. At least he hadn't eaten it. But then again, he might tomorrow. She shook her head.

The announcements ended.

Emmit clapped. Loudly. Everything was always loud with him. The woman in front with her expensive business suit and Gucci purse glanced back again. The woman pressed her lips together in the same look of disapproval Marnie's foster mom had often given her.

Of course, Doris had a lot to disapprove of. Marnie had made sure of that.

The woman scowled at Emmit, then stared at Marnie, probably noting the torn jeans, the comfy black T-shirt, the dark purple eyeshadow.

Come on lady, it's not like I've got a nose ring. Of course, if that woman kept gawking, Marnie would be tempted to get one, whether she could blow her nose right or not.

The woman smoothed her skirt. Marnie could almost hear her thoughts as she did so. About now, she'd be thanking God that she wasn't like that obviously sin-filled woman with the ugly black hair. She was offering thanks for her wealth, position, purity, social acceptability, and never imagining that there might be people who would never, ever want to be like her.

But Marnie knew the truth. At least she knew it now, learned it the hard way. Decency couldn't be bought at Saks; honor wasn't purchased at Nordstrom. It wasn't gained by knowing the right words to say, the right purse to carry, the right way to do your hair and nails. Instead beauty often hid in ugliness. And wonder often dressed in ratty clothes. The trick was seeing the truth, recognizing the beauty God placed in each person. Taylor was always good at that. Emmit was too. He saw through people, into them. Sometimes, she was afraid he'd see too much.

Emmit glanced at her from the far side of the pew and waved. The music started and everyone stood. He jumped up and down, tried to twirl, and landed back in the pew with a loud thump. He patted the wood, then scooted back and forth until comfortable.

Next he started to hum. Not quite in time with the worship song.

The woman in front straightened her shoulders and stared ahead.

Marnie sighed. "Maybe we should go." She motioned to Emmit.

Josephina squeezed her arm. "You aren't going anywhere. God wants you and Emmit here, and so do I."

"You're the only ones, then."

"You can't honestly care what that woman up there thinks." She peered into Marnie's face. "Yes, you can, and you do. How odd."

Marnie picked up her purse. Maybe Josephina was right. If a woman like that came into the coffee shop and looked askance at Marnie's hair or jeans or eyeshadow, she wouldn't care. She'd just serve her coffee, charge her credit card, and offer a cookie. Just like she did with everyone else.

Josephina inched closer so her voice wouldn't carry. "Why is this different, mija?"

"Because this is church."

"And nobody should look at Emmit that way, especially in church, sí?"

"Yes."

"Or are you just afraid that God looks at you the same way that woman does?"

"No, of course n—" She stopped because for an instant it wasn't Josephina standing next to her, it was Taylor. Taylor, who always saw more than the words she spoke, who saw deeper, who knew her better than she knew herself. Taylor, who had shown her God. And He was nothing like that stiff-backed woman in front of her. "How do you know?"

"Because I'm old and wise."

Because locking her regrets away didn't seem to keep them from being written all over her face as well. "You aren't old; you'll never be old."

"That's right, I just had a crow step on my eyes this morning and make those terrible marks."

"And you threw a lemon at him?"

Gucci-Purse-Woman glared back and hissed.

Josephina ignored her. "No, I don't keep lemons—they're bad for the constitution. So remember that." She tapped Marnie's cheek. "God doesn't look anything like that woman. Remember, Bible says manna's sweet like honey."

Marnie smiled. "And God only eats manna."

"You remember that when you think of Him looking at the daughter He loves."

Marnie's throat closed.

The song changed. "God of Wonders." God of the galaxy, holy, precious…loved her? Still? Didn't He know any better?

Emmit clapped his hands. Louder.

Josephina winked at Marnie.

The second verse flipped onto the screen in front. Everyone sang just like they were supposed to. Everyone clapped at the right moment, in time with the music. And a few people even swayed a bit in their seats. No one looked back.

Marnie relaxed.

Then it started.

A loud noise. A very loud noise. Strange and unexpected, an unplanned interruption in the sweet melody of music. Off-key. Awkward. Emmit singing.

And then it grew louder.

There were no words, just an odd squawking and groaning like a song that wasn't right but was a song all the same.

She moved to stop him but then paused. She watched him as the rebuke died on her lips. Shame did too. Because she was getting a glimpse of something far beyond the ordinary. Something fit for heaven itself.

Emmit stood there, his arms raised, his eyes closed, singing to his God for all he was worth. Emmit with his blond hair, thick glasses, and small ears. Emmit with a grin on his face big enough for the angels to see, shout-singing with all his might through that radiant, cheek-splitting grin.

For a brief instant, the music faltered, the other voices hushed. And then the guitar strummed again; the congregation's voices surged. Had others witnessed the wonder too? Had they beheld the beauty of a soul in love with his God?

I want to look like that. Desire whispered through her. Longing. Yearning to be free, with no regrets, no fear, no dark hidden past. Just arms raised, singing off-key, worshiping a God she loved.

Once, it had been like that. Almost anyway. Way back when love was new.

Rose was in surgery again, and Marnie and Taylor were walking barefoot on the beach. She left her boots by her bike while she and Taylor looked for clam holes. Today, they had no buckets, no shovels, but they looked for holes anyway. Looked for little signs that there was life down under the darkness, even though they couldn't see it. They looked for holes. They looked for hope.

"I think she's going to be okay, Marnie."

"How do you know?"

"I don't know. I hope. But we've prayed. We've done all we can do."

"Except find our mom."

"We'll do that too. Once Rose gets out of surgery, it'll be okay."

"Prayer doesn't mean God will answer. Why should He?"

He took her hand, pulled her close. His warmth penetrated her side as they walked together, her stride matching his. "Why shouldn't He?"

"Because…"

He turned her and looked into her eyes. And he saw. Just like he always did. He saw beneath the fear, the doubt, the worries. "He's your father. He loves you."

She dropped her gaze. "How can I believe in a loving Father when I've had no father at all?"

He sighed. "That's a lame excuse."

She lifted her chin. "Is not."

"Would a good father abandon you?"

"No."

"Would he ignore you when you talk to him?"

"No."

"Would he decide he doesn't love you anymore just because you've done wrong?"

"Of course not."

"See?"

"See what?"

"See-I-told-you-so. You know what a good father is."

Did she? Maybe she did. A good father didn't take off when you were a baby. He was there for owies and birthdays, your first day of school and your first date. A good father loved, protected, believed, and stuck by you.

"You don't have to have a good father to know what one is. God made you to know. He put that knowledge inside you. So it's not the knowing that's the problem, it's the trusting."

The trusting. It was hard to trust. She reached into her tiny purse and pulled out a pen and a scrap of blue paper from the charity banquet. She wrote words she'd memorized from the love chapter of 1 Corinthians in the Bible.

Love: Protects. Trusts. Hopes. Endures.

She folded the paper and tucked it back into her purse. And in that moment it felt right. She did know what real love was. Because she'd always known what it wasn't. Maybe God did place that knowledge in everyone. That, and the longing too.

She knew about the longing. It was the same yearning that drove her to find her mother. That emptiness, that desire to know and be known, to belong. Maybe she was really just searching for a father, her true Father, God Himself.

And if so, maybe God really did care about her after all. Enough to answer her prayers.

Marnie looked at Taylor and could almost believe it. Love, trusting, hoping, lasting. Love that stood by you no matter what. Love that got you a pet just because, when no one else would. Love that walked the beaches looking for clam holes. Love that held your hand, looked into your soul, saw, and cared anyway.

She looked into Taylor's eyes and saw the reflection of God's love, a love that acted, that stuck, even though her father abandoned her, her mother abandoned her, and Rose might abandon her too. But maybe God wouldn't.

Back then, she thought that meant He wouldn't let anything bad happen to her either. But she was wrong. God promised love, not happiness. He didn't promise perfection. He just promised His presence. He'd be there. That's what the years had taught her. She'd run away from Rose, Taylor, the pain, the past. But God remained. Always, always, He'd been there. Even when she tried to throw it all away.

"The Bible tells us that we love Him because He first loved us." The pastor's words brought Marnie back to the present. The music had stopped. Emmit had quieted. And the pastor now stood, his Bible opened, on the platform in front.

"But what does that love look like when things go wrong? Job lost his children, his livelihood, his health. And he wanted to know why. So, what did God do when Job cried out to Him?"

Marnie wanted to know too.

"What was God's answer?"

She didn't know. She always skipped the book of Job. It was too, well, too awful.

"God showed up."

What?

"God showed up and shared His wonder. The wonder of a God so grand He made the stars sing at the creation of the world. The wonder of a God so intimate He's there when the doe and mountain goats give birth."

Marnie shuddered. God was there when even the deer gave birth. That meant He was there when...

"Grand, yet intimate. Always present with His love. Think about that."

Was this what God was trying to say to her? That He was here, in Emmit's worship, in Josephina's touch, in the pastor's words? God drawing her to Himself, reminding her of what she once suspected to be true, God who could see into her just like Taylor used to, see and know and love anyway.

"You may ask how that matters to a man in pain."

It mattered. She saw that now. It was the only answer that mattered. Not the answer to why, but the answer to who God really is. That's what Job was really asking. And that's the question God answered. God of Wonders, as big as the universe, caring enough...even now.

And when God showed up, Job trusted. Taylor had been right all along. She didn't need to know that God loved her, she needed to trust it. She needed to look at her failures and trust God's love. She needed to see her mistakes and trust them too. She needed to look at Emmit and learn to trust there.

She glanced at him. He was studying his fingers and smiling a quiet, secret smile. He knew. Somehow, he knew the truth.

And she knew it too. God had given her Emmit to show her the truth about Him and the truth about her. Marnie and Emmit needed each other. But mostly, she needed him. Somehow, through the shout-singing, the frustrations, the memories, he was showing her the way home. He was showing her how to trust.

She closed her eyes. *God, I don't know how to face it all. I don't want to think about what happened in the past. I want to forget.* But she didn't, not really. Her regret box told her that. She'd carry those regrets with her always. Unless God could set her free.

Is that what You want for me, Lord? To carry them? To remember? Or is there a way to trust You to take the guilt away?

Emmit scooted close to her and laid his head on her shoulder. "Church good, Auntie Mar-ee. I like it."

I like it too. She put her arm around him. They sat together and listened as the pastor finished his sermon about Job, suffering, answers, and a transcendent God who was closer than their very breath.

Emmit sighed as the pastor ended his talk with prayer.

Marnie sighed too. Then she stood. "Stay right here, Emmit, while I go ask the pastor a question. Okay?"

"I like pastor."

"You stay here."

"I like beach."

"We can't go to the beach. You just stay right here."

"I like doughnuts."

Josephina scooted toward them. "I've got the remedy to that." She pulled the napkin-wrapped doughnut from her purse. "Here you go." She handed it to Emmit and moved back toward the end of the pew.

He grabbed it with both hands and stuffed half into his mouth. He chewed with his mouth open.

Marnie shook her head and glanced at Josephina as the woman exited the pew. "Thanks. That'll keep him busy at least." Josephina tossed her a grin and hobbled to the back door of the church.

Marnie turned and made her way up front. The pastor met her halfway.

"Good morning, Marnie."

She blinked. "You know who I am?"

He fanned the pages of his Bible. "Just because we've never spoken doesn't mean I don't know you're here every week. I've been praying for you."

Great. "I didn't know my problems were so obvious."

"Why do people think whenever a pastor says he's praying for them he's really shaking a finger at them?"

She crossed her arms. "What else would we think?"

He tucked the Bible under his elbow and smiled. "How about that we just give a hoot?"

"You guys get no credit, huh?"

He chuckled. "God doesn't either, so I guess I'm in good company."

"So, what are you praying for?"

"Blessings, of course."

She raised her eyebrows. "Blessings? I think God may have those stored up for someone else."

He looked into her eyes. "Now, why would you say that? You bless so many others at that coffee shop of yours." He nodded. "Yes, I know about that too—I'm a pastor, I hear about everything. I know about the job you gave to Joe even though you didn't need to hire anyone to clean, and the books you lend to Mrs. Gates, and the coffee you donate every month to the homeless shelter, the iguana you lend out for birthday parties, and even the baby showers you throw for free."

She hoped that was all he knew.

"So I've been expecting to see God's blessings on you too."

"Well, keep waiting."

"I don't have to. His blessing was sitting next to you in church today."

"You think?"

"I do."

She shook her head. "Crazy blessing, huh?"

"They always are." He glanced behind her at the pews. "Where is the boy, by the way?"

"Right there." She turned around.

Emmit was gone.

arnie raced out of the church. She shouted Emmit's name. That kid! You turn your back for a minute, and poof! He's gone. Of course, she should have known better than to turn her back at all. And whose bright idea was it anyway to put her in charge of a special-needs kid? Rose's. Or maybe God's. Well, she always knew God was crazy. Rose, though, was supposed to have more sense.

A pang went through her at the thought of her sister. But at least Rose couldn't see what a poor job Marnie was doing keeping tabs on Emmit. "Marnie, you're such a disaster," Rose would say. "Can't trust you with anything."

Rose would have been right. But she'd chosen to trust her anyway. Chosen to write the absent, wild, irresponsible sister's name into the will as guardian of her son.

Maybe Rose was crazy too.

Or maybe there was more to it than that. Because leaving Emmit to Marnie could mean that despite everything, Rose still trusted, still hoped, still persevered. And that would mean Rose didn't hate her after all.

Maybe Rose had still loved her. And that meant she'd have to trust Rose too. Trust that her sister had made her Emmit's guardian for a reason. Trust that it wasn't all a huge, horrible mistake.

But still, that kid was going to kill her. "Emmit!"

No answer.

No Emmit either.

She rounded the corner and called his name again.

This time, a voice answered. "I think I saw him heading toward the kitchen."

"Thanks," she shouted behind her without looking at who spoke. She turned in the direction of the fellowship building, with the kitchen in the back.

Groups mulled in front of the doors, blocking her way. She wove around them.

Then she halted. Stared. It couldn't be…

Someone was walking toward her. A man with a long ponytail and wire-rimmed glasses. The man she hated most in the whole world. The man who had mocked, scorned, and— She couldn't think about it. It was just her regrets throwing up images in her mind. *It's not him. It's an illusion.*

And still he came closer, closer. Around a group of ladies chatting, children hanging on their pants. Around a knot of sullen teens dressed in black. Around the well-dressed couple with their lemon-tasting faces.

"Marnie." The apparition spoke her name.

She didn't move.

He stopped in front of her. "It's been a long time."

"Craig." The name was bitter on her tongue. She almost reached out and poked him just to be sure he wasn't real. But she didn't because she was afraid he would be. Afraid he really had found her and was standing in front of her, three thousand miles away from where she'd seen him last. "It can't be you."

"Sorry to surprise you like this. I found out Taylor knew your address. He said he sent Emmit, after Rose…"

Taylor. Betrayed her.

"Is the boy here?"

"No." *You aren't real. Go on. Get away!* Her breath quickened. Her mind shouted. Her voice remained steady somehow. "How could you possibly be here? In California. In Pacific Grove. At my church."

"I tried the coffee shop first."

This was just wrong. Wrong, wrong, wrong. Her world here was supposed to be separate, safe, protected. But it wasn't anymore. She stared into Craig's face. She swallowed. Hard. "What do you want?"

"Nothing. I just, I just…wanted to see Emmit."

Stupid answer. Her imagination wasn't being very creative this morning. "What for?" *Because I'm not taking good enough care of him? Is Taylor having second thoughts? Why would he send you, of all people? No, this is just a nightmare. Remember, it isn't real.* "You can't take him."

"Take him?"

"He's mine."

"Yes, well, that's what—"

"Go away."

"Look, Marnie, I know it's been a lot of years, and I know you can't forgive me—"

"Forgive?" After all these years, he was talking about forgiveness, in front of a church. That really wasn't fair. But Craig had never, ever been fair.

"It was wrong. I was stupid."

You ruined my life. Ruined it with a single date won in a poker game. I paid for that mistake, paid and paid and paid. "I won't pay anymore."

"What are you talking about?"

She backed away. "You stay away from me."

"Marnie, wait. I didn't come all this way just to harass you."

"Really?" What other reason could there be for him to appear after all these years? Except that she was losing her mind, seeing things, dredging up images of pain from the past. Images that couldn't be real. *Could they, God?*

"I should have called. But I was afraid you'd refuse to see me."

"I would have." She closed her eyes. "I do."

"I'm still here."

She peeked at him through the slit of one eye. He was right. He was still there.

"Look, there are things you need to know. I promised Rose…"

She opened her eyes and glared at him. Craig, the one guy it had been safe to hate. The one who she promised herself she'd never listen to again, never give another chance to poison her mind. How could he be here now, talking, jabbering, like he had nothing to do with what happened before?

She straightened her shoulders. "I don't need to know anything you can tell me. I don't want to talk to you. I want you to go back to the hole you came from."

"Marnie, please. I'm sorry." He reached up and pulled at his ponytail.

"Just get away from me." She turned and stepped away. But not fast enough.

"Everyone deserves a second chance."

Her words. Her very own words, used against her. A second chance. Even Craig? No, not him. Because if she forgave Craig, she would have to forgive herself too. He'd done wrong, but she'd done worse.

She turned back around. "There are no second chances for either of us. You can't ask that of me."

"I know. But—"

"It's too late."

"You have to know."

"No!" She whipped around and ran toward the back of the fellowship hall. She ran as fast as she could.

And still his words chased her. "Marnie, Marnie come back." And then his final words shouted after her. Words thrown like daggers to pierce her soul.

"Marnie, the baby didn't die!"

~~~

The doughnut was gone. Emmit stared at the white stuff covering his fingers. He licked one finger. Sweet. Yummy. He licked another, then rubbed his face. Specks came off on his hands. He licked those too.

He was waiting. Just waiting. He didn't know why. But he did know he needed to wait.

He grabbed a small, white container from the counter in front of him. He turned it over and shook out bits of something through the tiny holes. They looked like the crumbs from his fingers. He stuck out his tongue, leaned over, and tasted the new white flecks.

Yuck. His nose wrinkled. It wasn't the same. This white stuff was bitter. Strange how things that looked the same could be really different. He should think about that more.

But not now. Now, he was waiting. Maybe he was hiding.

The door creaked open, then whooshed shut.

"Emmit!"

He turned and smiled. "Auntie Mar-ee. You find me." He held up his hand. "Fingers yummy."

"Don't ever run off like that again, do you hear me?" She rushed over, took him by the shoulders, and shook him real hard.

His head bobbed. Auntie Mar-ee was wrong. "I no run. I walk."

"You don't do that again! Never! Do you understand?"

He didn't like that loud voice. And he didn't like that she didn't smile. She didn't even look at him. She looked behind her. That was strange.

"We've got to go. Right now. Hurry."

He didn't like to hurry. Instead he wandered over to the window and pressed his nose against the glass.

"What are you doing?"

"Looking for the Son."

"It's cloudy today." She talked fast. Unhappy-like. "The sun's not going to come out."

"Oh." His lips trembled. Auntie Mar-ee's words made him sad. He didn't like sad. He needed another doughnut. "Doughnut?"

"Stop it, Emmit. Just stop it. We have to go. Quick."

He pressed his hand on the window and made smeary streaks on the glass. It was supposed to be like painting. It wasn't. It was just smudges. He sighed. "Why doughnuts have holes?"

She hurried toward him, but still she didn't look right at him. She just kept looking over her shoulder, back at the closed door. "They just do. Now come on."

"Go to beach?"

"No."

"Doughnut?"

She groaned. "We'll stop for one. We'll stop for a dozen if you want. One of each flavor, okay?"

"No. Auntie Mar-ee make them."

"Not now, Emmit."

He pushed his glasses up on his nose. "Man coming."

She held out her hand toward him. "Come on. Let's go get dough-nuts!"

He grinned. "I like doughnuts." He trotted after her out of the kitchen, around the building, out to the parking lot. He knew all the time that a man was coming behind them. And the man was very, very sad.

———~———

Murderer. The word clanged through Taylor's mind. *Murderer.* He couldn't believe it. Wouldn't.

But Doris had refused to say more. Still, only once before had he seen that look on her face. It was like she'd tasted spoiled milk at a fancy party where she couldn't spit it out. He saw that look earlier today, and he saw it sixteen years ago when they'd finally found Marnie's mother. Then Doris had curled her lip and said nothing. She swallowed the bitterness and turned away. Today, she'd just pointed to the door and told him to get out.

Now Taylor shuffled the papers on his desk, then stared at his computer screen. Outside his office, Nancy tapped on her keyboard. He should be tapping on his too. He should be writing to Marnie, getting some answers. But he wasn't. He picked up a pen and twirled it in his fingers. He glanced down at the scribbled list he'd made.

Birth certificate

Hospital wristband

What does Marnie know?

What did Rose know?

What does Doris know?

What about Craig?

What's it have to do with Emmit?

What's the truth?

The pen stilled. He gripped it in his fingers and added a single word to the list: *murderer?*

He crossed it out. Ridiculous. Because no one died except Rose, and Marnie had nothing to do with that. And further, he knew Marnie too well to think she'd killed anyone. Or did he? Had he ever? He'd often wondered through the years. Wondered if any of it was real. Maybe not.

But he did know Rose. And he knew people. People thought long and hard about who to name in their wills. Good grief, some people took a half hour to decide who would get a ceramic cat. Rose would never name Marnie as Emmit's guardian unless she was sure. Still, people didn't plan to die in a freak accident. They always thought they'd be there to raise their own kids. Usually they were.

But not this time.

So, how was that Marnie's fault?

Taylor dropped the pen and rubbed his forehead. He ought to just close the file, walk away, and let bygones be bygones, as the saying went. But he couldn't. Not this time. Because if there was anything Marnie had taught him, it was that God was found in second chances. And maybe, just maybe, this was his.

Show me the truth, Lord. Show me like You used to.

He closed his eyes and waited. Nothing came but the questions. More questions to add to his growing list. Had he been wrong about Marnie all along? No, he didn't believe that. But should he bring Emmit back? Was Doris right about that at least? Maybe he could forget about Rose's wishes and take care of Emmit himself. Maybe that's what God was asking him to do, that's why he kept seeing the boy.

God?

The windows in Taylor's inner office shuddered as the main room's outer door swung open. Nancy stopped typing. Taylor glanced out to see a delivery guy in brown handing her a slim envelope. She signed the clipboard, rose, and brought the envelope to him.

She held it out. "It's for you."

He took it, slipped his finger under the flap, and slit it open. A photo fell out.

Nancy left quietly and shut the door behind her.

Taylor picked up the picture and held it toward the light. Emmit sat on a bench outside his old school, his hair disheveled, his glasses askew. He wasn't looking at the camera. In fact, it appeared that he didn't even know the picture was being taken. The kid hated photos, but this was a good one. Emmit's collar was turned up, the breeze was tossing his hair, and he had a look in his eyes, as if he were contemplating the universe. Of course, any picture where Emmit wasn't making a face, or covering it, was a good picture.

Still, why would someone send him a picture of Emmit? He looked at the envelope. It was sent two days ago from here in town. Odd. Why would someone be in such a hurry to give him an old photo of Emmit? Or was it? Snow was on the bench and on the ground behind it.

Taylor set the photo on his desk. A sign glowed behind Emmit. It was distant, but he could make it out. Big, black letters read: "Twinkle, Twinkle…Get ready for the winter ball." He grabbed the picture and held it up to his nose. That was the theme of this year's dance, not last year's. He knew because a friend from church was helping to build some of the sets. And that meant the picture had to be taken within the last couple weeks. But how could it? He turned the photo over. Words were scribbled on the back: *I thought you should know.*

He dropped the picture.

Photoshop. The picture had to be altered by software. Someone was jerking his chain. But why? He scowled. Everything always started with a *why* lately.

And nothing started with *because*. It didn't make sense. Nothing did. *God, some answers would be great about now.*

He pushed the photo across his desk. Emmit's face taunted him. Emmit with that scar on his lip that was visible even in a picture. A scar he'd had for as long as Taylor had known him, since his surgery as a baby.

Taylor had seen a similar scar once. No, twice. A scar on a cranky woman in a T-shirt with a cigarette hanging from her mouth. He'd been so glad when that woman denied being Marnie's mother. He'd thanked God silently, and started to walk away, and put the woman out of his mind. Marnie's mother would be beautiful, kind, and a Christian.

He was wrong on all counts.

A few weeks later, he found himself back at that same door, in the same apartment complex, with Marnie beside him once again. This time, they didn't bother to peek through a knothole in the fence. They went straight to the front door. But they didn't knock, not yet.

Taylor wrinkled his nose. "Are you sure this is what Rose said? Here?"

"I'm sure."

"That old hag?"

"Taylor!"

"Well, she is."

"Maybe she was just having a bad day last time we came. Let's give her a second chance."

"Yeah, a real bad day."

"Maybe she'll be better this time, now that we know the truth."

He coughed. "Sure, and maybe the sky will turn green and rain violets."

Marnie grinned. "You never know."

"She was horrible. Admit it."

Marnie scowled at him. "You behave. Besides, I don't care if she's horrible. I just want to know if she's real. For me, and for Rose." She rubbed her palms together, then twisted the end of her hair around one finger.

"Are you okay?"

"Of course not." She threw him a wavering smile, straightened her shoulders, took two steps forward, and rapped on the door.

No one answered.

Taylor clapped his hands. "Well, that's that; we'd better go."

"Come on, Lawyer-Man, this is the moment we've been working toward all summer. You promised to find my mom, and you kept your promise."

Taylor grimaced. "I wouldn't have, if I'd known."

She looked at him for a long moment. "Yes, you would have."

He stared at her, then dropped his gaze.

Marnie knocked on the door again. Hard this time.

The woman answered, with the same dirty T-shirt, the same worn slippers, the same stringy hair, and that white scar on her upper lip. She glared at them. "What do you want?"

Marnie cleared her throat. "Are you Helen Wittier?"

"It don't say that on the mailbox."

"Are you?"

"Who's asking?"

Marnie moved closer. "My name is Marnie Helen Wittier. My sister's name is Rose. Do you remember us?"

The woman paled. "Remember ya? Sure I remember you. You're that fool girl who was here weeks back telling me you're my brat."

"Am I?"

"I ain't your mother." She flicked her cigarette onto the porch, then rubbed the tip out with her heel.

"Rose is at the hospital. It's serious, and the doctor needs to know her family's medical history."

"Too bad for her." The woman grabbed another cigarette and lit it. She pushed back a dirty lock of hair and tucked it behind her ear. Just like Marnie often did.

Taylor's stomach dropped. He stepped up to the door. He didn't want to. He wanted to just turn around and walk away. But he reached into his pocket and pulled out his lawyer-guy card, as Marnie always put it, and handed it to the woman.

She squinted at it. "What's this?"

"I'm Mr. Cole, a lawyer with Smith, Runkey, and Barnes, and I'd like to inform you that failure to come forward in a life-and-death situation, such as that of Miss Rose Wittier, can result in your being sued." It wasn't exactly accurate but close enough. After all, people could sue for just about anything; the real question was if they could win. But this cranky old woman didn't need to know that.

Her fingers trembled. "Sued, you say?"

"If you are Helen Wittier, mother of Rose and Marnie Wittier, it would behoove you to come to the hospital to answer some medical questions."

"That all I got to do?"

Marnie touched the woman's arm. "Please, just tell us the truth."

The woman flicked her second cigarette onto the porch and stepped on it. "Well, all right. You driving?"

Taylor put a hand on Marnie's arm.

She trembled beneath his touch. "Mom?" Her voice shook. "My real mom?"

Helen refused to meet her gaze. "I ain't never been no real mother to you or to anyone. You know that."

"It *is* you." Marnie stepped forward to hug her, but the woman skittered from her touch.

Helen crossed her arms over her chest and glared at Taylor. "I agree to talk to the doctors, but I ain't taking no trip down memory lane. You hear me?"

Taylor sighed. "It's natural for a daughter to want to know why her mom left her. You have to expect that."

"I don't have to do nothing." She tossed a glance at Marnie. "I was a junkie, all right? You don't need no more explanation than that. Ain't it enough that I'm ashamed of what I done? Ain't it enough that I never did bother you no more? Left you alone with that hoity-toity foster mom. Better off, you were."

Marnie caught her breath. "You knew where we were, and you never..."

The woman grunted.

"We were in five foster homes before Doris took us in. Five. So, how can you say...?"

Helen rubbed her nose. "Didn't know about that. Took me a few years to get cleaned up. Didn't know nothing 'bout nothing during those years."

"Still."

"Look I said I ain't taking no memory lane trip, and I meant it."

Taylor moved between them. "Let's just go to the hospital and talk to the doctors, okay?" He looked at Marnie, hoping she'd hear the words he wasn't speaking, words that would communicate to her to wait, to give the woman time, to get her in the car and moving toward Rose before Marnie let loose with all the questions that had been haunting her for years.

Marnie nodded.

Taylor stepped closer and spoke under his breath. "Bide your time."

Her lips pressed into a line. "If you say so, Lawyer-Man."

Taylor touched Helen's arm and motioned toward the parking lot. "I'm parked right over there. We can give you a lift to the hospital."

"How do I know you aren't some scam artists?"

Taylor raised his eyebrows. "And what would we be scamming you out of?"

"Humpf. You got a point there. All right, lead the way."

They walked to the car, and Helen climbed in the back.

Marnie's fingers brushed his arm. "Thank you, Taylor."

"For what?"

"For the chance to find my mother. The second chance."

"Are you sure you're glad?"

She smiled. "Nobody's perfect."

He glanced at the woman in the backseat. "No kidding."

"Except maybe you."

"Hardly."

She winked at him, then he opened the door and she slid into the passenger's seat. As he drove off he could see that she still had a hundred questions for her mother, including *the* question. But she didn't ask. Not yet. Mile after mile, she told about her motorcycle, her iguana, their friends, Rose's illness. She asked about Helen's apartment, her job, how long she'd been in the area.

But beneath the surface, Marnie's unspoken questions throbbed. *Why did you abandon me, why did you deny being our mother, why didn't you ever say that you cared? How could you just leave us and not come back? Was I so worthless to you that you never even bothered to try to get me back?* Taylor heard the questions as if they were shouted into the car's interior, though Marnie still didn't speak them aloud.

Still, *the* question couldn't wait forever. After all, the answer was supposed to solve everything, supposed to make her whole. Marnie wouldn't have admitted that, but Taylor knew it was true. He also knew it was impossible.

"I know you don't want to talk about the past, but you said something to me the day you left. It was important. Do you remember?" Marnie tried to say it casually, but the words came out strained anyway.

For a moment, no one answered. Taylor could almost hear Marnie's heart thudding in the silence between them.

Helen guffawed. "You gotta be kidding me. You expect me to remember something like that? I was so high the day I left, I could barely remember my own name."

Marnie's breath faltered. "You have to remember. You have to!"

Taylor glanced in the rearview mirror.

Helen stared out the window. "What? You gonna sue me over that too? You and the lawyer here?" She turned her head forward, and her gaze clashed with his as she jerked her thumb in his direction. She went back to glaring out the window.

Taylor reached over and took Marnie's hand in his. "Give it time," he muttered.

"But…"

His voice dropped to a whisper. "Second chances. Remember…"

She sighed. "Second chances. And this is only my first try."

Taylor gripped the wheel in one hand and kept driving toward the hospital. The women in the car grew silent as Marnie waited, believing in the power of a second chance.

Taylor stayed silent too, driving, waiting, pondering the strange allure of second chances. They'd gone to Helen's house once and failed. They'd gone again today and found out the truth. Marnie failed to get her answers today, but that didn't mean she would fail again tomorrow.

He glanced at her. "Do you think we all get second chances?"

She scooted closer to him and spoke in undertones. "Of course I do. My mother is getting a second chance, isn't she? She doesn't seem to see it that way yet, but it's true all the same."

He hadn't thought of it that way. "I guess so."

"Why?"

He shrugged.

Her hand tightened on his. "You're thinking of that case you messed up last year, aren't you?"

His eyes widened. "Can you read my mind?"

She grinned. "Sometimes."

That was scary. He hoped not. But she was right; he was thinking of the mistake he made last year while working for Legal Aid. What if God gave him a second chance to make that right? What if he could do something about that case he'd botched for those tenants? At the time, it had seemed like a simple dispute, and he'd treated it that way, on autopilot. But instead of an easy win, the couple had gotten thrown out of their apartment when the woman was seven months pregnant. He'd heard she went into early labor. All because the law had been twisted and he was too stupid, too distracted, to stop it.

Some advocate for children he turned out to be. He couldn't even protect the well-being of a little unborn baby. And he'd carried that burden, and the shame of it, with him all this summer. He'd run all the way up here to Maine to hide from it, ignore it, try to forget. But of course he hadn't.

"Are you thinking of going back?"

Was he? If he wanted a second chance, he'd have to go back, just like he and Marnie had to go back to the apartment complex to find her mother. If he wanted a chance to make things right, he'd have to finish school, return to Legal Aid, and see if there was anything he could do better. Then he'd return, marry Marnie, and dedicate his legal life to helping children.

But instead he'd finished up law school and when he came back, she was gone. And he ended up an estate planner, helping little old ladies decide what to do with their ceramic cats.

He lost something more than just love when Marnie left. He stopped believing in people, stopped believing in the vision God had for his life. He settled. He despaired. He gave up.

So he stopped asking the hard questions, taking the harder road, believing that good things could come in ugly packages. He let his mistakes and his loss define him.

And he was still letting loss define him.

He picked up the photo of Emmit and stared at the image. What he ought to do was stop hiding in Maine and go out to California to force the truth out of her. He ought to just get in her face and demand… He shuddered. It was safer here. Right here behind his safe computer screen, in his safe office, with his safe e-mail program keeping a safe distance between them.

Taylor set down the photo, pulled his keyboard toward him, and started to type.

Marnie,

I've been stupid. But now I need to know the truth. And I won't judge you for it, for any of it. It's all about second chances. I remember that now. Will you give me a second chance? Will you tell me the truth?

The truth. About Emmit, about Rose, about why Marnie left. That's what he was asking her. And yet what he truly wanted to know, but was afraid to ask, was why she took her special box and left his ring behind.

The phone rang. He picked it up.

"Dude, is that you?"

"Craig? Where are you?"

Craig's voice sputtered over the line, as if the man had run all the way across the country.

"I'm in California."

Maybe he had run all that way. "You didn't."

"I had to come. You don't understand."

"Did you see her? Did you talk to her?"

"I tried, but she won't listen. Look, man, there are things you don't know, things neither of you do, but it's time you found out. Time for things to get set right."

"And how do I do that?"

"The truth's out here in California. So you gotta get out here. You've got to confront her face to face."

Taylor dropped the phone into its cradle. Face to face? Maybe he didn't want the truth that much after all.

18

*S*omeone shrieked. A bell clanged. Whoops and shouts echoed from the bookstore beyond. Marnie glanced down at the list she was making and counted to three. She'd check out the bookstore in a minute. For now, she considered the list.

What to do about Ponytail-Guy

- ~~Run away~~—Forget it. That solution had led to disaster before.
- Don't listen—Fat chance. She hadn't been able to pull that one off in the past either.
- Yank on ponytail until he squeals like a girl and leaves me alone—That was still a viable option.

Marnie grimaced. She'd never do the last one, either, but there was no harm in imagining, especially since she'd been running out front to check the door of Books and Brew every time the bell jingled. So far, no ponytails on guys had entered. Yet, at least.

Daisy stuck her head through the office doorway. "We got a newbie over in the bookstore."

Marnie nodded. "I heard. About time." She crumpled up the list and tossed it in the trash. She strode through the coffeehouse portion of Books and Brew and into the bookstore. Italian opera played from the speakers. Every day she chose a different theme. Yesterday it was seventies pop, the day before, children's campfire songs. But today, the sounds of soprano seemed right. She rubbed her hands together. "Okay, who's our winner?"

A woman wearing sweatpants with a toddler on her hip raised her hand. She pointed at the creature in a glass cage beside the bookstore register. "It—it's alive."

Max flicked his tongue and moved his head a centimeter to the right.

Marnie walked over to him and ran a finger down his back. Used to be she'd shock customers by picking him up and slinging him around her shoulders, but not anymore. Now he liked to sit next to the small display of gift books and occasionally flick his tongue at customers. He did that now.

"Da-gon." The boy attached to the woman's hip pointed at the iguana, then stretched out until he was nearly perpendicular to his mother's side. "Pet. Pet."

Marnie motioned them closer. "Reach right in and scratch him right here above the eye ridge." She showed the boy the right spot. "He likes that."

The woman's eyes widened. "Are you sure?"

Marnie rubbed Max's eye ridge herself. "He doesn't bite."

"Okay, Conner. You can touch the dragon. Be gentle."

The boy's mouth opened in a look of wonder as he reached over and grabbed the iguana's neck. Marnie loosened his fingers, then showed him how to carefully rub.

Max closed his eyes.

The woman touched Max's back, petted him with one finger, lightly, tentatively.

The boy squealed and clapped his hands. "Mama pet da-gon."

Marnie laughed. "Free hot chocolate for the brave young man and a coffee for his mom. But Max has to stay here." She grinned at the mother. "Health codes and all. And we've got a little sink just inside that door"—she pointed at the french doors that separated the bookstore from the coffee-shop portion of the store—"for hand washing."

Daisy propped open the doors and allowed the scent of fresh snickerdoodles to waft into the room.

Marnie raised her voice. "And cookies on the house for everybody."

The other patrons all clapped.

Daisy stepped through the doors and glanced at Marnie. "Are you sure? Can we afford it?"

"Of course not."

Daisy frowned. "God loves a generous giver, though. Bible says that."

"A cheerful giver."

"Yeah, that."

Marnie turned back toward the woman with the toddler and winked. "We always celebrate when Max makes a new friend."

The woman shook her head. "I'd better pay for my own, then."

"Conner is friends enough for both of you." She nodded toward Max.

Conner was sitting on the counter now with his body half in the glass cage and his arms thrown around the "da-gon."

Marnie chuckled. Conner looked so much like Emmit the first time he'd encountered Max. Of course, Conner was in a much smaller body, but other than that, they both beamed, they both threw their arms around Max's neck, they both thought Max was their new best friend, and neither of them could say *iguana*. She should have known, way back then on Emmit's first day, that he'd be dancing his way into her heart too. After all, any friend of Max's was a friend of hers.

She shook her head and went into the coffee shop to wash her hands. Then she moved around the counter to the coffee cups and picked up a cup and a purple marker. The woman followed with Conner a moment later.

Marnie smiled at her. "So, what'll you have?"

"What's Josephina's Heaven?"

"Our specialty tea. We named it that because that's what they'll be serving in heaven."

"I'll have one of those."

"Good choice."

The woman pulled out her wallet.

"On the house. In honor of Max and Conner. And Emmit."

"Who's Emmit?"

"Another iguana lover."

The woman smiled. "Wow, when Joe said I had to come here for Conner's books, I had no idea I was in for an adventure."

Joe waved his rag from a table near the wall. "Told ya." That man, always cleaning, always working. He was worth every penny Marnie paid him. He rubbed at a spot on the tabletop. "Ask her why she does it."

The woman raised her eyebrows. "Well?"

Marnie handed the hot chocolate Daisy had just made to the woman. "Because it doesn't matter if you scream at him the first time, Max always gives you another opportunity to be his friend."

Joe piped up again from the corner. "And that's the way we do things around here, ain't it, Miss Marnie?"

She nodded. "That's right."

The bell on the front door dinged.

Marcus walked in with Emmit. Emmit had yellow paint smudged all over his face and dribbled down his shirt. His new shirt.

Marnie grimaced. "Don't tell me, he was trying to paint the sun again."

Marcus shrugged and swept the hair out of his face. "That's what the teacher said."

"Well, thanks for picking him up. You want a snickerdoodle, Emmit?"

"Doughnut."

"Of course."

Daisy set the woman's tea on the counter and smiled at Marcus.

He smiled back. Shyly.

The woman at the counter picked up her two cups. "Is he your son?"

The question shot through Marnie like a blade. "Son, no, um, he, he just works here." Son. Why would the woman ask if she had a son?

"No, not him, the retarded boy."

Marnie bristled. "He has Down syndrome."

The woman swallowed. "I shouldn't say *retarded,* huh?"

Good thing Marnie gave second chances. "His name is Emmit."

"Emmit. Is he your son?"

Emmit pushed his glasses up on his nose, tugged at his ear, then wiggled his fingers at Marnie.

Warmth flooded her. Her son? She turned to the woman. "Yes. Yes, he is." She almost choked on the words. And yet she was glad. It was crazy but true. There he stood with his glasses still crooked, paint all over him, and his hair sticking up. In a moment, he'd probably do something that would make her want to scream. Still, she was glad.

She waved back at him.

"My friend's niece's stepsister has a kid with Down's. I've heard it's challenging, huh?" The woman moved back toward Conner.

Marnie tapped her fingers on the countertop. Challenging? Yeah. "But worth it."

Mrs. Gates stepped up to the counter. "Ice water, please."

Free ice water. As always. "We have some new fiction in."

"I miss Phyllis A. Whitney. That woman knew how to write a story. But I guess these newfangled authors are okay too."

They should be. Mrs. Gates had read every one. One of these days, that woman would actually buy a book and not just read them and put them back on the shelves. And she'd order something she'd have to pay for too. Then the sky would fall.

Marnie hid her grin and handed Mrs. Gates the ice water.

Marcus glanced her way, then put his arm around Emmit's shoulders. "Speaking of new books, hey buddy, you want to help me shelve them?" He motioned toward the bookstore side of the shop. Three boxes sat open on the floor.

"Ask Vi-let too."

Daisy twitched.

Marcus sighed. "Sure, I'll ask Daisy too. Remember, her name is Daisy, not Violet."

"Vi-let."

Daisy stepped around the counter. "Don't worry about it. He can call me whatever flower he wants. Lily, Pansy, Tulip, Marigold, Rose."

This time, Marnie twitched.

Daisy sidled up to Marcus. "Just as long as *you* get my name right, okay?"

"I think I'll start calling you Dandelion."

"Oh, come on, a weed?" She punched him in the shoulder.

"But they're the only flower you can wish on."

She glared at him. "Okay, that's sweet, but you're not. You'd better behave or I won't help you both with the books."

Marcus flung his arm around her shoulder too. "Sure you will."

Marnie shook her head.

"Are those two going steady?"

Marnie refocused on the older woman before her. "Not yet. But soon, I think."

She'd been noticing it for weeks, the way Daisy looked at Marcus, the way he'd sneak glances back. The way they teased and let their fingers touch, just a little as they handed coffee cups back and forth. She remembered that feeling from a million years ago. Except it wasn't coffee cups, it was seashells. Seashells meticulously glued to the box that held her few little mementos from childhood. Her box of regrets.

Their fingers had brushed as Taylor handed it to her over the coffee table in his tiny little cottage by the sea. She sat on one side, he on the other. Behind him, the curtains rustled in the breeze that came from the open window. She could smell the briny scent of the sea and feel the dampness that fluttered through the opening and settled on her skin. A dish of smooth stones sat on the table. Coffee steamed from the machine in the other room. Decaf, and beside it, the chocolate she would add to his.

Even now, she could remember every detail as their fingers touched when he handed her the box.

"It's beautiful. How did you get it?"

He scooted up. "I snuck it from your apartment the other day when I stopped by. Those are all the shells I've gathered this summer."

"I can't believe you knew about this box."

"Of course I did. I saw you slipping things into it all summer."

"You never said anything."

"You didn't seem to want me to."

"And still, you made my box beautiful. Why?"

"To remember me, while I'm gone."

She made a face at him. "Like I'd forget."

He put his elbows on his knees, leaned forward, and folded his hands together. "You know I don't want to go. But I need to go back and make things right."

"That's what you keep saying. Along with the part where it's somehow my fault."

He looked at her for a long moment, then grinned. "I guess you could put it that way. Second chances. You taught me that. You and that crazy search for your birth mom. You showed me that sometimes you've just got to go back and try again. So that's what I'm going to do too."

"I know, and you're right. I'm proud of you for going back and trying to help those people who got evicted, and others like them." She turned the box in her hand and stared down at it. It was beautiful, the way he'd glued all the shells together so carefully, so intricately. As if he really, truly cared. Crazy thought. "But that doesn't mean I have to like the thought of you leaving."

"I'm coming back. I promise. After I finish my law degree, I'll come back here to start my law practice. And then…" He paused and took a deep breath. "Look, Marnie. There's something in that box. I don't want you to open it until I return, okay? But I want you to keep it for me."

"So, you're giving me back my box, but you don't want me to open it?"

"Promise?"

She smiled at him. "No."

"Come on."

"Okay, maybe."

"Close enough."

But she peeked anyway, months later. And she saw a perfect solitaire nestled in black velvet. It took her breath away. She never tried it on, but she did take it out, look at it, and die a little on the inside. And then she left it behind. She left it right on the coffee table where he'd first handed it to her. And there was no note, no message. Just a little black box to tell him she was sorry, he deserved better, and she'd messed up too badly for him to ever give her a second chance.

Funny how the past always had a way of catching up with you and sin a way of reaching through the years and never letting go. She'd tried to keep it locked away. Hidden forever in a box on a shelf. Still, she deserved this painful reminder, this nagging knowledge that it could have been different.

If only...

19

*Y*oung ones these days."

Mrs. Gates's voice shocked Marnie out of the memory. Thank goodness. If she lingered too long on that old memory, she was sure to start feeling sick. Because she'd been that close to having the love most people take for granted. So close. If only...

"What about you, Miss Wittier?" Mrs. Gates tapped the counter with her knuckles. "What's good for the young goose is good for the old one too."

Marnie blinked. The woman did *not* just say that. She stuck her pinkie in her ear, wiggled it, and stared at Mrs. Gates's rouge-covered cheeks.

"Well?"

"Umm."

"I'd say a woman nearing, what, forty?"

"Thirty-five."

"Like I said, nearing forty. Woman like that ought to hurry up and get herself a good man. Clock's atickin', if you know what I mean. You looking at least, dearie?"

"No."

She pushed out her chin and squinted into Marnie's eyes. "What's the matter, all the good ones taken?"

No, just three thousand miles away. If only…

"Woman your age can't be too picky. I've got a nephew…"

Oh, here we go. Lord, please. She closed her eyes.

"Tsk, tsk. Just not right, you not having a special someone in your life."

"She does." A woman's voice cut through Mrs. Gates's comments.

Marnie's eyes flew open. Kinna. *Thank You, God.*

Mrs. Gates huffed. "Whatever are you talking about, Mrs. Henley?"

Kinna smiled into Mrs. Gates's face while her eyes stayed as hard as granite. "Whatever are *you* talking about, Pearl? Marnie has Emmit. And if that's how God wants it, that's how it'll be. The rest is none of our business."

"Well, but—" Pearl's words sputtered to a halt.

Kinna pointed to a table near the bookstore. "Now you'd better hurry back over to your sunflower table before someone else sits there. I saw that young man who just came in eying the pressed flowers."

Marnie's gaze shot to the door. Not Craig, just the kid from the computer repair shop down the way. Whew.

"Oh, my." Pearl grabbed her ice water and hurried over to the table. "That's my table, sonny," she called to the kid browsing through the magazine rack. "You just find another spot." She settled into her chair, then got up and rushed through the french doors to the fiction section of the bookstore and snatched a book from the shelf.

Marnie shook her head and focused on Kinna. "Thanks."

Kinna threw her a half grin. "It's amazing how much infertility and being single are alike. Change a few words and it's the same questions, the same comments, the same prying, know-it-all advice."

Marnie pointed to the stroller behind Kinna. "Nice to have that all behind you, huh?"

Kinna gave her a long look. "I'll tell you a secret. A baby isn't the answer to infertility, just like a man isn't the answer to singleness."

"What is, then?"

"Surrender."

Great, just what she needed. A riddle. She frowned. "Surrender to what?"

"Grace. Love."

"Love can hurt."

Kinna nodded. "So can healing, but it's still a good thing." She looked down at her baby in the stroller. "You know what? I've learned that God works in the barren years. When He seems the most absent, that's when He's doing His most intimate work." She turned back around and tapped her chest. "In here, where no one else can see."

"If you say so."

"Listen, honey. If your future husband walked through that door right now, would it change who you are or who God has made you to be in all these years of being single?"

For a moment, Marnie envisioned Taylor striding through the door. Same intense brown eyes, same wavy hair but now with a little gray at the temples, same special smile just for her. Her heart nearly stopped at the image. "I guess it wouldn't change me, except for the heart attack."

Kinna laughed. "That's why we just take the gifts God gives as He gives them. Infertility, singleness, or a boy named Emmit. We do it because we surrender to love. His love. We accept it, even when it hurts." She glanced over her shoulder. "Sometimes, God's love-gifts aren't what we want, but they're gifts all the same."

Marnie wrote Kinna's drink order on a cup from memory. "So, are you calling your infertility a gift?"

Kinna shrugged. "I don't know. But I am calling Emmit one." She pointed in his direction with her thumb.

Marnie's gaze followed the gesture, through the doors to the bookstore. And there was Emmit, carefully taking books from a box and placing them spine first, pages out, on the shelf. They were probably even upside down. "Yeah, some gift." Just like God to give her an upside-down, backwards kind of present.

Emmit paused, opened a book, and tore out a page. The sound of ripping paper hissed across the room.

Daisy rushed toward him. "No, Emmit. You can't tear out the pages." She gripped his hand and eased the book from his fingers. Then she glanced at the books he'd put on the shelf. "How 'bout you come help me put the travel books away, okay?"

Emmit lifted up the page he'd torn. "I like this one. I keep." He turned toward Marnie in the other room. "I keep nice picture, Auntie Mar-ee! Look!" He held it up higher until she could see that the page was a simple watercolor of Jesus and the children from a storybook.

"You can keep it." Between Mrs. Gates and him, she'd go bankrupt for sure.

Joe stuck his head out of her office doorway. "Hey, Marnie, your computer's playing the theme from *The Twilight Zone*."

Ah, that meant she had mail. She used to not care, but now… Well now, it might be Taylor. And how sad was that? She'd never been one of those girls to wait, staring at the phone. Yet here she was rushing from the counter back to her office just because it might be "him." Pathetic.

She slowed. She wouldn't rush. She'd maintain some semblance of dignity. Not that anyone was watching, but still. She wasn't in junior high anymore. After all, what did Mrs. Gates say? Nearing forty. Ouch, that hurt. Perhaps she'd better slow down and stop acting like a giddy teen.

Marnie glanced over at the shipment of books she was sending back to the publisher. Then she paused beside her open checkbook. Still behind in rent. Mr. Karloff would be in again today. Well, she'd pay him and Marcus and Daisy too. And she and Emmit would survive on ramen noodles and four-pounds-for-a-dollar carrots. Poor kid, all he wanted was doughnuts and all she could give him was ramen.

She supposed she deserved it. He didn't, though, except when he tore up books. She glanced at her desk. Okay, she'd waited long enough. She hurried over and stared at the computer screen. Three new e-mails. An advertisement. An invoice. And…the third was from Taylor. She sat down and clicked on the message.

His words flashed on the screen. Second chances and the truth. Two things she thought she'd left behind in Maine. Still, Taylor wouldn't like the truth. She didn't either. He'd hate her for it. She hated her too. And that's why she didn't want to remember, didn't want to confess. Ever. She rested her fingers on the keyboard and started to type.

Taylor,

Don't ask me about the truth or what happened. It was a long time ago.

And yet she carried the memories around with her as if it were yesterday.

Isn't it enough to know that it was nothing you did? Things happened. I changed.

Except she didn't. In some ways she'd never changed. She just kept going around and around on the treadmill of her guilt.

By the way, Craig's here and I don't know what to do. I can't believe he's still got that stupid ponytail. But that's not the reason I
don't want to see him, don't want to listen to anything he has to
say. Listening to him never turns out well. I should know.

But what's worse, he's asking questions about Emmit.
I think he wants to take him. Didn't you say Craig and Rose
were together?

He had. Those words were seared into Marnie's mind. What in the
world had Rose been thinking, hooking up with that loser? Didn't she
know… Marnie closed her eyes. No, Rose didn't know. Marnie hadn't
told anyone the part Craig played in ruining her life.

I know that I've been wanting to find another home for
Emmit. But now I'm not so sure.

Was that true? Did she really want to keep him? Well, at least she
knew she didn't want him to go with that awful Craig.

Emmit ambled into the room and dropped his backpack on the desk.
It tipped and spilled pencils and paper, candy wrappers, and a pair of
dirty socks over her desk.

She stopped typing. "Why are socks in your backpack, Emmit?"

He sat on the chair and tucked his legs up so he was sitting cross-
legged on the seat. "Auntie Mar-ee not happy."

She stuffed the socks back in his pack. "I'm not sad either. How
would you like some Chinese food tonight?"

"Okay."

"Ramen."

"Carrots."

She picked up his pencils and papers and returned them to the bag. "Yeah, I guess we've had that one too many times this week, huh?" Her fingers brushed something sharp and plastic. She moved a candy wrapper and stared. Her breath stopped. There, gleaming on her desk, lay a tiny purple sword, the kind that once was used to spear olives in martinis or maraschino cherries in a nice, tall Shirley Temple. She used to love those. "Where did—?" She swallowed and started again. "Where did you get that, Emmit?" She pointed but didn't touch it, didn't ever touch it again. It hurt too much.

"I get from Auntie Mar-ee's box."

"Why?"

"For sun."

Of course, he'd probably seen something just like it in a drink on a hot day. There's no way he could have known how much the sight of that stupid plastic sword pierced her.

"Sun change it. Make it better."

"It won't melt in the sun. It's too hard."

"Not melt."

"No."

He picked it up and held it in his fist. "Sharp. Makes ow."

Oh, Emmit. She put out her hand and turned her head away. "Give it to me."

"Auntie Mar-ee?"

"Please."

The slim plastic dropped into her palm. She closed her hand. One silly little sword. To remind her of one simple little date, one simple little night. One not-so-simple mistake that changed everything.

Taylor had pushed the box covered with shells to the middle of the table and stood. "Come on, it's my last night here, let's make it count."

"What do you want me to do? Help you pack?"

He stretched his arms out in front of him. "Sure."

"No way. I'm not doing anything to help you leave."

He held out his hand to her and lifted her off the couch. "Like I said, it's your fault I'm going."

She glared at him. "Ouch."

He grinned. "I don't mean it that way, and you know it. What I mean is, I was perfectly happy with my guilt until you convinced me I might have a chance to make things right."

She scowled at him. "I did no such thing."

He raised his eyebrows. "Really?"

She crossed her arms. "Fine, I'll take the blame, but you had another year left in law school anyway. Don't tell me you would have blown that off just to stay here with me."

His grin broadened. "You never know. Though my lease is up on the bungalow."

"You know Doris would rent it to you indefinitely, if only to keep me out of trouble."

"So, that's what I've been doing all summer, huh?"

She punched him in the arm. "If you say so. Now what are we going to do to make your last night memorable?"

"You're going to help me pack, remember?"

"You're nuts."

"You are too."

"Let's go clamming."

"The tide's not right."

"So?"

He laughed. "Okay, but only if we go on your motorcycle. You've been promising me a ride all summer."

"I'm driving."

"No fair."

"It's my bike."

Taylor grabbed a bucket.

Marnie grabbed her helmet and tossed it toward him. "You'd better wear this."

He caught it. "What about you?"

"Don't say I never did anything for you."

"I'll never say that."

She shook her head and moved toward the door.

He beat her to it, opened it, and let her pass.

A few minutes later, they were riding down the winding street, the wind in her hair and Taylor gripping tightly around her middle. She loved the feel of him there, warm against her back. She should have done this before. And she probably should have let him drive. But this was too much fun.

"Whoo-hoo!" He whooped in her ear as the Harley turned a corner and picked up speed. "You sure you won't let me drive?"

"Not until you come back. Give you something to look forward to." She shouted the words back to him over her shoulder.

His rib cage jiggled as if he were laughing.

"Be careful, or you'll get bugs in your teeth." She squeezed the gas until the landscape became a blur around them and the roar of the engine drowned anything else he might have said. Through hills, across a bridge, until she could see the ocean, whitecapped and vast in the distance.

She slowed. A tiny town loomed before them with its one stoplight down Main Street. She let up on the gas. Of course the light was red. The bike rumbled to a stop.

A group of teens gathered on the street corner. One of them shouted to her. "Hey, nice ride!"

"Thanks."

"Dude, wouldn't she let you take the bars?"

Taylor didn't answer.

One of the kids stepped off the curb. "What you got there? An upchuck bucket? Bike's a little much for ya?"

Taylor tightened his grip. "No, but the girl is."

The teens laughed.

Taylor did too.

The light turned green. Marnie revved the engine, then the Harley sped off again. Three more turns and they were at the beach. She parked and shut off the engine. Taylor got off the bike behind her.

Together, they looked out over the shore and surf. No one was out clamming now because the tide was almost all the way in. But it didn't matter. Clamming was what they did together. The beach was theirs. It always would be.

Marnie took the bucket from Taylor. They rolled up their pant legs and walked out onto the sand. The strip of beach was narrow now with the tops of rocks peeking from the damp surface and broken shells littering their path.

Taylor took her hand in his, the way he always did, and drew her closer. "So, what will you do while I'm gone?" He tried to say it casually, but she still heard the strain in his voice.

She shrugged. "Take some more classes at the community college, I suppose, and keep working at the bookstore."

"I thought you wanted to open a coffee shop."

"I do. Someday."

He squeezed her hand. "I'll help."

She laughed at him. "How? Are going to sue the cows to get cheaper milk? Or maybe the Colombian coffee lords?"

He grunted.

"Besides, I've tried your coffee. Blech, even the chocolate doesn't help." She stuck out her tongue.

He flicked her tongue with his finger. "Hey, that's not fair. I make great coffee."

"You make great Shirley Temples. Leave the coffee to me."

He put out his other hand toward her. "Deal."

She shook it. "Deal."

They kept walking, listening to the tide coming in, with the bucket swinging from her arm, neither of them looking for clam holes. The sun dropped low in the western sky, then vanished altogether. The breeze picked up and made her hair dance around her face and stick against her mouth. She shivered.

Taylor took off his light jacket and put it around her shoulders. "Let's go back to my place. I'll make you the best Shirley Temple you've ever had."

"You just want me to help you pack."

"You caught me." He winked at her. "Two Shirley Temples."

"Well, how can I refuse?"

So they went back to his little bungalow on the beach. She helped him pack. He made her Shirley Temples, with maraschino cherries skewered by a tiny plastic sword. She made some coffee, his decaf with a dash of chocolate. He put on the music.

They sat there, 7UP bubbling, coffee steaming, reminiscing about the summer.

"I remember when you first came riding up on your Harley. My jaw about hit the ground."

"I think it did."

"You didn't like me much."

"Had you fooled, did I?"

"My boss was really gaga over you. He talked about you for three days after the kids' charity gig."

She chuckled. "Well, I thought he was cute too."

He leaned closer. "But not as cute as me."

"Of course not." She stayed still. "And you found my mom."

"Not so sure *that* was a good idea."

"I'm giving it time, like you said. She won't get away again."

"Hmm."

"You got me my first pet."

"I can't believe you picked a big ol' nasty lizard."

"I can't believe you bought me one."

"You know, that night I almost…" He paused and turned toward her. His face flushed.

"Almost what?"

He looked into her eyes. "I'm really going to miss you."

"I know." Her gaze slipped down to his lips. Her breath quickened.

He moved closer. Closer. Then he kissed her, long and deep and passionate.

She kissed him back.

"I love you, Marnie." He whispered the words against her cheek.

Her heart hammered, but she couldn't say it back. She just couldn't. She was too afraid.

He kissed her again. And again. Until it turned to more.

The music changed, deepened, slowed. Her shirt hit the Shirley Temple glass and spilled ice over the coffee table. The plastic sword skittered over the surface.

But neither of them stopped to clean it up.

Taylor took her hand and led her to the bedroom.

She woke up in his bed the next morning. Alone. The bags they'd packed the night before were no longer by the door. His toothbrush was missing from the sink in the tiny bathroom. And that silly plastic sword was sitting on the nightstand beside her. Beneath it was a note. "I'm sorry, Marnie. I love you."

That night was the last time she'd seen Taylor Cole.

20

*I*t never snowed in Pacific Grove. Except for today. But this wasn't real snow. It was the kind that drizzled from the machine on the far side of a field. Marnie parked the car and pointed to the section of whiteness that was about a quarter of the size of a football field. Christmas Wonderland. At least that's what they called it here on the Agostini Ranch. Once a year in December they gave pony rides, made snow, and sold crafts in the big red barn. If they made money, they sent it to missionaries in some far-off corner of the world, but Marnie suspected they mostly did it to bring a little extra joy to the California coast where Christmas never, ever meant snow. She always let Ally, the Agostini's daughter, advertise the event at Books and Brew.

Usually, Marnie just came for a few minutes, bought a few token crafts, threw a few smiles, and slunk off again. This year, however, was different. This year, Emmit was here, and he'd found out about the snow.

And she found out how good Down-syndrome kids could be at nagging. For days and days and days.

"Go to snow, Auntie Mar-ee?" he'd ask. "We go to snow now?"

"No, Emmit."

"I like snow. I want snow. I go to snow. Let's go to snow. Go to snow today? I don't see snow. I want snow. Snow come from sky. I catch snow on my um-um-um." He stuck out his tongue so far that the last word was muffled. Then after a few minutes, he'd start again.

That went on for four days until she finally agreed to take him to the snow. Of course, then she had to convince him to wait until the day of the event. It took two hours and a drive out to the ranch three days early to make him believe that the snow wasn't there now but would be there soon.

"On Saturday," she said about five hundred times. But he didn't know what Saturday meant, so the nagging started again.

"Today?"

"No, not today."

"Today we go to the snow."

"No, in three more days."

"Snow not there now. Snow there later."

"Yes."

"Snow there later today?"

"No, in two days."

He held up three fingers. "Two."

She folded one of his fingers down. "Yes, two days."

"I like snow. We go today?"

"Not yet. Tomorrow."

"Tomorrow."

"Yes, tomorrow."

"Then the snow will come."

"Yes, then the snow will come and we'll go out to play in it. Okay?"

"Not today."

"No, not today. Tomorrow."

"I want to go today."

"Emmit."

"Okay. Tomorrow."

And now tomorrow was here. Finally. She'd barely parked the car when he leaped out and raced toward the white field.

She got out and called after him. "Emmit, you left your glasses." And his hat, and his mittens, and his coat.

He didn't care.

He ran with his funny stiff-legged gait all the way across the field to where the snow spat from the machine and sparkled in the bits of mid-morning sun. He sat under the spray, lifted his face, and let the flakes drizzle down all over him.

Marnie shook her head, gathered up all his things, and followed. Crazy kid.

"Hi, Marnie."

She waved at a couple she knew from the coffee shop.

Another group of customers turned toward her. "Hey, great seeing you here. The hot chocolate's good, but it doesn't hold a candle to your coffee." A couple of them lifted up their steaming foam cups as if in salute.

"Thanks. Dollar discount at Books and Brew if you buy a craft today for the missionaries."

Two of the younger guys in the group whooped their appreciation.

Marnie grinned, then continued toward Emmit. The sky darkened as the sun hid behind clouds.

Emmit had gotten up from under the machine's spray and was now running back and forth through it, waving his arms like a bird.

She giggled. "Hey, Emmit, whatcha doing?"

"I fly." He didn't pause as he answered.

"Just like an angel from heaven."

This time, he did stop. He grinned. "Snow angel."

She smiled. He was a snow angel. At least today.

He held up his arms and let the snow flutter down around him. He laughed, clapped his hands, and twirled in the flying whiteness.

The sun peeked through the clouds again and made the snow glitter. Emmit basked in the light.

Marnie moved closer. "There's your sun, Emmit."

He turned and looked at her over his shoulder. "Not my sun. God's sun."

God's sun. Maybe he was right. God's sun, God's snow, God's gift to her in the form of a fifteen-year-old Down-syndrome boy who loved sun, snow, the beach, and doughnuts. God's gift, that came at the expense of her sister's life. Rose, who had raised a Down's boy all these years and Marnie had never known. Perfect Rose, with her imperfect son, who loved him just the same.

A pang went through her. *I miss you, Rose. I'm sorry I didn't keep in touch. It wasn't your fault. Nothing that happened was your fault.*

Yet she'd blamed Rose back then. For having such stupid friends, for making her go to those stupid parties, for getting sick and needing pain pills even though that wasn't her fault either.

But no matter what, Rose had stood by her. Recovering from surgery, hurt, weak, tired, and still on bed rest, yet Rose stuck by Marnie during the dark days after Taylor left.

Six weeks after his last night with her, Marnie took a pregnancy test. It was positive. *Positive.* Others tried for months and months, even years, before they got pregnant, and she conceived after just once. It wasn't fair. But if life had taught her anything, it was that it was rarely fair.

Still, she took the test again. Positive again.

She decided to tell no one but Rose. She'd just wear those baggy shirts and stretch pants that were so popular back then. No one would know, especially Taylor. She didn't want to burden him, didn't want him to think he had to rush back and be with her. He needed to do the right thing where he was. Just because they'd done the wrong thing, done what she'd always swore she'd never do until the ring was on her finger and the "I do's" were all said and done, didn't mean she had to make things worse by crying to Taylor and guilting him into coming back. At least that's what she told herself, the reason she gave for why she didn't tell Taylor.

The truth was something different. The truth was that getting pregnant proved how unworthy she was of his love. Good girls didn't get pregnant out of wedlock. Good girls stayed pure, stayed clean, got married. She wasn't a good girl. Taylor should know that. His church-deacon parents, his pastor brother, certainly would. She could almost hear the whispers about white trash trapping an up-and-coming lawyer. She could almost see the looks. Better if he didn't know. Better if no one did.

So she kept quiet. But still her foster mom found out. "We'll get you right in for an abortion," were the first words out of the woman's mouth as she poured a cup of tea.

For the first time, Rose stood up to Doris. "She's not having an abortion. We're not going to take one mistake and turn it into two."

"At least we agree that this pregnancy is a mistake."

Rose scowled from the bed. "The baby isn't a mistake. What happened to Marnie to get her pregnant was a mistake."

"Well, it was her own fault."

At that, Marnie turned her back and walked away. But she couldn't escape the accusations. Her fault for being irresponsible. Her fault for not being careful. Her fault for seducing men with those evil black boots. God was punishing her for all of it.

Rose wouldn't hear that either. "A baby is punishment?" She practically screamed the words as her torso lifted from the mattress.

Doris rushed over and pressed her back into the bed. "Just calm your-self." She glared at Marnie, as if Rose's actions were Marnie's fault too.

Marnie moved back to Rose's bedside, but Rose wouldn't be silenced. "You tell all those people out there struggling with infertility that a baby is punishment. You tell them you want to kill this baby, that somehow just because it wasn't planned, it doesn't have a right to live. That's the stupidest thing I've ever heard." She grunted. Quiet, genteel, composed Rose ac-tually grunted. Then she reached out and grabbed Marnie's hand. "A baby is always a gift, Marnie. Don't ever forget that. It's going to be okay."

Only Rose cared, only Rose stood by her. "We'll get through this," Rose kept saying. "A baby is always a miracle."

But in the end, there was no miracle. Only shame. Only guilt. Only fear.

And it wasn't okay. It could have been. If only Marnie had believed Rose. If only she had believed God.

Instead, it had taken her fifteen years and her own private snow angel to understand Rose was right.

She'd been right all along.

~~~

It was almost like being home again, with the snow falling around him. He loved the snow, and he loved the Son, and he missed home.

Emmit flung out his arms, stuck out his tongue, and tasted home.

Soon, he'd be going back again. He could feel it. Soon, he'd fly all the way back, just like he flew all the way here. It wouldn't be long now.

He'd known that ever since he'd peeked out of the church kitchen door and seen the man with his funny glasses and funny dark-colored long hair. Emmit had seen that man before. Lots of times. His name was

Egg. He didn't look like an egg, but that's what everyone called him. Eggs were round and white and didn't have any funny colored hair except at Easter. Maybe he was an Easter egg.

Emmit had seen Egg again at the cookie shop, but Egg didn't come in. He just watched through the window. Didn't look at Emmit. Like he didn't know him. He just stood there and stared and then wrote something on his hand.

Still, Egg was here. And that meant Emmit was going home real soon. He would miss Auntie Mar-ee. But Mar-ee wouldn't need him anymore. She'd be okay. She wouldn't go home.

For her, home would come here. And then everything would be all right.

Emmit picked up a fistful of snow and threw it in the air. It fluttered back down like a hundred tiny angels.

And that made Emmit very, very happy.

～∾～

Taylor was being stupid. He sat outside Emmit's old school anyway. He hunkered down in his car, watching the faces, waiting. Waiting for a boy who was three thousand miles away. Stupid.

But he'd dreamed about Emmit again last night. Emmit making angels in the snow. They didn't have snow on the California coast, so he took it as a sign. And speaking of signs, he tapped the picture of Emmit in his hand and glanced up at the sign for the winter ball. The same sign in the picture. The same everything. Except today there was no boy who looked like Emmit sitting on the bench outside the school. Just a girl frantically texting and another jabbering on her phone, both with coats zipped, noses red, and hands clumsy with gloves. He just had to come, had to see for himself. And it had to be today, the last day of school before winter break. So here he was. Stupid.

Taylor sighed, pulled out his laptop, and opened it. No new messages. Funny how he was always checking e-mail these days. If he was "with it," he'd get her cell phone number and text her. But that would be too close, too immediate. He avoided that. And so did she. As if they both knew that door was best left closed. If they got too close, well, who knew what would happen next?

Her last note had come three days ago. She'd written to tell him about Craig showing up. Idiot. What was that guy doing making trouble all the way out in California? He'd made a promise to Rose? A promise to what? Muddy the waters, that's what. It was just nuts. But the good news was that Marnie had seen Craig at her church. And that meant she was still going. He'd wondered if she'd given up on God too over the years. But from the sound of it, she hadn't. She'd stuck with Him, wrestling, struggling, and most of all, hanging on. He'd gathered that much from her note.

He clicked over to it and reread the part where she talked about Emmit. That was another thing he liked about e-mail. You could read it again and again. And if you read it often enough, you could almost hear the other person's voice speaking into the silence. He'd always loved Marnie's voice.

He focused on the words and tried to remember the sound of her speaking.

It was a beautiful thing to see, Lawyer-Man.

Lawyer-Man. He hadn't heard that in too long, but he could easily remember the sound of it.

His arms were raised right up high, and he had his eyes

closed. His glasses were slipping down his nose, but he didn't care. What abandon! I miss that in myself. I've grown too guarded, I think. Emmit showed me that. He's helping me to open up. Of course, I don't have much choice. He's pretty much turned the sanctuary of my little bungalow upside down. Every time I want to withdraw, he's right there giving me a hug. That boy loves his hugs! And did you know he never gets dizzy when he twirls? It's amazing.

He hadn't known that. In fact, he couldn't remember ever seeing Emmit twirl.

The painting is still a disaster, though. I don't know why you ever suggested that. Of course I gave him a second chance at it, but that turned out worse than the first. Now all my windows at Books and Brew are painted with blobs of yellow. My customers think the look goes well with all the tables I've made for the place, so I think I'll leave it. At least I can wash off the paint if I want, but the table I made from a bicycle is beyond repair.

Emmit tried to ride it. And now he wants me to make a new table out of seashells.

The letter skipped a line, then ended with a final sentence.

I won't make one out of seashells. I can't. You know why.

He did. Because even though she'd left the ring behind, she'd taken the box he decorated with shells. It had taken him half the night to glue on all those ridiculous seashells. But it didn't mean anything without the ring, the ring she'd found inside a small velvet box. And then she ran away. He'd always wondered if the ring made her run. Was it because she didn't want to marry him and didn't want to face him to tell him so? Or was it because he'd taken her to the bedroom before the altar?

He'd always promised himself he wouldn't be one of those guys who slept with a girl without marrying her. Sin was sin for a reason. He knew that before. But he'd found it out for certain after that night. Sin would tear you apart, leave you bleeding, snatch your future, and drain away the life. It would make you an estate planner when you could have been an advocate for children. It would make you alone when you could have had a family at your side.

Marnie ended her e-mail with just her name, followed by a short postscript.

P.S. The truth is ugly, best to leave it masked.

The bell rang. Kids poured from the building. Taylor watched, but none were Emmit. They couldn't be. So, why was he even here?

Because you're losing your mind, Lawyer-Man.

He shook his head, hit Reply on the computer screen, and began to type.

Emmit sounds like he's adjusting well.

But was he? The Emmit Marnie described didn't sound like the Emmit he knew at all. Emmit didn't paint on windows. So, why was the boy acting out like that? And why didn't Marnie seem to care? Well, she never was one to hold things against people. Just look at how she'd treated that horrible mother of hers. It wasn't like that woman had turned into some sweet fairy godmother the moment she was found. Not hardly.

Yet Marnie kept wanting to see her, would invite her over, bake clams, make a nice dinner, and then Helen wouldn't show up. Or she'd come late and say she'd already eaten. And she'd smoke like the proverbial chimney no matter how many times Marnie asked her not to. Taylor hated that.

"Let's just give her another chance," Marnie would say. "I'm going to ask her again tonight, see if she remembers."

So she gave her chance after chance, right up until the day he left. And still the woman smoked and cussed and never made it on time to dinner. And she still refused to talk about the past. Refused to recall what she'd said to Marnie when she was a girl. And still Marnie treated her with love, biding her time, waiting.

Taylor smiled. In a way, that's what he'd always loved about Marnie. She lived with that same abandon she'd described in Emmit and always looked for the good in people. Except maybe for Rose. But he heard that had changed after Rose took sick. Doris had told him that much. While he was gone, Marnie and Rose had become close, but in the end, even Rose hadn't known where Marnie had gone.

She may have shattered him when she left, but before that she'd also made him whole. And he was grateful for that. Her coming into his life was a gift. He had no regrets.

He should tell her that. He never had. He started typing again.

I asked you for the truth, but I didn't offer you any in return. That was wrong. So let me start, Marnie. I never got to tell you what happened to me those months after I left you to go back to school.

I failed. You know about how my mistake got those renters evicted. Or maybe you don't. I can't remember what I told you back then and what I didn't. But the gist is, I made a mistake and someone else paid for it. But what I didn't see then was that I was too busy studying for my next exam, too busy planning out my own life, too focused on what I wanted, to truly see the people I was supposed to be helping. That's why I really failed. Here I thought I was "saving the world" getting my law degree to help "those poor kids." Sounds awful, doesn't it? Well, it was. I pretended to be noble, but really I was just arrogant. In some ways, I guess I thought I was God. I wouldn't have admitted that, I couldn't even see it, until you showed me love in how you dealt with your mother. You saw her, I mean, really saw her, and valued her for who she was, even though she was nothing like a mother should be. Even though she didn't give you what you wanted.

I remember that one time when she took the twenty out of the jar on your dresser. She thought no one saw her. But you did. And instead of demanding she put it back, you asked her if she needed more. And she said yes! I don't think you gave her more, but you did give her some groceries and you went over and helped her clean that horrible little hole she called her apartment.

You know what I learned that day? I learned that I'd hurt those renters not because I hadn't learned enough, but because I didn't care enough. You also showed me that God gives second chances and third chances and fourth chances. He cares for all of us no matter how messed up we are, and I needed to be a lot more like Him.

I left to try to make things right, but I couldn't. There,
I've admitted that too. The tenants were gone, the building
sold, and there was nothing more I could do. You see, I still
wasn't God—I couldn't fix things in other people's lives
either. I always thought God wanted me to, that's why
He made me a lawyer, to get justice for others, to fight for
them, to be the person who rode in and saved the day. But
I'm no Savior.

He paused and stared out the window without seeing the school, the
bench, the sign, anything. All he wanted was the truth. Finally. Not the
truth about what had happened to Marnie, but the truth about himself.
She was teaching him truth again, despite all the miles between them.
Just writing to her, reading her e-mails, was enough. She was amazing
that way. Still.

He refocused on the screen.

After all this time, I finally get it. It's what you wrote about
Emmit. Life isn't about making things perfect. It's about
living with the blobs of yellow. It's about rejoicing in the
life God gives you, even when it's not the life you wanted or
expected. It's about throwing your hands up in abandon even
when your glasses are askew and you can't see the reason, the
meaning, behind what you're going through.

He stopped again. He hadn't done that. Instead he'd been stuck back
there in the mistakes of sixteen years ago. But why not just throw his
hands up and let go? He couldn't change the past, but he could care for
others in the present.

You found the ring, so you know what I'd planned. I was
going to go home, fix all my mistakes, then ride back to you
like a prince on a white horse. But I'm not a prince. You
know I wasn't then, after what we did on the last night. And
I'm not now either. I guess there's only one Prince, and that's
the way it should be.

He needed to let God be God, the King be the King. His plans
weren't God's plans; they never were. Even way back then, he'd been making his plans and expecting God's blessing. He'd never bothered to look
for God's plans. Maybe he still wasn't. Maybe he was afraid that what
God wanted would get him hurt again.

Someone rapped on his window. He jumped and glanced outside.
There stood Myrtle with an ugly ceramic dog tucked under one arm.
With her other arm she made big round motions like she was cranking
down the window in an old car.

He pushed the button and rolled down his window.

She peered in at him. "Heavens to Betsy, whatever are you doing
here, Mr. Cole?"

He shut his computer. "Just on my way back to my office."

She tapped the side of his car. "Why that's just where I was headed
too. But here you are instead, just as convenient as convenient can be."
She glanced up at the sky. "Thank the heavens."

Taylor glanced up too. But he didn't see anything except a few clouds
through the branches of a giant maple.

Myrtle set the dog on the edge of the door where he'd rolled down
the window. "Well then, here you go, Mr. Cole. Looks like Harold is all
yours."

He stared at the dog. "What?"

"Yep, I was there wondering and wondering about who should inherit my precious Harold, and a voice said in my head that I should give him to you. So here's Harold." She leaned in and dropped it onto his lap. Then she turned and walked away.

He looked at the dog and grimaced. What did a guy searching for the truth need with an awful ceramic dog?

He didn't know. But it looked like God intended him to find out.

21

*M*arnie sat at the small desk in her cottage and listened to the pounding on the door. Craig had been beating on it for five minutes. She didn't care. There was no way she was opening it. Not for him. Not for anyone.

So he shouted, he pounded, he begged, he whined.

She paced the room, dusted the bookshelf, moved her regret box from the top of the cabinet to the drawer behind her desk and back to the top shelf of the bookcase in the living room. She tugged on the lock on the box, then checked the knot on the thick ribbon she'd tied around it, twice. Then she sat back at the desk.

He kept knocking.

She organized her bills.

He called her name.

She checked her e-mail. Nothing from Taylor. Good.

Emmit wandered in from his room. "Egg loud."

"Do you want to paint?"

"No."

"How about the new Jeremy Camp CD?"

"No." He shuffled back into his room.

Craig's knocking turned to beating. "Marnie, I know you're in there."

Emmit started singing from the other room. *"Mary had a little lamb, little lamb, little lamb…"*

Marnie smiled. *That's right, Emmit, you sing. You sing real loud.*

Max crept across the floor and disappeared into Emmit's room. For a moment, the singing stopped.

Marnie moved her chair until she could just see through the doorway to his room. There the two sat, Emmit and Max, basking in the sunlight that poured from the window. Then Emmit started to sing again. Funny how she didn't mind it as much now. Not the singing, or the hollering for doughnuts, or the mess he made when he ate.

She still missed going to the movies occasionally or out to her favorite fancy restaurant on Cannery Row. Emmit was no good at nice restaurants. She'd discovered that after he'd thrown the whole basket of complimentary bread to the gulls and decided to send the shrimp "back home" to the sea the one and only time they did go out. And of course, he didn't do it quietly. Emmit didn't do anything quietly, unless it was getting into her private things at home. So they'd stuck to the dollar menu at McDonald's and Burger King as a treat after the shrimp incident, and she'd changed the lock and tied two ribbons around her regret box.

Truth was, Emmit hadn't gotten any easier to have around. And yet here she was, refusing to answer the door for fear Craig would somehow steal him away. After all, he'd done it before. Sort of.

She shook her head and focused on the sound of Emmit's voice to block out the knocking. Nothing Craig could say would be good to hear. It never had been. And this time, she had a locked door between them. This time, she wouldn't let him push her. This time, he wouldn't make her stupid.

Emmit glanced through the bedroom doorway and saw her. He waved and kept on singing.

Craig's voice got louder at the outer door. "Marnie, we have to talk."

Go away.

"Don't make me do this at your coffee shop."

He wouldn't. Would he?

"I want to see Emmit."

No.

"There's something you have to know."

I don't want to hear it.

"I have to tell you and Emmit together."

Why?

"I promised Rose I would. Now open the door. Come on, Marnie."

I can't. Don't you know I can't? Leave me alone. Leave us alone.

"You can't still blame me for what happened."

I can. And I do. Go away, Craig. I don't want to remember.

"Have you told Taylor the truth? You have to. This is about him too."

Shut up.

"You owe him that. Don't make me do it for you."

Don't you dare!

"I can call Child Protective Services."

Oh no.

"I'm a Child Services worker in Maine. All it takes is one call."

No. Don't let him do that. God?

"You don't deserve him, Marnie."

"I know." This time she said the words out loud.

The pounding stopped. And all that remained was Emmit's voice singing about Mary's lamb, his fleece as white as snow.

Marnie picked up her laptop and walked back to her bedroom. It was quieter here but not empty. Before Emmit came, there was a bed, a dresser, a nightstand, and that was it. No pictures, no little doilies, no personal items scattered on the surfaces of the furniture. There were still no doilies, but a painting of yellow globs now leaned against the dresser mirror, a clay lump the teacher said was a model of the sun sat on the nightstand, and a photo of Emmit and her together, snapped by Daisy at Books and Brew, was tucked into the lampshade. In the picture, Emmit had crumbs on his cheeks and a smear on his glasses. And he was grinning. She loved that grin. Ten seconds before the picture was taken, he'd just finished smashing up a cookie and tossing all the bits into the air, saying it was snow. Then he rubbed his fingers on his glasses, picked up two chunks of cookie from the floor, and shoved them in his mouth. That was her Emmit.

She plucked the picture from the lampshade, sat on her bed, and re-opened her computer. She opened a new e-mail and typed in his name. Taylor Cole. His address came up. She stared at it. *I can't do this. Craig can't make me.*

But he could.

No, she'd kept her secrets for fifteen years. She could keep them for another fifty.

Unless Craig tells what he knows.

But the truth would destroy Taylor, just like it had destroyed her.

And yet, God was rebuilding. In Emmit, she saw a glimmer of hope, of healing. But if she never confessed her sin, how could He heal her?

God?

A knock came again. Except this time it wasn't Craig at the front door. It was Emmit, standing at the entrance to her bedroom, holding something silver in his hand.

"What's that?"

He came forward, his arm extended. "From Auntie Mar-ee's box. I give to you now."

"Not again, Emmit." And how did he get into her box this time? Maybe she needed ten tied ribbons and five new locks. "When are you going to stay out of my box?"

"Not yet."

Of course not yet. She held out her hand. "What do you have this time?"

He dropped something into her palm. A dirty silver chain with a heart on it. Her fingers trembled. Of all things, he had to bring her this. This one thing that hurt her most of all, a cheap silver-plated necklace Taylor had won for her at a silly carnival game. He'd tossed a few dimes at tiny glass bowls and one went in. The necklace was his prize. She closed her eyes and remembered how he clipped it around her neck, looked at it, looked at her, and called her beautiful.

She didn't take it off after that, even when the silver started to wear and the heart turned black. She should have known then, but she didn't.

She kept wearing it even after Taylor had gone back to his last year of law school. She wore it the last night she was with Taylor. She wore it when she took the pregnancy test. And she wore it at the ultrasound.

At twenty-two weeks along, she already felt like an elephant, especially as she lay on the table and pushed up her top. Nobody outside the family knew she was pregnant. She wore her clothes loose in the style of the day and avoided parties and gatherings. But as she exposed her stomach for the ultrasound wand, it was obvious that new life was growing inside.

Marnie ran her fingers lightly over her distended skin, then read the name tag of the technician operating the machine. Paula.

Paula smiled at her. "Let's take a look, shall we?" She squirted goo on Marnie's bump and ran the end of the wand around her bellybutton. "Ah, there we are. See." Paula turned the screen toward Marnie.

Marnie caught her breath at the black-and-white image. There it was. A baby. A real baby. Her baby. Kicking, squirming, wiggling. Little fists flailed. Little feet pushed. A little heart beat.

"It's real. I can't believe it's real."

And for the first time Marnie felt a glimmer of wonder. It wasn't a thing; it wasn't an "it." It was a baby. And it was incredible. This was why Rose said she couldn't abort. This was why she couldn't call the pregnancy a tragedy. Because this was breathtaking. This new baby, this new life.

"I can't even feel him moving like that."

"You will soon enough." Paula lifted the wand and the image vanished into gray fuzz. "Do you want to know the sex?"

"Yes." Marnie barely breathed the word.

Paula replaced the wand and moved it to Marnie's side until the baby's bottom was clearly visible. "There you go. It's a boy."

A son. Marnie's mouth went dry. *My son.*

And at that moment, her world changed. Forever.

Paula continued to move the wand. "His heart looks good. Kidneys too." She positioned it over his head. "Brain's good." She moved it down to look at the baby's face. "Oh." Her voice lowered.

Marnie tried to sit up.

Paula pressed her back. "Hold still, please."

"What's wrong?"

Paula turned the screen away so Marnie couldn't see. She leaned closer to the machine and moved the wand with her right hand.

Marnie's heart pounded in her chest. "Is the baby okay?"

Paula sighed. "This is why they tell me I shouldn't say anything and make you wait for the doctor instead." She lifted the wand. "It looks like baby has a cleft lip. It's probably nothing life threatening, but…"

"But?"

"We can't tell for certain, but cleft lip is often a sign of other problems. I'm sorry. The doctor will be able to tell you more."

Something cold and horrible settled in Marnie's gut. "Is there anything we can do?"

"Baby boy will have to have surgery for his lip after he's born. And we'll keep checking for other problems too. So far, his heart looks okay and so does the rest, so we'll just have to wait and see."

Wait and see. Hard words, ugly words. "You suspect a problem with his heart too." She tried to make it a question but failed. She could read it in the woman's face.

"Sometimes they go together, but not always."

"Wait and see."

"That's all we can do now."

All we can do. That one sentence rang in Marnie's ears as she spoke with the doctor, as the doctor said the same thing, as she gathered her purse, as she paid her bill, as she walked out of the office, got into her car, and drove back to her apartment.

Wait and see. Pause and feel. Wonder and terror. Awe and despair. Belief and disbelief. Mixing, warring, tearing through her until she was left with a single question, a single cry: *God, what am I going to do?*

She wanted the baby. She didn't want the baby. It was her son. It was a child with problems she didn't know how to deal with.

Her mother was waiting for her when she got back to her apartment that day. Helen stomped out her cigarette as Marnie approached the front door. "Well, what did the doc say?"

Marnie pressed her lips together. "I don't want to talk about it."

Helen followed Marnie into the apartment. "Baby got problems?"

"Why are you here?" She didn't turn as she spoke.

Helen shut the door behind her. "Needed some cash."

Marnie threw her purse onto a chair. "I don't have any. Not today." She sniffed. *Just leave me alone.*

Helen shuffled into the living room and sat down. She dug in her shirt pocket for another cigarette, pulled it out, and lit it. "You got an ashtray?"

"Don't smoke in here. Not with the baby." She turned her back and started toward the kitchen.

"I knew that baby'd have problems."

Marnie whirled. "How could you know something like that? How can you even say that? What is wrong with you?"

Helen put the cigarette in her mouth and spoke around it. "Here it comes. Let me have it, girlie. It's about time."

"You…you…you…" Her hands balled into fists.

"That's right. It's my fault."

Marnie closed her eyes and steadied herself. "Of course it isn't your fault. That's ridiculous."

Helen pinched out the cigarette and stared up at Marnie. "But it is. Baby's got a cleft lip, don't it? Heart problems too? Or don't they know that yet?"

"How could you know that?"

"Runs in families. Runs in mine. That's why I told you—" She stopped and sucked in a quick breath.

"You told me what?" Marnie stepped closer, then lowered herself to a chair opposite her mother. "You remember, don't you? You know what you told me that day."

Her mother looked away. "'Course I remember. Never forgot. Too bad you didn't listen. Done got yourself knocked up anyway."

"Mom?"

Helen sighed. "I was having lots of health problems back then, heart troubles and a lot of pain with the old surgery for my cleft palate and lip.

Doctor had done something wrong when I was a baby and it was hurting. Got hooked on the pain meds and couldn't get off. Lying, cheating,
stealing, trying to get the meds any way I could. Finally used up all the
doctors in town. Needed to go somewhere else for my fix. A big city, I
thought, where I could try out some free clinics, fake my name, get what
I needed."

"And that's why you left us?"

"Seemed like a good idea at the time. You didn't need me. I was no
good to you at all. Plus, I found out that my condition was genetic, that
I probably passed it on to you two. You didn't have the cleft lip, and we
didn't know about the heart. But I did know you could pass those bad
genes on to your kids. So I warned you. Thought that was the least I could
do for you before I went off."

"Yes, I remember now." Marnie's voice dropped to a whisper. "You
took my shoulders. You squeezed them real hard. And you told me, you
told me…"

Helen's rough tone became even rougher. "I told you that you had
something bad inside you. I said I was going away to get something to
make you better. And I made you promise you wouldn't have no kids of
your own until I came back."

"I was ten. How could you make me promise that?"

"You didn't know what you were saying, but you promised anyway.
And I went away. Never did find no cure. Didn't look for one, really. Just
looked for the drugs to make the pain stop."

"And I thought you left because there was something bad inside me.
You made me believe that." That explained a lot. Too much.

"I guess I did."

"How could you?"

"I was right, wasn't I?" She pointed at Marnie's belly. "You broke your
promise and now look what happened. It's just like I said."

Marnie put her hand over the bump on her midsection and felt a flutter beneath her fingers. Her baby. Her son. Something bad inside her. Something that shouldn't be. Her mother had told her, warned her. But she hadn't remembered. And now her baby had problems, maybe a lot of problems. Deformity. Pain. Sickness. Sorrow. A baby who, at the least, would have a scar the rest of his life. Scars that were the result of a mother who had something bad inside, something she couldn't fix, couldn't change, shouldn't have forgotten.

I'm sorry, baby. I'm sorry, God.

Taylor. She cringed. She could never tell him now. Never.

Helen stood and walked toward the door. She paused as she reached for the doorknob and glanced back. "I didn't want to tell ya. But you kept badgering me. And now you know. I warned ya. All those years ago, I warned you. But you never did listen to me. And now that baby of yours is gonna pay." She opened the door. "You should have kept your promise, Marnie. If only you'd done what I said." The door slammed behind her.

Marnie could still hear the slamming of that door as if only a moment had passed instead of fifteen years. The worn necklace slipped through her fingers and slithered to the floor. She closed her bedroom door, so quietly, pressed her back against the frame, and slid down beside it. She shut her eyes and rested her head on her knees.

A tapping came from her bedroom window. She looked up.

And there was Craig, glaring at her through the pane.

~~~

Taylor hated where he was going. But he was going anyway. He should have gone there first. He should have stopped being such a wimp and gone to see the last woman on earth he'd ever wanted to lay eyes on again.

Well, he was going now. He could avoid it no longer. He pulled his car into the ugly little lot and rumbled along to the last trailer on the left. It looked like something from a bad B movie. *Attack of the Killer Weeds.* Thistles poked from around the trailer and an old, rusted out Monte Carlo sat in the driveway. The car looked like it hadn't been driven in years. He parked and glanced up at the trailer's dirty windows. A curtain fluttered.

She was here.

Taylor tucked Harold under his arm and got out of the car. He didn't know why he was bringing the ceramic dog. Maybe to shield him from the woman inside. Maybe just to give him something to put between them. Or maybe so he'd have something to throw if she went crazy again. She'd certainly become loony in the past fifteen years. She still lived on her own, though Taylor couldn't see how she managed. Half the time she didn't know what day it was. The other half she thought it was Tuesday.

He went up the rickety steps, Harold in place, and knocked on the door.

The woman answered, with her hair just as stringy, her face just as sour, the smell a lot worse than he remembered. And she still smoked. Behind her, trash littered the room, and the stink of rotten eggs and cigarette smoke blended together and wafted out to him.

He gagged. "Hello, Helen."

She squinted at him. "Who are you?"

"Taylor Cole. Remember? I used to know your daughters."

She tapped the ashes from her cigarette onto the rug. "You that lawyer who was supposed to marry Marnie but never did?"

"That's me."

"You're a jerk."

He grimaced. "Yeah. Well, now that we've dispensed with the pleasantries, I need to ask you some questions about Rose."

She sniffed. "Rose is dead."

"Yes, I know. I'm the one who contacted you about that."

"You were the stuffy lawyer-voice on the phone, huh? When was that?" She scratched her head with a dirty fingernail. "Tuesday. You called on Tuesday."

He sighed. This was going just great. "Yes, that was me." Months ago, on a Monday.

"So, what do you want?"

"I want to know when Emmit was born."

She took a long drag from her cigarette and blew the smoke in his face. "What does it say on his birth certificate?"

"March thirtieth."

"Yeah, that sounds right."

"But Rose always said his birthday was in June. He was just born when I came back, remember?"

"Rose lied."

"Why would she do that?"

Her eyes narrowed. "Why should I tell you?"

"Why shouldn't you?"

"What's that you got under yer arm?" She poked her cigarette at Harold.

"A dog." He lifted it to give her a better look.

"Humpf. I had one like that when I was a kid. A Yorkie."

It was a schnauzer. "If you tell me what you know about Emmit's birth, I'll let you have it."

She tilted her head and considered him. "To keep?"

"Sure." Myrtle was going to kill him. Her precious Harold going to a home like this.

"All right." Helen snatched the dog out of Taylor's grip. She ran her fingers over his shiny surface and smiled.

"So, when did Rose really give birth?"

She blinked at him. Her eyes unfocused. "Rose? Why we talking about Rose?"

"You're telling me about when she had Emmit."

"She never had Emmit." She kissed the dog on the head with a loud smacking sound.

"What?"

Helen stepped back and slammed the door in Taylor's face. "Go away."

"Hey!" He beat on the wood. He pounded and pounded until his fist smarted. He called her name, but she didn't open it again.

Her face appeared for a moment at the window. "You idiot!" She shouted out to him one last time before she disappeared. "Emmit ain't Rose's kid. Rose couldn't have no kids."

If he'd still been holding Harold, the dog would have dropped and smashed to a million pieces.

22

Everything was going fine until Egg showed up. Again. And this time at the nice store where Auntie Mar-ee couldn't just lock the door and pretend because other people were there too. They gathered around the funny tables, smiled, and drank that yucky brown stuff. Emmit had tasted it for the first time last week. Ick. It smelled a lot better than it tasted. But people drank it anyway and smiled about it.

Sometimes people didn't make any sense at all.

But he still liked to hug them. This morning he hugged everybody, a great big tall man with suspenders, a shorter man who smelled like dirt, a woman who didn't seem to like to hug, and especially that pretty girl with the yellow hair and sky-colored eyes. Vi-let. He liked Vi-let. Everybody else called her Daisy.

He liked hot chocolate too. And doughnuts. Except Auntie Mar-ee still hadn't made him a single doughnut. He had to have cookies instead.

He sat at the crayon table with his legs folded in front of him, a nice cookie, and a picture book with really thick pages. He breathed in cookie smell and that dark stuff they called coffee. He listened to people talking and laughing and his friend Marc-Marc telling jokes. He turned the stiff pages of his book and smiled at the pictures of Jesus.

Then Egg came in.

And Auntie Mar-ee shouted "You get out of here!" in a scary voice like no one had heard before, not even Emmit. And her face turned all red like he'd painted it that color.

Everyone got real quiet, except Egg who said, "Hi, Marnie. You didn't return my calls."

And she hollered "Get out!" again.

Emmit's book fell right on the floor and he couldn't see the pictures of Jesus anymore.

Auntie Mar-ee rushed over to him, shoved another cookie in his hand, and hurried him right back into her little office while everybody's eyes got all round and wide.

She shut the door with a big bang that scared him. And he couldn't see his friends anymore. And he couldn't smell the coffee. And she left his nice book on the floor.

But he could still hear what they were saying out there. They were saying it real loud. He didn't like loud, unless he was the one making the loud. This loud was bad.

He wandered around the room, opened drawers, and ruffled through papers. He picked up the phone and dropped it back down in its cradle a few times. He broke up his cookie and hid it in the top drawer of her desk. He put a pencil up his nose. He poked some buttons on her 'puter.

The screen lit up. Lots of words were on it. He couldn't read them. He recognized one word, though. Taylor.

Mr. Cole was a nice man. He missed him. But he'd see him again real soon. Real, real soon. Emmit pulled a torn piece of postcard from his pocket. It had a picture of buildings, like a school. The letters *L-A-W* were on one of the buildings. He turned it over. Words were there too. And Mr. Cole's name. That's all he could make out. He'd gotten it from Auntie Mar-ee's special shell box.

He tore it up into little pieces and threw them up in the air. They came down like flakes of snow. He liked snow.

He stooped to pick them up again. But the sound of Auntie Mar-ee's voice from the big room stopped him. Her words were all shaky and hissy, like the sound of the air when it came out of the little spout on the coffee machine.

He trembled. He didn't want to hear it anymore. Not yelling, not mad sounds, not sad sounds either. He wanted nice sounds.

Emmit opened the office door and stepped out into the hallway. Auntie Mar-ee stopped talking. Egg stopped talking too. But nobody saw him. Then the loud sounds started up again.

Emmit pushed his glasses up on his nose, turned, and walked straight out the back door.

~~~

If Marnie had a shotgun, she would have nailed him right in the gut. Or maybe a little lower. But she didn't. All she had was a platter full of macaroons. So after she had shoved one in Emmit's hand and pushed him back into her office, she threw three at Craig.

Two missed. The other hit him in the chest.

Her customers stared and fell silent. For a moment, no one moved. Except Craig. He brushed the crumbs off his shirt and kept coming. He didn't even slow but strode right up to the counter and pressed his palms on the stone. "Good grief, Marnie. What's with throwing cookies and rushing out the Down-syndrome kid?"

Marnie took a step back. "Don't you dare talk about him like that."

Craig put his hands on his hips and peered into her face. "What are you talking about?"

She glared back. "Emmit. Like you don't know."

"Good, because that's just who I want to discuss."

"He's fine here with me. Don't you dare call Social Services. Don't you dare interfere. Don't you dare say another word about anything." She sniffed. "And what I tell Taylor is my own business."

His lips twitched into a short smile. "So you did hear me yesterday."

She scowled. "How could I not, with you shouting your head off and then doing the Peeping Tom thing at my window?"

"You ran away fast enough." He crossed his arms. "I guess you're good at that."

His words hurt her. She pushed the pain deeper, buried it. "That's right. And I can run again, so why don't you just go back where you came from and let us be."

"I'm not leaving until I see Emmit."

"You already saw him. That's good enough."

"I did not, and no it isn't."

"Why do you need to see him at all?"

"I promised Rose that if anything ever happened to her, I'd make sure Emmit was okay."

She raised her eyebrows. "You're the hero?" She took a step toward him. "Not in this show. So listen up. Emmit's okay. I'm okay. We're both okay. No thanks to you."

He sighed. "All right, maybe I deserved that. But you said you didn't want him before, so what's to say you don't want him now?"

How could he know that? Had he been snooping around her friends, discovering how she'd tried to get Emmit into a home? She wouldn't put it past him. Her fingers wrapped around a thin plastic jug. "You'd better get out of here, or else..."

He grimaced. "Or else you'll throw that vanilla syrup at me too? How do I know you won't try to get rid of Emmit, like you did—?"

Her hand trembled. "Don't say another word."

His lips pursed. "Marnie…" He shook his head, then turned away and looked out the window. For a long while, neither spoke.

The bell on the door jingled, and a policeman entered.

Thank goodness. Marnie focused on him. "Hey, Pete, the usual?"

Craig moved aside, just a little.

Pete glanced around the room. "Yeah, the usual. Everything all right in here?"

Marnie threw a look at Craig. "Everything's A-Okay." She emphasized the *okay,* narrowed her eyes at Craig, then grabbed a cup and moved behind the espresso machine.

Craig tapped his knuckles on the counter. "We're not finished yet. I can wait."

She added espresso and caramel to the cup and topped it with frothy milk. "Then you can wait until you-know-where freezes over with long, skinny icicles."

"Get out your snowsuit."

"There's nothing you can say that I want to hear. There never has been."

"Things change."

"Not enough."

Pete stepped up to the counter. "Got any macaroons today? The guys were asking for them at the station."

Marnie let out a long sigh and capped Pete's cup. "Sorry, Pete. They're all gone."

"Sold out already?"

She frowned and handed him his drink. "Not exactly. I've got chocolate chip ready, though."

"Those will have to do. Two dozen." He glanced at Craig. "Don't remember seeing you in here before."

Craig glanced down at his shoes. "My first time."

Pete took the cookies Marnie handed him, then picked up his cup. "We cops love it. We're in here all the time."

Craig cleared his throat. "Thanks for the tip, Officer."

"You're welcome." He tucked the cookie bag under his arm and strode toward the door. The bell jingled again as he left.

Marnie refocused on the man in front her. The man she'd gotten used to not thinking about, not remembering, pretending he never existed.

But he existed now. And again he wanted to take something. At least that's what she suspected. "What's Emmit have to do with you, anyway?"

He stared at her. "You know, in some ways, I've got as much right to him as you have."

She knew it. He did want to take the boy. "That's just stupid. I'm his family."

He moved closer. "You should be. I want you to be. But you ran away, remember? What's to say you aren't going to run away again?"

"He's happy here. And so am I."

"Yeah? Where were you on his third birthday when he almost choked on a piece of cardboard? Where were you on his first day of school? Where were you when your sister slipped on that patch of ice and Emmit had no one? Huh?"

"That's not fair."

"Life isn't. You know that."

"Of course I know it. You taught me that."

"I've tried to make amends, Marnie. I've been there for Rose and for Emmit. I've tried to be a good guy."

"And that makes up for everything you said that night?"

His jaw hardened. "No. I was stupid. And mean."

"Yeah, you were."

He smoothed his hand over his ponytail in a way that irritated her even more. His nose wrinkled. "I know why you can't forgive me. It's because you can't forgive yourself."

Heat rose in Marnie's face. She took a deep breath. "Nothing good ever comes from seeing you, Craig. Every time you come into my life, I lose. Do you understand?"

"It doesn't have to be that way."

"I won't lose Emmit. You can't take him."

"That's not what I'm saying. I'm not here to—"

"You leave us alone. You. Get. Out."

"Not until you promise me."

"Promise you what?"

"The truth, Marnie. We have to tell the truth."

"I have." Her voice rose.

"You wanna bet?" His did too. "They deserve the truth, Taylor and Emmit. When that's done, then I'll back off." He glared at her.

Marnie shivered. Not this time. *I won't play for the truth again. I don't have the right cards.*

She wrapped her arms around herself and squeezed. For a moment, she was back at that table again, all those years ago, with its dimes and nickels, cards and chips. But now Craig demanded truth and she was the one who wanted someone to just drop it. But then her life changed forever and she didn't know it. Now it was changing again.

Her throat closed. She forced words through it anyway. "This is not a poker game."

"You'd better fold. You can't win this one."

Except this time, she had to. It couldn't be like before. She couldn't lose a son. Not again. *Oh, God, not again...*

Marnie blinked as the memory rushed back, engulfing her, drowning her, making her ache with a pain she'd tried for over fifteen years to hide in a box on a shelf. But the box was opened, and its images spilled into her mind.

She could hear her mother pleading, begging, crying. Confessing. "I couldn't help myself. The drugs were right there."

She could smell the cigarettes on the woman's breath. She could see her red-rimmed eyes as her gaze burrowed into the floor and her fingers gripped a prescription bottle so tightly her knuckles turned white.

"You took them all?" Marnie held out her hand.

Helen rubbed the scar on her upper lip.

"Give it to me."

Helen's arm shook as she raised it and dropped the empty bottle into Marnie's hand.

Marnie glanced at the bottle. "You had it refilled too? And stole all those pills as well? How could you? Rose needs these pain pills. You know that."

Her jaw hardened. "I need them more."

"I thought you were clean."

Helen shrugged.

Rose moaned from the other room.

Helen licked her lips. "We can say the others fell down the sink. Doc will give us a new prescription."

"So you can steal those too?"

Rose's voice grew louder. "Marnie, is that you?"

"I'll be right in, Rose." The baby kicked. Marnie touched her belly and felt a tiny foot pressing against her palm.

"My chest hurts. I need something for it." Rose's words ended in a groan.

Marnie dropped her hand and glared at her mother. "Rose was right. I should have never tried to find you." She shook her head.

"Better get her more pills."

Marnie squeezed the bottle in her fist. "And keep them under lock and key." She stomped toward the phone.

Her mother followed. "There's just one thing."

She turned. "Yeah, what's that?"

"When that Richie-Rich boyfriend of hers and his longhaired friend were here the other day, the ponytail guy caught me taking the pills."

"Craig? He knows?"

Helen nodded. "Promised not to tell the police or that stuck-up William."

"That's good."

Helen sniffed. "'Cept there's a catch."

Of course there was. "What?"

"Seems he wants the date he won. Said you'd know what he was talking about. Something about a poker game."

The baby kicked again. "He told you about that? Did he mention the ride on my bike too?"

"Said something about that being part of the deal. Guess he doesn't know you're knocked up." Helen rubbed her nose. "You'll do it for me, won't you? Won't do no harm." Her tone turned wheedling.

She pointed the empty prescription bottle at her mother. "I'll do it if you promise to stay away from Rose and her medication from now on. You don't step foot in this house unless someone else is here watching you. You don't call and ask if you can come over. You don't 'pop in for just a minute.' Nothing. Do you hear me?"

"My goodness, you're the bossy one all of a sudden. What happened to all your talk about second chances?"

Rose called again from the other room.

Marnie grimaced. "I won't let you hurt Rose anymore. I'll go on the date, but that's it. We're done. Okay?"

"Okay."

Except that wasn't it. And it wasn't done. Not by a long shot.

In some ways it all seemed inevitable. And yet for fifteen years she'd gone over every detail wondering what she should have done differently, how she could have stopped it from happening at all. But in each replay, events still unfolded just like they had that night. Craig was still as horrible, and she was still as stupid.

All because she bailed out her mother and paid her poker loss with one fake date. Because how could it hurt? He'd drive her motorcycle to the club just like she'd promised. She'd take a taxi and wear a baggy shirt to cover her seven-month bulge. Then they'd spend a couple hours in a loud nightclub with loud music, loud voices, loud dancing, and loud, sweaty bodies. She'd endure some shouted conversation with a guy she could barely stand. Maybe a couple drinks—his something amber and strong smelling, hers a simple Shirley Temple. What could go wrong?

But "wrong" started as soon as she refused to dance with him.

He grabbed her arm and blew sour breath in her face. "Hey, I thought you were supposed to be the wild one."

"What are you talking about?"

"At the party, remember?"

She did. She was Rose's wild and crazy sister. Of course.

"So loosen up a bit, would ya?"

"I don't dance."

He snorted. "And you don't drink. Some fun you are."

He shoved his glass into her hand. "Come on, just a little sip. Think of it like medicine."

She shoved it back. "No way."

The music changed from one loud, obnoxious song to another. He dropped his glass onto a table and pulled her closer. "Dance with me. You owe me. I won that poker game fair and square."

She tried to wriggle away. "Sure. Real fair. Now let me go."

"We're going to dance." He yanked her against him. Then his eyes grew wide. He shoved her away.

And that's when she should have been suspicious, should have known something was wrong by the way he was looking at her, like a cat who just stopped licking his chops because the milk was sour.

"What's that under your shirt?"

The breath whooshed out of her. "What do you mean?"

"Are you pregnant?"

"What business is that of yours?"

"You went and got yourself knocked up by that namby-pamby lawyer dude, didn't you?"

"What if I did?"

Craig shook his head. "You make me sick. You think he's gonna marry you just because you got a baby?"

Her jaw tightened. "That's not why I—"

"Yeah, right. Try telling him that. Does he know?"

"Not yet. Why do you care?"

"Wait till I tell William that this is the way the Wittier girls try to snag a husband."

Ice settled in Marnie's gut. "Don't." She wouldn't ruin it for Rose, not this time. It was bad enough when he'd met their mother, just briefly, and hadn't shown up again for a month. But now…

Craig leaned closer. "Just because William is slumming, doesn't mean he'd accept some brat kid if your sister forgot to take the pill. And

I'm betting Cole won't either. He left you before he knew, and he ain't coming back once he finds out. No guy in his right mind would."

"Taylor will be back." But would he?

"Right, and what are you going to tell him then? 'Here's your baby, honey cheeks.'" Craig's voice became high and mocking. "'Guess you have to marry me now.'" He snorted.

Marnie swallowed. It wasn't like that. Taylor wouldn't think… She imagined handing him the baby with its cleft lip and who knew what other problems. She imagined him looking at her, thinking, believing she'd tried to trap him. With a child. Taylor, who wanted nothing more than to defend kids. Taylor, who would look at her and know she didn't want this baby. That she didn't love it like she should. Would he believe she was just using the child to trap him? He'd hate her for that. And she'd deserve it.

And then, maybe William would believe Rose would try the same thing. How could her one mistake ruin not only her relationship with Taylor, but spoil Rose's chances with William too?

"Guys don't marry girls like you. Or Rose."

She'd always known it. That's why she'd always protected herself from the danger of love. Why she promised herself she'd never get pregnant like this, never have a baby out of wedlock. Never fall into the stereotype of the girl from the wrong side of the tracks.

Except she was that girl. No good. Not worthy. And knocked up. Craig knew it. And soon Taylor would know it too.

"Get out of here. You disgust me. And if you think I'm going to let that slutty sister of yours pull this same trick, you've got another thing coming."

Marnie stumbled backward. "I didn't want to go out with you anyway."

He picked up his glass and downed the last bit of alcohol. "Yeah?

Well, this is the last date you'll be seeing for a long, long time." He shook his head and sneered. "Guess that's what I get for slumming too. Maybe Cole deserves what he got. Crazy broad." He threw the motorcycle keys to her and turned his back.

She stared down at the keys. They called to her, beckoned her. *Run away. Flee. Get away while you can.* Away from the images he'd created in her mind, away from the accusations, away from the fear that Taylor would never understand, away from the certainty that she'd become everything she always dreaded she would be. And it was the baby's fault.

"I never wanted this baby anyway!" She turned and raced out the door. "I never wanted—" Her voice choked. "I never…"

She spotted her Harley and ran toward it. The doctor said not to ride while pregnant, and she'd been good about that. But now she didn't care. Didn't care about herself. Didn't care about Taylor. Didn't care about the life growing inside her. It was a mistake. She had something bad inside, and that something bad was a baby. Sick, deformed, wrong. Just like she was. She didn't want it. Didn't want him.

She started the bike, kicked off, and revved toward the street. Craig's face swam before her vision, then morphed into Taylor's. "You tried to trap me, Marnie. How could you? How could you use a child to get to me?" She saw a baby's face, marred with scars and a huge hole in his upper lip. The baby screamed. Tears formed in Marnie's eyes, blurring her vision.

She turned a corner, kept riding, not knowing where she was going. It started to sprinkle. She drove faster, not caring when the sprinkle turned to rain and mixed with the tears running down her cheeks.

The bike rose over a hill and she saw the ocean, wide, vast, and angry. Angry like Craig, angry like Taylor, angry like God. Angry at her.

She turned away from the ocean. The bike's wheels slipped out from under her. The world tipped, spun, with the bike twisting, whirling into a blur of metal, rain, and black pavement. Pain lanced through her. And she knew nothing but the whine of the bike, the agony of it crushing her, the scrape of pavement, and blood everywhere.

The baby.

The thought of him came to her through the pain. Her hand reached toward her stomach. But there was nothing but blood. Blood and pain and brokenness and the sickening knowledge that she killed him. Because she didn't care enough, didn't love enough. But it wasn't the baby who was bad. It was her. Just like her mother said.

She killed her son. And worse, she killed Taylor's.

The image faded, left her nauseous, trembling, her palms sweaty on the coffee shop's counter before her. And the question, deep within her, that she never wanted to face, never wanted to acknowledge.

Had she crashed her bike that day on purpose?

Because sometimes, in the back of her mind, she suspected she could have stopped it if she'd tried hard enough. She could have saved him.

Craig stepped closer. "The truth, Marnie. That's all I'm asking. I want to see Emmit, and then it's time for the truth."

She shook her head. How could the truth help her now? Taylor would hate her. Emmit would hate her. Her friends would look at her with disgust in their eyes. She stared down at her hands. They would know about the something bad. They would all see it.

"It's time. You know it is."

"Why?" Her voice cracked and fell.

"Because Rose is dead, and you can't hide anymore."

She raised her head. "All right, you want the truth?" Her voice wavered. "I killed my son." The words sickened her. "How's that for the truth?"

"Get Emmit."

She focused on her customers, her store, the wild tables, the mismatched chairs, the lines of books on the shelves on the far side of the shop. She would lose them all. But that would be better than losing Emmit. He was hers now. They belonged together, despite her sin, despite her mistakes, despite everything she had done and regretted.

Marnie swallowed and raised her voice so all could hear. Craig was right. It was time for the truth. "I killed my son." There, she'd confessed. Wasn't that enough? "I won't run anymore. I can't. Not this time."

Craig's eyes narrowed. "What's changed you, Marnie?"

She refused to look at him. "Emmit has."

"Why?"

She drew herself up to her full height. Her heart hammered in her chest. A month ago she was looking into group homes. A month ago he was driving her crazy. He still drove her crazy. And yet she'd risk everything to keep him. She'd even risk the truth. Because now, now...

She took a deep breath. "Because I love him."

The words shimmered between them.

And they were true.

A stocky man with bright blue eyes strode toward them and tapped Craig on the shoulder. Jimmy Henley, still smelling like the construction site.

Craig turned.

Jimmy pointed to the door. "I think the lady wants you to leave."

An older man rose and approached Craig as well. Jerry Boutry. He stepped to the door and opened it. "Get along now."

Then another man stood, and a woman, and even one of the teens who only came in to drool over Daisy.

Marcus came from around the bookshelves. Daisy joined him.

Finally even old Josephina waddled up and jabbed Craig with the cane she was using. "Young man, we'll have no quakes in here today. That boy belongs with Miss Marnie, and that's the way it's going to be."

They all had heard her, yet they stood by her anyway. All of them. How could they? Why did they?

A soft hand touched her shoulder. "You don't worry about a thing, honey."

Marnie blinked. Warmth flooded through her. She turned toward Craig. Her voice trembled. "You heard them."

Craig stared at her with narrowed eyes. "You *have* changed. I'm glad." He nodded once and walked to the front door.

Marnie turned away and headed for her office. "Emmit?"

He didn't answer.

"Emmit." She frowned and opened the office door.

But Emmit wasn't there. Not on the chair, not on the floor, not even climbing the shelves or hiding under the desk.

She stepped back out into the hall.

The door at the back of the hall was open, leading to the alley beyond.

Marnie ran toward it and through the open doorway. She glanced down the alley. Nothing was there but a white-and-gray seagull perched on a green dumpster. "Emmit!"

No one answered her call.

She should have known. Craig had come, and again she'd lost her son.

23

*T*aylor had gotten so used to the madness he didn't notice it anymore. Except for today. Today, he heard, and it made his stomach turn.

He clutched the papers in his lap and listened to the three children of Mrs. Flora Higgins bite and devour one another. It didn't matter that the will he'd just finished reading was fair, evenhanded, and generous to all. It didn't matter that the sum total of Flora's possessions equaled far less than any of them would make in the next few months, and everything she owned could be purchased new down at the local Furniture Mart for a few thousand dollars. It didn't even matter that the sun splashed through the window in Taylor's inner office and there was nothing Flora liked better than to sit in the sun and soak up the rays.

Which was probably why she'd died of skin cancer.

But all that mattered was that Flora had left the dining room set to John when it was Linda who really needed it. After all, Linda's table was made from particle board and was fifteen years old. John's wife, Lisa, just bought a new set last year. Ah, but that set was for the entertainment room, not the dining room. And poor Debbie didn't have a dining room set at all, never mind that she didn't even have a dining room to put it in. Apparently she'd make it fit into the tiny one-bedroom apartment she was renting after her divorce. Except Linda was sure her mother had meant to leave the set to her. Hadn't she said so nearly on her deathbed?

John slammed his hand down on Taylor's desk. "Fine! But I want the grandfather clock, then."

And so the bickering started again until Taylor was tempted to slam his own hand down on the desk and tell them Flora had left everything to charity.

Instead he kept quiet until the arguing turned to nasty accusations.

"You should have…"

"You weren't even there…"

"You're the one who said the doctor should…"

"I was only trying to…"

"So I deserve the…"

"Mom would have never left that to you."

"If she'd known…"

"The truth?"

At that, Taylor stood and walked out into the front office. No one noticed. He wandered to the far end of the room and gazed out the window. From here, he could just glimpse the cold Atlantic between the buildings and busy streets. Out beyond the push and press of people lay the wildness and mystery of the ocean. Yet here's where he stayed, in this crowded little building, on this crowded little street, with his private inner office now crowded with bickering little people who couldn't come to grips with the loss of their mother.

He sighed. Sibling relationships were strange. They loved, they hated, they grasped, they stole. It had always been that way, from when he first took over the estate-planning practice until now. And even before that. Marnie and Rose had been no different, squabbling over their mother, their friends, the parties, the clothes, the shoes. Borrowing and complaining, deciding what the other deserved and what they didn't, judging and—

Taylor's thoughts screeched to a halt. Sibling relationships *were* strange. And maybe that explained everything. The birth certificate, the hospital wristband, the secrecy, the warnings. Because if Emmit wasn't Rose's, then maybe...

Taylor pressed his hands into the windowsill and leaned forward until his forehead touched the glass. It was impossible, crazy. Emmit couldn't be Marnie's.

Because she would have told him, wouldn't she?

No. The answer came to him in a flash of certainty. Marnie wouldn't have told him a thing if she was ashamed. He let his breath out in one long whoosh.

If it's true, it changes everything.

Everything he thought. Everything he'd assumed about Marnie, about himself, about God. Everything would change.

God, do I have a son?

"Are you okay?"

Taylor turned from the window toward the red-haired woman behind him. "You aren't God."

Nancy smiled. "Good observation. Does that mean you're okay?"

"Nope, I don't think so."

She raised her eyebrows. "Shall I go out and get you a coffee? The usual decaf mocha from around the corner?"

"No. But I need you to cancel my appointments for the next week."

"You going somewhere?"

"Maybe."

"You want me to get rid of the Higgins clan in there too?" She stabbed her thumb in the direction of his personal office.

Taylor grimaced. "No, let them argue. They may as well get it over with." He sighed. "I'll never understand why death makes people so greedy."

Nancy wrinkled her nose. "It seems like that, doesn't it? But in the twelve years I've worked for you, I guess I've learned one thing."

"What's that?"

"It's not about the stuff."

"You could have fooled me."

She glanced back at his inner office door and lowered her voice. "They just lost their mother. They've had a loss they couldn't control and didn't want."

He knew what that was like. "So?"

"So they do what people do. They grab on to anything they can. They clutch, they horde, they grasp."

"A dining room set won't bring their mother back."

She looked at him. "Of course not. But people would rather hang on to things that mean nothing than admit they haven't the power to hang on to the things that do."

A chill skittered through him. "What do you mean?"

Nancy skewered him with her glance. "It seems to me that most folks would rather be king of a pile of junk than acknowledge they aren't king at all."

"Than accept another King?"

She clucked her tongue. "Because then there's no control. Another King might do anything."

Taylor nodded. "Even let a mother die." Or a life plan. Or an engagement. Or a dream. Loss was loss. And Nancy was right. It wasn't about the stuff. It was about clinging to control. False control. John, Linda, and Debbie couldn't stop the loss of their mother, but they thought they might control the loss of her dining room set, her grandfather clock, her sofa, her teaspoon collection. So they bickered and fought, grasped and grabbed.

Nancy adjusted her glasses. "What choice do they have?"

Taylor paused before answering. "To let go?" He couldn't do that. He couldn't just let go, release the loss, move on. Could he?

"Yes. They have to. Because she's already gone."

Long gone. Fifteen years gone. "That doesn't seem to matter, does it? They're still grasping."

"The sad part is that all the grabbing and griping isn't going to make any difference at all, even to the one who keeps the dining room set, the clock, and whatever else they're going on about in there."

"It's crazy, isn't it?"

Nancy shuddered. "More than that, it's ugly. Can you hear what they're saying to each other?" She nodded in the direction of the room.

Taylor quieted and listened to the siblings.

"Mother always thought you were a two-bit loser anyway." Debbie's words ended in a whine.

"She never said that."

John's tone sharpened. "Do you really want me to tell you what she thought about you?"

"She always liked you best because you were born first."

"You were the baby."

"I want the sofa set. I don't care what it says in the will."

This time, Taylor shuddered. He turned toward Nancy. "I'm like them, aren't I?"

She made a face. "Of course not."

But he was. Just like them, he too had lost the one he loved, and instead of honoring that love, he'd clung on to the meaningless furnishings of a woman long gone. Here he was, stuck in the same place he'd been fifteen years ago, not married, not taking any chances, not doing any of the things God once called him to do. He just kept hanging on to the little bit of nothing she'd left him—this town, this place, this practice.

He really was just like John, Linda, and Debbie in the other room. Except he'd had no one to struggle with except God. God, who wanted him to let go. God, who had never stopped pursuing him. God, who wanted the past for Himself.

But Taylor had hung on to the hurt, the memories, and the old hopes of that summer for all he was worth. To Emmit. To his business. To the trappings of a past long gone. And all the while, the will, God's will, read that all those hurts, those dreams, the disappointments, and the doubts belonged not to Taylor, but to God.

And then Taylor lost Emmit too.

So, what was God asking of him now? To finally hand over what was never his? To let go at last? To place the past, the present, and the future into God's hands and walk forward in freedom from all the "stuff" of the past?

Taylor looked around the main office, at the bookcases, the files, the desks, the shabby carpet, the faded window coverings, the worn sign on the glass door. He took a deep breath. How were they any different from a dining room set and a grandfather clock? They weren't, because he was hanging on to them just as tightly. He needed to follow the dream God had given him so long ago.

"Nancy, don't cancel my appointments for next week. Cancel all my appointments. Period."

She glanced at him and smiled. "It's about time. You know I've been wanting to retire for years."

"I know."

"So, can I tell Ted to plan that cruise to the Caribbean?"

"I thought he wanted to take you moose hunting in Canada?"

She grinned. "That too." She stepped closer and hugged him. "Been waiting a long time for you to stop hanging on to this old place."

He hugged her back. "Guess it's not easy to let go."

"Kinda hard to receive something new when your hands are closed tight around something old."

He turned again toward the ocean view. "That it is, Nancy. That it is." It was time to let go and live the life God gave him now, in all its joy, in all its sorrow, in all its wildness.

He couldn't let the loss of her define him anymore. Because maybe, just maybe, he had a son.

Taylor pressed his hands into the windowsill and stared out at the bit of ocean he could see. *I loved you, Marnie Wittier, with all my heart. Thank You, God, for giving me time with her. Thank You for showing me love, even if it came with loss. And now I'm done with hanging on. I don't need to be stuck here anymore, wallowing in this place, in the past. Help me to go forward, to leave the dining room set, the sofa, the china, and even...* He paused. *Even a sixteen-year-old diamond ring in Your hands so I can be who You want me to be, do what You want me to do, go where You want me to go.*

And he knew exactly where that was. Pacific Grove, California.

Nancy touched his arm. "I'll make the arrangements."

He smiled. "Thank you."

The phone rang. Nancy hurried to answer it. She mumbled a few words into the receiver, then pointed to the earpiece in Taylor's ear. "It's Craig from Child Services. He says it's urgent."

Taylor tapped the button on his earpiece. "Craig?"

"You've got to get out here quick." Craig's voice sputtered in his ear. "Marnie has lost Emmit."

"What do you mean?"

"Emmit. He's gone."

Taylor pushed back the hair on his forehead and stared out the window into the busy street. His heart thudded in his chest. He took a deep breath. "I think I know where we can find him."

24

*T*hey'd searched everywhere. The doughnut shop, the music store, the store where Marnie had bought Emmit a new pair of shoes. She'd been back to the bungalow five times, then over to Books and Brew, to the church and back, to every store within a mile of the coffee shop, every home around her house. And no one had seen a boy with thick glasses and blond hair.

Her police friends had called in on their radios, others combed the streets calling his name, Jimmy enlisted his construction buddies, and Kinna called the hospital. But Emmit was nowhere to be found.

Marnie paced back and forth in front of the bookcase in her bungalow and tried to think. Where could he have gone? It had been eight hours since she shoved him into her little office to keep him from Craig, and she was no closer to finding him than the moment she realized he'd escaped out the back door. Despite all the running, all the fear, all the panic, all the desperate looking, Emmit was still gone.

Lord, help! What am I going to do? How am I going to find him?

She glanced up at her box of regrets, a box full of reminders of everything she'd ever done wrong. It was supposed to help her not to make those same mistakes again. But it didn't help. All the regrets in the world hadn't stopped the worst thing from happening a second time. Despite every bit of paper, every memento, every word scribbled in black ink, she'd lost her son. Again. She'd lost Emmit.

Marnie paused and picked up the dirty pair of socks Emmit had left on the coffee table. She scrunched them in her hand. Then she ran her fingers over the funny picture of a dog he'd drawn at school. She straightened the small stack of his CDs on the middle shelf of the bookcase. And she waited for the phone to ring.

It didn't.

She paced some more, imagining all the horrible things that could have happened to him. Hit by a car, kidnapped, fallen in a hole, broken, bloody, hurt, and lost. Crying for his mother when all he had was a worthless aunt who didn't know how to find him.

I knew I would fail him someday. She didn't know someday would come so soon.

The doorbell buzzed.

Marnie raced to the door and threw it open. "Did they find him?"

Josephina stood on her front stoop. "Sorry, mija. This earthquake's not over yet."

Marnie's stomach turned. She ran her hand through her hair. "Where could he be? How could I have let this happen?"

Josephina frowned. "What do you mean 'let it happen'?"

She clenched her teeth. "I should have stopped it. I should have—"

"Should have, would have, could have—none of them do any good." Josephina waved her hand in the air, then reached out to tip up Marnie's chin with her finger. "Look mija, Down's kids bolt. So there's no use placing blame. All we can do is look, and hope, and pray. I came here to pray."

"But this is my fault. God's not going to listen to me."

"Fault doesn't matter. God always listens. What matters is that we do what we can to find Emmit." She dropped her hand and glanced around at the room behind. "Are you going to invite me in?"

Marnie drew a trembling breath. She'd never had anyone in her home before. Except Emmit. He changed everything. "Of course, come on in. Have a seat."

Josephina walked through the door, across the entry hall, and settled onto the couch. Marnie shut the door and followed.

Josephina looked up at her. "Any more ideas where he might be?"

"I've been over it and over it. We've looked everywhere I've ever taken him. I should have put another lock on that door. A big, huge lock. I should have kept a better eye on him. I have never—"

"Mija."

"What if he's hurt or someone took him or he's, he's—"

"Mija."

She clasped her hands together and squeezed. "What?"

"This quake will pass. Regrets about what happened yesterday and fears about what may happen tomorrow keep you from living now. And that sweet boy needs you in the now. You've got to let the rest go."

"Let it go? How?"

"You believe in God?"

"Of course."

"And is this God of yours big enough to hold the past and the future both?"

"Yes."

"Why?"

Marnie frowned and sat next to Josephina on the couch. "What do you mean, 'why'? Because He's God. He's supposed to be big enough for anything. He's omni-something-or-other."

"I think they call it *omnipotent*."

"Yeah, that's it."

"But how do you know? When has He ever held the past and the future in His hands?"

Marnie looked down at her white-knuckled fingers. She loosened them, turned her hands over, and let her gaze rest on her palms. "He did it at the Cross." The darkest moment in all of history, when the Son of God bled, cried out in agony, and died. The moment when all hope seemed lost and everything that had ever happened appeared meaningless because the darkness had won.

But it hadn't. The darkest moment was also the brightest, because all the past, present, and future changed in that moment. It was redeemed. Death defeated. Hope reborn. And if God could do that, then maybe her past, her future could be redeemed too. And perhaps this darkest moment could lead to the light.

Josephina's voice lowered to a whisper. "That's right. So give them to Him. Give Him yesterday, give Him tomorrow, and give Him this moment too. That's what I do every day. It's what I have to do. All I can do is do my best now and trust God to take care of the rest."

"Trust Him, huh?"

"Pete and his officers have been searching for Emmit for most of the day. They haven't found him yet. But God knows where the boy is. We've got no choice but to trust Him now, do we?"

Marnie rubbed her hands over her upper arms, then squeezed. "I guess not."

"Well, let's pray." She lifted her hands and looked up to the ceiling. "Lord, we put Emmit's safety in Your hands. Bring him back to us. And help Miss Marnie to ride out the quake." Josephina dropped her hands, patted Marnie's knee, and rose. "There you go. I'll get back to looking, and you get back to hoping and trusting." She winked, then started toward the front door.

"Thank you, Josephina." Marnie moved around her and opened the door. "I'll call you if anyone hears anything."

Josephina stepped outside and smiled. "I'll be expecting your call soon, then." She nodded, then turned and ambled back out to her car. "Trust Him, mija. Just Him." She pulled open the car door and, a moment later, drove away.

Marnie stood in the open doorway as the breeze blew in from the bay. Could she do it? Could she stop trusting her regrets, stop clinging to her fears, and put it all in God's hands? Could she trust Him enough to leave the should-haves, could-haves, would-haves behind?

She didn't know. She'd clung to them all for so long, but now Emmit needed her. He needed her to let go. And if she could, maybe this time it would be different. She could be different. Not run, but trust. Not regret, but hope.

Help me, Lord. Help me to trust You enough to find Emmit. Help me to stop blaming and start seeing. Show me the truth at last.

Marnie lifted her head and gazed out toward the faraway waves of Monterey Bay. She saw the incoming fog, the rocky shore, the sandy beach.

And she knew where Emmit had gone.

~~~

Marnie parked her Bug and stared out across the beach to the high rocks that jutted out into the water at the far end of the cove. An early evening fog had settled now, obscuring her view of the end of the beach and making the rocks into dim outlines against the water. She slammed the car's door.

Emmit, are you out there?

She wrapped her arms around herself and walked across the parking lot, through the opening in the fence, and down toward the long beach. Sand squished under her shoes. Water rumbled against the shore. She glanced down. No clam holes. There were no clams on California's coast. *God, what am I doing here?*

Finding Emmit.

Why?

Because you said you loved him.

And she did.

It had felt good to say it. She never had, not to Rose, not to her mother, not even to Taylor way back when they crossed that line they should have never crossed. She'd kept silent even then. It took one crazy, aggravating, sweet, annoying, forgiving, frustrating, innocent Down-syndrome boy to break through to her.

Thank You, God. Thank You for Emmit, Your gift to me. I do love him.

"We love because he first loved us." The Bible quote from Sunday's service whispered through her mind. She loved Emmit because he loved her first. Despite her mistakes, her anger, her yelling at him and trying to get rid of him, he still loved her. He forgave. And taught her how to love him. To love again.

She never dreamed she'd be able to. Never thought she could heal. But then he loved, and he showed her the love of others—the love of her friends at church; the love of her regular customers, who defended her when she needed them; the love of Marcus; Daisy; Joe, who stood by her when she thought she was alone. And in some ways, the love of Taylor Cole, who she'd hurt more than anyone, and yet in all his e-mails he never accused, never blamed, never lashed out.

Of course, he didn't know the truth, but God did. God knew every last horrible detail, and yet He'd surrounded her with a love she never recognized before. His love. And all He asked was for her to trust Him, to let go. She closed her eyes.

Lord, as soon as I find Emmit, I'm going to write that e-mail to Taylor. I won't wait anymore. Craig was right. Taylor deserves the truth.

Marnie hurried down the beach, composing the note in her mind.

Dear Taylor, it's time you knew the truth and how sorry I am…

She kicked a bit of sand with her foot and imagined Emmit racing along the sand in front of her, with that awkward stiff-legged gait of his. He would run along the wet shore with his pant legs rolled up, dashing in and out as the waves washed toward him. Then he'd turn and laugh and push his glasses up on his nose. Next he'd probably start singing about Mary and her lamb, and his voice would mix with the roar of the bay and the squawk of the sea gulls and the bubble of surf against shore.

Marnie breathed in the scent of the sea. She'd forgotten how much she loved the beach, with the ocean rolling, the waves frothing, and the sand tickling her toes. She'd forgotten the briny smell of it and the refreshing chill of the breeze off the water. She'd forgotten why she once loved to let the coolness kiss her cheeks as she danced along the water's edge. This was wild, free, wondrous. And even without the clam holes, it spoke to her of hope. Hope that maybe, just maybe, she'd find love again. She'd find Emmit.

She glanced out across the sand. Several yards away, a family was playing in the surf. A mom, a dad, and four small girls. The older girls raced into the water, squealing their delight while the younger two, maybe twins, sat just out of reach of the water and tossed sand into each other's hair. Their mother turned, and Marnie spied the sling around her middle, with a baby peeking from its folds. A baby boy.

Marnie allowed her gaze to rest on the baby. *A son.*

Lord, help me…help me heal…

Tears welled in her eyes. She wept for Emmit, for Taylor, for the son they never had. Then the pain eased. She glanced at the baby again, and this time it didn't feel like a knife plunging into her gut.

One of the twin girls scooped up two handfuls of sand and tossed them into the air. She laughed and raced along the water's edge.

Marnie watched the girl, her head flung back, her arms out, her small feet making shiny indentations in the wet sand.

Then another wave came in and washed her footprints away.

She glanced behind her. Her footprints, too, were being washed away by the water. If only her past mistakes could be like that too, washed clean by the waves of what God had done for her on the Cross. If only her life could be like the smooth sand again, regrets all gone, sins forgotten, shame and pain pulled out to sea.

That's all she'd ever wanted, all she asked for as the ambulance sped her toward the hospital all those years ago, as the EMTs rushed her into Emergency, as the doctors frantically worked to stop the bleeding, put her back together, and save what was left of her life. Those moments were a blur now. She barely remembered the bright lights, the mask-covered faces, the pain that slipped away with the IV in her arm.

But she did remember a voice screaming, crying out for a second chance. Crying about a baby. That voice was hers.

She woke in a hospital room, a cast on her arm, bandages over her forehead, her stomach no longer rounded. Had she gone into labor? Had they taken her dead baby by C-section? She never knew. She didn't want to know. Because she was sure of one thing. The baby was gone. Forever. And it was her fault.

The nurse came in and said she was going to be all right. A familiar face, a friend of Doris's. But the woman was wrong. Marnie would never be all right again. How could she be? An hour later, Rose came to see her. She must have been pregnant with Emmit then, but she didn't say so, and Marnie was too wrapped up in her own problems to even notice. That was the trouble all along. She never could see past the bump in her middle to the road beyond. So neither of them talked about a baby. And neither of them said a single word about the life she killed.

Doris never came.

But her mother did. Not long after Rose arrived, her mother slumped through the door. Even now she could remember the one question she asked her mom. "Do you think Taylor will ever forgive me?"

And her mom answered, "How could he, after what you did?"

Marnie left the hospital twenty minutes after Rose and her mother walked out. Broken and bruised, still with blood crusted in her hair and on her face, Marnie took the clothes Rose brought, took the IV out of her arm, and left. Simply left. Before they could confront her with the death of her baby. Before she could see the looks of disgust in their eyes.

She ran away.

She went back to her apartment, packed her bag, and placed that worn silver necklace into her box. And that's when she found it—the ring Taylor had bought for her. A perfect diamond solitaire in a setting of white gold.

She stared at it, not believing, not wanting to believe.

He would have married her. Nothing Craig had said was true. So her baby died for nothing. For nothing. And she could never marry Taylor now.

He deserved better.

She took the first bus out of there. Rode it all the way from ocean to ocean, until she couldn't run any farther. It had brought her here to the very edge of the West Coast, where despite everything she'd tried to do to put the past behind her, she was still bloody, bruised, unable to heal, at least on the inside. At least until now.

She'd hung on to her regrets instead of her joys. She'd kept them locked away. But Emmit poured them out for all the world to see. Through his stubbornness, his inadequacies, his annoying little habits, he showed her that love was more powerful than regret. Love covered a multitude of sins.

"We love because He first loved us." Emmit and God too. Their love had brought healing. It was time she stopped hiding not only her regrets, but herself, her heart, away. You could choose to hide or you could choose to love. Emmit taught her to choose love. The past was gone. She couldn't hang on to it anymore.

Marnie started to run. "I love you, you crazy kid!" She yelled it at the very top of her voice. Then she yelled it again. The words echoed off the ocean and mixed with the sound of laughter. His laughter.

Emmit?

She raced toward the outcropping of rocks. She turned the bend, and there he was, sitting on a stone at the very edge of the water. "I heard you, Auntie Mar-ee. I been waiting for you." He stood.

She threw her arms around him.

"I like hugs."

She squeezed tighter. "I know you do. I do too." She let him go.

He rubbed his nose. "I say, 'Come to beach,' and Auntie Mar-ee comes. I like the beach."

"I like the beach too." *I do now, anyway. I do again.*

Emmit strode up to a sandy part of the beach. Then he started to dance. He threw his arms up and twirled, around and around and around, never getting dizzy, never toppling over.

She caught up to him and flung her arms out too. She twirled and dipped and joined his dance. And she sang. *"Mary Had a Little Lamb."*

She sang it badly.

Because at that moment she knew she didn't have to be perfect. She didn't have to sing in harmony. She just had to love, and even then, not perfectly. She just had to dance.

So Marnie sang. She danced. She moved to the song of the ocean, to the waves, and the odd, lilting sound of the laughter of a Down-syndrome boy.

Taylor's hands shook as he read her message on the tiny screen on his phone. Around him voices on intercoms paged passengers, flights flashed on huge mounted monitors, and people hurried by with suitcases in tow. Normally he'd study the faces of those around him as they rushed off to meet loved ones or jogged past to catch another flight. Today, though, all that mattered was the e-mail on the screen, and he hoped nobody was watching his face as he read it.

He took a deep breath, clutched the boarding passes in one hand and his phone in the other. He read her message again. It said the same thing it did the first time.

He and Marnie had had a son. That son was dead.

No wonder she had run. For a moment, he'd begun to hope…but no, that was silly. Emmit couldn't be his son. And this e-mail proved it. But oh, why hadn't she told him all those years ago? Why hadn't she given him a chance to forgive, to comfort, to stand together with her in their loss?

But what she did made sense in its own way. Marnie knew better than anyone how to stand alone, take care of herself, rely on no one. She'd always been able to give, but rarely could she receive.

And now he was going to her to reveal a truth as startling as the one she'd written in her e-mail. And the question would be, had anything changed? Would she be able to accept him now, accept what he would say, believe the truth he'd offer her in return for the confession she'd made?

Truth. He saw it now. Old truth. New truth. And it scared him. But he'd make the trip anyway. All the way to California to share with her the one thing he knew. And to see her face when he did it. Then he'd know. For certain.

God, go with me, go before me, prepare the way. I put this whole trip into Your hands. I won't grasp on to faulty expectations. Not anymore.

The intercom above him hummed. A woman's voice crackled from the speaker. "Now boarding Flight 1062 to Chicago Midway, then on to San Jose."

This was it.

Taylor tucked his phone back into his pocket and touched the elbow of the person next to him. Then he strode forward to board the plane to his destiny.

He walked down the long ramp. He found his seat. He sat down. In six short hours, he would see her again, face to face. And then only God knew what would happen next.

25

*E*mmit moved his hand over the pretty box. He felt the shells. He touched the smooth wood surface. Then he opened the lid.

It had taken him three tries to climb up the bookcase and get it from where Auntie Mar-ee hid it behind the big stack of books. He had to get the scissors down from on top of the refrigerator. Then he had to sneak back to his bedroom and cut the ribbons and open the lock.

She made it hard.

He did it anyway.

Soon Auntie Mar-ee wouldn't have to hide the pretty box anymore. She wouldn't have to lock it. She wouldn't have to tie it up with thick ribbons.

Because Emmit was going to fix it real good.

He put his fingers inside the box and rumpled the papers inside. They seemed cold against his skin. He paused and took his hand out.

He could just hear the sounds of water running in the bathroom down the hall. Auntie Mar-ee was in the shower. She'd be out quick. But not quick enough to stop him.

Emmit tipped up his face to the sunlight streaming through the glass doors. It was warm today. Clear. Just like he liked it. Last night it was cold when they came back from the nice beach and went to Books and

Brew. All his friends had come, even the nice man with the shiny badge and blue shirt and pants that matched. He was a policeman. He told Emmit to never ever run off again. He wanted Emmit to promise.

Emmit didn't promise.

All his other friends patted him on the back and gave hugs and laughed and cried. Sometimes people cry when they're happy. It seemed strange, but it was true. Then Auntie Mar-ee gave everyone free cookies and yucky coffee and everyone talked real loud for a real long time.

He finally got to go home and go to bed. He had to rest because he had big plans for today.

Emmit pushed the glasses up on his nose, then took the box in both hands.

Finally it was time.

He turned over the box and dumped out everything in it. Stuff scattered over the floor. He ran his fingers through the little pieces of paper, over the napkin, to the necklace, the little sword, a seashell, then back to the papers again.

He placed each piece, ever so carefully, in the stream of sunlight.

He pushed them straight, turned them over, and waited. He counted while he waited. "One. Two. Seven. Green. Five. A. B. C. Three!"

Emmit clapped his hands and grinned. Then he gathered up all the papers, the napkin, the necklace, the sword, and all the other stuff and put it back in the box. He added a pretty purple flower he'd picked outside that morning.

He smiled a big, happy smile and closed the box. This time, Auntie Mar-ee would be glad about what he'd done. This time, she wouldn't yell. Maybe she'd even dance.

Because God answered prayer. And He was about to answer a big one.

Emmit put the box in the middle of his bed, grabbed his pants from the dresser, and went out to play with Max.

26

*M*arnie rubbed the towel over her head, then ran her fingers through her hair to make it spiky. She threw on an old pair of sweats-turned-pajamas-turned-sweats-again and stepped out of the bathroom. "Emmit? Are you staying out of trouble?"

She couldn't hear him, and that was never a good sign. She had put two more locks on the door, though, to make sure he didn't escape again.

He wandered out of his room.

"Where's your shirt?"

He looked down at his white chest, as if noticing for the first time it was bare. "Got my pants on."

Well, that was something anyway. Last time they went to the park, she came out of the shower afterward to find him sitting in the middle of the living room with only his underwear on. After that, she figured out that she only had to get him pants he didn't have to zip, button, or snap. She cleared his pant drawers of everything except loose-fitting jeans with elastic waists, sweatpants, and dress pants that he could just pull on.

"You still need a shirt."

"I want this one." He held up a brightly colored Hawaiian shirt with buttons down the front.

"Where did you get that?"

"Vi-let."

"Of course." That girl was always bringing him something. Marnie slapped her hands together. "I guess it's time to learn to button your own shirt, then. Come here." She motioned for him to come closer.

She put the shirt over his shoulders, then lined up the buttonholes with the buttons over his chest. Garishly colored parrots and huge red and yellow flowers stared back at her. This had to be the ugliest shirt she'd ever seen. She hid a smile, then picked up a button and the fabric of the corresponding hole.

"I'll help you with the first one." She took his fingers and moved them to work the button into the hole. "This is called a buttonhole. The button goes into it."

"Like doughnut hole." He stuck his finger through one of the holes and jiggled it around.

She sighed. "Yes, like a doughnut hole." Why was everything always about doughnuts?

"Not a doughnut."

"No."

"Button."

"Yes, now you try."

He grunted, then picked up a button from halfway up the shirt and attempted to shove it through a hole at the bottom. The button went partway in. He huffed. "This hard."

His face turned pink.

Marnie smoothed out the fabric on his shirt front. In a moment, if she wasn't careful, he'd get mad and then he'd throw a fit. She didn't want that. His fits were enough to make her want to run away and hide. But she wouldn't do any more running. And no more hiding either. Not ever again.

No matter what? A voice whispered through her.

"No matter what."

Emmit looked at her. He frowned. "I don't like buttons."

She cleared her throat. "I have some good news for you. It's about doughnuts."

His face brightened. "I like doughnuts."

Ah, that did it. She chuckled. "Yes, I know. And did you know that the doughnut shop on the other side of town is shutting down?"

"That good news?"

"No, but this is. I'm getting their doughnut-making equipment on loan for Books and Brew."

"For store? Doughnuts?"

"Yes, we're going to be able to make doughnuts now. Chocolate doughnuts, sugar doughnuts, glazed doughnuts, any kind of doughnut you want."

He licked his lips. "Yum."

"They'll be the best doughnuts ever. You'll see." She patted his tummy.

He giggled. "Doughnuts good."

Yes, they were. Good to eat, and good for business too. Who would have guessed? But what Emmit didn't know was that making doughnuts might just save her shop. She'd already talked to the churches in the area. Her own church, plus five others had contracted her to provide doughnuts for their Sunday morning fellowship times. And they would let her supply the coffee too. And if that weren't enough, they were even asking her to bring books along she thought would help their congregations. All because of the doughnuts. Those crazy doughnuts Emmit had been bugging her about for months.

Maybe she should have listened sooner. Now because of them, because of him, she'd be able to keep paying Marcus and Daisy and Joe and the rent, and maybe even take Emmit out for real Chinese food instead of cooking ramen in the microwave.

"I eat doughnuts."

"You'll be able to have a doughnut anytime you want. How do you like that?"

"I like it."

"You'd better be careful or you'll turn into a doughnut."

A look of horror passed over Emmit's face. "I'm not a doughnut. Mar-ee doughnut."

She unbuttoned his middle button again and placed the button and buttonhole into his hands. "Now I'm a doughnut, am I? Sweet on the outside, big hole in the middle?" She stopped as the words penetrated.

Emmit's voice softened. "Mar-ee not doughnut anymore."

She sat back on her heels. He was always saying the funniest things. Her tone quieted as well. "You may be right, Emmit. I guess I have been just like a doughnut, sweet on the outside and empty in the center." Empty because of guilt, because of shame, because of what she did all those years ago. That guilt, that regret, was a burden God never meant her to carry. It had eaten right through her.

But now that she saw the hole, acknowledged it, God could make her whole again. God had been wanting to fill that emptiness with the truth for years—His truth, His love, His healing. Emmit had been telling her that all along. And maybe that's what God had been trying to tell her too, as Emmit hollered for doughnuts and wouldn't settle for cookies. Crazy Emmit. Crazy God.

Emmit grinned. He concentrated once again on the button in the middle of his shirt. He picked it up, then stuck out his tongue. He worked the button into the hole. He worked and worked and worked.

"I did it!"

She clapped her hands. "Yay! Good job!"

He beamed. "I look nice."

She buttoned his top button for him as he worked on the bottom one. "Yes, you do."

He raised his chin and adjusted his glasses. "I have to look nice to see the sun."

She stepped back. "Oh, really? You think you're going somewhere today, huh? Who says?"

He smiled. "Sun says."

She laughed. "Well, maybe we can take another stroll on the beach. Would you like that?"

"Not today. Today sun."

"Okay, how 'bout we go down to the pier? Looks like the fog's going to burn off early today."

"No fog. Only sun."

She sighed. Once he got something in his mind, there was no convincing him otherwise. "Okay, you can see the sun."

"Yes."

A knock sounded from the front door.

Marnie shivered. Craig? Again? She thought he said he was going back to Maine. She put a finger to her lips and looked at Emmit. "Shh."

The knock came again, sounding nothing like Craig's incessant pounding.

Emmit stroked his shirt and straightened his shoulders. "He's here. Open door."

Marnie shook her head and lowered her voice to a whisper. "Hush. I'm not opening the door. It might be Craig." Either that, or someone selling something, and she didn't want to open the door for either.

Emmit spoke, just as loudly as ever. "Not Egg. Egg not here anymore."

She grimaced. "How do you know?"

Emmit just smiled. He tugged on the bottom of his eye-wateringly bright shirt and sat on the floor with one hand on Max and a clear view of the front door. "Waiting all done. Big prayer answered now."

Another knock.

She shook her head and turned toward the door. "You're impossible."

His voice tiptoed behind her. "I love you, Auntie Mar-ee."

She paused, glanced back. "Thank you, Emmit. I love you too." She walked up to the door. If Craig was on the other side, she supposed she'd have to face him sometime. It may as well be now. She took a deep breath and gripped the door. *God, help…*

Then she opened it.

And saw him.

"Taylor!" She threw herself into his arms, smelled the musky scent of his aftershave, felt his warmth against her. She squeezed him tight. And for a moment, sixteen years fell away and they were just Taylor and Marnie, in love.

The moment passed.

"Hi, Marnie." His voice was deeper now and held a hint of laughter.

She loosened her grip. Her face flushed. "So, um, are you married?"

"No."

"Engaged?"

"No."

"Girlfriend?"

"Just a horse right now."

She let go and stepped back. "Whew, otherwise that welcome would be a lot more embarrassing." She smoothed her hand over her ugly sweatpants and swallowed. Hard. "I see you still like hats."

He smiled that same smile she remembered, the one that made a dimple just in one cheek, and touched the flat brim. "It's good to see you too."

"I can't believe you came." She didn't mean to sound so breathless, so schoolgirl silly. But she couldn't help it, with her heart doing that wild tap dance in her chest and chanting "he came, he came, he's here" in her ears. She cleared her throat. "Yes, um, good to see you." Really, really good. And he wasn't scowling or angry or red in the face. Maybe he hadn't gotten her e-mail.

"I had to come."

"About time."

"I know."

"Did you get my last e-mail about, about—?"

"Yes."

Her breath stopped. "And?"

"And God owns that furniture now."

She quirked an eyebrow. Maybe he'd gone a little nutty in the last sixteen years. "What?"

"I'll explain later." He moved to the side to reveal a boy standing behind him. "I brought someone." He touched the shoulder of the kid and brought him in front of him. He rested his hands on the boy's shoulders. The boy looked to be in his midteens, with glasses, dark hair, and…and…and an obvious scar on his upper lip.

It couldn't be. "Who's this?"

The Adam's apple bopped in Taylor's throat. He shifted his weight. He pushed back the hair under his hat, just like she'd seen him do a hundred times before. "Marnie, this is Emmit, the real Emmit."

That single sentence sliced to her very core. "No." She breathed the word. This couldn't be Emmit. Emmit was a blond boy with thick glasses, small ears, and an infectious smile. Emmit had Down syndrome. All this boy had was…was a scar on his upper lip.

She gripped the door handle to steady herself. "Emmit?" Craig's words came back to her, shouted at her as she ran from him at the church. *"The baby didn't die."*

Marnie reached out and touched the scar on the boy's lip. Emmit's lip. A scar just like a boy would get from surgery to repair a cleft lip. A scar just like she'd once seen on a woman named Helen Wittier.

She traced the white line with her fingertip as all the pieces fell into place. "Taylor, this is our son."

mmit squeezed his hands tight to keep from clapping them. He grinned wide enough to make his cheeks hurt. Then he hugged Max with a great big hug.

Because it had happened. It finally happened! The big prayer had been answered, and he'd done what he was supposed to do. A family had been put back together. And Auntie Mar-ee had learned to love. Now her family could be whole again. It would be right. And real-Emmit would have his real mother, his real father, his real family. Just like he'd prayed.

God always hears prayers. Even when the answers didn't look anything like what people expected, God answered all the same.

Because of the Son.

Emmit stood and watched so quietlike as Auntie Mar-ee grabbed real-Emmit and hugged him tight. He had taught her to hug like that. Mr. Cole hugged them both. And then they cried. They cried until their noses turned red.

It was a good cry.

But he was too happy to cry. He was happy enough to dance, but he didn't. Instead he waited. He watched. And he tried not to clap and sing. He would sing later. He would sing real good.

Auntie Mar-ee touched real-Emmit's face again and laughed and cried at the same time. It was funny how people could do that. Mr. Cole laughed too. Then he put his arm around both of them and shook his head like he couldn't believe it. Like he was having some kind of dream.

But it wasn't a dream. It was the Son, making things right.

Emmit took a step down the hallway to his room. He paused and watched Auntie Mar-ee look deeply into real-Emmit's eyes, smile, and whisper two words. Words that made real-Emmit cry too.

"Welcome home," she said.

Marnie wiped her nose and hugged her son again. Her son. It was incredible, wondrous, and a bigger quake than even Josephina could measure on the Richter scale. Her son…and Taylor's.

"Our son." Marnie heard Taylor's words, as if they were an echo coming down through the years. Like a dream from a lost memory.

Our son. The words shimmered between them, binding, healing, making her whole. Their son, who didn't die after all. Who lived and breathed, laughed and cried, loved and…finally had come home.

Taylor blew out a long breath. "Wow."

The boy looked up at him and pushed the hair off his forehead just like Taylor used to do. "I always wished you were my dad."

Taylor squeezed his shoulders. "I did too."

Marnie reached back and opened the door wider. Rose. Rose had done this. All of it. "Rose never told you, either of you?"

Taylor moved closer. "Your mom said Rose couldn't have children, not after the surgeries."

Marnie nodded. "So she took mine." It made sense. Rose had tried to protect her from their mother, just as she'd protected Emmit from his. "Because she loved him. She always wanted him, knew he was a gift even when I couldn't see it."

She remembered that night with the motorcycle, the rain, and her own stupidity. When she saw the blood, felt the pain, she believed the baby was dead. And when she woke up without him in the hospital, she knew it to be true. And then she got up and left, ran away. Before the doctor could tell her of the baby's death. Before he could ask her any questions. And before he could even tell her the truth. She had run. Because she was so sure she'd killed him.

But he didn't die. And then no one was left but Rose to claim him as her own, to raise him, to protect him, to love him as a mother should. Until death got in her way. "Rose did what she thought was right, all the way to the end." Rose had always been right. About so many things.

Emmit's face reddened. "She was a great mom."

Marnie sighed and focused on the boy in front of her. The boy who looked back at her with Taylor's eyes, her dark hair, and maybe, if she was lucky, a dimple on his right cheek when he smiled.

Except he wasn't smiling now.

"She was a great sister too." Marnie stepped back and motioned for Taylor and Emmit to enter the bungalow. "But there's still one problem: If you're Emmit, then who have I been taking care of all this time? You saw the boy sitting on the floor behind me, didn't you?" She pointed behind her, then glanced back.

Of course, her Emmit was gone. Probably off to his room to sit in the sunlight again. But Max was there, flicking his tongue, waiting.

Taylor moved around her. "The boy with Down syndrome? Blond hair, glasses, and a big watermelon-slice smile?"

"You saw him."

"He was sitting there, then he got up and walked down the hall. That's the boy you've been writing to me about for the past months?"

Marnie shut the door. "That's him." Her Emmit. The one who changed her, challenged her, and in the end, taught her to love. But if he wasn't the real Emmit, then who was he? And how did he get here? She started toward his room.

Taylor and their son followed.

"I see you still have Max."

"The only pet I've ever owned."

She glanced back at the boy. "I hope you like iguanas."

He grinned, and for a moment, she could almost see a glimmer of Emmit, the old Emmit, shining from the eyes of the new one. "Cool." But he didn't have the dimple.

She stepped into the second bedroom. And there was her Emmit, her sweet Down-syndrome boy, sitting, legs folded up, in a ray of bright sunshine.

"Emmit?"

"All put right now. Family together. Prayer answered. I all done." He stood.

Marnie caught her breath. Her Emmit looked taller now, stronger. "Who are you?" The words came out as a whisper.

He grinned and pushed up his glasses. He walked over and put his hands on real-Emmit's shoulders. "The Son sent me when you prayed. You thought He didn't hear. He heard. He cared. He loved." He paused and glanced from Taylor to Marnie. "And He healed. Your family is whole now."

Tears coursed down real-Emmit's cheeks. "I thought, I thought I was alone."

Down's-Emmit grabbed him in one of his signature hugs. "Never alone." He turned back to Marnie. "I fixed your box for you." He pointed to her box of regrets, now perched in the middle of his bed. "Open it."

"Emmit? I don't understand."

"No questions, just open the box. Box good now. See?" He waved at the box with one hand, while leaving the other arm around her son's shoulders.

Marnie walked over to the box and lifted the box off the bed. There was no use arguing with him; she'd learned that much over the last couple months. She turned the box in her hand. The lock was off, the ribbons cut.

Her Emmit grinned again. "Fixed."

Marnie opened the box and took out the papers. Papers just like the ones she'd put in over the years—purple ones, yellow ones, a bit of napkin, a torn envelope. Exactly the same as all the papers she had, except these were completely, utterly blank. Not erased, not whited out, but clear and smooth and perfect, just as if she had never written on them at all.

All her regrets were gone, her sins as if they'd never been.

She ran her fingers through the notes, then picked out a purple flower. "How? How did you do this?"

His arm dropped from real-Emmit's shoulder. He clapped his hands. "I gave them to the Son."

The Son. Now she understood. Not the sun shining in the sky, but the One who died for her, died to make all her papers blank. Not whited out, not smudged with eraser scum, but clear, smooth, perfect. The Son who gave His life so she could live regret-free at last.

He took off his glasses and laid them on the table beside him. "Now you see. Now, understand." He raised his arms, just like he'd done before, all those weeks ago in church when the music played and he sang off-key. This time, he didn't sing. And he didn't close his eyes.

He simply looked her in the eye and whispered, "Bye-bye, Mar-ee. Don't look for me." Then he dropped his arms, opened the glass door, and walked out onto the patio.

Marnie followed. "Wait. Who are you?"

He paused for a just a moment, glanced back, and smiled. "Just a messenger. From the Son." He turned away and kept walking.

Taylor touched her arm. "Don't go after him. Look."

Marnie watched as the rays of the setting sun reflected off the distant ocean and silhouetted a figure taller, broader, more brilliant than the boy she remembered.

The light grew brighter.

Then she could see him no more.

~~~

Marnie Helen Wittier didn't hate baby showers anymore. She still wasn't very fond of her middle name, but well, she was learning to live with it. What mattered now was that despite her confessions, despite her evasions, despite everything that had happened in the last couple months, she was again weaving in and out of tables at Marnie's Books and Brew while offering friends cookies and specialty lattes. But this time, they were Christmas cookies, and this time the party wasn't for a new baby girl; it was for a new fifteen-year-old son.

Josephina poked her cane toward a spot on the wall. "Hang it there, Joe, where he can see it when he comes in."

Joe grunted and adjusted the welcome banner to the left. "Poor kid's gonna think we're all nuts." He pulled a small hammer from his back pocket and tapped the pin through the banner and into the wall.

Josephina sighed. "Well, it won't stay up in an earthquake, but I guess it'll do."

Marnie grinned. "We aren't having any earthquakes today. I promise." She walked over to the espresso machine, then turned back and glanced over the welcome signs mixed with Christmas decorations all over her shop. Emmit, the real Emmit, probably would think they were all a little batty, but at least he'd know that he had friends here who cared.

Over the past days, she'd looked for the old Emmit, Down's-Emmit, a couple times, but she didn't find him. Taylor said she wouldn't, and he was right. But sometimes in the distance, on the beach or at the shopping mall or across the street, she'd think she saw someone watching her. But when she looked back, the figure was gone. And she wondered...

The bell over the front door jingled. She looked up. Taylor walked through the doorway with the real Emmit. Both wore matching cowboy hats, Aussie style, and both touched the brims in just the same way when they saw the welcome signs.

Marnie grinned and waved them over. "Come on, I just took some cookies out of the oven."

She picked up a spoon and banged it on the side of a cup. No one looked up. Apparently the universal sound for "pay attention, please" worked a lot better when you weren't beating cardboard. She picked up her steaming pitcher and banged the spoon on that instead.

Her customers and friends craned their necks and quieted. Marcus and Daisy peeked out from the book section. Joe came down from the ladder, a rag in his hand, as always.

Marnie cleared her throat. "Everyone, I want you to meet my friend Taylor." She motioned toward him. "And our son, Emmit, the real one." The one who had been hiding out in Maine with friends for all these months while another Emmit took his place.

Murmuring broke out around the tables. Josephina clapped. Jimmy whooped. Kinna beamed and held her baby, and Pete the policeman whistled.

Emmit blushed.

Mrs. Gates held up a quavering hand. "But what happened to the other Emmit, the Down-syndrome boy?"

Marnie smiled. "Don't worry, he went back to where he belonged." Where he came from. He went home.

"His real family must have been worried sick. But good thing he's back now." Mrs. Gates shook her head. "Imagine us being fooled like that."

Marnie set down the spoon and pitcher. Yes, imagine. Imagine the lengths God went to in order to heal her, to make her whole.

Josephina caught Marnie's gaze and winked. "Everything's as it should be, isn't it, mija?"

Marnie nodded. "God knows what He's doing."

Pete and Jimmy got up and shook Taylor's hand and clapped Emmit on the back. A few others called out their "welcomes," "good to meet you's," and "so you're why Marnie's looking so happy's."

Emmit tossed her a grin, then hurried over to the books side of the store. That boy loved books. And painting, just like Taylor had said. He'd already painted three beautiful pictures that now adorned the walls of his room. All she had to do was keep him supplied with books and paint, and he'd be happy. At least now that he'd decided living near the beach in California was better than holing up in a basement in Maine.

Joe stuffed his rag into his back pocket, propped open the french doors, and went over to Emmit.

Warmth flooded Marnie as she watched Joe pointing out some of his favorite books. He hadn't read a book in twenty years before he'd gotten here. But now he read at least two a week. And the reading was transforming. It seemed like that's what Books and Brew was all about lately: transformed lives. And she was hoping that Taylor's and Emmit's lives would be next. Because even in this short time she found she loved the real Emmit. She loved her son, because the first Emmit taught her how.

These initial days were hard for him, hard for them all, but good too. Right. Taylor and Emmit and her together. As it always should have been. Except sin, regret, and fear had kept them apart.

So God had sent a miracle to clear the way.

Marnie turned back around to see Mrs. Gates standing at the counter before her. The woman squinted at her through her bifocals. "So, finally found your man, did you?"

Marnie winked at Taylor. "He found me."

Mrs. Gates huffed. "'Bout time, I'd say."

Taylor moved around to the back of the counter and stood beside Marnie. "That's what I say too. About time."

Mrs. Gates tapped her fingers. "I'm glad to see you did the right thing at last. Hated to see Marnie here without her man." She stared up at him and narrowed her eyes. "You are going to be her man, aren't you? No backing out now?"

"Well, I did find some land with a little house on it out on Highway 68. Make a nice ranch for troubled teens. Emmit wants to help with that."

"Troubled teens, eh? Haven't you had enough trouble, young man?"

He put his arm around Marnie. "I'm planning on keeping my trouble close these days."

Mrs. Gates laughed her high, wheezy laugh. "I knew you were the right guy the moment I laid eyes on you."

Marnie shook her head. "Which was about thirty seconds ago."

"I've got the eye, I tell you." She tapped her temple twice. "Not been wrong yet."

"If you say so." Marnie turned to Taylor. "Can you please get me a cup for Mrs. Gates's ice water?"

Mrs. Gates raised her chin. "No, today I'm having tea."

Marnie raised her eyebrows. "Tea?"

"Tea." She dug in her purse, then plunked down two dollar bills and a quarter onto the counter.

Marnie stared at the money. That made two miracles in under a week. "Tea it is." A cheap old woman paying for her drink, and one not-as-old woman who had finally found out how to live a life regret-free. It was crazy. And wonderful.

She poured the tea for Mrs. Gates, then turned and looked at the picture she'd pinned onto the bulletin board behind the register. A picture of her with her arm flung around a boy with Down syndrome, a boy with crooked glasses, yellow hair, and a grin on his face. She reached out and ran her fingers over the image.

What a gift that boy had been. A wondrous, incredible gift. Just like her baby had been a wondrous, incredible gift too. It hadn't seemed so at the time, but Rose knew the truth. A baby is always a gift, even when it's one you don't think you want, don't think you'll like. And both times, Marnie had tried to throw that gift away. Both times, she thought she'd lost it. And both times, God gave her a second chance. Incredible. Wondrous. And just like God.

Taylor came up behind her. "Do you regret that I didn't come sooner? Part of me wanted to. And the rest of me was afraid to."

Marnie dropped her hand from the picture. "I don't have any regrets. Not anymore. I got another chance."

He put his arm around her. "Everyone deserves a second chance. That's what you taught me."

"I was wrong."

"What?"

"No one deserves it. But God gives us one anyway. Me, you." She paused. "Us?"

"Definitely us."

She turned toward him and looked up into his face. "Have I ever told you that I love you, Taylor Cole?"

He smiled. "I don't think you have."

"Well, I love you. I always have."

Emmit came up and stood on the other side of her. She put one arm around his waist and the other around Taylor's.

They stood there together, looking at the photo while the coffee brewed, while Mrs. Gates sipped her tea, and while a fresh batch of doughnuts rose in the proof box beyond them.

Epilogue

Emeth sat on an outcropping of rocks and watched the white-tipped waves washing in from the bay. A breeze came off the water and swirled the sand at his feet. Two otters dipped in and out of the waves a quarter mile out. He saw them clearly, without glasses. He could hear the song of the gulls clearly too and could sense the beauty in their cries as they swooped overhead.

And now he could sing again. Beautifully, perfectly, making music to the Son he loved. He'd spent hours, days, eternities in worship, knowing that the Son was pleased with him and basking in the One who was love. It was good to sing again, sing to Mary's lamb.

But now he waited. A few more moments and they would come. She would come.

Emeth listened to the sounds of the water washing the sand, the rush of the waves against the rocks, and the still-distant voices of a man, a woman, and a boy.

"Race you to the rock!"

"You go ahead."

"Can we try kayaking?"

"Maybe Saturday."

"Do you think we'll find a sand dollar today?"

"Look, I found a shell."

"What's that for?"

"My gratitude box, of course."

"Is that what happened to my favorite tie?"

"You can always check for yourself. The box is open for all."

"No more secrets?"

"No more lies."

"No more regrets."

"Emmit, slow down!"

They came closer, the boy running out front, the man and woman walking hand in hand just like they used to when they were young and in love. They were older now, wiser, and more firmly in the hand of the Son. They strolled barefoot, their pants rolled up, their footprints making divots in the wet sand.

Emeth couldn't look away as they came closer, closer. They couldn't see him, sitting here watching them. If they could, they'd see a man strong and tall and dressed in brilliant white. Then they'd fall down, afraid. So he was glad they couldn't see him. Glad that he could watch unnoticed and wish for them all the joy the Son had planned for them.

The boy ran past him. Then the man and the woman passed too. She looked happy now, peaceful, radiant. The boy dashed out into the tide.

She called out after him, "Wait for me!" Then she waved. A ring flashed in the sun.

Emeth rose. "I love you, Mar-ee. But the Son loves you more." His words flew away, unheard in the wind.

And yet, for a single instant, she looked back. And she smiled.

Emeth closed his eyes and imagined the snow falling, like white angels fluttering to earth. Then he raised his hands, palms up, and was gone.

ACKNOWLEDGMENTS

A new story is always a gift. It comes from the heart of God through the generosity of others who give of themselves, their time, their talent, their knowledge, to bring that story to life. Here, I'd like to thank just a few of those who gave of themselves so *Shades of Morning* could become a reality:

As always, to my husband, Bryan. Thank you for your encouragement, support, and insights as my first reader. And thank you for being the "hero" in God's love story for me.

To Tracy Higley and John Olson. Thank you for brainstorming the details of this story with me years ago in Central Lounge at Mount Hermon. Your insights and ideas brought this story to life!

To Patti and Bill Risinger. Thanks for the quick read when I needed it and the insightful comments on the book's ending. I am so grateful for our friendship!

To Laurie Hohstadt. Thanks for watching the twins, especially in those last months before deadline!

To my excellent editor, Julee Schwarzburg. Once again you helped me dig deeper and make this book more of what God envisioned it to be.

To the rest of the team at WaterBrook Multnomah. You are such a blessing!

And to Rick and Diane Pate. Thank you for sharing your wisdom, stories, insights, and knowledge of what it's like to parent a boy with Down syndrome. Your friendship is such a gift!

And finally to Andy who inspired this story with his joyful abandon. This book is for you.

Note from the Author

Dear Reader,

People often ask me where my ideas come from. Sometimes they come from conversations, sometimes they come from dreams, sometimes they come from images that spring into my mind. But *Shades of Morning* came from Andy.

It was an ordinary Sunday morning. I didn't expect to see anything different, or special, or extraordinary. I figured I'd come to church, sing the songs, shake some hands, listen to the sermon, and that would be that.

But God had other plans. And so did Andy.

It started off as expected. I walked into church and sat in my usual seat, halfway back from the front and on the right side of the church platform. Soon the singing began. Then some announcements. Then another song. Just like always. Eventually we came to the fourth song in the worship set. Something about our God of wonders. I sang quietly, as I do every Sunday, because my husband tells me I can't carry a tune. I didn't want to disturb the other worshippers. Everything was going so smoothly. So...normally.

The second verse flipped onto the screen in front. Everyone sang just like they were supposed to. Everyone clapped at the right moment, in time with the music. And a few people even swayed a bit in their seats. Just as planned.

Until Andy.

At the third verse, a noise came from the far side of the church. A loud noise. Strange and unexpected—an unplanned interruption in the sweet melody of music. And then it grew louder. I furrowed my brow. Was that someone singing...badly?

I stood on tiptoes and peeked toward the sound.

And there was Andy. His arms were raised. His eyes were closed. And he was singing to his God for all he was worth. Andy, in his middle teens, with blond hair, thick glasses, and small ears. Andy, with Down syndrome and a grin big enough for the angels to see. Andy, shout-singing with all his might through that radiant smile.

As I watched and listened, I had to smile too. A small smile at first. Then, like Andy's singing, my smile grew. And grew. And grew. Until the angels could see my smile too. Because at that moment, I knew I was seeing something precious, beautiful, incredible. I was getting a glimpse of something far beyond the ordinary. Something fit for heaven itself.

For a brief instant, the music faltered, the other voices hushed just a bit. And then the guitar strummed again, the congregation's voices surged, and I knew that some, at least, had seen what I had. They'd witnessed the wonder, beheld the beauty, of a soul in love with his God. An extraordinary moment, an extraordinary gift wrapped in an unexpected, off-key package. It took my breath away.

So my hope for you, dear reader, is that you will recognize the gifts of God in your life that come in unexpected and unattractive packages. May you see His glory in the off-key moments of life, may you leave regret at the Cross, and may you embrace the wonder of His amazing love for you.

If you were touched by Marnie's journey in *Shades of Morning*, I hope you'll send me a note and tell me about it! You can e-mail me at marlo@marloschalesky.com or send a note to me via my publisher at:

Marlo Schalesky

c/o WaterBrook Multnomah Publishing Group

12265 Oracle Boulevard, Suite 200

Colorado Springs, CO 80921

And to find out more about me and my books, please visit my Web site at www.marloschalesky.com, and my "Tales of Wonder" blog at www.marloschalesky.blogspot.com. I'd love to hear from you!

READERS GUIDE

I was in college when I first fell in love with God. Before that, I knew about Him, I believed that Christ died for my sins and rose again, but He hadn't yet captured my heart with the breathtaking wonder of His love…until 1986, my freshman year. Part of that process happened just outside the Stanford post office. I sat on a bench, praying, thinking, and reviewing all the things I had done wrong in life, all the sins Christ died for. I thought about what the "book" of my life might look like—pages filled with black marks and smudges, covered over with the "whiteout" of God's grace. And while I was glad the sins were covered, it made me sad to think about what the book would have been like if only I'd done better, chosen better, been better all along.

I closed my eyes and prayed. And as I did, an image came strongly into my mind. The book of my life, with God turning the pages. But these pages weren't smudged and whited-out. These pages were crisp, clean, and new. They were beautiful. They were pure. They were pristine. I caught my breath, and for the first time I understood the true beauty of what Jesus did for me on the Cross. He didn't just white out my sins. He made me new. The sins vanished as if they'd never been, and my heart, my life, was transformed and renewed. My "book" was completely clean and ready for Him to write His words, paint His images, and make it into a thing of exquisite beauty.

That's the image that birthed the theme for *Shades of Morning*—the wonder of how God doesn't just erase or white out, He makes new. He makes beautiful. He's in the business of amazing transformation for me, and for you. So if you'd like to dig deeper into the themes and spiritual nuances in *Shades of Morning,* here are some questions that may help:

1. In chapter 5 we learn that real-Emmit prayed he might have a complete family. How might have Habakkuk 1:5 been an answer to real-Emmit's questions about God in that chapter? "Look…and watch—and be utterly amazed. For I am going to do something in your days that you would not believe, even if you were told." How might this quote apply to your own prayers that God doesn't seem to be answering as you wish?

2. In chapter 9 Taylor relates how his mom once told him that you can't compare apples meant for pie with apples meant for candying. She meant that God's vision and purpose for one person isn't the same as for someone else. How does this address the question of why God may answer one person's prayers in one way and another person's in another?

3. In chapter 10 Marnie asks, "Why couldn't we have just kept the past buried? Buried in a box on a shelf forever." But she realizes that the past wasn't truly buried, and it never had been. She carried it with her always, no matter how she tried to forget. How does her inability to release her regrets to God interfere with her relationships and her spiritual growth? Have you experienced times when your regrets harmed relationships with people close to you? Explain.

4. Think about how Marnie's guilt takes her away from Taylor and how Taylor's guilt keeps him from pursuing Marnie. Then consider the guilt in your own life. What is the proper role of guilt? In what ways can it be destructive? In what ways can it be helpful?

5. In chapter 15 Marnie sees God as the One who looked at baldness and saw beauty. The One who knew her and loved her anyway. When God views you, do you think He sees beauty or baldness? If you lived every day believing that God saw beauty, how would that change the way you live?

6. In chapter 16 Marnie realizes that "Decency couldn't be bought at Saks; honor wasn't purchased at Nordstrom… Instead beauty often hid in ugliness. And wonder often dressed in ratty clothes. The trick was seeing the truth, recognizing the beauty God placed in each person." Consider James 2:1–4 in conjunction with Marnie's thoughts. If we truly believed as Marnie did, how would that change the way we interacted with others?

7. In chapter 16 Marnie realizes that even though she didn't have a good example in an earthly father, she still knew what a loving Father is. Do you think God put the knowledge of real love, a real father, in all of us? What are some characteristics of a good father? How is God like that?

8. In chapter 19 Kinna tells Marnie, "I've learned that God works in the barren years. When He seems the most absent, that's when He's doing His most intimate work." Think of barren times in your own life. How has God changed you in those times? Can you now see how He

was doing intimate work inside you? How might the realization of His work in you help you during barren times in the future?

9. In chapter 20 Taylor recognizes that "Sin was sin for a reason… Sin would tear you apart, leave you bleeding, snatch your future and drain away the life." Why do you think God calls certain actions "sin"? How would your attitude toward sin change if you defined it as "that which hurts me or others" rather than "things God says I can't do"?

10. In chapter 20 Taylor writes, "Life isn't about making things perfect. It's about living with the blobs of yellow. It's about rejoicing in the life God gives you, even when it's not the life you wanted or expected. It's about throwing your hands up in abandon even when your glasses are askew and you can't see the reason, the meaning, behind what you're going through." Have there been times in your life when you couldn't see the reason for what you were going through? Consider Philippians 4:4–9. How might those verses help you the next time life takes an unexpected and unwanted turn?

11. In chapter 20, Taylor realizes that "he'd been making his plans and expecting God's blessing. He'd never bothered to look for God's plans." What is the difference between looking for blessing and looking for wisdom? How do you follow God's will in your life instead of your own?

12. Taylor's assistant, Nancy, says it's hard to receive something new when your hands are closed tight around something old. In chapter 23, Taylor learns that he has to release the past, his disappointments as well as his hopes and dreams,

completely to God. Is there a place in your life where you're clinging to "the meaningless furnishings" of a past time? If so, how can you let go of those things in order to embrace the new things God may have for you?

13. In chapter 24 Josephina says to Marnie, "Regrets about what happened yesterday and fears about what may happen tomorrow keep you from living now." Later Marnie realizes that "She'd hung on to her regrets instead of her joys." Consider Matthew 6:34. Have regrets and worries kept you from living to your fullest in the "now"? If so, how might you let go of both? How does hanging on to your joys help?

14. In chapter 24 Marnie realizes that the Cross is the ultimate example of how God transforms tragedy into triumph. She considers the Cross "the darkest moment in all of history, when the Son of God bled, cried out in agony, and died. The moment when all hope seemed lost and everything that had ever happened appeared meaningless because the darkness had won. But it hadn't. The darkest moment was also the brightest, because all the past, present, and future changed in that moment. It was redeemed. Death defeated. Hope reborn." Think about what Jesus did on the Cross. Then consider how the cross itself was once a sign of the most grisly type of execution, but has now been transformed into a symbol of redemption and wonder. What does that say about how God might transform the ugly things in your past as well? Think about how He might redeem the mistakes, the tragedies, the sins, the disappointments. How might your darkest moments be transformed into light?

15. In the end, Marnie realizes that no one deserves second chances, but God gives them to us anyway. Think of a time when you had another chance to do something right. Did you deserve that opportunity, or was it a free gift from God? How might God be giving you another chance today to do right?

16. In the epilogue, notice that angel-Emmit's name changes to Emeth, his true name. The Hebrew word for *truth* is pronounced "Em-it" but when scholars write it in English, they usually write "Emeth" as Hebrew doesn't have a "th" letter or combination. So *Emmit* and *Emeth* are the same Hebrew word but written differently. How does Emeth's name change reflect the change in his character? How is he different? How is he the same? And how does the word *truth* reflect his role in the story? Similarly, how has God's gift of truth changed your life and your view of the past?

They say love is *blind.*

This time they're right...

A woman lies unconscious in a hospital bed. A man sits beside her...between them lies an ocean of fear and the tenuous grip of memories long past. Daylight flees. Darkness deepens. And mystery awaits...beyond the night.

They say you should reach
for your *dreams.*

This time they're wrong...

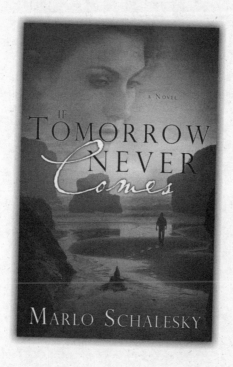

A NOVEL

IF
TOMORROW
NEVER
Comes

MARLO SCHALESKY

Childhood sweethearts Kinna and Jimmy Henley had simple dreams—marriage, children, a house by the sea. What they didn't plan on was years of infertility stealing those dreams, crushing their hopes. All that's left now is the memory of young love—until Kinna rescues a mysterious old woman from the sea and the threads of the past, present, and future weave together to reveal the wonder of one final hope. One final chance to follow not their dreams, but God's plan.